HIGH PLAINS
HEARTS

THREE-IN-ONE COLLECTION

JANET SPAETH

BARBOUR
PUBLISHING

Angel's Roost © 2003 by Janet Spaeth
In the Cool of the Evening © 2011 by Janet Spaeth
Sunshine © 2011 by Janet Spaeth

Print ISBN 978-1-62416-734-8

eBook Editions:
Adobe Digital Edition (.epub) 978-1-62836-347-0
Kindle and MobiPocket Edition (.prc) 978-1-62836-348-7

All scripture quotations are taken from the King James Version of the Bible.

This book is a work of fiction. Names, characters, places, and incidents are either products of the author's imagination or used fictitiously. Any similarity to actual people, organizations, and/or events is purely coincidental.

Published by Barbour Publishing, Inc., P.O. Box 719, Uhrichsville, Ohio 44683, www.barbourbooks.com

Our mission is to publish and distribute inspirational products offering exceptional value and biblical encouragement to the masses.

 Member of the
Evangelical Christian
Publishers Association

Printed in the United States of America.

Dear Readers,

Welcome to North Dakota! I've lived here most of my life, and I'm still stunned by how beautiful it is. A clear Dakota blue sky arches above the open stretch of land that goes on forever. The seasons are here in full force—from the gentle, green spring that comes after a fierce, cold winter with wild blizzard winds, to the glorious, brisk autumn that follows a warm, sun-blessed summer.

From the eastern part of the state, with some of the richest farmland in the United States, to the wild Badlands in the west, this state is incredible. Imagine a field of sunflowers, towering high above the ground, or an expanse of blue-blooming flax. You'll see them here.

My favorite time in North Dakota is night. Every evening I go outside and spend a few minutes marveling at the nighttime sky. It's dressed up at night in its finest jewels. Stars aren't sprinkled across the sky—they are glowing clusters of sparkling diamonds against an inky velvet sky, and the moon is a glowing pearl. If I'm lucky, I'll see the aurora borealis. The northern lights are stunning, with blazed streaks of sapphire and turquoise and emerald, and they remind me that our Father loves us and cares for us. Always.

I'm blessed to live here, and I hope you enjoy your visit to North Dakota in these stories!

Janet Spaeth

ANGEL'S ROOST

Dedication

This book is dedicated to those angels, seen and unseen, who have shaped and changed my life. I am especially grateful to Cleo Rowe, whose faith is constant and unwavering and who believes in angels because they believe in her.

Cleo, this is your book. Thank you for being my friend. You are an angel yourself.

Chapter 1

Now faith is the substance of things hoped for,
the evidence of things not seen.
HEBREWS 11:1

Yes, her halo was definitely tilted.

Tess leaned into the display and straightened the halo on the three-foot-tall angel that stood inside the door of her store. It was always an eye-catcher, but sometimes it seemed as if it had a mind of its own—kind of a renegade angel.

"There," she said at last, leaning back and admiring the angel, which grinned at her from under its wild raffia hair, not at all repentant. "Now try not to get into any more trouble."

She opened the door that led from the store into the rest of her house. It was nice having the store only footsteps from where she lived. She walked the short distance to the kitchen and put the teakettle, painted with whistling angels, on the stove to boil.

Tea would be nice, she thought, as she shivered in the back room. It was the day before Thanksgiving, and in North Dakota that meant winter had already arrived, no matter what the calendar said. Heat didn't quite penetrate into the far rooms of her old Victorian house, but she wouldn't trade it for the world. The rooms were still alive with precious memories—of Grandma and Grandpa and the very happy childhood they had given her.

The tinkling of the angel chime over the shop door broke her reverie. She turned off the burner and dashed back into the store.

A man, his hat and shoulders dusted with large white snowflakes, stood in silence, looking around the room. Tess smiled. Her store had this effect on many people.

"Welcome to Angel's Roost," she greeted him.

He continued to take silent inventory of the store. "This is incredible!" he said at last, removing his snow-sodden hat and revealing disheveled hair that was mostly black but shot through in places with early silver. He tried unsuccessfully to straighten it. "Hat hair," he said briefly in apologetic explanation before turning his attention back to the store. "Is it all angels? Everything in this store?"

"Every last bit of it."

"This is incredible," he repeated.

"Are you trying to find something in particular? A gift for your wife perhaps?" she asked.

"No wife, not even a girlfriend—sorry to say." He looked at her, and under the droplets of melting snow she saw that his eyes were dark and fringed with long lashes. Gorgeous. Absolutely gorgeous. The kind of eyes she usually saw looking back at her from the pages of magazine advertisements.

Then the corners of those eyes crinkled, and she knew that under the thick muffler he was smiling. "This must be what heaven looks like." He gestured in a sweeping motion at the hundreds of angels of all sizes, shapes, and colors that filled the shelves, tables, and chairs of Angel's Roost.

His motion stopped when he saw the angel with the halo that was, once again, tilted.

He tugged his mittens off and pulled the snowy muffler down under his chin, revealing a face that was not traditionally handsome but already had deep laugh lines etched into it.

"This is a wonderful piece of work," he said as he leaned over and straightened the out-of-kilter halo. "How much is she? I've got to have her—I can just see her greeting my customers as they walk in!"

An odd sensation of possessiveness about the crazy angel washed over Tess. She did some unnecessary neatening of the angel's ecru and pink ruffled skirts.

"She is for sale, isn't she?" the man asked. "She'd look perfect right inside the front door."

"Her halo won't stay straight," Tess said softly.

"That adds to her charm." He knelt and closely examined the angel's face, studying her mischievous eyes, her tousled hair, her lopsided smile. "Yes, this is an angel that knows exactly what's what in the heavenly realm. Want to bet she's hidden Gabriel's horn more than a few times?"

Tess laughed. His description was perfect.

He stood up and stuck out his hand. "I'm Jake Cameron, by the way."

He said it as if expecting the name would mean something to her. Quickly she ran it through her memory: *Jake Cameron, Jake Cameron.* In the dim recesses of her mind a light began to glow. Food, something to do with food.

"Tell me where the angel will fit into your store," she improvised.

"It's not a store, exactly, although we do sell some items. You've been in Panda's, haven't you?"

Panda's! The upscale coffee bar was a big draw for college students on the far end of town, near the mall. All the new development out there had attracted most retail and new eating establishments when the downtown had fallen out of favor and into disrepair.

It had become a division of the town's loyalties in which sides had been taken, battle lines drawn. Tess was firmly on the side of downtown.

The history of the community itself, a river town established by a long-ago fur and commodities trade, was still evident, preserved in the stately structures that had crowded together in the early days of the Dakota Territory to form a business center that had eventually deserted it.

Tess delighted in it. Its bricks and ornate moldings had much more character than the plastic and glass of the End, as the new area had come to be called.

She'd been in Panda's once, almost a year ago, and she was overwhelmed by the choices. All she'd wanted was a cup of coffee, but she'd ended up with a brownie-type creation and a mocha drink topped with a dollop of whipped cream and a sprinkling of cinnamon. She had to admit that both were wonderful, even if she didn't know exactly what she'd eaten or drunk.

Tess nodded. "I've been there."

He studied her for a moment. "You're not a regular, though. I'm sure I'd remember you."

"To be honest, it's a bit out of the way for me," she responded. "I don't get over to that part of town very often."

She knew she was understating her disdain for the End, but this man was a customer, and she was not about to get into an argument about the town's two diverse business sectors.

"I know what you mean. I don't get downtown much either, or, believe me, I would have been in here before. It's astonishing what all you have in this store. I've never seen so many angels gathered in one place." He looked around curiously and picked up a small packet from a calico-lined basket near the cash register. "What's this?"

"Smell it," Tess suggested.

"Wow! This is great! What is this stuff called?"

" 'Angel's Breath,' " she answered. "Potpourri. The manufacturer calls this little package a sachet, but to me a sachet is something you put in a drawer to scent your clothing, and this is too potent for that. One little packet will scent an entire room. Some people buy it for their cars too."

The potpourri was one of her best-selling items. She even used it in her bedroom.

"Well, it's wonderful, whatever it's called." He put it back and asked her directly, "How do you like being downtown?"

He had touched on one of her favorite subjects. "I love it! It has a special ambiance that, quite frankly, the newer development doesn't have—yet," she added hastily, recalling that was where his business was located. "I really do like it. I suppose it's not for everyone, but it works for me."

He nodded and picked up a terra-cotta angel, which he studied with casual interest. "But hasn't it gone to street people?"

She warmed to her topic. "Actually, downtown has always catered somewhat to street people. Not too long ago people strolled up and down Main Street, window-shopping even at midnight."

"That's not the same thing."

"You're right. It's not. But what I'm getting at is that the downtown has always had a nightlife that other parts of town haven't had. It's part of the downtown identity. And," she acknowledged, "as time's gone on, those people on the streets at night have changed. That's true."

"It's not safe." His statement was blunt.

"It's not totally unsafe either. But the mayor's renewal project has taken this into account, and I'm hopeful about seeing changes down here."

"You know a lot about this."

"I'm a member of the task force."

"Do you think Panda's would fit in downtown?"

Before she could respond, a large gray cat sauntered in. Its plumed tail waved back and forth, dusting dangerously near a set of fragile china angels that hovered protectively around and over a detailed porcelain nativity set.

She scooped the cat up as it began to weave through the display and affectionately rubbed her face in the cat's fur. "This is Cora."

"Hi, Cora." Jake reached out and scratched the cat's nose. A loud purr rewarded his efforts.

"You must be a cat person," she said as Cora wiggled free to wrap herself in and out of Jake's ankles.

"I adore cats." Cora investigated the puddles of melted snow that had dripped off Jake's coat. He stood still, exhibiting the instinct of a cat lover not to move quickly and startle an investigating cat. "And this one is terrific."

"She's been with me since I moved in here." After two years Tess was finally able to tell the story without tearing up. "This was my grandparents' house, although I grew up here, too. When Grandma died—Grandpa'd died about a year before—she left me this house. I came back here after the funeral, and Cora was waiting. Sunning herself right in this front area, as if she'd always been here."

"Was she your Grandma's cat?"

Tess shook her head. "No. Grandma loved cats, but she'd been living in a nursing home since Grandpa died, and she couldn't have a cat there." As she remembered, she couldn't help smiling. "Grandma always said there'd be a cat waiting for her in heaven, a cat the color of pussy willows."

Jake knelt and stroked Cora's gray head. "The color of pussy willows, huh? What an extraordinary story!"

The cat meowed imperiously and meandered over to the large angel with the rakish halo. Jake watched her. "Cora's got good taste. I truly do want to buy this wonderful angel. Are you going to tell me how much she is?"

She paused, and he pulled out his wallet, clearly misunderstanding her hesitation. "Oh, I suppose it really doesn't matter. I'll take her at whatever price you're asking."

"I really didn't have a price put on her," Tess said. "To be honest, she's been here since I opened, and she's almost a fixture in Angel's Roost." She made some quick mental calculations and named a price she almost hoped was too high.

He didn't flinch. "No problem." He handed her several bills, and Tess tried not to let her eyes widen at the amount of green she saw in his wallet.

Then he smacked his forehead. "I can't take her!"

Tess breathed a mental sigh of relief, and she turned from the old-fashioned cash register.

"Here's your money back, then."

He shook his head. "Oh no. I still want her in Panda's, but my car is packed with boxes I have to mail. For once in my life I'm ahead of the game with my Christmas shopping. Too bad too, because I see lots of things here that would have been great. My mother, for example, would adore that angel with the emerald green wings, and—"

"Would you like me to deliver the angel?" She tried not to wince as she spoke. Parting with the angel was hard enough; having to take her to her new home was almost unimaginable.

"No. No need to. I've decided I want to come back and do a little more Christmas shopping. When do you close?"

She had to smile. "Around five, but it doesn't matter. I can stay—"

He scratched Cora's neck as he thought. "No. You probably want to get home."

"I am home."

He looked up, startled.

"I live here."

"I didn't realize this was an apartment building," he said.

"It's not. It's a house—my house. As I say, I live here. Well, Cora and I live here."

Cora looked at Tess as if challenging her words. Jake caught the glance, too, and his chocolate brown eyes twinkled with amusement.

"I have the feeling that you live here only through her largesse."

"Basically. In exchange for vast amounts of tuna and Cat-Cat Yums, I get all the kitty kisses and snuggles I could ever want."

They exchanged laughing glances.

"In other words she tolerates me."

He grinned as the cat happily scraped the side of her head on the big angel. "She's a character, that's for sure. So may I pick up Faith tomorrow?"

"Faith?" Tess was at a loss.

"That's what I'm naming this angel. Faith. Doesn't it fit her?"

Tess tilted her head and studied the wayward angel. "I don't know. I always thought of faith as being light and airy and pure, not crazy like this one." Mechanically she once again straightened the angel's halo. "But let me think about it."

"When I come back tomorrow, let me know what you've decided. But Faith seems right for her, so Faith she is."

"Well, she is your angel now." The words cost her dearly.

"As a matter of fact, let's put a SOLD sign on her," he said. He took one of the business cards from the angel-wings holder near the cash register and scrabbled in his pocket until he found a pen.

"SOLD!" he proclaimed as he wrote the word on the back of the card. He bent over and tucked the card into the angel's raffia grasp.

As he stood up, he looked out through the prism edges of the piano window that graced the front of the store. "Still snowing. Not that that's any big surprise, right?"

She nodded mutely, relieved he didn't seem to expect much of an answer.

"I'd better be going," he said, wrapping the muffler around his neck again and settling the sodden cap back on his head. "The snow isn't stopping, and I want to get to the post office before it closes."

His warm brown eyes met hers. "By the way, I didn't get your name."

"Tess Mahoney," she said, somewhat breathlessly. Had her heart always beat this irregularly? Maybe she should get a checkup.

"Tess Mahoney," he repeated. "Sounds a bit Irish."

"You've got it right with 'a bit.' The name is Irish, but the rest of me is a mishmash of everything."

"Well, Tess Mahoney, I'm very glad to have met you and your angels, and I'll be back tomorrow to pick up Faith and do some more shopping."

"I'll be here."

With a wave he opened the door and left, the cold November air swirling in to replace the warmth that left with him.

Cora leaped up to the counter and leaned against Tess, her body heat welcome as the chilled early night air invaded the cozy store.

"Well, Kitty-Cat," she said as she locked the store's door and turned off the light, "thanks to Mr. Cameron you'll be in Cat-Cat Yums for quite a while."

There was nothing to take her from her snug house that night—no choir practice, no urban renewal meetings, no shopping to be done. So she curled up on the couch under one of the many colorful afghans her grandmother had crocheted, with Cora cozied in beside her and a cup of spiced tea heating her hands.

It had been a long time since she'd gone out with anyone. She smoothed Cora's already silky fur. Thoughts crowded her mind.

He wasn't married. He liked cats. He didn't seem to think her store was silly.

But one major question was still unanswered, and she posed it aloud to Cora: "Does he believe in angels? What does he believe?"

The answer made all the difference in the world.

Cora's even purring became hypnotic, and Tess felt herself drifting off to sleep after she'd downed the dregs of her tea.

Her last thoughts were of Faith. Why would he think Faith was an appropriate name for an angel who seemed to be always challenging her? No, he was wrong. Faith was constant, unchanging, not an angel whose halo refused to stay put.

Chapter 2

Tess woke as a thought broke into her dreams with the clarity of a fire alarm. She had told Jake Cameron to come back for the angel today. But this was Thanksgiving! She was going to help serve dinner at her church.

She found his phone number in the telephone book and whistled at the address. Panda's must do a fairly decent business, she realized, for him to be able to afford a home in the Pines. It was the newest housing development in town, far down along the river, and houses there began at more than she could make in fifteen years even if she saved every penny she earned.

She waited until ten o'clock to dial the phone. He answered on the second ring, but his voice was thick with sleep.

"Oh, I'm sorry—I woke you up," she said, her words falling over each other.

"No, well, yes, but that's all right. I had to get up now anyway. What time is it?"

"And how do you know you have to get up now if you don't know what time it is?" She couldn't resist teasing him.

"The sun is up," he responded, the grogginess clearing from his voice. "I'm always up at the crack of dawn."

"Well, dawn has cracked. About four hours ago." She grinned at Cora, who lifted one exhausted eyelid in response.

He muttered something she couldn't understand and probably didn't want to. "The roaster blew a bearing last night around midnight. Wouldn't you know it, just as we head into our biggest season. So I stayed up to work on it."

"Did you get it fixed?"

"Oh, I cobbled it together to last until I can get a replacement part." His voice softened. "So how are you today, Angel Lady?"

"You recognized my voice!" Tess couldn't hide her astonishment.

"Sure. Even the combined voices of the guy at the post office yesterday, telling me that 'Sorry, sir, these boxes need extra tape,' and the college student at Panda's, notifying me that 'Hey, dude, your big machine has just gone blooey,' couldn't erase the memory of your angelic tones. Seriously, I do have a good ear for voices."

His dead-on imitation of the postal worker and the Panda's employee caught Tess off guard, and she laughed. "Have you considered comedy?"

"Some people say that's what I'm doing at Panda's, but they're just jealous. So how's my angel doing? Is Faith's halo askew again?"

"I don't think it would stay on straight if you glued it on," she said. "It

13

seems destined to go off to the side no matter what I do."

"I'm anxious to get her here."

"That's what I called about. I said you could take her today, but I forgot—this is Thanksgiving."

"Oh, that's right. I guess I could pick her up tomorrow, but I'd kind of hoped to have her already in place when I opened on Friday."

"You could take her this afternoon," Tess suggested, "unless you have other plans."

"No, I don't. I was just going to loll around the house and watch ball games on TV, but now I'll probably go in and tinker with the roaster. I don't want to interfere with your plans."

"Well, I do need to be at the church by three."

"Church? They have services on Thanksgiving afternoon?"

"We serve an open dinner. I'm in charge of salads and desserts this year. Plus I'll be going in to make sure everything is in place and set the tables, put up the chairs, that kind of thing."

"Sounds like fun. Can you use an extra pair of hands?"

"You're volunteering?" Tess couldn't believe her ears. "Of course we can! But what about your roaster?"

He laughed softly. "It's undoubtedly safer without my hammering and fiddling around on it. I'm not exactly Mr. Handy, unfortunately. All around, the best choice—the wisest choice—is for me to help out at your church. It'll make me feel useful."

"Fair enough. Can you be here at Angel's Roost shortly before three?"

"With bells on."

She hung up the phone and swept Cora up and whirled her around until the cat meowed a clear complaint. "He's coming to my church! He's coming to my church!"

She hugged Cora to her chest and buried her face in the soft fur as her thoughts led into prayer. "Dear God, I sense something is moving here by Your power. Guide me in the way I should go."

She felt the soft glow of prayer heard and answered, and her heart relaxed.

Cora's impatient wriggle reminded her of the earthly demands of a cat that needed to be fed.

The rest of the morning and the early afternoon sped by. Tess had just slipped into her favorite sweatshirt, a bright yellow one festooned with angels in rainbow colors playing musical instruments, when she heard a car pull up in front of the house. She flew to the front door and motioned him around to the side, where the outside entrance to the house was.

He hadn't even reached the door yet, and her heart was already singing. Did he have any idea how happy he was making her this day?

He came into the entryway off the kitchen and stamped the snow from his feet.

"I'm ready," he announced, kneeling and rubbing Cora's waiting ears. "We can take my car. I left it idling so it'd be warm."

A smile curved her lips. "Better turn it off because we're walking."

"Walking? Are you serious? It's freezing outside, and there's this white stuff called snow all over the sidewalks. Say, this isn't one of those 'work up an appetite' ploys, is it?"

"No, Silly. Trust me."

She pulled on her boots and coat and, after saying good-bye to Cora and promising her turkey leftovers, led him back to the sidewalk. He reached inside the late-model sedan, which Tess knew carried a very expensive price tag, and turned off the ignition.

"Okay, let's go!" Tess said. "Just pretend we're arctic explorers. It'll be fun."

"Way cool. Too way cool," he grumbled. "And the pun is definitely intended. We've just met, and already you're trying to kill me for my insurance money. Well, it won't work. It just won't work. Mom's my beneficiary, so there." He glared at her with mock suspicion. "She didn't put you up to this, did she?"

"You nut," Tess answered, poking him with her elbow.

They crossed the street and trudged through half a block of snow-covered sidewalks before Tess tugged on his arm. "Let's go in here."

Jake peered at the white stone church in front of him. "Nativity Church," he read from a sign by the steps. "Why, this is charming!"

"Ah, you're just saying that because you're cold, and if this is our destination, it means you don't have to walk anymore."

"That might color my opinion," he confessed playfully, "but I am truly serious. This is an absolutely delightful church!"

A tall man with thinning hair and an open smile met them inside the door. "Hi, Tess! The others aren't here yet, but if you want to go on down and—oh, in the glare of the sunlight I didn't see your friend." He stuck out his hand toward Jake. "I'm Reverend Barnes."

"Jake Cameron," Jake said, taking Reverend Barnes's hand and shaking it enthusiastically. "I hope you don't mind my coming. Tess said—"

"Everyone's welcome. Glad we could treat you to a hot meal and some fellowship. Not necessary to explain why," he continued as Jake tried to stop the well-meaning pastor's words. "We all have times when we need a little something. Maybe food, maybe companionship. Certainly in these hard—"

Tess interrupted gently. "Reverend Barnes, Jake's here to help with the dinner."

Reverend Barnes wasn't at all nonplussed. He tilted his head back and laughed with a joy that seemed to boom to heaven itself. "Welcome, welcome," he said, grasping Jake's hand again. "Glad to have you with us, son."

Another couple arrived, and the minister's attention turned to them. Tess guided Jake down the stairs to the kitchen.

"Who comes to this dinner, anyway?" he asked as Tess tossed him a large white apron.

"Well, as Reverend Barnes already said, some people come because this is the only way they'll get a decent meal today. Others come because of the companionship that's offered." Her eyes met his. "I come because it reminds me that one of the things I have to be thankful for is that I am blessed with food and friendship."

His gaze didn't waver. "But shouldn't it be more than that? Those in need—surely their purpose isn't to remind us of our blessings."

His words took Tess by surprise. She'd never thought about it that way. Certainly he had a point. She hadn't examined this closely enough.

"Can you explain?" she asked.

"Not really," he answered, and she appreciated the honesty in his voice. "But it does seem rather egocentric to think the role of the hungry is to make us aware of how good it feels not to be hungry."

"You've posed a good question, son." Reverend Barnes's deep voice filled the kitchen as he joined them. "Sorry to eavesdrop, but I might be able to help."

"Please do," Jake said.

"Maybe if you flip the picture over, it'll make more sense. For the hungry what purpose does being fed serve? Rather than thinking of what this does for us, we should be asking what it does for those in need. We should focus on them. Being hungry is a wrong that must be righted. And we here today are simply agents of that change. In serving this food we serve at a greater table."

He smiled benevolently at Tess. "It should make us feel better, helping out today, but it shouldn't make us complacent. For many people hunger is an ever-present enemy of happiness. We need to do what we can to feed the hungry. It's what Jesus wants."

He handed Jake a folding chair and smiled. "Now that I've solved that problem, it's back to work for me. I've got to come up with some inspirational words for tonight's dinner."

"Wow," Jake breathed as Reverend Barnes turned and raced back up the steps, like a man half his age. "It seems to me he's already come up with some incredibly inspirational words."

"He is astonishing," Tess agreed. "He has the ability to see right through to the center of things. Even if I hadn't been a member of Nativity since I was born, I'd be here because of him."

Jake nodded thoughtfully. "Where do I start with these chairs?"

A twinge of concern creased through the satisfaction of the day. He had changed the subject so quickly—but why? He didn't seem to be trying to avoid the matter; yet he certainly didn't seem inclined to pursue it.

Her musings were interrupted by a stream of people carrying foil-wrapped turkeys and mysterious casserole dishes that smelled wonderful. The kitchen exploded with the joy of many hands cooking.

Jake fell into the role of chief chair-placer quite easily. Tess found herself taking pleasure in the relaxed way he became part of the group and the openness with which her church friends accepted him.

She found herself watching him and the way he interacted with the others. A small movement behind him caught her eye: Reverend Barnes moved toward his wife. For a slice of a moment the minister and his wife glanced at each other, and Tess could tell that volumes passed unspoken—in a muted language only they understood. Then Reverend Barnes sloped his head down and dropped a gentle kiss on his wife's forehead.

A surprising, new hunger washed over Tess. That same degree of closeness and understanding the minister and his wife had—she wanted it, suddenly wanted it, but with whom? Could it be that having Jake there today was bringing this to the forefront? A hole in her life had become a gaping, aching wound of lonely need.

"He's a keeper, I think." The voice belonged to Ellen Smalley, the organist. The tiny woman had always reminded Tess of a wren, small, drab, and twittering but completely harmless. Tess had adored her since she had been a small child in the Carolers' Choir in grade school.

Tess tried to collect her scattered thoughts. "He's not mine to keep."

Mrs. Smalley's brow furrowed. "He's not married, is he?"

"Oh no." Tess couldn't stop the bubble of laughter that arose at Mrs. Smalley's obvious relief. "I mean he's just a customer of mine. There's not anything going on between us."

Mrs. Smalley nodded, clearly not believing a word Tess was saying. "Give it time, honey—give it time."

"No, no." Tess tried to object, but the furious heat she felt pouring up her throat was making things worse. Why on earth had God decided to make her a blusher?

To make things worse, Jake chose that moment to look at her and wink. Mrs. Smalley laughed out loud. "You know," she said close to Tess's ear, "there is a phrase 'match made in heaven.'"

This was too much!

But heaven intervened and saved her as the first of the hungry and lonely trickled past on their way to the small dining room.

Thanksgiving dinner had begun.

For the next two hours Tess was too busy to give Jake much thought, although their eyes did meet frequently over steamy bowls of stuffing and corn as she passed them from the kitchen to the serving area.

Eventually, however, the area moved from organized chaos to a diminished roar and then to an exhausted but satisfied calm. The workers drooped into the now-vacant folding chairs, and Tess smiled as Jake collapsed into the one adjoining hers.

"Whew." He ran his fingers through his work-ruffled hair.

A single voice began to sing softly, and soon the others joined in: " 'We gather together. . . .' " Tess's soft alto was joined by Jake's strong baritone, and they smiled at each other as they united in the familiar Thanksgiving hymn.

He sang the hymn from memory. Tess's heart lifted again.

But her hopes were deflated quickly as, when the song ended, he sighed. "I learned that early on. We sang it every year in school at Thanksgiving. I've always loved it."

He learned it in school.

She fought against the disappointment. But before she could phrase a prayer, words of assurance came, this time from Reverend Barnes.

"We've done a good thing here today, but feeding over a hundred people a rollicking good turkey dinner isn't enough. I hope we've done more than send them out with warm food in their bodies. A full stomach doesn't mean a lot if there isn't a full soul to go with it. Let us pray that today we fed those whose souls were already full, and those whose souls were hungry. Let this food be our testimony to Jesus Christ."

She heard several fervent amens.

Reverend Barnes continued as he reminded them of one of Tess's favorite passages from the Bible: "When Jesus said, 'I was hungry, and you fed Me,' was He talking about turkey dinners only? Or should we search for more in His words? What lesson do we take forward with us from this day?"

The group silently considered the minister's words. Tess found herself returning yet once more to Jake's presence today and her role in it. Was he one of those Reverend Barnes had referred to as those with hungry souls? If so, had her words and actions been witness enough?

"Bless you all for what you have done. No matter how small, every effort grows when united with others. Have a blessed Thanksgiving, my friends, and don't forget the leftovers. You've earned them!"

Soft laughter spread through the small gathering, and, one by one, people stood up, stretched, and returned again to the kitchen for one last stop—the take-home containers Tess and Mrs. Smalley had packed during the last minutes of the dinner for each of the workers.

Neither Jake nor Tess spoke until they were out of the church. The night sky overhead was clear and cloudless, and stars sprinkled the deep indigo with dots of silver. If she looked hard enough, she could see all the way to heaven, she thought.

Their breath plumed outward as they stopped, by silent mutual agreement, and took in the view.

"Thanks for inviting me," Jake said at last.

"Actually I didn't. You invited yourself," she teased him.

"So I did." He chuckled softly. "Are you sorry?"

"No. I'm not." Her eyes met his in an honest gaze. "I'm glad you came."

"You know, I'm beginning to rethink my opinion of downtown," he said.

"I'm starting to see what you find so appealing here. It does have a life of its own I was never aware of." He chuckled again. "And I don't feel at all threatened by this great long walk at night."

As they started the short trek back to her house, her foot found a slick patch on the walk, and she began to slip. He took her hand to steady her.

He held her hand, mittened fingers closed in mittened fingers, the entire way to her house.

"Thank you again," he said, still holding her hand. "This has been a Thanksgiving I will never forget."

"Nor will I," she agreed.

"Your church is as friendly and warm as you are." His dark eyes seemed to be saying something she couldn't read so she took the plunge.

"You know you're always welcome at Nativity." When he seemed still to be waiting for her to say more, she added, "If you'd like, you can go with me to a service."

"That's an invitation I may take you up on someday," he said, and his fingers tightened around hers before letting her hand go.

He turned and walked away.

Tess stood outside and watched him drive off. His car seemed so big, and so empty.

She went inside her house and gave Cora the leftovers. As the cat gulped down the turkey tidbits, Tess went into the store to double-check the front-door lock. The glow from the streetlight outside caught on a sideways gleam— that of a halo, once again tipped.

Faith. They had both forgotten about her.

He'd be back. He didn't have any choice. She still had his angel, his Faith.

Tess's evening prayer centered around Jake as she sought guidance on living as a witness. The answer was not quite what she had expected: She remembered another Bible verse, this one from Hebrews, that Reverend Barnes could have easily used. "Be not forgetful to entertain strangers: for thereby some have entertained angels unawares."

Could it be? Maybe the one needing the witness had been her? Had she, the expert on angels, been in the presence of some tonight? Which stranger might fit the bill? One of those in need of warm food? One in need of a warm heart?

Jake's image sprang into her mind.

"Flip the picture," Reverend Barnes had advised.

"Wow," breathed Tess. "Wow."

Chapter 3

Not that Tess thought he was an angel! No, if anything, Jake was on the other end of the celestial spectrum.

Actually, that wasn't fair. He had volunteered to help out at the church dinner, and so far he'd given her no indication he wasn't a Christian. And, that little annoying niggling voice inside reminded her, he'd also given her no indication he was a Christian.

But she was getting off track. "Maybe," she said to Cora, who had finished her feast of turkey leftovers and was cleaning her whiskers with satisfaction, "I should be worrying less about his soul and more about mine."

Cora was too stuffed even to meow, it seemed. Instead she strolled over to her spot beside the heating vent and collapsed in sated ecstasy.

"You glutton," Tess said. "Here I am in moral turmoil, and all you can do is purr."

Cora opened one heavy eyelid and stared at her.

"You're right, as usual," Tess told the cat. "I can't expect God to answer my prayers just like that"—she snapped her fingers—"and in a way I'm necessarily going to like. Maybe what I need to do now is get out of God's way on this and let Him work through me, instead of trying to make Him work through me."

She flopped down beside Cora. "You are the smartest kitty in the world," she cooed as she ran her fingers through the soft fur.

She was certain the cat smiled, just a bit.

✒

The day after Thanksgiving was traditionally the busiest shopping day of the year, and this year was no different. What Tess didn't know as the day began was that the evening news had aired a special about downtown regrowth and the mayor's plan. She hadn't watched the news because she'd been at the Thanksgiving dinner at Nativity when the story ran.

But her first customers told her about it. Angel's Roost had been one of the shops mentioned, and over and over she heard the same comment: "I didn't even know you were down here."

Clearly she needed to advertise. With only the brief mention on the news her business had tripled. What could it do with an effective promotional campaign?

During breaks in the flow of people stocking up on angels for decorations and gifts, she began to sketch out an advertisement.

But, as the afternoon trade died down, so did her enthusiasm.

"I'm no artist," she told Cora. "If I want to get Angel's Roost in the public's mind, I'll have to hire an advertising agency or get on the news every night."

She chose a name at random from the phone book's listing of ad agencies. Their conversation was short and anything but sweet. "Well, Toots," she informed Cora, "I'd better hope for lots of news coverage because there is no way I can afford a professional advertising agency."

The price of an original ad from an agency wasn't high, but it was more than she could pay right now. Maybe after Christmas she'd look into it. She'd have more time then. Unfortunately, when things were quieter at the store, her bank balance dropped accordingly.

The tinkle of the door chime ended in a crash.

"Uh-oh." Jake picked up the legs of the metallic angel, now separated from her body, which swung freely over the door.

"Poor thing." Tess took the pieces and examined them. "Oh, no problem. I can put them back together. This ring came apart here."

"Whew. I was afraid I was responsible for bringing an angel earthward. That weighs heavy on the old conscience, you know."

She grinned at him. "You lowly mortal. Don't you know it takes more than a human being to bring down an angel?"

"I'm not going to argue." He held up his hands in mock surrender. "I'm delighted I haven't taken an angel out of more than temporary commission. And speaking of angels"—he patted Faith on her curly little head—"I've come to take this gal with me."

"I'm going to miss her, you know." Tess was surprised at how true that was.

"I don't blame you. But she'll have a good home with us at Panda's. She has her own niche all set up right inside the door."

Tess was struck with a sudden horrible thought. "She's not going to be holding a coffee cup, is she, with a sign at her feet saying something like 'World's Most Heavenly Coffee'?"

Jake looked aghast. "Do you really think I'd be guilty of a cheap trick like that? No, let me assure you. She is going to be there as an angel, not as an advertising gimmick. If she wants to take over as Panda's guardian angel—that is, if one hasn't already been assigned to us—well, that'd be fine with me."

"I'm not sure businesses have guardian angels," Tess said doubtfully.

"But their owners do, don't they?"

"Everybody does." She couldn't resist adding, "And some people must have a whole host of them guarding them. Children, for example. How else do they live through childhood relatively unharmed?"

He chuckled. "I bet I sent at least one angel into early retirement."

She motioned to a famous print of a guardian angel guiding two precious children, a boy and a girl, along a path. "How often do you suppose something like this happens? One angel assigned to two children?"

"If that were a picture of my sister and me, that poor angel would be a nervous wreck. What you don't see is the itching powder the little boy put inside the girl's clothing, and the Kick Me sign she taped to his pants." He studied the picture. "Matter of fact, why don't you wrap that up, too? I'm going to give it to my sister for Christmas, just to remind her of how angelic we were as kids."

"Does your family live around here?" Tess asked as she took the painting down and wrapped pink and gold angel-printed tissue paper around it.

"They're all over the country," he said, paying her once again with cash. "Sis and her family are in Mississippi, my two brothers are in New England, and Mom and Dad are in Southern California."

"Will you be seeing them this Christmas?"

He shook his head. "No. The big family gathering takes place every summer at the family cabin in Montana, but I'll try to buzz out and see Mom and Dad later in January." His eyes twinkled. "Right about then I'm ready for some basking in the sun without a parka, and, oh yeah, it's great to see my parents, too."

"Sounds fun."

"It is. They have a big ranch-style house with a swimming pool. It's quite a nice break from the icy depths of winter. Although I have to say it gets harder and harder to go out there to visit, what with Panda's taking so much of my time."

"Being a sole practitioner in business means vacation time is severely curtailed, that's for sure."

"True." He reached down and patted Cora, who had joined them. "Besides, this grand lady might not be as flexible as your customers."

"That's the truth!"

She handed him the package. "Want some help carrying all this to your car?"

"I can get it." As he gathered up the large angel and balanced the print under his arm, he said, "By the way, come out to Panda's soon and see how Faith is doing out there. I think you'll like it."

"I'll try." She held the door open for him. "It was nice doing business with you."

He stopped and turned to look at her. "Oh, I'm not finished yet. I still have more shopping to do. See you later!"

Cora joined Tess at the door but cringed back at the gust of cold air that swept into the small store.

"Brr. You're right, Cora. It's way too cold today." She shut the door and, through the window, watched him struggle with the angel as he tried to wrangle it into the car without bending the wings or totally tearing off the halo.

She grinned as he finally gave up and put it in the front seat, like a passenger.

What was he doing now? She laughed out loud as he stood up and moved away from the door. He'd even fastened her in with the shoulder strap of the seat belt!

He glanced back at the store and, catching her eye through the window, gave a jaunty wave before pulling away from the curb.

He'd no sooner left than another figure loped up the walk to the front of the shop.

"Reverend Barnes!" Tess cried in delight as the minister stooped slightly at the door. "You don't have to duck today. The door angel broke."

"Oh no." He looked in consternation at the body of the angel still swinging over the transom. "She always seemed to say hello when I visited."

"Oh, she'll be back. It wasn't anything I can't fix. Actually, it's a good sign. I've been so busy today that she got a workout, the likes of which she's never seen before."

"I heard you had some good coverage last night on the news. It's great that it brought out customers in droves."

"Well, not in droves, exactly. Clusters. That's it. Clusters of customers. So what can I do for you, Reverend?"

"I want to buy Mrs. Barnes a really special angel this year. This will be our thirty-seventh Christmas together, you know."

"Thirty-seventh! I'm impressed. You both deserve angels for that. What did you have in mind?"

"Something with gold and diamonds and emeralds for putting up with me all these years," he said jokingly.

"Gold and diamonds and emeralds," she mused. "Gold and diamonds and emeralds. Hmm. Let me think what I have in stock right now."

"I'm just teasing!" he protested.

"So am I. Crystal and colored glass, maybe. Hey!" She snapped her fingers. "I have an idea that might work."

She reached high overhead and felt around until her fingers closed around it. "How about this?"

She handed it to him. It was a shining silver bell, a bit dusty now. At the top of it, serving as a handle, was an elaborately sculpted angel's head, her hair made of hundreds of delicate gold wires fused together lightly. The bell was her skirt, a lacy gold mesh network overlaid atop the silver background.

"I could engrave it here"—she pointed to the hem of the gleaming skirt where a band of smooth silver ran along the border—"with whatever you would like. That would personalize it."

"Perfect!" The minister's eyes shone with enthusiasm. "What should I put on it?"

Tess shrugged. "Whatever you want is fine; it just can't be too long, or it won't fit. What would you like to say to her?"

"You know, she's been my angel all these years, but I wonder if she knows it."

"How about 'My Angel'?" she suggested.

"Perfect! How soon will it be done? And this is a secret, you know."

"I'll have it done early next week. And my lips are sealed," Tess promised solemnly.

"And, speaking of secrets, why have you been keeping your young man a secret?"

"What young man? Talk about secrets! I didn't even know I had a young man! Rats. I'm always the last to know." Tess laughed lightly and tried to suppress the telltale flush she knew was edging its way up her neck.

"Don't play coy with me, Tess Mahoney." The minister waggled his finger under her nose. "You know good and well who I'm talking about. I mean that fellow who came to the dinner with you and helped us out so much. That young man. What's the story with him?"

"There really isn't a story, Reverend Barnes." Tess sadly acknowledged to herself that this wasn't an actual lie. "He's a customer. As a matter of fact, he just bought that big angel that's usually there"—she pointed to the empty spot and tried to ignore the twinge in her heart—"and a print, and that's that."

Reverend Barnes studied her shrewdly. "No, that's not that. There's more, but I'm not going to pry. I did promise your grandmother I'd keep watch over you, you know."

"Yes, I know." Tess's heart gentled. "And I am telling you the truth. I've only known him since the day before Thanksgiving. And I do like him—a lot—but there's really no more to the story."

"It's still early," he said.

"He's a customer," she repeated, with slight emphasis on the last word.

"I meant early in the day," he said, his bright blue eyes dancing with impishness. "Why, whatever did you think I meant? Girl, you've got to learn to relax!"

She could not become irritated with him. He was a rascal, and she absolutely adored him. Besides, she knew he had only her best interests at heart.

She made a split-second decision to confide in him. "Reverend Barnes, I do like him. A lot. I like his sense of humor, his thoughtfulness." She struggled for the words. "He even likes Cora."

"More to the point, does she like him?" He was all too familiar with the way the cat ruled the household.

"She adores him. Well, she lets him scratch her ears. And her nose. And her forehead." She pretended to frown. "Reverend Barnes, I do believe the man is courting my cat."

"This sounds like it's getting serious," he answered, and Tess realized he was only partially kidding her. "When a man woos a woman's cat, he's building the base for an all-out campaign to win her heart."

"Do you think so?" Her fingers clasped together so tightly that her ring cut into her palm. "I mean, I almost don't dare to hope, and, let's face it, I'm out of practice with all this. But I do like him."

The minister pried her tensed fingers apart. "Just take it easy, Tess. Let

God guide you through this. I'll be praying for you."

"I also wonder if he's a Christian," she said softly. "It does matter, you know."

He patted her hands. "You were born into the faith, my dear, and it's always been part of you, like your red hair and your blue eyes. But even if I didn't know your religious background, I'd have to say I'd be more surprised if I learned that you weren't a Christian than that you were."

"I don't follow."

"I can't say for sure, but I have that feeling about Jake. He's a good man, Tess, at least from what I saw of him last night. Certainly there are consummate actors who can fool you into thinking they're saints when the only view of heaven they've seen is a perfume ad. But I don't sense that about this young man. I think he's all right."

His assessment tallied with hers, she had to admit. Jake did seem ethical, so why was she looking for something to be wrong with him?

"Just let God lead you," the pastor advised. "And let this relationship develop without complicating it early on. Have faith in God's wisdom."

There was that word again. "Faith."

"You're still young," Reverend Barnes continued. "You need to get out, have fun, go to dinner. And, speaking of dinner, I'd better be going. Mrs. Barnes is making her famous stuffed pork chops."

Tess smiled. "World famous, I'd say. She's going to have to give me that recipe."

He shook his head as he pulled up the collar of his overcoat. "Not a chance. That recipe ranks right up there with the CIA's most-secret secret. About the other matter"—he grinned widely—"I'll check back with you later. Meanwhile, try to relax and have a good time. If you get the chance to share your faith, do it, but don't push it too hard too fast."

He winked at her. "Your grandparents raised you to be a good Christian girl, and your faith shows through you like a beacon. That alone does more to move a seeking soul than a year of my sermons. Why, I'll bet that right now your faith is having a nice visit with that young man, Jake What's-His-Name."

She stared after him, her mouth agape. How did he do that? She looked at the empty spot where Faith had stood. Nice visit, indeed. Sometimes that man was downright spooky.

The phone rang, interrupting her contemplations. She picked it up and held it to her ear, still absorbed in the minister's words.

"Hello? Hello?" A disembodied voice floated from the telephone receiver. "Tess?"

"Angel's Roost," she answered, snapping back to reality. "May I help you?"

"Tess, this is Jake." The connection spit and crackled. "Sorry. This car phone is giving me all sorts of problems. Anyway, I wanted to know if you had plans for tonight."

"No, no." The minister's words revisited her: *"Have fun—go to dinner."* *Easy for him to say,* she thought. "No, I don't have any plans."

"How'd you like to go to dinner tonight?" Jake asked. "Tess? Tess?" How did that man do it?

Chapter 4

Tess pawed through her closet one more time. Well, there was nothing to be done at this stage: She'd wear her green silk. She slipped into it and preened at her reflection in the hall mirror. She had to admit it. No matter that the dress was four years old; it did look good on her.

She told herself she was cool, calm, and collected. She pulled back her shoulders, tilted her chin upward, and tried for a haughty look, like a lady of society.

A furry shadow moved into the mirrored image, sniffed Tess's ankles, and twitched her tail crossly, as if angry that her owner would be leaving her alone on a cold winter night.

"Don't worry, sweetie. I'll only be gone awhile," Tess crooned, smoothing Cora's already silky gray coat. "It's just a date."

Just a date. Her stomach flipped up and flopped down.

A slight whisk of makeup, a quick brush through the tousled auburn curls, and she was ready. She'd just sprayed on a light spritz of cologne when she heard a knock at the back door.

Jake whistled as he saw her. "You, my friend, are a knockout!"

"Why, thank you!" she responded, trying not to smile too much. A knockout! No one had ever called her a knockout before. She felt ridiculously flattered.

He helped her into her coat and then paused as she opened the door. "I hate to be making fashion suggestions to such an elegant lady, but wouldn't you be more comfortable walking to the car with shoes on?"

"Shoes?" she asked blankly. Then she looked down at her feet and saw her stockinged toes. "Shoes," she repeated.

She must be more flustered than she had given herself credit for. She dashed up the stairs and pulled a pair of shoes from her closet, making sure they matched. She wasn't taking any more chances!

She said good-bye to Cora, who glared at her through slitted eyes, and they left her house. His car was parked in front, and it was still warm.

"Where are we going?" She settled herself into the leather luxuriousness of his car. The dashboard had more lights than Las Vegas. She didn't have any idea what half of them were for, but she didn't want to ask.

"To Whispering Winds."

Wow. Tess formed the word silently.

"Ever been there?"

27

"No, can't say I have."

He turned slightly toward her, taking his gaze off the road momentarily. "Guess why I chose it."

"Because it has good food?" she ventured.

"Partially. Guess again."

"Good service?"

"Nope. Keep trying."

She was stumped. Because it was probably the most expensive place in the area? Because he thought she'd probably never eaten there? Because she'd be impressed? No, all those reasons sounded so shallow. She made one last effort.

"Because you own it?"

He burst out laughing. "I wish! No, guess again."

"I give up. Tell me."

"Because it's not downtown and not on the south end. It's middle ground."

That was true. Even as he spoke, they left the city limits and drove on the old highway access toward a darkened county road.

Jake slowed down and peered at the small blue reflecting markers that glowed alongside the road. "If I'm not careful, I'll miss the turnoff. They should mark it better."

He located the road sign and turned down the county road. Without the street lamps or even occasional lights of the highway, the night sky surrounded them so completely she couldn't tell where sky ended and earth began. Only the headlights of the car cut through the darkness like a searchlight.

"Are you sure this is right?" Tess asked tentatively. "It's really, really dark out here."

"Well, I'm pretty sure," Jake responded, but his words held a trace of hesitancy. "It can be hard to tell out here, though. You get on the wrong road, and you can go miles before you get your bearings. Even during the day. Why, last summer I was out—oh, here it is. I recognize that white-painted rock."

Tess felt the car begin to climb a small rise—almost a hill, if there could be such a thing in eastern North Dakota.

And, sure enough, at the top of the rise, there, spread out before them like a sparkling lake of glittering lights, lay Whispering Winds.

He slowed down and pulled into the expansive parking lot. Even at night Tess could tell the place was spectacular. She had the impression of a ring of pines and spruce edging the parking lot and circling behind the restaurant.

Small trees, possibly maples, although she couldn't tell without their foliage, dotted the freshly snowplowed parking lot. Tiny white lights glittered in the leafless branches.

A young man in a military-style overcoat and hat met the car as Jake pulled into the looping road by the front door of the restaurant. As the keys were exchanged between Jake and the valet, Tess let herself out of the car, over their objections, and stood near the entrance.

She heard a soft murmur as the evergreens brushed against each other in the evening breeze, undoubtedly the source of the poetic name of the restaurant.

"You didn't need to wait outside," Jake said as he joined her, taking her elbow and guiding her toward the restaurant's door. "It's too cold."

She shook her head. "No. I was listening."

"Listening?" For a moment Jake seemed lost; then he nodded in understanding. "Oh, you heard the whisper. That says a lot, you know. Not everyone can be quiet enough to hear it. Legend has it that only a truly peaceful soul can hear it."

They entered through the massive brass and etched-glass doors. Tess paused and looked around her.

"This is magnificent!" she breathed.

The restaurant was constructed as a great room. The ceiling arched a full two stories overhead. Each table was draped with a pristine white tablecloth, and the chairs were upholstered in a muted mallard green. Over the hardwood floors Oriental rugs of a thousand colors and patterns were scattered, adding an underlay of hues that contrasted with the stark monochromatic vault above them.

They checked their coats and allowed a server to lead them to a table. It was tucked back into the corner, and Tess wondered if Jake had requested it. But every table seemed to be situated with an awareness of privacy, so maybe she was reading too much into it.

"Would you like a cocktail before you order?" the hostess asked.

Jake looked at her, and Tess shook her head slightly. "If they have mineral water, that would be wonderful."

"Mineral water for both of us, please," Jake directed the hostess, and she left.

"You didn't have to skip the drink because I did," Tess said, though she was secretly glad he did.

"I don't drink," Jake said and paused, as if weighing what to say next. "I grew up in a house where drinking was a problem for a while. My dad was a borderline alcoholic, although he's come around since then."

"I'm sorry to hear your family was in that situation," Tess said, "but I'm delighted to hear it's different now."

"Yes. Dad has changed in a lot of ways. I'm glad the period when he was at rock bottom was brief. Still, it's something that stays with me, and I consider it every time I'm offered a drink."

Once again Jake rose in her estimation. If there were a ladder to measure his standing, he'd be climbing it steadily, rung by rung.

"Thank you for sharing that," she said softly. "You didn't have to, you know."

"Oh, I'm sorry." He reached across the table and covered her hand with his. "I didn't mean to get too personal."

"Don't worry. It didn't offend me. I just realize how painful personal topics can be to disclose."

"It's not a subject I usually chat about, but something about you makes me want to tell you everything about me." His look was intense and a bit unsure. "But, to be honest, we're edging into an area that makes me uncomfortable."

He might as well have dumped the crystal pitcher of ice water in her lap. Her face must have registered her shock, because he explained quickly: "I'm afraid this conversation is going to give you the wrong impression of my family and me. I had a very happy childhood, all in all. This one stage was blessedly short-lived, but memorable. I like to think it made me stronger. I know it served that function for my father."

"Well, I also had a pleasant childhood, although it was, at the time, unconventional. My parents were both killed in an automobile accident—"

"Oh, I'm sorry," he murmured sympathetically.

"Thank you, but I wasn't even two at the time, so I don't have anything but vague unshaped memories. My grandparents stepped into the breach and took over, never letting me have a moment that wasn't filled to overflowing with love."

She smiled as the memories washed over her. They were wonderful people, her grandparents. She wished they could have met Jake, and she said so aloud.

"I can see their love in you still," he said, his gaze resting softly on her face.

It was the best thing he could have said. Tess felt their legacy daily, the strong basis of faith and trust they had instilled in her early.

The waitress chose that moment to appear at their table and take their orders. Tess quickly studied the menu and selected the salmon pasta in pesto sauce.

"That does sound good," Jake said. "Maybe I'll switch my choice from the filet mignon."

The waitress stood by patiently while they sorted through the side dishes and salads that accompanied their entrees, leaving them in solitude at last.

The conversation took a lighter turn, as they discussed television shows they enjoyed. Both admitted to liking half-hour situation comedies, and when Jake allowed that his favorites were the late-night reruns of the old black-and-white shows, Tess agreed happily.

They ran through some of the more memorable *I Love Lucy* episodes and were just reliving the famous assembly-line sequence in the chocolate factory when their salads arrived.

Tess didn't know it was possible to do such wonderful things with a salad. The heated dressing was heavenly, and the butter flavored with sun-dried tomato and a hint of Parmesan cheese was exquisite on the warm rolls, clearly fresh from the oven.

"You know, I could have a whole meal of this alone," she said at last. "I'm going to try adding seasoning to butter at home, but I doubt I can do this justice. This is scrumptious!"

"I'm glad you're enjoying it. You said this is your first time here?" he prompted.

She nodded. "I've been meaning to come for a long time, but I've never gotten around to it. Do you come out here often?"

"Not as often as I'd like," he confessed. "Panda's keeps me pretty busy." He pushed his salad plate to the side and lowered his voice. "I'd like your feedback on something. But first I need your promise that this will stay confidential."

"Sounds pretty serious."

"It is."

"Then I can't promise." At his look of surprise she explained. "I decided a couple of years ago not to put myself in morally compromising spots. And part of that was not making promises that make me uneasy. This one does that."

"There's nothing morally compromising in this!" he protested.

"But I don't know that," she reminded him gently. "You haven't told me anything. For all I know, you may be about to tell me your plans to rob First Central Bank next Wednesday."

"Rob a bank!" His words rang out loudly, and several diners turned to him with surprised looks on their faces. He grinned sheepishly and waved his hand apologetically to them.

"Well, now that they all think I'm a master criminal—"

"Hardly a master criminal," she interrupted. "I don't think a master criminal would announce his plans to a crowded restaurant."

"That's true. But what I want to talk to you about isn't criminal or anything like that. It's business," he said.

She laughed. "A master criminal you're not, and a master businessperson I'm not. Why on earth would you ask my opinion about a business matter?"

"Here's the deal. I'm thinking about moving Panda's downtown."

She sat up straight. "You're kidding me! Panda's downtown?"

"Sssh!" He glanced around the crowded dining room, but no one seemed to have heard. "I'm not sure yet. I'm just tossing the idea around."

"Well, a coffeehouse downtown would be welcomed by the business owners—I can assure you of that," she said, trying to sound calm when in fact she wanted to shout with anticipation. The idea was spinning cartwheels in her head.

Panda's downtown! The contribution that move would make to economic regrowth was nearly unfathomable. If Panda's moved, other trendy restaurants and shops in the south end might follow. It could be the initial step in a trend that signaled the necessary revitalization of the historic downtown!

"So you do think it's a good idea?" he persisted cautiously.

"What do I have to do—a wild dance of joy?" She grinned at him.

"That would be interesting but unnecessary, I think. No, I'm serious.

31

What do you think?"

"I love it! Do you have a location selected yet? There are some wonderful old buildings that would be ideal. There's one down on the riverfront with a wide span of a back wall. You could break through it—I'm sure the owner would allow construction—and be able to serve in the back, alfresco, in the summer."

She warmed to her subject, becoming more enthusiastic by the minute. When she finally began to run down, she realized he was staring at her, his chin cupped in his hand. "Wow," was all he said.

Tess fussed unnecessarily with her napkin. "Well, it is a topic near and dear to my heart. I'm a downtown girl, you know. I honestly don't see what the appeal is in the south end. Not a single tree grew there naturally, except for some old homesteader's shelterbelt trees that escaped the ax, and they exist only through the good graces of who knows what."

"The End is safer. It's cleaner. We have a lot more traffic out there. I see an excitement there that I honestly don't sense downtown."

She had done it. She had unwittingly insulted him and his original business decision. She quickly tried to make amends. "I'm sorry. I don't get over there very often—" She bit her tongue to keep from speaking the rest of the thought, that she purposely avoided that part of town.

"That's all right. I know there's a solid division in the city between downtown and the End. Each thinks it has the advantage over the other."

She nodded. "Considering how you feel about the End, why are you considering bringing Panda's downtown?"

The vigor came back into his demeanor. "I do appreciate the historic setting of downtown. And I like the mayor. If anyone can make this new project work, she most certainly can. It would be exciting to be part of it."

"But—?" she prompted.

"But I have no assurances—and a lot of questions. What if she loses the next election? What if she can't get the rest of the business community behind her? What if, despite the city's best intentions, the whole thing flops? What then?"

They weren't questions she hadn't heard and fielded a hundred times, but for once, the ready, pat answers wouldn't serve. It became real, this chance they were asking businesspeople to take. Invest in downtown. Invest their money. Probably most of it. And with nothing to promise in return.

Now the doubt had a face and a name. Jake's. And her answer became vitally important. She sent a quick prayer heavenward, asking for guidance in what she was about to say to him.

She chose her words carefully. "Beginning your business in the End was a risk. You had no guarantee it'd go."

He shook his head. "No. It was a risk, but not a great one. There was no other coffeehouse, and the time was right. The only risk now if I stay there is that the appeal may fall off in a few years. But then the challenge would be to adapt."

"Okay," she conceded. "Let's talk about moving Panda's."

"On the downside," he said, "I risk losing my established customers."

"No," she argued, "they'll follow you."

"Maybe, but a great number of them will simply move to another place in the End. I no longer have the monopoly on coffeehouses out there."

"But you would downtown," she pointed out. "No other place there is like Panda's."

"And, on the other hand," he continued, "although I might lose some in the move, a significant number downtown would come to Panda's, not just businesspeople like you, but those who live there."

"What you want is a guarantee," she stated at last, sensing an impasse. "You don't lose anything, but you gain substantially."

He grinned. "Well, that would be nice. Is the downtown commission by any chance offering something like that?"

"Nice try, but no."

"So what do you say to me, to make me bring Panda's downtown?"

She deliberated before she spoke. "I say, follow your heart. You're right—it's going to be exciting for the downtown in the next couple of years. If you want to be part of that excitement, then join us. But don't do it if your heart isn't in it 100 percent. This is going to be a long-range commitment, and you need to be willing to be in it for the duration. About the last thing this project needs is people who will fall away as it begins rolling along."

"I understand all of that," he said uneasily, "but is it enough for me to be committed to the project? Isn't there more to it? I do have my own financial future to consider. I don't have a wife and children now, but I hope to someday. I don't want to go into that relationship in debt."

The thought of him married and with a family brought a shimmer to Tess's heart.

"I guess," she said at last, "it's like a lot of things in life. You've got to have faith. There are no guarantees about how things will turn out, but there you have it. Faith. That's what it's going to take."

His dark eyes met hers. "I bought her at your store, remember?"

She smiled at him, glad for the way the tone of the conversation had quickly lightened. "How could I ever forget?"

"I'm wondering if Faith belongs downtown or if there's a place for her out on the End."

She heard the seeking in his words. "Faith can be anywhere, Jake. Anywhere."

"Even in a coffeehouse on the other end of town? Guarding a roaster that's held together by a wire coat hanger and duct tape?"

"Even there," she said.

Chapter 5

Tess put aside her turmoil-bound thoughts and turned her attention to her dinner. The pasta was just as wonderful as she'd hoped it would be, the sauce perfectly spiced with basil and a hint of garlic, and an array of pine nuts sprinkled over the top.

The server brought a tray laden with desserts of all kinds: caramel cheesecake dripping with honeyed sauce, apple pie with a crust that flaked at the slightest motion, and the piéce de résistance: something called chocolate truffle elegance. Neither Tess nor Jake could resist it, but their stomachs ached in protest at the thought, so they agreed to share a slice.

Soon it arrived, a heart-shaped deep chocolate concoction, which Tess realized was exactly the color of Jake's eyes, dusted with pale pink-tinted powdered sugar and drizzled with an even darker chocolate sauce. Atop it were two cherries perched on a pure white cloud of whipped cream.

"How many calories do you suppose this bite has?" Tess groaned as she reluctantly destroyed the picturesque presentation. "Thousands and thousands?"

"Like you care," Jake retorted, his eyes dancing. "You probably won't have to spend the next month at the gym doing penance for this."

"Well—"

"If you're about to tell me about the lucky metabolism you inherited, can it, lady." He growled menacingly at her. "I inherited a metabolism meant to carry me through the endlessly harsh winters of my prairie ancestors when there wasn't anything to eat but a buffalo tail and a dust bunny. Why, I could live on this little snack alone for a month or two, if I didn't move too much."

" 'Little snack'? I can't eat another bite, although it does seem criminal to leave even a crumb. It's so good."

He leaned over and whispered conspiratorially, "Wrap it up in the napkin and put it in your purse."

"That does it!" Tess wiped her mouth and leaned back, trying to stop the laughter that bubbled up.

He signaled to the server, and when she came over he murmured some low words to her that Tess didn't catch. Undoubtedly something about the bill.

As they stood up to leave, the server returned with a small foil package shaped like a heart. "No way!" Tess cried. "You didn't."

"Maybe I did, and maybe I didn't," he said, guiding her toward the door where the valet was pulling up with his car. "Just keep that pretty little nose out of it."

A few people were outside, their voices carrying clearly in the night air. Somewhere in the distance, a cow mooed, and Tess laughed. "A not-so-subtle reminder that we are not alone," she said to Jake as he held open the car door for her. "No matter how elegant the surroundings, no matter how fluffy the whipped cream atop the chocolate truffle elegance, there will be a reminder that somewhere a big old cow is responsible for that whipped cream!"

Once they had topped that slight rise that constituted the county hill, they were again left in the pool of absolute night sky. Jake drove for a few minutes before pulling over to the side.

"What's wrong?" Tess couldn't keep the alarm out of her voice.

"Not what's wrong—what's right. Come on—let's go." Jake turned off the motor of his car.

"Go? I'm stuffed, Jake! I can't walk anywhere!"

"We're not going anywhere. Come on!" He opened his door and stepped out.

"Okay." Tess undid her seat belt and joined Jake at the side of the car.

"Look at this," he said, his arm sweeping around them. "Is this magnificent or what? Just look at all those stars. How many are there? We don't know. All we know is there are lots of them and they're beautiful, and that's enough."

He was right. The stars had never glittered so brightly, she was sure, as they did that night. There were stars behind stars, and the more she looked, the more she saw.

"There's Orion," he said, pointing to the row of three stars that made up the hunter's belt. "And the Big Dipper, and the Little Dipper, of course. And there's Cassiopeia, right over that big tree—can you see it? The celestial queen on her throne."

She leaned against him as the frigid air crept in around her coat.

"Cold?" he asked.

"A bit."

"Good." Jake grinned as he held her closely to him. With his arm wrapped around her, she basked in the warmth of their togetherness.

The sensation of absolute romance swept over her and through her. She felt light-headed, almost giddy, ready to dance, to sing.

How was he feeling right now? She stole a glance at him and discovered he was already looking at her.

"I really want to kiss you," he said softly.

"Then do."

Meteor showers probably fell that evening. That would explain the brilliant flashes and fireworks Tess saw, even through closed eyes.

"We'd better go," Jake said at last as the kiss finally broke. She nodded, trying unsuccessfully to keep her teeth from chattering as the cold reasserted its icy grip.

He led her around to the passenger's side of the car, and when she got in, he leaned over and fastened her seat belt.

"One more," he said. "Just one."

And he reverently laid a light kiss on her lips.

Conversation seemed unnecessary on the way back to town. He selected a radio station that played mellow orchestral music, which fit her mood precisely, and she rested her head against the glove-leather seat.

He had kissed her.

Over and over her mind replayed the scene, and with each replaying it just got better.

He had kissed her!

She was so engrossed in her happiness that she was surprised when the car came to a stop.

"Home, sweetheart." His voice shook her back to reality.

He opened the car door for her and walked her to the side door of her house. He waited patiently as she fumbled in her purse for the key. On the other side of the door came a plaintive meow and frantic scratching.

"I think somebody missed you," he said, his voice low in her ear.

"Usually she's not this crazed," Tess said as her fingers finally closed around the elusive key. "I hope nothing's wrong."

She opened the door, and the cat launched herself—not at Tess, but at Jake.

"What in the world is up with her?" Tess wondered aloud. Cora had never acted like that. She reached out to prevent the cat from attacking Jake, but to her astonishment Cora was rubbing against his arms and shoulders.

"Here, I'll try to pry her off you," she said. "She's usually not like this. Actually she's never been like this. I don't know what's gotten into her."

He tossed her the foil-wrapped package from the restaurant. "Maybe it's something she's hoping to get into her."

"Chocolate?" Tess asked. "She's a cat. She can't have—"

Cora jumped down from his grasp and pawed at Tess's knees.

Tess opened the package and laughed. It held bits and pieces of salmon. "Would you by any chance like some salmon, sweetie?"

"They're fillets that fell apart before cooking and couldn't be used," Jake explained, "so I asked them to save them."

"That's amazing. I didn't know they'd do something like that."

"Well, I may not own the place, but I do know the owner, and he's a cat lover from way back. He saves these portions all the time. You just have to know to ask for them."

He was extraordinary, no doubt about it.

"This is so sweet of you," she said to him.

Jake cooed at the cat as he fed her the scraps. "Nothing but the best table scraps for this exquisite cat, right, Cora?"

The cat gazed lovingly at Jake.

Tess had to smile. "I have never seen that cat look so googly-eyed before, not even with a major dose of catnip under her belt."

"I'm just trying to buy her affections. She's an amazing cat, you know. I think she has definite celestial connections, and, let's face it, we can use all the help we can get on that end."

"I prefer to get my help through more traditional means," Tess said quietly.

"More traditional means? Like what?" The question seemed almost throwaway; he asked it so offhandedly.

"Prayer." The single word was barely more than a whisper.

"Ah." He nodded but didn't volunteer anything else. He toyed with Cora's ear thoughtfully.

"It works." She sounded more defensive than she had intended to so she tried to soften it. "It really does, you know."

"Oh, I believe that."

"I'm still somewhat befuddled," she confessed. "Are you telling me you're a Christian?"

"Of course I am," he said. "I've been baptized, confirmed, the whole nine yards. I can still recite the Apostles' Creed from memory. We had to learn it in membership classes in sixth grade."

Her mind spun. She'd never been challenged like this before. Usually her conversations about religion were with people from Nativity, where everyone agreed on their terms.

"Are you active in your church?" she asked, teasing a salmon-stuffed Cora into activity with a fuzzy ball.

"No. Much of weekly trade comes from the post-church crowd, which begins early and lasts until shortly after lunch. I couldn't make it to any of the services in town, I'm afraid, and definitely not to the ones at the church I grew up in."

She asked which church that was, and when he named the largest, wealthiest church in town, she nodded. It was known for the strength of the pastoral care and its outreach projects specially designed to reach generally underserved groups; those targeted to college students, young parents, and single mothers were the best known among their many programs.

She had met the minister several times and had been impressed with the care he expressed about his congregation. She'd never seen him be depressed or sad for long; he was a man truly uplifted with joy by his knowledge of Jesus Christ.

"Don't they have midweek services there, too?" she ventured as a faint memory floated to the surface of her mind.

Jake shrugged. "I suppose so. I just don't get over there very much."

She didn't respond.

"Okay," he said, "I haven't been there for a long time. This Thanksgiving at Nativity was the first time I've set foot inside a church—any church—in probably fifteen years."

"You're right—that is a long time," she agreed.

As much as she longed to scold him for not going to church, she didn't. Perhaps if she kept quiet, he would lead himself back into the church. And, sure enough, he continued to talk.

"I liked what I saw of Nativity," he said, filling the unbearable silence, "and Reverend Barnes seems like a very inspiring person. What are your services like?"

She told him about the structure of a traditional Sunday service at Nativity and gave him a brief overview of the congregational belief.

"I don't know," he said. "I'll have to think about it."

"Come to church with me," she offered. "We'd all be delighted to have you join us for worship."

"Thanks. Maybe someday I'll take you up on that." He rubbed Cora's nose.

"I was raised in Nativity," she said, quietly remembering Sunday schools with dedicated teachers who painstakingly taught her the Ten Commandments, the Lord's Prayer, and, yes, the Apostles' Creed.

"We—Grandma, Grandpa, and I—would dress in our finery every Sunday morning and walk the half block to Nativity. Grandma carried her white leather Bible, Grandpa his great black one, and I'd proudly tote my pink one with my name on the front. My grandparents got that for me the Christmas I turned five."

"May I see it?" he asked, his question catching her by surprise.

"Honestly, no. I don't have it anymore." She raised her eyes as she spoke.

He leaned back, clearly shocked by her revelation. "Why not? I'd think someone as religious as you are and as admiring of your grandparents would hold on to that Bible until you died."

"I gave it away."

"You what?"

"A woman and her two children came into our church one very cold, very wintry day about two years ago. Their home had burned to the ground, with all their belongings in it. Poor woman. She was a widow whose husband had been shot during a convenience-store robbery, and she was trying so hard to hold it together for those dear children."

She smiled a bit at the memory. "Reverend Barnes made her a little apartment downstairs at Nativity—actually, the dining area where we served Thanksgiving dinner—until she could put her life back together."

"And the Bible. . . ?" Jake asked.

"The little girl sat by me on Sundays and called it the pretty pink book. She liked to look through it during the service and study the pictures. Her favorite was the one of Jesus surrounded by the children."

"So you gave it to her."

"Sure. Why not?"

He shook his head in amazement. "It still astounds me. Couldn't you have given her another Bible, maybe a new one? That would have worked as well."

"No, Jake, it wouldn't have. I wasn't just giving her a book. I was giving her more than that. See, the mother had decided to go into church service, and this was my way of supporting them when I wasn't there to give them a hug or read them a story." The more she tried to explain it, the muddier it sounded to her. "I was giving her my love, my confidence in her, my support."

"It's wonderful," he said. "I think that Bible has gone deeply into places no other book, no other copy of that book, could go. I'm sure it went directly into their hearts and souls and took up residence. And," he added softly, "the greatest compliment they could give you would be to give the Bible away again, right?"

"I occasionally have twinges of nostalgia about that sweet old Bible. But now I carry Grandma's when I make my weekly pilgrimage to church, and Grandpa's is in the place of honor in the house, over the mantel in the living room."

Out of nowhere a yawn overtook her. With great embarrassment she covered her mouth and tried to stop it, but it was too late.

"It's almost midnight," he said. "It's time for me to go anyway."

He ran his hand over Cora's smooth fur as the cat slept peacefully between them, her stomach distended with the salmon scraps.

"She's snoring!" he said softly.

"She does that when she's overindulged herself," Tess said lovingly.

"Well, here's to a snoring night for all of us," he said, standing up. "I don't know about you, but I'm still stuffed."

"Me, too."

She handed him his coat. "Thanks for taking me to dinner. I apologize for the conversation getting so serious here at the end."

"No need to apologize. I'm just delighted to be getting to know you."

He touched her cheek with his fingertips. "Good night, sweet angel. I'll call you later." His lips barely brushed the top of her head before he turned and left.

She couldn't help herself. She yawned widely and openly.

It had been a wonderful and strange night. And it was clear to her that she was falling for this man more quickly than she had ever imagined possible.

Did people fall in love this rapidly? It was one question too many for her overworked brain.

"Come on, Cora," she said to the slumbering cat. "Race you to bed."

Even stopping to brush her teeth and wash her face, Tess won the race easily. Cora didn't, in fact, try. Instead Tess padded downstairs in her robe and slippers, picked up the slumbering cat, and carried her upstairs.

The two ladies slept, their tummies full of gourmet salmon. And both snored softly.

Chapter 6

Saturday. Tess was usually up and around every day of the week by seven, but this morning Cora had to notify her the day had begun without her breakfast. Some loud meows in her owner's ear and a few well-placed swats with a thick furry paw, and the situation was well on its way to being remedied.

Tess was awake—sort of.

She ambled downstairs in her robe and fuzzy slippers, yawning in the bright sunshine that flooded the dining area as Cora followed her, reminding her of her very important errand.

She dumped a can of Meow Meals into Cora's bowl and was met with disdain. Had the cat actually sniffed with haughty contempt over her food?

"Come on, Cora—you've had Meow Meals every morning for three years. Are you all right?" Suddenly filled with concern, she knelt and put her hand on the cat's brow. Maybe that wasn't the way to test a cat for a fever. She'd never seen a veterinarian do that, at any rate.

The cat gave her one long annoyed look and, turning her back to Tess, began to scratch the floor around her dish as she pretended to bury the food.

"Oh, Cora, this is really too much." She tried to pick up the cat, but Cora slithered out of her grasp and leaped to the floor with a thump.

"I can't figure out—oh, wait a minute—yes, I can." She remembered the silvery heart filled with salmon scraps from the night before.

Tess retrieved the package, now considerably smaller, and emptied it onto Cora's plate. "I can't believe my weirdo cat has a better memory than I do," she told Cora, who was now gobbling the fish with relish, her earlier bout with hunger averted.

She nudged the cat's side with the tip of her slipper. "Just don't get used to it. When that's gone, it's back to Meow Meals and Cat-Cat Yums for you."

She yawned and stretched. Coffee, that's what she needed. The thought that Jake must have wonderful coffee every morning popped into her mind. He probably had all sorts of exotic varieties at his fingertips, and a grinder, too, she thought as she measured the store-brand coffee from the can. She did appreciate good coffee, freshly ground and brewed, but what she needed right now was immediate coffee.

A shriek sprang from her lips as she noted the clock over the stove. It was nearly nine!

Her toe caught in the rug, and she stumbled over Cora, who didn't so much as twitch a hair. Nothing was going to move her from her salmon breakfast.

A quick shower and speed dressing got her in the store in half an hour. She flipped the sign on the window from Closed to Open and unlocked the door.

Saturday mornings were generally slow, times when she dusted the inventory and wiped down the display cases and shelves. She tried to keep up with it on a catch-as-catch-can basis through the week, but she relied on Saturdays to do a more thorough job.

She took all the birthstone crystal angels off their shelf for detailed cleaning with the tiny brush she used specifically for the delicate items. A slight movement startled her.

It took a moment for her to identify the source of the motion—Cora had plopped herself in the spot vacated by Faith's departure.

Tess thought about how easily she had moved into calling the angel Faith, although the logical part of her still considered it foolish and misguided. But something about the zany angel made the name fit. It didn't make sense.

Neither did the fact that she missed the angel. The hole it left was more than in the display area. How many times had she greeted it when opening? How often had Cora blissfully rubbed up against the rough grain of it, as if brushing herself on the textured robe? And straightening the wayward halo was part of the daily ritual.

Rats. She wanted to see Faith again.

The bell on the door tinkled a welcome as Jake walked in the front door.

"Are you always as hungry as I am the morning after a big meal?" he asked without preamble, sliding a bakery box across the counter to her.

"Oh, you didn't need to," she answered. The most delicious aroma wafted from the box to her nose, and her stomach replied with a loud growl that startled Cora out of a sound sleep. "But I'm glad you did," she added hastily, tearing into the box.

What met her eyes was a true sweet tooth's delight indeed. The selection of doughnuts and other pastries was astonishing. It was enough to stop any diet dead in its tracks. Twisted cinnamon rolls were nestled next to white frosted cake doughnuts sprinkled with tiny decorations.

He picked one up and held it out to her proudly. "Check it out."

The little candies were white angels! "I've never seen these," she marveled. But, even as she spoke, the businesswoman in her was taking note. "I wonder where they came from. I should—"

He pulled a slip of paper from his pocket and handed it to her. "Here. I already asked. And I called my distributor—he's making a delivery to us on Monday—and he said if you want him to bring some then, he sure can do that."

"To sell? For me to sell?" she asked numbly, feeling as if the morning had suddenly gone into fast-forward—but she hadn't.

He nodded. "They sell them in large bags for bakeries, but he said he thought they might have some in smaller packets for retail sale."

"Wow." That was all she could manage as he moved in a blur. Maybe she was still too groggy from sleep to keep up with him.

"You look like you could use some coffee," he said sympathetically. "I didn't know what you had here so I also brought—ta-da!—a thermos from Panda's. It's a blend called Spice of the Season. It has some cinnamon in it and nutmeg, ginger and a few other mysterious ingredients I couldn't divulge to anyone, including my own dear mother. Trade secret."

He had even brought cups.

She pulled out two chairs from a wrought-iron table set and pushed the display of angel-animal beanbags on the tabletop out of the way. "We can sit here."

Cora was over like a silver flash.

"Is it okay if I feed her?" he asked as the cat looked lovingly up at him.

Tess could see her having to feed Cora only gourmet food and pastries for the rest of her life, and she fought it as hard as she could. Her cat needed healthy food, not this table-scraps stuff.

But the fight was lost as soon as she saw Cora's goo-goo gaze resting adoringly on Jake. "Sure, go ahead," she heard herself saying.

She took a sip of the coffee and almost choked. It was twice as strong as the way she usually drank it.

"Don't you like it?" Jake asked as her eyebrows shot up at the bitterness.

"It's a bit thick," she said.

"It is?" He poured himself a cup. "I haven't tried it yet, but we try to keep it at a constant level of strength."

He took a sip and sighed. "No, this is right. Try it again."

She did, and to her surprise she liked it.

"I guess I'm not used to tasting the coffee flavor so much, but I do like it."

"How late are you open today?" he asked.

"Five-ish. Why?"

"Would you be interested in seeing Panda's? I know you've been there already, but I'd like to show you the roaster and the back rooms. It's really quite an operation."

"Do I get to sample?"

"Everything."

"Only if I can have decaf. If I drink coffee after four in the afternoon, I get wired and will be up all night."

"Decaf?" He said the word with scorn. "That's like artificial coffee." But then he grinned at her to let her know he was teasing. "We have decaf. And it's pretty spectacular if I do say so myself. And if you want to, we can eat supper at Panda's, too."

"I didn't know you served dinner," Tess said.

"We do now. A woman moved here from Santa Barbara who does incredible things with sun-dried tomatoes and sprouts that will set your tongue singing."

He'd hit upon her second food weakness, sun-dried tomatoes. A day with sun-dried tomatoes and angel-decorated pastries was almost too good to be believed.

He picked her up at five o'clock sharp.

Panda's was larger than she'd remembered. The grounds were landscaped now with small trees draped with lights. "At dusk they'll come on. During the Christmas season each tree has a different color of lights. Otherwise, when the leaves are off the trees, they're all white."

She looked at the trees curiously. "What color are they?"

He began pointing them out. "That one is purple, that one turquoise, and that one green. That one is gold."

"Not exactly the traditional Christmas colors," she noted.

He nodded. "But at night, when they're all glowing, the scene is rich and spectacular. Those colors remind me of the three kings—now here I go getting sentimental about Christmas, but I remember three gigantic Wise Men Mom always had inside the front door. One had a turquoise robe, one a purple robe, and one a green one. And each was highlighted with gold."

"So these colors remind you of those Wise Men?" she asked.

"They sure do." His mouth broke into a wry grin. "Then one memorable Christmas my sister and I came flying in the front door, covered with snow. As soon as our boots hit the tiled floor, the rest of us hit the floor, too. We crashed right into the display. Broke Melchior's head off, gave Balthasar a ding in his elbow, and took a chunk out of Gaspar's foot."

"What did your mother do?"

He laughed. "Replaced those plaster statues with brass ones. She said the next time we did something like that, we'd be the ones with the gouges."

"She sounds like a neat lady," Tess commented.

"She is."

She could smell the coffee even before they reached the door. She wrinkled her nose, and he chuckled.

"The aroma is a bit strong when the roaster's going. For some it's better than perfume. Others would rather have a face-to-face encounter with a skunk."

He guided her inside the store. The building was made of rosy brick and smoked glass, a combination that shouldn't have worked but did. She said as much.

"I wish I could take credit for it, but it has to do with an argument between the contractor and the architect. I don't know all the details of it, but it sure did make for a striking building," he explained.

The interior picked up the same color themes, pink and gray, she noted as her eyes began the slow adjustment to the dimmed lights after the bright sunlit glitter of the snow outside.

And there she was. Faith. Looking just as zany and happy as she had in Angel's Roost. Tess was relieved to see she wasn't holding a sign advertising "World's Most Heavenly Coffee."

He hadn't lied when he said Panda's had a place for her. In a little sheltered alcove off to the side of the entrance, she held court. Her nook was lined with pink and green flowered tiles that matched the colors in her face and dress exactly.

And below it, a discreet card with carefully written letters done in a flowing calligraphic hand that said merely "Angel's Roost" and her address.

"Oh, you didn't have to do that," she protested. "You own her."

"As much as one can, I guess. We had the card made, and I'm glad we did because we get many comments on the angel and questions about where we found her. Having the card there frees up my staff from those endless questions about where we got her, are there others like her, what kinds of things are at Angel's Roost, and on and on."

"I wish!"

"Truly Faith has generated a sizable interest since she arrived. We're delighted she's here."

She walked over and straightened Faith's halo, which was once again tilted. "I miss the old girl," she said. "And I think Cora does, too. She used to wrap around Faith when the late-morning sun poured in through the window and take her morning snooze. Now she just sprawls in the space."

"Maybe she's enjoying having it all to herself," he suggested.

"Who knows what Cora thinks? Her mind doesn't operate the same way mine does, that's for sure. I think her brain operates mainly on a need basis: 'I need food; I need a nap.'"

He led her back through the dining area. Most of the seats and booths were filled. Mixed in with the college crowd were families, people on their breaks from work, and some older women sharing a chocolate concoction that looked as if it had a week's worth of calories.

As they went through the swinging doors into the kitchen area, a tall, gangly young man stopped Jake. "Dude, I've got five finals this week. I cannot believe it. Cannot. So I've got to, like, cut back on my hours this week. Majorly. Is that cool?"

Tess bit her lip to avoid laughing. This youth was obviously the same one who had told Jake, "Your big machine has gone blooey." Jake had nailed the student's inflections down to the very last detail.

She glanced around while Jake and Todd, as his name turned out to be, hammered out the workweek schedule. The kitchen was spotless. Chrome and glass gleamed. The cups were neatly aligned inside glass-fronted cupboards, and the countertops sparkled like those on television advertisements.

"So what do you think?" Jake asked, rejoining her after having finished talking with Todd.

"Is it always this clean and shiny back here?"

"Todd. He is an absolute clean freak so I let him sanitize his little heart out. Panda's always earns top ratings by the health department, and I value that highly."

She nodded. She'd seen the scores published in the newspaper, and it always made her cringe when one of her favorite eateries was given a low mark.

He led her to a large barrel-shaped machine. "This baby is the roaster. I'm the only shop in town that has one of these. It used to be that if you offered freshly ground coffee, you were on the cutting edge. That's old news. Now people are discovering how rich and tasty freshly roasted coffee is, and that's one of my major attractions here—besides Faith, of course."

"Of course," she murmured.

She walked around the impressive machine. "Is it fixed now?"

"Yes. Cost me an arm and a leg. I had to fly the certified repairman in, but it was cheaper than packing the machine up and freighting it to Minneapolis for warranty work. Besides, then I wouldn't have it while it was on its way, being fixed, and sent back."

"I didn't realize how competitive this business is." She frowned. "To have your entire business revolve around a roaster. . ."

"Well, I like to think it's more than that. Panda's offers some terrific food, too, especially desserts and now sandwiches. Speaking of which, are you ready for dinner?"

"Thought you'd never ask."

Her sandwich was a masterful creation of sun-dried tomatoes, sprouts, and some interesting cheeses she'd never heard of before. He insisted that she try a new dessert, chocolate cake drizzled with pastel-blue mint syrup.

He disappeared into the kitchen with it and came out a few moments later, bearing it as if it were a royal gift of gold.

She smiled as she saw what he had done. Topping it was a sprinkle of those tiny white angel candies.

"Give me your opinion, please," he begged as she ate the first forkful. "Do the angels add anything to it?"

She gave him her response, which was enthusiastic. He sat back in the seat, satisfied.

"I'm glad you like it," he said. "I hope now I'll see more of you here."

"I'll certainly try harder. But the problem is, I just don't get down to this part of town very often."

"I know what you mean." He crossed his arms over his chest and lapsed into unhappy thought for a while. "This is part of my problem."

"That I don't get to this part of town?"

"Well, sure, but I mean the way this town is divided into two clear business parts." He motioned to the others seated around them. "I don't know if I can give all of this up. I don't know if I should. Panda's is doing well here, but can it sustain itself? What if someone else gets a roaster?"

"Oh, it can't be as simplistic as that," she protested. "There's an ambiance here. And you said yourself that you've developed a clientele."

"Sure. But look at them. For the most part this is their section of town. Maybe the college students would follow me downtown since the university is as close to downtown as it is to the End. But maybe not."

He pushed his chair back and stood up. "But the fact of the matter is that it's been a bright and beautiful winter day, and I'm with a bright and beautiful woman, and I don't want to talk about anything that is not bright and beautiful. Let's go!"

She hastily swallowed the last of her coffee and wiped her lips. "Where are we going?" she asked as she shrugged into her coat.

"Shopping!"

Chapter 7

She tried to object as he bustled her into the car. "But I don't have any money with me. I'm not ready to do my shopping. I haven't given it any thought. I don't want to go to the mall on a Saturday."

The truth was that the last reason was the real one. She abhorred going to the mall on the weekend, especially when it was busy. And the first Saturday after Thanksgiving, the mall was going to be wild, especially as people began their Christmas shopping in earnest.

He apparently didn't hear anything she was saying, or he chose to ignore it. Instead he began singing "The Twelve Days of Christmas" as loudly as he could.

" 'Six geese a-laying—' "

"I said I don't want to go sho—"

" 'Five goooooolden rings!' "

She gave up and glared out the window. She hated the mall, absolutely, completely, totally hated it. She had to carry her coat because she was too hot with it on. And if she bought anything, then she had to carry that as well as her coat and her hat and her mittens and her purse. Her arms ached at the thought.

And her feet got sweaty in the mall, and then she'd climb into her unheatable van where her toes froze into ice chunks on the way home because they'd been wet inside her boots.

She couldn't believe her eyes. He drove right past the mall.

"Um, Jake, the mall—?"

" 'Four calling birds,' " he warbled. " 'Three French hens—' "

"You went by it already. Jake, Jake." She tugged on his sleeve. "It was back there."

" 'Two turtle doves and a parrrrrtridge in a pear tree.' " He flung his right arm out in a triumphant finale. "Sorry, Tess—did you say something?"

"The mall was back there. You drove past it."

"You wanted to go to the mall?"

She could have throttled him. "You said you wanted to go shopping," she reminded him, her words measured and spoken with a calm she didn't feel.

"You don't strike me as the mall type," he said. "Do you want to go? I can turn around, although I must admit this surprises me. This is a side of you I've not seen before."

She couldn't tolerate it any longer. She growled at him. Bared her teeth and snarled.

47

"Okay," he said, whistling through his teeth. "We won't go to the mall."

She rolled her eyes so hard she thought she'd pulled some kind of eye muscle. He was infuriating.

But he put on his turn signal and swung off onto a frontage road.

Her curiosity got the better of her. "What's out here?"

He pulled into the parking lot of a large brick building. It seemed nondescript until he drove close enough for her to see the front of it clearly.

"Welcome to the Animal Kingdom," she read. "Oh, I've heard of this. It was mentioned in the paper, but I've never been here before."

"You have to get out more often," he said as he switched off the ignition and opened his door.

His comment stung a bit. She was a downtown businesswoman as well as a member of the mayor's task force on rejuvenating the city's heart. Not only didn't she have the time to visit every business in town, but her loyalties were firmly on the side of downtown. Whenever she could, she patronized those businesses in the heart of the city.

She knew there was truth in what he said, though. It was almost too easy to let herself cocoon in the downtown district, what with Nativity half a block away and a grocery store only a few blocks past that. Most of her clothes she bought from mail-order catalogs and had them delivered to her home. She was well on her way to becoming a hermit if she didn't watch it.

She trailed after him as he strode across the lot. Snow that hadn't been scraped off by the plow crunched under her feet.

Just as a few well-chosen words were about to escape concerning men who walked ahead of their companions, he stopped and waited for her to catch up. "I thought you were right beside me! This is embarrassing—I've been talking away to you, and here I am, jabbering to myself. I'm sorry. I didn't realize you weren't with me. I'll be more considerate—I promise."

The words died on her lips. He was too good.

She stopped to read the sign on the door: "We do not sell animals here. We recommend you visit your local humane society." Below that, the address of the animal shelter was lettered in neatly.

"That's great!" she said, feeling more enthusiasm for the visit. She was an avid supporter of the humane society.

Her eyes widened at the sight that met her inside. It was a warehouse of pet supplies that stretched wall to wall and floor to ceiling.

Jake clutched her hand. "Help me pick out some gifts for a very special young lady."

She fell easily into his game. "Tell me something about her."

"Well, she's about this big—" He carved in the air a shape the size of a small calf. "And she has lovely gray hair and white whiskers and an attitude that tells me she doesn't suffer at all from low self-esteem."

"I see. And you were thinking of getting her—?"

"Something edible."

They located the cat section, and Tess's eyes widened at the aisles of cat treats. They lined the shelves in bags and boxes and cartons of many differing sizes and shapes, and they came in an even greater variety of flavors.

"Fish Medley. Poultry Delight. Beefy Bouquet. Halibut Hearties," he read. "Whatever happened to tuna, chicken, and beef?"

"Well, it's not that easy. Apparently combo meals have come to kitty land. You've got choices here of tuna and liver"—she shuddered—"or salmon and chicken on this row, or, ooh, now this sounds good: mackerel and cod with cheesy cheddar bits."

"Actually they do sound appealing." He picked up a foil packet and studied it. "Hey, this one even cleans their teeth. Like dog bones but for cats, I guess. Wouldn't that be neat, if you could just eat a snack, and you wouldn't have to get up and brush your teeth because the snack's already done it for you?"

"Now there's something for your cook to work on!" she said.

"Which do you think Cora would like the best?" He walked a bit farther down the aisle and picked up a diamond-shaped package. "Here are some herbal treats."

"Trying to predict what Cora will like is folly. She's fond of anything expensive. That much I know."

"These are $12.59."

"That's expensive, I'll grant you, but I don't think herbal anything will fly with the lady, unless it's catnip, of course. In which case, she'll fly."

He picked up a basket from the end of the row and began throwing packets into it. She tried to intervene, but he continued until he had an assortment that filled half the basket.

"Now to the toys."

They found the section with cat toys. Jake gave each one serious consideration and eventually selected several felt-covered, catnip-stuffed mice, some soft spongy balls covered with fuzzy metallic threads, and a windup mouse that Tess was sure Cora would bat into the wall and destroy within seconds.

Then he chose an elaborate contraption that allowed the human to dangle a stuffed glittery toy from the end of a flexible stick. But more than that, a system of pulleys and relays changed the height and sway of the toy.

He didn't stop there. He added a scratching post, since Cora still had her claws, and a special tray for enjoying her catnip without spreading it all over the house. And, of course, a bag of catnip, guaranteed to make her a very happy kitty cat.

Tess watched in amazement as the bill was totaled. "All this for Cora?" she asked. "I mean, I love her dearly myself, but this is too much!"

He flashed her a grin as he signed the credit slip and returned his wallet to his pocket. "I like doing this. One day maybe I'll have a cat of my own, and chances are I'll spoil him or her instead. But for now, if it's all right with you—and Cora—I'll pamper her. Indulge me. I'm having fun."

She shrugged. "Well, okay. But you know she's going to be awfully mad when all the treats come to an end."

"Why would they?" He thanked the salesclerk and picked up the bag.

As they walked to the parking lot she tried to choose the words that would convey what she meant.

"Well, someday you'll, uh, I'll, uh, we. . ." Her voice trailed off. The day he wouldn't be stopping by every day to see her, surprising her in some way or another, was bound to come eventually. Putting it into words was painful, and the syllables caught in her throat like dry shreds of paper.

He stopped and faced her squarely. "At this moment, Tess Mahoney, I plan to continue seeing you as long as I can. Yes, I'm growing very fond of you, and I do hope, fervently, that this relationship will grow and develop into something permanent. There. Does that explain it to your satisfaction?"

Tess had the unshakable impression she was standing in the parking lot of the Animal Kingdom, her mouth open as if she were waiting for an out-of-season fly to come along. She tried to shut her mouth, but it wouldn't cooperate.

"Is that all right with you?" he asked.

She tried to speak again, but she could only nod. She knew how she was feeling about him, and she knew how she hoped he was feeling about her, but this declaration was so sudden that she was caught off guard.

He smiled. "Okay, then. Let's go wrap these for Cora. We'll go to my house since she'll probably insist on watching the whole operation if we try to do it at your house, and that would spoil the surprise."

He chattered the entire way to his house about this and that, items in the news, the sweater he had bought his father for Christmas, the prospects for his favorite team, the Minnesota Vikings. He didn't mention his proclamation in the parking lot, but that was all right.

She had heard, and now she knew, and that was all that was necessary.

He turned into the development known as the Pines. Some of the down-towners called it Snooty Acres, poking fun at the people who lived there. It was heavily populated with doctors, lawyers, and car dealers.

He pulled into the driveway of one of the smaller homes. It was a tidy brick colonial, its pristine white shutters marked now with the deep forest green of wreaths that adorned the side of each window. The sidewalk and entrance were neatly cleared of snow.

The front door opened into a large antechamber with a bench and coat tree. She sat on the bench to pull off her snow boots and tried not to envy him for this.

The two entrances to her house led directly into the store and into her kitchen. Whatever people had on their shoes or boots followed them in. It was an unavoidable problem unless she remodeled, and even then that would steal some precious space from the room.

A stack of drywall leaned against the closet door, and beside it were a can of paint and a brush. "The basement was pretty much unfinished when I moved in," he explained, "so I'm having some work done on it. The theory is there'll eventually be a guest room downstairs, but it's going so slowly I've about given up hope."

He showed her through the house. It was larger inside than it appeared, and it was amazingly clean. It was so spotless it looked almost unlived in.

She began to get nervous. She was anything but a neatness nut. The store she had to keep in shape, and she managed that by a strict cleaning schedule she adhered to.

But her own living quarters were another matter. She shuddered at the thought of the upstairs, where her bedroom and what she used as a den were. Some people decorated with antiques. She decorated with clothes. And books. And a lot of unclassifiable stuff.

So far Jake had seen only the downstairs, which stayed fairly neat by virtue of the fact that she didn't use it. If he were really this neat—she saw trouble ahead.

He offered to take her coat, and she hugged her arms to herself after she gave it to him. The house was chilly.

He noticed. "Let me turn up the heat." He paused, as if trying to remember where the thermostat was, before excusing himself to turn it up.

Could it be this was not his home? Why would he pretend it was? A photograph sat on the fireplace mantel, and she studied it. The couple in the picture was posed in front of a boat, their arms draped over each other's shoulders. The man's grin was familiar; it must be Jake's father.

He entered the room and confirmed the identification. They were his parents, standing in front of their new boat. The snapshot had been taken only a few months ago.

His arms were filled with two rolls of wrapping paper, some tape, and a bag of bows.

"Let's do this in the dining room."

The large table was cleared. "Wow," said Tess. "I didn't know you could see an entire tabletop anywhere but in a furniture store."

As soon as she said it, she wanted to bite back the words. They sounded horrid and critical.

But he didn't seem offended. Instead he offered an apology. "I'm really not here very often. I spend most of my waking hours at Panda's, and I come here only to sleep and shower. I don't even eat here generally. I do that at the restaurant, too."

He looked around as if seeing it for the first time. "It doesn't feel like home, you know? That's one of the reasons I'm doing the remodeling downstairs. Maybe if I can put my own touch in here. I don't know. What do you think?"

She decided to stay noncommittal. What she thought was that it had all the warmth of a model home on display for a builder, but she didn't want to say that. "You probably need to stay here for a while. Sit in the furniture. Read a book in bed. Have pizza in front of the television. That kind of thing."

He nodded miserably. "But I hate to be alone." The admission cost him dearly, she could tell.

"I could come out, and we could sit in front of the television and eat pizza. Make cookies in the kitchen." She grinned. "Trust me. I can slob up a place in seconds flat. If there were an Olympic competition for uncleaning a house, I'd win the gold medal."

"I'm going to take you up on that offer," he declared. "Sometime this week let's rent a video and pop popcorn—the whole shebang."

"Sounds good to me." She rubbed her hands together. "I can feel it starting to warm up now. Let's get wrapping."

After they had finished, she started to pick up the scraps of wrapping paper and throw them away. He put his hand on her arm and stopped her. "I like the way it looks now—lived in. Like people have been here and had a good time. Leave it."

He picked up the packages and piled them in a corner of the living room. "This is where I'm going to put the tree," he said. "And these presents will be a good reminder to buy one."

"I need to get one too," she said. "A school down the street from Nativity is selling trees. The profits go to the school library so I thought I'd get mine there."

"It's kind of late," he said, glancing at the clock. "Almost nine. Won't they be closed?"

She shook her head. "They're open another half hour on the weekends."

"Let's go then." He sprang up from the pile of presents and retrieved their coats from the entryway. He waited while she pulled her boots back on.

"How are we going to fit two trees in this car?" she asked.

"We'll go to Panda's and pick up the delivery van. And we'll be buying three trees—Panda's needs one, too, don't you think?"

"I think everybody needs a tree," she said, that wonderful sense of bliss settling over her again.

After a quick stop at Panda's to switch to the van, they were headed back downtown. Jake found the school easily; they had a series of CD players hooked together playing Christmas carols full blast.

Because it was still early in the season, the selection was wide. It was as if a mini-forest had sprung up alongside the playground equipment.

Tess had the search narrowed to two candidates: a blue spruce that was full and elegant and a Douglas fir that was tall and narrow. She leaned them both up against the school wall and paced back and forth between them, comparing them.

"I don't know which to choose," she said as Jake rejoined her. "I like them both."

"Then buy them both. We'll figure out later which one goes where. I need your help. I can't decide either. I found this one flocked tree that is either incredibly gorgeous or incredibly awful, and I don't know which. I can't take my eyes off it."

"I don't really care for flocked trees," she began, but the words died in her throat as he stopped in front of the most amazing tree she'd ever seen. It was thickly flocked in dazzling white, and the ends of the branches were tipped in gold.

"Oh, wow," she breathed.

"So tell me, good or bad?"

"This tree defies the usual value system of a simplistic good or bad," she said at last. "It exists totally outside that realm."

"Well, should I get it? And for my house or for Panda's?"

"I can't make that decision for you, but I'm terribly afraid if you don't take it, I will. Wait. I wonder if Cora would eat flocking. With her appetite I'd better not take the chance. It might hurt her. I suppose I should pass on it then. I don't want to take any chances." She leaned her head to one side and studied the tree. "What an incredible tree."

"Okay. Here's my suggestion. We take these three trees and sort them out later."

She nodded. "That sounds fair. I want all three of them, but that's overkill. And there's no room in the store. But this white and gold tree would be an eye-catcher in there, wouldn't it? Couldn't you see it all decorated with angels? And a large gold and white angel on the top—you know, I have one that would work perfectly."

He looked at her, an idea clearly dawning in his mind. "I think I have it. Let's put this in Panda's and have you decorate it with angels from Angel's Roost. Can I hire you to decorate it?"

"Oh, I'll do it for free," she said, but he shook his head.

"No, it's a paying deal, or it's no deal. It'll look super with Faith there and the lights outside."

His enthusiasm was infectious.

"It won't be too garish, will it?" he asked, his voice suddenly worried.

"Well, no one's ever going to accuse you of being overly subtle, but this is campy garish, I think. And with the angels it'll be wonderful. You don't need to worry about it."

"When can you set it up?" he asked.

"How about Monday night? I'll have to go through my stock first and see what I have left after this weekend." The day after Thanksgiving had been so busy she'd lost track of what was left.

He smiled happily. "Terrific. If you have everything selected and boxed up and ready to go, I'll pick you up after you close, and we can come down to Panda's and set the tree up."

He reached out and took her hand. "Something is happening to me, Tess Mahoney, and it all has to do with you." He kissed her lightly on her nose. "Thank you."

It had to happen eventually. Her heart exploded with joy.

Chapter 8

She slipped into the red choir robe the next morning in the small anteroom at Nativity, mindless of the Christmas chatter that surrounded her—who had finished their shopping, who had the impossible person to buy for, what would someone else give his boss.

If only Jake had decided to join her in church this morning. She berated herself for not extending the invitation again, but she had twice already, and he hadn't taken her up on it.

"If only God believed in phone calls."

She didn't realize she'd spoken aloud until one of the other members of the choir, a teenage girl with baby blue fingernails that matched her eye shadow, looked at her curiously.

"Well," Tess explained, "if God would call me and tell me exactly what to do, life would be so much easier. Right?"

The girl looked at her with much the same disdain Cora had shown that morning when Tess had delivered a plate of Meow Meals instead of gourmet salmon. "But if He did that," she drawled, "your friends would never get through. The line would be busy all the time. Unless He has call-waiting."

Tess stared at her. What on earth—? Then it struck her, and she let the laughter roll out from deep inside her, cleansing her from her worries.

"What's so funny?" the girl asked, her pastel-painted eyes wrinkled in a frown.

"I think I just got a call from God," Tess said, wiping tears of laughter from her eyes.

The girl stepped back from her. "Whatever."

But the message had been clear. Stop. Enjoy. Rejoice.

Tess's heart was light and free when she entered the sanctuary. The first sight of the Christmas decorations always took her breath away. She was never quite prepared for it.

She sang the processional, "O Come, All Ye Faithful," with gusto. It was one of her favorite hymns, especially the line, "Born the king of angels."

Reverend Barnes invited one of the children up to the front. A little boy, his red hair slicked into place, joined the minister at the pulpit.

"Do you know what Advent is?" Reverend Barnes asked the young lad.

"Yes, sir. It's the time of the coming. Jesus is coming. In four weeks and three days. That's 'til Christmas Eve. Four weeks and four days, and it's Christmas morning. We're going to Aunt Edie's, unless Uncle Ned has to work, and then she'll come here, and we'll drive out to Grandpa's. He gots horses, you know. Six of them, but they don't all have shoes. But a horse's shoe isn't like a person's shoe. It doesn't go on with Velcro."

The congregation was roaring, but the little boy didn't hear, so intent was he upon his story. He had the minister's entire attention, and he wasn't about to let it go. Tess couldn't hear his words anymore, but she saw one hand make a little fist and pound it on the sole of his sneaker, obviously exhibiting how a horse was shod.

Reverend Barnes regained control by offering to let the little boy light the first candle. "We light the candle of Hope today," he said as he guided the boy's hand to the wick. "And what are we hoping for? This week I want you to focus on that in your prayers and meditation time. Let this be a week of crystallizing your priorities."

The little boy looked at him, puzzled, so Reverend Barnes clarified. "Deciding what's really important. What are you hoping for this year?"

"I want a race car," the boy said loudly. "Not a toy one, but a real one. I want to drive it—vroom! vroom!—to my sister's school. I could drive real fast if I had a race car. I would—"

His mother, red-faced but laughing, held her arms out for her child, and he happily went to her, wrapping his arms around her neck.

"At least he knows why he wants a race car," Reverend Barnes said, smiling at the little boy as he settled between his parents. "Let's take a lesson from him and examine our own wishes and motives—not just for Christmas, but for all aspects of our lives."

Tess pondered his words as he ended the sermon and moved into the announcements. She listened only vaguely as he ran through the notices of meetings, Sunday school outings, and special projects.

"If any visitors are among us today, we invite you to stand and introduce yourself so we might greet you and welcome you after the service." It was his traditional ending for the announcements, and Tess automatically looked up to see which family had visiting relatives.

To her astonishment Jake stood up. "I'm Jake Cameron. I was invited by Tess Mahoney, and I'm delighted to be here with you."

In one motion the entire congregation turned and looked at her. Tess cringed as the dreaded flush crept up her neck and spread onto her face.

Reverend Barnes beamed at her, then Jake, and told the congregation, "This young man helped us with the Thanksgiving dinner on Thursday. We've already come to enjoy him, and we look forward to his presence again among us. Welcome, son."

Jake nodded and stuck the visitor's label the usher handed him onto his jacket.

Tess didn't know whether to be ecstatic or furious at Jake. Why hadn't he told her he was coming—or even that he was considering it?

But, her mind argued back, what difference would it have made? None.

Tess was discovering something about herself—she was a busybody, always wanting to know why people did what they did and preferably knowing what they were going to do before they did it.

Well, maybe not everyone.

Maybe just Jake.

But at this moment that was more than enough.

From across the sanctuary, his gaze caught hers. He met her still-surprised eyes with a smile, almost as if he were proud of himself for being at Nativity on a Sunday morning. Actually, she was proud of him too, or she would be as soon as she could get over her astonishment at seeing him there.

For the rest of the service she kept stealing glances at him. He seemed genuinely interested and followed along closely with the bulletin and the hymnal.

He was here! She allowed herself to revel in the knowledge. He was here! The analytical part of her wouldn't leave it alone without pestering her purely emotional side with questions. Why was he here? Was it because he had been impressed with Nativity and Reverend Barnes on Thanksgiving evening? Or was it because he had felt a tugging on his soul to give himself to the Lord? Or was he here because he knew it would please her? And which one meant the most to her?

She recalled the situation in the choir room before church began, and once again she took the Lord at His word. She would relax and let Him do His work. All the Lord was asking of her was that she welcome each movement that brought a hungry soul closer to His presence.

Keeping her attention on the remainder of the worship was difficult, at best. When Reverend Barnes pronounced the benediction, she was almost glad.

She left the choir area—Nativity was too small to have a true loft—and instead of returning to the music room to hang up her robe, she hurried over to him.

"It's great to have you here!" she said, trying to strike a median note between gushing with happiness and sounding accusatory. "I didn't expect to see you here, though. You didn't say anything yesterday about coming to church."

"It was a spur-of-the-moment thing. I got up, showered and shaved, and was ready to head out the door to Panda's when I thought I'd give this a try instead." One of the men he had worked on the dinner with stopped to greet him, and Tess was impressed by how easily Jake spoke with him although he had met him only briefly that one evening.

Tess didn't hear the first part of their conversation, but she caught the later words, when the man asked if Jake was going to start coming to Nativity.

"This is a wonderful church, and I've certainly enjoyed it," Jake replied, and Tess noted, with a heart that sank just a notch, that he didn't really answer the man's question.

She reminded herself that she had known him only a few days, but those days seemed like years. Was it possible to fall in love this quickly?

This man with the chocolate brown eyes and dark hair silvered with early gray, could he be the one intended for her? Maybe, she thought somewhat ruefully, at her age God sped up the clock and ran courtships at breakneck speed. It was probably necessary when you were on the outer fringes of the dating stage of life.

"This is all too grand," the birdlike voice of Ellen Smalley twittered in Tess's ear as she fluttered in place, adjusting the lace collar on her nut-brown dress, and tucking an escaping strand of faded brown hair back into the bun at the nape of her neck. "You know, you can go sit with him after the choir sings. Many couples like to do that. Then they're together for the rest of the service. It can be so cozy."

Jake was still in conversation with the man, but Tess saw him watching her curiously as she spoke with the organist. As much as she loved the woman, she wanted her to do nothing more than go away and forget she ever saw Jake Cameron.

It was clear that Ellen Smalley had no intentions of going away, and she certainly wasn't going to forget Jake. "I believe I'm remembering correctly"— flutter, flutter, adjust sleeves, tap hair—"that he has a splendid singing voice. A baritone, as I recall."

"I'm sorry. I don't know," Tess replied, trying to smile serenely although her teeth were clenched so tightly that her latest round of dental work was in serious peril.

"We could use a strong baritone in the choir. Well, we could use any strong male voice in the choir. Ted Walman is the only loudish voice we have, and"—the organist's voice sank to a whisper that everyone in the narthex could hear—"he can't sing for a hill of beans."

Tess smiled her fake smile at those who lingered nearby, obviously eavesdropping on their conversation. She fervently hoped none of them was a friend of Ted Walman.

"He's visiting," Tess said. "He's a member of another church elsewhere in town."

Mrs. Smalley drew back in reproof, her arms crossed over her plump bosom that did, for all the world, round out into a shape that looked like a bird's chest. "You're not thinking of leaving us and going there, are you?" she asked bluntly.

"No!" Tess's sharp reply turned heads.

"Well—" Mrs. Smalley said with a sniff, turning her attention to Tess's clothes and plucking a stray thread from the sleeve of her choir robe—"I hope not. We love you here at Nativity, and we want you to stay with us forever and ever and ever."

Tess hugged her. "I won't leave. Don't worry." Her heart melted as she realized how much she cared for the organist, even if the woman did often drive her crazy with her snoopiness.

"I'm glad to hear that," Mrs. Smalley replied, brushing some invisible dust from a nearby tabletop. "He seems like a good fellow."

Jake had finished his conversation with the man and moved back closer to Tess. Seeing her opportunity to make her getaway, she told him, "I need to put away my robe."

"Oh, honey, let me do that," Mrs. Smalley chirped, holding out her arms. "I don't want to be the one who stands in the way of love's progress."

"We're not—" Tess started to object. But Jake took her elbow and smoothly interjected a "Thank you" to the organist and steered Tess out of the church as if she were a small canoe.

"There's no arguing with people like that," Jake said. "Bless their souls—they care so deeply for others they can't quite separate what's helping and what's meddling. I'm going to have to watch my p's and q's in this church; they love you so very much."

They walked to her house together, not saying much because it was too cold to do more than walk home as quickly as possible. Although the temperature was barely above zero, the sun had never been brighter, the sky bluer, or the clouds fluffier than they were that morning.

Nor any cat hungrier. Cora meowed loudly at both Tess and Jake as they walked in the door. When she realized Jake hadn't brought her any food, she stalked away, her tail twitching angrily.

"A cat the color of pussy willows," Jake mused. "What was your grandmother like?"

Tess laughed. "Well, she certainly wouldn't have gone off in a huff just because you hadn't brought her food! No, Grandma was a very mannerly, very polite, very gentle, and sweet woman."

Jake knelt and tried to lure Cora out from under the Hoosier cabinet with his key chain. "Cora is a lot more like my grandmother. Now there's a personality fit."

"You're kidding!"

"When I was a teenager, Grandmother had advanced diabetes and kept trying to bribe me into bringing her chocolates, if you can believe it. And not sugar-free ones either. No, they had to be those expensive specialty ones."

"Did you?"

"No! I loved the lady. I didn't want her to die, and I certainly didn't want to be the angel of death for her. But she kept trying to get me to do it, and I kept refusing, and she kept getting angry."

"That must have been hard." Her heart melted with sympathy for the young man whose grandmother asked such a difficult task of him. "Didn't it hurt to be put in that position with her?"

"Well, I loved her. Besides, she was sick, and that probably wasn't making her mind work all that great. What hurt the most was seeing her like that, not the way she treated me. I could go out and do something to take my mind off my problems, but she was her own problem, and she couldn't get away from that."

"Wow. Pretty deep thinking for a teenager," Tess commented. "I'm impressed!"

"Mom counseled me through it. It was during Dad's rough patch, so we were all having a hard go then. Mom would put her arm around my shoulder, give me a little hug, and tell me, 'This, too, shall pass,' and it did."

She was filled with admiration for the woman who held together the family when members of it were falling apart. What a remarkable person she must be.

Cora finally succumbed to curiosity and strolled over to investigate Jake's keys. She took her time, though, as if saying to him she was in no hurry to look at the keys, but if it would make him happy, she'd humor him and bat them around for a while.

"This is a wonderful cat, you know," he said to Tess as he teased Cora with the ball on the key ring.

"Why don't you have one?" she asked. "You seem to be crazy about cats."

"I moved from a no-pets apartment to my house about a year ago, and I've been having some more construction done on it. I thought I'd wait until that was done, since the workers were in and out all day long with the doors open. Not good for a kitten."

"How do you like living in the Pines?" She felt as if she were being as curious as Cora, asking all these questions, but she really wanted to know the answers. "Aside from going to your house, the only time I ever get out there is to look at the Christmas decorations at night."

He grinned as Cora swatted the key ring, trying to get the ball free from the keys. "Done your sightseeing, or should that be light-seeing, yet this year?"

When she shook her head no, he stopped playing with Cora and looked up at her, his dark eyes gleaming with an idea. "Tonight we can drive through town and check out the Christmas lights. It's still a little early in the season, but down in the Pines a few folks have put up some pretty elaborate displays."

It sounded like fun. She hadn't yet made the annual Christmastime circuit of town, gawking at the lights that brightened the winter nights, and going with him sounded even more fun.

Especially if they went in his car. Not only were the leather seats incredibly comfortable, but his heater actually warmed the car. This was a wonder to her. Her old van's heater vaguely blew out tepid air, only neutralizing the icy interior. She couldn't stay in it long in the heart of winter, not without losing the feeling in her fingers and toes.

He gave Cora one final loving nose rub and stood up. "I'll come back around six thirty. We can do the grand tour of the lights and then have a late supper. How does that sound?"

Cora looked up at him and meowed sweetly.

"Sorry, old girl—you need to stay home and guard the angels. If you're a good kitty, I'll bring you a treat," he told her.

"You are going to make that cat as big as a barn," Tess interrupted. "She's already the size of a shed."

Cora's tail switched once in haughty disdain before she walked away.

"Guess you've been told," Jake said laughingly.

"Oh, I never listen to anything she says," Tess responded, sniffing with contempt. "Cora is always so—oh, how can I say this—catty?"

Chapter 9

True to his word, Jake appeared at Tess's house at six thirty. He reached into his pocket and pulled out a package. "Cora, sweetie, want a treat?"

"Jake, you're going to make it so that she'll never eat Meow Meals again. She's going to expect only gourmet food and special snacks pretty soon. Already she's getting snooty about Cat-Cat Yums, and she used to be wild about them."

"You're right." He looked properly chastised. "Well, I can't very well go back on my offer now. I'll have to give her these."

She grinned. "Indeed, you are a man of honor. I suppose it'll be all right this last time, but you've got to go slower, or she'll be the size of a horse and eat about as much, too."

Cora watched him somewhat suspiciously.

He tore open the bag and sniffed it heartily. He grimaced and gagged. "How on earth can this be a treat? It smells like someone was sick in it!"

He had Cora's interest, and she trotted over. She batted the bag out of his hands, and the treats sprayed across the floor.

Tess quickly covered her nose. "They're horrible! What are they?"

Cora, however, gobbled them up quickly from the floor, and within seconds the offending treats were gone, safely inside her stomach.

He picked up the bag and, holding it at arm's length, read the label. " 'Giblet Niblets.'" He shuddered. "I wonder if they all smell this bad."

"If they do, Cora gets one chance to eat them, and if she doesn't snarf them down the way she did these nasty things, out they go. I think I'll flush them. Are you sure they weren't bad or something?"

"I think they were okay."

"Maybe they were spoiled. Come here, sweetness—come to me." Cora ambled over and climbed lazily on Tess's knee. "I wonder if they were okay. I hope she won't get sick."

The cat looked up at her and yawned happily. Tess turned pale. "I hope her breath will smell better by the time we come back, or else she's sleeping outside."

Cora's eyes drooped, and Tess put her on her blanket by the heat register. "I think she's okay. She probably just has horrible taste in food, no pun intended."

Jake quickly mapped out his plan for the rest of the evening.

"We'll do the Pines and then the End. By the time we finish with that, the memory of Giblet Niblets should be gone, and I'll be ready to eat again without gagging. Sound okay to you?"

"Sure." It sounded heavenly to her, spending this much time with him.

"Do you have any suggestions about dinner?" he asked her.

"How about Stravinski's? We'll be late enough that we probably won't need reservations. I like it because you can get a salad or pasta or whatever. The food is wonderful there."

They agreed on Stravinski's and bundled up again to face the inevitable cold. After a quick trip into the coffeehouse on a mysterious mission, he returned with a familiar white box, a thermos, and two cups.

"I can't understand why you don't weigh four hundred pounds," she grumbled as she investigated the contents of the box. "Ooh, look at this! And this! I don't know what it is, but it's chocolate, so it has my attention."

"They're cookies and fudge," he said. "We're offering ready-made tins filled with them for people who need quick Christmas gifts. The thermos is filled with hot chocolate, and here's a bag of marshmallows and a can of whipped cream," he added as he reached in his pocket, pulled them out, and laid them on the console of the car.

"Chocolate to eat, chocolate to drink. And Christmas lights to look at. Life is good, very good," she commented happily.

As they left, Jake drove around to the front of Panda's so she could see how it looked with all the trees lit up.

It was an amazing sight. The rich tones he had chosen were strikingly beautiful. She could see why the hues he had chosen reminded him of the three Wise Men and their camels. The jeweled hues were majestic.

The Pines was aglow with Christmas lights. Jake pointed to one house on the first block they visited. Full-size snowmen made out of wire and colored bulbs guarded the front yard. On the roof a Santa and sleigh were parked—not the usual plywood cutout, but a real sleigh and a mannequin to portray Santa.

He pulled over to the side so she could see it better. "Look," she said, pointing to Santa, "he seems so real." She nearly passed out from shock when Santa got out of his sleigh and waved at them.

Jake laughed. "That's Mike Summers up there. He does this every evening between six and seven. Great fun, isn't it?"

One yard had an elaborate nativity scene with animated animals. "Mary and Joseph look chilly out there in the snow with only their robes on," Tess said.

Jake agreed. "Makes you want to throw some coats on them, doesn't it?"

In a neighboring yard the owners had used the snow to sculpt a three-dimensional scene of Bethlehem in white that extended the length of their property. It was backlit with a soft blue light. Over one section a bright golden light shone, signifying the star that led the shepherds to the stable.

Another house was wrapped entirely in lights, like a gigantic present.

Tess quickly picked her favorites. The Bethlehem scene showed great creativity, she said, and Jake nodded. "The owner is a doctor with no creative ability at all except in healing, but he's very religious. He hired some college students to do it."

Knowing that took nothing away from her enjoyment of it.

As they drove through the area, large white flakes began to fall.

"Look at that. It's truly the Christmas season," she said as she cradled her hands around the warm mug of hot chocolate.

"I can't imagine living someplace where it was warm at Christmas," he said. "As much as I complain about the snow, this is one time when I want to see it."

"Isn't it interesting that we do depend upon it to bring us to the season?" she asked. "Like for us, anyway, there are cues. Would it be Christmas without the snow and the lights and the trees?"

"Yes," he said reflectively, "it would be, but would we truly feel it? I hear people all the time saying they don't have the Christmas spirit or they're not in the mood right now for Christmas."

"I wonder about that because it's true. I know I've felt it myself. Why do we need these cues? I've even heard children say it, so it's not because we're jaded or shopworn."

"Could it be that this is not a solitary holiday, that we need to share it with others? There's such a universal joy surrounding this time of year. Maybe that's it. We pick up on other people's droopiness." He shrugged. "I never really thought about it, but you're right. It is an intriguing phenomenon."

"I've been giving Reverend Barnes's sermon this morning some thought. Remember how he asked us to focus on what we want?"

"Yes."

"I'm glad he did."

"And what have you decided?" he asked, his head cocked as he listened carefully.

"I don't know yet. But it is a challenge. It's like shopping in the world's biggest candy store. What do I want? About the only thing I'm sure of is that I know I want more than a racing car." They both laughed at the memory of the little boy who had amused the congregation that morning.

"There is so much I want. The usual good things like health and happiness for my family and friends," he said, "but I think Reverend Barnes means more than that. What do we want for ourselves?"

"It's a hard thing to know and even harder to put into words. But I think that's part of what he was getting at," she mused thoughtfully, watching the Christmas lights as he continued to drive slowly.

"The minister who taught our confirmation class many years ago said our prayers are a good way of finding out what's truly important to us. What matters enough to pray about? And do we care enough to take whatever action we can?" Jake slowed down to avoid a cat that dashed across the road.

"Can you explain?"

"Well, he gave the example of someone who is in a nursing home. We may care enough to pray about that person, but do we care enough to leave the comfort of our homes and visit him? And then he also said we should ask how God must feel about our priorities. A good exercise might be to compare ours to His."

"It's a wonderful concept," she said softly. "I'll have to keep that in mind as I work through my wish list this week."

"Unfortunately," he continued, as they left the Pines and traveled back toward the rest of the End, "this doesn't do much good when my most fervent prayer is something like, 'Oh God, please let this roaster work,' or, 'If You let my car start, I will love You forever.' Selfish little things like that. I wonder sometimes if God gets a bit annoyed with me."

She chuckled. "Well, God is probably annoyed with 99 percent of the population then. I do that all the time, pray dumb things like that. Sometimes I catch myself trying to make deals with God: 'God, if You'll let the pilot light on the furnace ignite on the first match, I'll pray more each day.'"

"Does it work?" Jake asked, tilting his head and smiling.

"Of course not! Actually, my grandparents trained me well enough that I almost always catch myself in the act of praying that way, so I'm not too bad in that realm. I have more problems with the flat-out, spur-of-the-moment demands on God's powers: 'Let this person buy this angel because then I can pay the utility bill.' Or worse, 'Please let these pants fit.'"

"I can't imagine you doing that," he said, reaching across the car and patting her hand. "First of all, you're much too pious—"

"Pious!"

He had the grace to look embarrassed. "Well, what word would you use?"

"Not pious. Faithful, maybe. Devoted. True. Loyal. Trusting."

"That's better? That list makes you sound like a cocker spaniel."

She laughed. "Maybe we should all be like cocker spaniels. I'm a cat person, but I have to admit that cocker spaniels are the epitome of loving adoration mixed with exuberance."

"Good way to phrase it."

"Maybe they're good spiritual models for us. And maybe even earthly models."

"I guess the greatest danger would be that people would feel compelled to pat your head and give you nice meaty bones to chew on."

"And make you eat snacks like Giblet Niblets. There is undoubtedly something similar for dogs that is just as stinky as that stuff." She shuddered again at the memory of the fetid treats.

"I had a black Lab when I was a kid, and I can tell you from past experience, dogs will eat anything. I won't go into details. Just be a good dog and trust me."

"Or I could be a good cat and ignore you," she teased in return.

They entered a section of the End where small houses sat next to each other, no two exactly alike but not entirely different, like brothers and sisters.

Each house was decorated with what was apparently an obligatory string of lights along the lower edge of the roof. In the yards were illuminated plastic snowmen or Santa Clauses.

"This is low-income housing," he told her. "The End's Community and Business Organization, CBO, discovered that the people who live here really wanted to decorate their houses but couldn't afford it. So we gathered together donations and bought Christmas lights for anyone who wanted them. The only hitch was they had to put them up themselves."

He stole a glance at her. "What was truly heartwarming about this story is every single house accepted them, and every single house put them up. We heard that in houses where elderly people lived, their neighbors volunteered to put the lights up."

"This is truly a neighborhood where the Christmas spirit abounds," she whispered, seeing new meaning in the gleaming colors that stretched ahead as far as she could see like an endless rope of light, all at roof level, and all indicating a unified neighborhood celebrating the extraordinary joy of this holiday season.

She stared out the window of the car, drinking in the view as if it were water for a hungry soul.

"Stop!" she cried.

Jake slammed on the brakes, and the car fishtailed on the frost-slicked road before coming to a stop.

"Sorry," she said. "Didn't mean to startle you. But look!"

She pointed to a figure in the yard. It was a snowman, obviously fashioned by children, and around its neck hung a hand-lettered sign.

She had to struggle to make out the letters through the thickly falling snow. "Jake, look at that," she said in delight as she figured it out. "It's a birth announcement. Listen!"

Jake leaned forward as she read the words aloud: " 'Born December 25. Name: Jesus. Parents: Mary, Joseph, and God. Weight: Our endless sin and His forgiveness. Length: Eternity. Welcome, Jesus!' "

Her throat closed up as she fought back tears. Whoever had written this had captured the true sentiment of the season perfectly.

She had heard the downtowners referring with scorn to the End and particularly to this part of town, the assisted housing. She'd always imagined it to be like the housing projects she'd seen on the news, ill-kept and overrun with who-knew-what. She'd never expected to see the pride and care evidenced by the vista she now beheld.

"You seem taken by this all." His voice revealed his surprise.

"I've never been out here before," she confessed, "and what I'm seeing is totally at odds with what I'd envisioned it would be like."

"It's nice, isn't it?"

"Very nice. As a matter of fact, I wish many places downtown were maintained as well as this neighborhood."

He drove to another section of the End. Here middle-class families had bedecked their homes with several strands of lights, and the yard scenes were larger. Wreaths hung from every house, and many sported electric candles shining from curtained windows.

Then the houses became much larger and the decorations more ostentatious. On many houses were rooftop displays, although none of these Santas stepped out of the sleigh to wave.

Some arrays were downright garish.

Tess blinked as one house came into view. The owners had obviously decided to spare no expense, and their electric bill would surely show it.

The house was entirely wrapped in lights. Animated elves climbed up and down the walls, bringing toys to Santa's workshop, which was stationed on the housetop. A relay system must have run down the back of the house because the elves worked in an endless loop, bringing dolls and baseball bats up the wall and climbing back down for another load.

The yard itself had been turned into a candy-cane garden. Nearly fifty candy canes, seven feet tall, sprouted through the snow, and Tess and Jake watched as children played tag through the maze.

Over it all a loudspeaker played "Jingle Bells" continuously, as gigantic cut-out silvery jingle bells swung back and forth over the garage doors, not quite in time to the music.

"That's, well, that's—" Tess was at a loss for words. All she could do was stare at the display.

"Bizarre?" Jake suggested.

"At least. What do you suppose their neighbors think of it? It would drive me absolutely bonkers in one night. By Christmas I'd be a basket case."

"Well, his closest neighbor is the president of the electric company."

"Ohh." She nodded understandingly. "I see. And so does he, I suppose. I bet every time he looks out his window he sees a bonus in his future."

"And the person who lives in this house is also a business owner." Jake named the largest electric equipment supply company in the northern region. "So you can probably write this scene off as part wild Christmas spirit and part economic grandstanding."

"I've certainly done my share of goofy decorating blunders, but that place is downright tacky. I can't imagine living there."

"Hey!" Jake protested laughingly. "This is prime real estate."

"It's definitely prime something. All I know is after seeing that I need chocolate. I need some fudge, and I need it quick!"

"Chocolate will make you like that house better?" he asked her.

"No, but I do like fudge. Almost anything is bearable if you're eating fudge."

"Oh." He nodded in mock seriousness. "That explains chocolate's mass appeal."

They drove farther down the street where the houses sprawled a bit more and the decorations became as expansive as the property allowed. These houses had grounds, not yards.

One house was technically perfect. The pristine white front of the three-story Edwardian was lit with soft cream lights. Evergreen ropes wrapped around the columns in precise twists. The polished brass fixings of the entrance reflected the light and offset the deep green wreath that was easily five feet across. Tess tried to determine if the musical instruments tied to the wreath were real. They certainly looked that way.

There were no garish lights here, no animated displays of the North Pole. It looked like a picture from a Christmas card, especially with the snow continuing to fall, light and fluffy, but it felt hollow and icy. This house seemed to be on the other end of the spectrum from the electrical extravaganza down the street.

And both were, in their opposing ways, pretentious.

"That's about the extent of the Christmas-lights tour of the End," Jake announced as he pulled away from the final house. "So what did you think? Of course it'll all be beefed up in a week or so. Lots of folks went out of town this weekend for Thanksgiving."

"You know what my favorite was?"

"The Electric Elves visit Candy Cane County?" he guessed.

"Wrong-o. Although that one will live in my memory forever," she said dryly, "kind of like those Giblet Niblets."

They grimaced in unison.

"And to think they both happened on the same night. That's a bit too much coincidence for me," he said, shaking his head. "I'm not a superstitious guy—don't believe in it—but let's hope these things don't come in threes. So which of these holiday houses was your favorite, although I think I already know?"

"My favorite was the section with only the string of lights and the hand-made decorations. Especially the snowman holding the birth announcement."

He nodded. "I hadn't seen that before, but it's wonderful."

"I'm going to call Reverend Barnes tomorrow and tell him to go take a look at it." She glanced sideways at him, chagrined. "But I don't know where the house was. Can you write down the directions for me?"

"I'll go you one better," he promised. "I'll call him and tell him. And if he wants, I'll drive him over there to see it."

"You're a nice guy, Jake." And he truly was. Over and over he was showing her his compassion for others, a kind streak that ran a mile wide and a mile deep.

"Do nice guys finish last?" His eyes were twinkling like the lights they'd seen.

"Not at my table. And speaking of finishing last and eating, let's go to Stravinski's."

"But we haven't seen the downtown lights," Jake protested.

She was grateful for the darkened interior of the car so he couldn't see the betraying flush that was creeping up her neck and washing over her cheeks. She could feel the heat from it.

"I'm hungry, okay?" It came out more defensively than she'd intended.

He saluted. "Yes, ma'am!"

She softened her approach. "There's one thing you'll learn about me, or maybe you already have. I think it's probably hereditary, a defect I was born with."

He glanced over at her with concern. "What is it, honey?"

"Where some people have a stomach, I have a bottomless pit."

"You scamp! You had me worried there!" he threw back at her, but she could tell he wasn't angry. The edges of his eyes turned up with amusement. "I thought it was something serious."

"It is when I'm hungry. Then everybody had better watch their step!"

"Luckily for me I own a restaurant," he muttered playfully. "It's closer than Stravinski's. Should we go there instead?"

She shook her head emphatically. "While I loved Panda's, my stomach is all set for Stravinski's Caesar salad and white northern soup."

"And I wondered where Cora got her appetite." He winked at her. "Are you two related?"

"Close. By a whisker."

He groaned. "That was bad, Tess. You had me feline real, real awful."

She smiled impishly. "Ah, just drive, Mr. Cameron. No more puns. I want the rest of this evening to be absolutely, totally purrfect."

Chapter 10

An hour later Tess wiped her mouth with her napkin and sighed in satisfaction. "I am stuffed."

The server walked over, balancing a tray with one hand. He lowered it enticingly near Tess's face, close enough that she could see and smell the mouthwatering aromas of the elaborate desserts.

"But no one can be too stuffed for a serving of tiramisu," she amended after the server left with their orders. "I've been on a tiramisu binge since October when I first tasted it."

"I like tiramisu, but I'm going for that cheesecake concoction—what did he say it was? Cherry almond? It sounds wonderful." He sipped his coffee and grinned. "It's hard for me sometimes to enjoy a dinner at a different restaurant because I'm always comparing everything to Panda's, like this coffee."

"This decaffeinated is good." The brew was so rich and full she couldn't tell it was decaffeinated.

"It should be. They buy it from us. We bring a fresh roast over every other day, sometimes every day. It's one of the areas we've been branching into, doing wholesale to restaurants."

"Really. I didn't know that, but it makes sense. This coffee is terrific."

"Thanks. See, having a local roaster makes all the difference. I hope this is a wise move, moving into wholesale, but it's hard to know. I can only do so much before I burst. I'm wondering when my limit will come and what will happen."

"Are you trying to do all this without an assistant?" she asked, suddenly concerned. She was hearing an exhaustion in his voice that either hadn't been there before or she had missed.

"I'm trying to be conservative about this while it's in the trial phase. I'd hate to get someone involved and then have the whole thing fall down around our heads like a pack of cards. It's my risk now. It has to be, until I know if it'll be a success or not. Then, and only then, will I hire someone."

"But if you need the help now—," she said, feeling protective of him.

"Tess," he said earnestly, "I can't in good conscience hire someone only to have to let him or her go within a couple of weeks. I want to be able to offer that person a good job, a stable job. And I'll wait until I can."

"I admire that, Jake—I really do. I can't help but think you've chosen a suicide course, though." She couldn't keep the concern from entering her voice. "The human body can do only so much, you know."

"I know. That's one of the reasons I spend so much time at Panda's and hardly any at my home. Every waking minute I spend down there. Until I get established enough, until I feel confident in this new venture, that's the way it'll have to be."

A wave of suspicion washed over her. "You've spent most of today with me. This morning you were in church. How much time have you spent at Panda's today?"

"Some."

"How much?" she demanded. "In hours and minutes. How much?"

His brow furrowed. "Well, I went in early—"

"How early?"

"Five-ish."

"Five in the morning?" She couldn't keep the amazement from surfacing in her voice. "I'm just starting to dream deeply at that time. Okay. You went in a little after five—"

"Uh, before five." He spoke almost guiltily.

"Before five. Which means you got up at—?"

"Four or so."

"And you went to bed when?"

"Around midnight." At her glare he modified it. "All right, twelve thirty."

She totaled it up. "So you've had a whopping three-and-a-half hours of sleep. Jake, that stinks. Big-time. And now you've spent the day with me when you could have been catching a nap."

"But I'd rather be with you."

"Sweet, and I appreciate it, but that's not the point." A new worry struck her. "We're still supposed to tour this part of town and check out the lights. And then what—what are you going to do?"

"I didn't have any particular plans." He avoided meeting her eyes and toyed with the linen napkin, folding it first one way and then the other.

"You were going back to Panda's and work, weren't you?"

When he didn't answer, she repeated the question. "Tell me the truth, Jake."

His chin lifted. "Yes."

She touched his hand and took the napkin from his edgy fingers. "Do me a favor," she pleaded. "Take the rest of the evening off. Let's go for our drive, and then we'll go to my house and make sure Cora hasn't starved to death in our absence. We'll sit and talk, and then you will go home—do you hear me?—go home and get in your jammies and go to sleep."

"But they expect me at Panda's," he objected. "What if something needs my attention?"

"I have a phone at my house. Hey, you even have a phone in your car. Call Panda's. See how things are going. Who's in charge right now?"

"Well, I guess that would be Todd."

"He's capable, right?" she persisted.

The uneasiness began to fade from his face. "Yes. He's good, a little flaky but good."

"Do you trust him?" She felt as if she were leading him, step-by-step, along this path.

"Sure." He shoved back his chair. "I know where you're going with this, and I get your point. But you know what it's like to own a business."

"I know that since I've owned Angel's Roost I've been the strictest boss I've ever had. I understand what you're feeling, but, Jake, you need to take care of yourself, or all you've accomplished won't matter."

He stared at her, and she watched as the challenge drained from his face. When he spoke at last, his words were so quiet she had to strain to hear him. "You're right."

The relief that flooded through her body made her weak. "Let's pay our tab then and go. More Christmas lights await us."

Main Street had been decorated earlier the week before. Great ropes of silvery lights and green garlands looped across the road, hooked on to the old-fashioned street lamps that lined the street.

A few businesses had decorations in the windows or a strand of lights draped over a door. But for the most part their only bow to the season were signs advertising loans to help with Christmas shopping or a holiday sale on washers and dryers.

She saw it for the first time through new eyes. "If it weren't for the city's decorations, this whole area would be bland, bland, bland."

"Maybe they need some encouragement," he suggested. "Like what we did out in the End, but modified, of course. I'm not trying to say the downtown merchants and businesses are low income, but maybe if they had some incentive. . . ?" He left the sentence hanging.

"What a great idea. We do a lot with First Night, but even that doesn't involve too much decoration of individual stores. It's not a business festivity, so many aren't really involved."

"Are you going to First Night?" he asked, referring to the city's gala downtown celebration of New Year's Eve. This would be the fourth year the town and its businesses, churches, and offices had put on the nonalcoholic festival as a way to salute the change of the year, and it had already become a treasured tradition throughout the community.

"Wouldn't miss it for the world. What about you? Do you go?"

"I haven't so far," he confessed. "As you might imagine, that's a fairly busy night for us. People consume a lot of coffee. And the pastries, too. It's like the last caloric blowout of the year."

She must have looked disappointed because he added, "But this year I think I'll try to go. It'll depend upon how the help list looks."

When she looked confused, he explained. "The help list is something I use for holidays when we're open, as well as special times. My workers use it to tell me if they can work that night, so I don't have to call through the entire list when I need someone. If enough people are on the help list, I'll take in First Night. . .or at least part of it," he qualified at the end.

They drove to the residential section next to the city center. The houses were small and close together, but they rose tall.

"The houses along here remind me of the people who must have built these houses, needing each other for warmth and companionship, so they huddled together, like these houses. And they're tall because on the prairie you can see forever, but first they needed to see over the trees that lined the riverbanks." She couldn't keep the pride out of her voice as she spoke of her neighborhood.

"Their height may also have made the upper floors, the sleeping areas, easier to heat," Jake commented pragmatically, "because hot air rises. That way they could take advantage of the stored heat from the day's activities. If they'd been spread out, the outer corners would have been icy on a night like this without additional heating and thus cost."

She made a face at him. "I like my version better. It's more poetic."

"It is," he acceded, "but mine is more practical, more realistic about why the houses are built the way they are. Don't you agree?"

She tried not to let her face reveal the truth, that she had never thought of it that way. Her vision of how the community had grown and shaped itself had always been a romantic one. Never once had something as everyday as heating the homes entered her thoughts.

"I'm somewhat embarrassed," she confessed. "Heating was too prosaic, I'm afraid, for my fanciful mind. Of course you're right."

The houses seemed immediately smaller, dingier, grayer, just tall scrawny buildings lining a river.

He glanced at her. "And I'd never seen them with such an artistic eye. These houses suddenly have character, personality, and a quiet steadfastness about them I'd never noticed before. Thank you for sharing this with me."

The holiday decorations were simple on most houses. Some had decorated their homes traditionally, while others had used modern themes and colors, like the one house that was lit with purple and turquoise bulbs.

The fresh snow in the moonlight made the houses that lined the street look homey and Christmassy. Her heart warmed as she surveyed the area where she had lived her entire life.

As Jake pulled up in front of her house, she realized she hadn't put up her own lights this year. She mentioned it to Jake, and he immediately seized upon the opportunity.

"I'll do it."

She took his arm in her mittened hand and pulled him toward her door. "Not tonight. This is our time to relax and take it easy."

Cora met them with a chorus of meows and complaints that let them know she'd been alone the entire evening, it had been horrible, and she had almost starved to death.

While Tess refilled her dish with Meow Meals and replaced her bowl of water, Jake picked Cora up and talked to her. Tess had to turn her face to hide the grin on her face as he cooed to the cat. "You poor baby cat. Were you all alone in this big old house and not a thing to eat? Poor, poor baby cat. Don't worry—Tessie is home now."

She couldn't stop herself. "Tessie? It makes me sound like that Loch Ness monster."

"What's that, sweetums?" Jake bent his ear to Cora's mouth, then reported, "Cora says you are the Loch Ness monster."

"Cora is a flat-out opportunist who will say anything for a treat. Remember that you're the one who gave her Giblet Niblets. You rank right up there with the guy who invented salmon takeout. In fact, as far as she knows, you might be the guy who invented salmon takeout. I'm getting her some Meow Meals, tuna flavor, by the way, and some water. May I get you anything?"

"Sorry, no. If you have any of those Giblet Niblets left, though. . ." He pretended to look hopeful.

"No, thankfully. The piglet ate them all—bless her little heart. I do have some brownies."

"Okay, you've convinced me."

They went into the living room with the plate of brownies, Cora trailing after them. When she realized she wasn't getting any tasty tidbits from them, she curled up on her blanket in front of the furnace vent.

Jake walked around the room, checking out the decorations there. "These are your grandparents, I assume?" he asked, picking up a black-and-white photograph of an older couple.

"Yup. Those are the sweethearts. I miss them a lot, but I know they're in good hands in heaven."

He sat down on the overstuffed couch draped with a few of her grandmother's crocheted afghans. "Do you believe in angels?"

Her answer was simple and direct. "Yes."

"Have you ever seen one?"

She weighed his question. Some people asked her the question, searching for the answer as some reliable indicator that a spiritual force was truly at work in human lives. Others asked it with disbelief, their minds already made up that angels were no more real than, say, leprechauns.

What was his motive?

He seemed to be asking it honestly, wanting to hear the answer.

"Yes," she said at last. "Perhaps."

Many would have stopped her there. How could her answer be both yes and perhaps? But he considered her reply and seemed to understand.

"Do you mind telling me more?" he continued.

"I have seen children escape injury by what could only be an angel's hand. I'm talking about suddenly stopping midfall and missing the corner of a table by no possible physical means."

She took a deep breath. "I've heard stories of people who have, during times of stress and spiritual trial, had someone with them who, upon later investigation, could not be verified as existing. The extra nurse in the hospital who talked someone through a difficult recovery. The roommate at the recovery center who kept a fellow from crashing mentally. The woman who pulled a child from a burning car and then vanished."

She paused, studying his face for his reaction. She couldn't read it, but he didn't appear to think she was insane.

"Now none of these instances I've mentioned proves the existence of what we call angels," she went on. "A strong spiritual force is at work in each of these stories, and whether you call them angels or spirits or simply God's intervention, they're visible signs of the strength that comes from God."

"Have you ever seen an angel?" he repeated.

"I've seen a child's fall stopped. Jake, it was the strangest thing. A little boy was standing on a chair in the kitchen at church. It tipped over backward, and suddenly he was falling, the back part of his head aimed right at the sharp corner of the counter. No one could get there fast enough; but apparently someone did because he stopped falling, only a fraction of an inch from the corner. We all watched as his head moved over just far enough to miss the corner, and he fell the rest of the way without hurting himself. He sort of sat down, too—he didn't even get a bump."

She shivered at the memory. It was still so real. She had thought they'd be going to the hospital with him, and instead he wasn't harmed at all.

"And there's one other time. This happened when I lived in St. Paul, going to college. I hadn't been to church for a while—I was in my rebellious period—and I finally decided to go back, to see if it was what I was searching for."

She paused. This, too, was vivid.

"I walked into the sanctuary, and as I stood at the door, wavering about whether or not I'd stay, an elderly woman said, 'Here—sit by me.' She shared her hymnal, and when she sang, Jake, it was the sweetest sound. I've never heard a voice as clear and sweet and pure as hers was. Her caring made me give church a second chance. And when I tried to find her the next Sunday, to tell her what she had done for me, I couldn't find her. I asked the minister, and he said there wasn't anyone like her in the church. To me, she was an angel."

He didn't speak right away. Then he said, "Those stories are pretty convincing to me. I've never seen an angel."

"That you know of," she said. "My favorite Bible verse is from Hebrews, and it goes: 'Be not forgetful to entertain strangers: for thereby some have entertained angels unawares.' You may have encountered an entire host of angels and not known it."

"I doubt it."

"Think about the dinner on Thanksgiving. Any one of those people could have been an angel. How would you have known it? An angel could be symbolic, too, I suppose."

"Explain, please." His head was cupped in his hands, as he waited for her answer.

"I'm not sure about this, but maybe it could be that a human being could act as an angel, too. Like that woman in the church in Minnesota for me. Maybe she truly was a human being; maybe she was just visiting, and that's why no one knew her; but she performed God's deeds."

"That's an interesting theory. Actually, that is probably the most logical explanation. Well, except for that falling child thing—but I suppose there could be some theory about reactive neutrons or something."

"Reactive neutrons?" she repeated. "What are reactive neutrons?"

"Made up," he replied cheerfully. "I just made it up. I'm simply saying there might be some physical response we haven't identified. But that's not to deny the possibility of angels."

"You can't quite believe in them."

"But I can't quite not believe in them," he countered. "I think I'm too pragmatic, though, to accept this angels thing totally. I guess I want proof. You know, pictures on the ten o'clock news. Full coverage by *Newsweek* with photographs and scientific capitulation. The *New York Times* carrying the story on their front page with an in-depth explanation that will answer once and for all whether there is such a thing as an angel."

"They exist whether you believe in them or not," she said. "In some form or some fashion they do. Call them what you will, but they exist. They don't flap down with gigantic wings, although that would make identification much easier, and they're not wearing halos nowadays. But I believe in them."

"Are you upset with me?" he asked, his warm brown eyes studying her.

"No." It was true. At the basis of the ability to believe in angels was the ability to believe in God. And she wasn't yet sure of where Jake stood in his faith journey.

"I guess that surprises me," he said. "You know, as heavily invested as you are with angels and all."

"Invested? Financially or emotionally?"

He shrugged. "Both, I guess, but I did mean emotionally. Isn't it all tied in with your religion, whether you believe in angels or not?"

"Considering they're the messengers of God, yes, it would help if you believed in Him first." The words sounded testy, and she immediately regretted them as she saw his face. "Of course, I'd rather you agreed with me 100 percent, but your arguments are valid, I think. They're definitely much more considered than those I usually hear."

The clock bonged softly, and she leaped up.

"It's after eleven! Remember—you were going home early to get some sleep."

He hedged a bit, but she took his face in her hands and turned it so he was looking directly at her. She could feel the stubble of his beard beneath her hands. It felt wonderful.

"How late is Panda's open tonight?" she asked.

"Midnight."

"And Todd can close, right? You could check the till tomorrow, couldn't you, to make sure it balanced? Or ask him to let you know if it's off wildly?"

"Yes."

"Call. See if there's any reason you need to go in." She pushed him toward her phone.

Tess eavesdropped shamelessly.

When he hung up the phone, she confronted him. "I know everything is all right, so you don't need to go there. Go home. Sleep."

"I'm not tired," he protested.

"Yes, you are. You need to remind your body you are. Have a big glass of milk before you go to bed." The image of his cold, unlived-in house came into her mind. "You do have milk, don't you?"

"I can go to Panda's and get some."

"You will do no such thing. Wait here."

She went into the kitchen and retrieved the thermos he had brought on Saturday. As she opened the refrigerator door and took out the carton of milk, Cora padded in to join them.

Tess filled the thermos for Jake and a bowl for Cora.

"Now, both of you, drink up. And go to sleep."

Now that she was aware of it, she could see the little lines that worry and exhaustion had carved into his face. Automatically her fingers strayed up to soothe them.

"Please, for me, get some sleep."

"I am tired," he admitted. "So tired I may kiss Cora and scratch you behind your ears."

But he got it right.

Chapter 11

She took her own advice and went to bed, but sleep was maddeningly elusive. Even when Cora thumped onto the bed and curled up beside her, like a living hot-water bottle, she couldn't stop thinking about the evening.

Had it been only a few days she'd known him? In that short time he'd become very dear to her. And when he acknowledged how tired he was, she'd nearly cried.

He was such a good man, such a good man.

Her thoughts floated around the word *love* but refused to settle on it.

Cora began to snore softly, her mouth open just enough to allow leftover snatches of the aroma of Giblet Niblets to escape. Tess pushed her carefully so as not to awaken her, but so she'd sleep with her mouth facing the other direction.

Cora stirred from her sleep, sighed, and stood up enough to circle three times and resume her earlier spot, breathing happily into Tess's face.

Tess gave up. Maybe she'd get used to it soon. She had other, more pressing problems to deal with.

Something she was seeing in Jake was an emerging pattern of his inability to move into faith. He wanted proof of angels; he wanted numbers to guarantee his move downtown would be successful; he wanted assurances that his new venture into wholesale was going to be prosperous. Proof. He wanted proof.

But he wanted a proof that didn't exist, not the way he envisioned it. Very little in life came with a guarantee—it was a concept so basic it almost seemed cliché. Could he ever make that important step past the necessity of proof and into faith?

Her mind turned it over and over, but fruitlessly. Finally she buried her face in the warm fur of Cora's side, away from the cat's mouth, and slept.

❧

Quite a bit of snow had fallen overnight. She'd have to clear the walks before her customers arrived. She cleaned the kitchen after breakfast and pulled on her snow-shoveling outfit, a gray one-piece snowsuit that had been her grandfather's, and arctic lace-up boots in military green and yellow. She waited until the last minute to put on the orange woolen hat with the pull-down mask that covered her face—it itched mercilessly.

She caught a glimpse of herself in the hall mirror. "Stunning. Absolutely stunning."

One advantage of the narrow houses clustered together, the hallmark of downtown homes, was not having much public sidewalk to shovel. But the paths to the doors were another matter.

She cleared the sidewalk of snow and turned her attention to the front walk and steps. The path going to the kitchen could wait. Actually, as cold as she was, it could wait forever. Like until April. Or May if necessary. She could use the front door.

Right now she needed to warm up.

The telephone was ringing as she stepped inside. She flung her snow-crusted mittens off her hands, snatched the phone from the hook, and tried to balance so she could untie frozen laces from her boots.

"Hello!" she shouted. Her lips were frozen into thin blocks of ice, and it was difficult to modulate her voice. "Hello!"

"Tess?" He sounded unsure.

"This is Tess." The phone fell from her icy fingers and clattered onto the floor, startling Cora who had come into the kitchen on her eternal quest for food. "Oh, sorry. Hi, Jake. Cora, in a minute."

"Did I call at a bad time?"

"I was shoveling." She had to say the word three times before she could get it out. Apparently even her teeth were frozen.

"With a snow shovel?" Disbelief resounded through his voice.

"No, with my tongue." Clumps of snow fell from her jacket and began to melt in icy pools on the freshly cleaned floor of her kitchen. Why had she decided to mop before shoveling?

"Don't you have a snowblower?"

"No. Where would I keep it, in my kitchen?" She tried not to sound angry, but she knew she was losing the battle. Shoveling snow, especially when it was frigid like this and blowing icy particles into her face, frustrated her. "My garage is too small, but a shovel fits just fine by my back door, so I shovel."

She tried for a more cheerful attitude. "Besides it's good exercise."

The feeling was starting to return to her fingers and nose. Good. She wasn't frostbitten. She blew on her hands and rubbed them together, trying to speed the warming process.

"Tess, it's seventeen below. That arctic front is here."

"I know it's seventeen below. And with the windchill it's even worse. Believe me, I know. I just spent half an hour in it. Major chunks of my body are frozen and may never recover properly. I see my fingers, but I don't feel them. I haven't checked, but I'm not sure there's anything below my ankles. It's not like I have any other options, though. I have to shovel, or the city fines me. And my customers stay away. Either one of those is too much for me."

He apparently got the idea not to pursue the subject because he changed the topic. "I did what you said. I went home, drank the milk, and you know what? I went right to sleep. Slept until six thirty this morning. And I stayed away from Panda's until eight!"

She resisted the urge to utter a sarcastic "Congratulations." She knew how difficult this had been for him. And she realized he was doing it for her. She should feel glad, proud, relieved, instead of wallowing in this anger that was misdirected.

So she forced herself to relax and try to feel cordial. It wasn't his fault the cold front had arrived in full force.

"I'm glad. Now don't you feel better already?"

"Actually I do. Although I'll have to be here tonight. I have a very important business meeting, so we'll need to delay setting up the Christmas trees."

He sounded mysteriously vague, and she couldn't help but be interested.

"May I ask what's going on?" she inquired curiously, giving way to the snoopy side of her nature.

Cora licked one of the puddles formed by the snow melting from her boots. "Ick, ick, ick!" Tess said to her, trying to push her away from it without dropping the phone again.

"Well, it sounds as if you're busy so I'll talk to you later," he said cheerfully and hung up, leaving her with her curiosity unsatisfied.

"Humph," she said to Cora. "It sounds like we're on our own tonight. That's okay, though, because there's a good movie on the classics channel. You and I can snuggle up with a bowl of popcorn that's swimming in butter and have girls' night in."

Cora didn't seem too impressed, but she would be when the popcorn made an appearance. Cora loved buttered popcorn.

Tess quickly changed out of her snow-shoveling outfit, and just in time, as the first customer of the day came into Angel's Roost.

She was almost too busy to miss Jake. Almost. There were corners in the day when he'd appear in her mind or moments would replay. And she'd catch herself leaning against something and smiling goofily at the air.

Maybe it was best they take a break from each other. Tonight would be good. It would be difficult, but good. And tomorrow night she had the mayor's commission to go to, and Wednesday night was choir practice. Unless he stopped by the store sometime, she wouldn't see him until Thursday.

He did. The following morning he struggled in with her Christmas tree, the blue spruce she'd finally decided on. He left quickly afterward, pleading short-staffing at Panda's.

She missed him when she struggled to bolt the tree into its holder, when she decorated the branches with her collection of heritage ornaments, when she placed the special piece on top. But she did get to see him. Each day he popped in with some pastries and coffee, and each day she lost a little more of her heart to him.

He wouldn't, however, tell her what the secretive meeting had been about, but it was easy to see he was excited about it. He seemed almost glowing with happiness and anticipation.

She didn't have to wait until Thursday night to see him. He met her at Nativity's church door after choir practice on Wednesday night with the news that he wanted to put up the Christmas trees.

Fortunately she had laid aside some angels for the tree at Panda's, afraid they'd be snapped up by anxious shoppers if she didn't. She dashed inside, got the box, and blew a kiss to Cora, who regarded her sleepily.

"I'll be back in a while, punkin," Tess told her. "Christmas calls!"

Jake's house was warmer than it had been before, not just in temperature, but in emotion. She could feel his touch in the rooms, which, she noted happily, were no longer showroom perfect.

He brought her a paper bag imprinted with the name of a local discount store. "Here's the stuff for my tree. What do you think?"

She opened it. "It's all new." She looked up from the sack of boxed multicolor ornaments and tinsel.

He nodded proudly. "I bought it today."

The reality finally sank in. He didn't have any ornaments of his own!

She thought quickly. With some quick juggling she could use a few of the ornaments she'd designated for Panda's and sprinkle them in amidst these sparkling new ones. It should lessen the cold, austere sensation of a tree with all-new decorations.

She presented the idea to him, omitting any mention of her intent to bring his tree some holiday warmth. "It would be a theme then. If you don't mind angels, of course."

Jake laughed. "Could you do anything else?"

Within an hour of working steadily they had decorated his tree with a melange of old and new. She stood back and admired it. It was astonishing what the angels had done to make the tree less brittle-looking.

They hurried on to Panda's. The decorating was easier there because the branches were so thickly laden with flocking that only gilded tips could carry the ornaments. The angels were suspended, hanging only from slender invisible wires, as if ready to take flight. To finish it off, Tess looped a strand of golden beads through the white and gold branches, balancing the effect of the angels dangling from the outer edges.

Jake contributed a gold-lettered sign: "Decorations by Angel's Roost." He tried to pay her, but she refused his money.

Together they stepped away from the tree and studied the effect.

"It's incredible," Jake said at last. "Who would have thought something as garish as that thing was could ever turn out as, well, celestial as it looks now? Tess, I could kiss you."

She turned to him. "Now that's a payment I can accept."

And she did.

They made a date to go to a movie on Thursday night.

But early in the morning the phone rang.

He started right in. "Tess, have you seen the morning's paper?"

"No," she said sleepily. She hadn't even seen the morning sun.

"What have I done?" Anguish laced his voice.

Immediately she was wide-awake. "What's going on, Jake? Are you in trouble?"

"In a sense, yes. Tess, I need to talk to you. May I come over?"

"Sure. Just give me a few minutes for a quick shower."

"Thanks. I'll be over in half an hour."

She was about to hang up when he said, "Tess, sweetheart, one more thing. You might want to unplug your phones for a while."

"Jake! What is going on? Tell me! What? What?" But the only response to her questions was a dial tone. He'd hung up.

Questions abounded as she raced through her shower and tugged on a sweat suit. She didn't bother with makeup. Her hands were shaking too much with worry.

She met him at the door, and he handed her the morning paper. He had folded it open to the business section, displaying one article in particular: "Is Panda's an Endangered Species in the End?" The subtitle read: "Panda's to Bolt Downtown."

She scanned the article: "Panda's, a popular trendy coffee spot in the End, is planning a move downtown, reliable sources say. Jake Cameron, owner of Panda's, will close his south-end restaurant and coffeehouse by April of next year and head downtown where growth initiatives are attractive for business owners. The move will leave a hole in the End's growing economy, but it is expected to be a boon to the city's center. Why this sudden departure from an area that has served him well for the past five years? Perhaps his newest companion, a downtown business owner and member of the mayor's commission, has something to do with it. Whatever the reason, the move is expected to be positively angelic."

Her mouth dropped open in horror. "Can they say that? Is it true? It isn't! It is? You haven't—oh, you have! Oh Jake, I'm so happy and so furious right now."

She was dimly aware that she was making no sense at all, but it didn't matter—her emotions warred with each other as they jockeyed for prime place in her brain. Her speech was only a mirror of what her thoughts looked like, chaotic and disordered.

He was moving Panda's downtown. That was good. He had told a newspaper reporter before he told her. That was bad. He hadn't told her at all. That was even worse. He had somehow implicated her in it, although weren't people implicated only in crimes? That was bad, but it meant he cared for her—didn't it?—which was good. Wasn't it?

Oh, she was so confused.

"It's true. Somewhat true," he corrected himself. "That's what the big news was I've been so mysterious about. I was going to check into that building you told me about, but I hadn't done anything with it. I don't even know which building it is. All I'd done was make a call to a Realtor, and we played some phone tag. We never did connect so I'm not sure what this is all about."

"Why didn't you tell me?"

"I didn't want you to know," he said glumly. "When it was a done deal, all signed, sealed, and delivered, I was going to make a big production out of it. I thought you'd be surprised."

"Well, it worked. I'm surprised." She handed him back the paper. "I'm delighted with the news, of course, although I am livid over the snide innuendoes that I influenced you."

"You did. If I hadn't met you and talked to you, I wouldn't even have considered moving down here."

"But I didn't make you do something you didn't want to do," she reminded him. "And there's a humongous difference."

"I'm trying to figure out how they got this story. I talked to the real estate agent handling the deal, and he claims he didn't talk to the paper, and I believe him. So who—?" He slapped his forehead. "Stupid, stupid, stupid."

"You figured it out? Who told the reporter?" She leaned forward eagerly. "I did."

"Jake!" How could someone with his business savvy sabotage his own project? "What on earth are you talking about?"

"People from the newspaper come to Panda's all the time," Jake said, "and I spent a lot of time on the phone with the real estate agent there. The reporter probably overheard us talking about it."

"But, even so, this is still slimy journalism. Did they ever contact you to verify the story?"

He wouldn't meet her eyes, and she knew something was wrong. She persisted until he explained he had cut back his time at Panda's and had missed the reporter every time.

Her stomach rolled over and sank. She was the one who had been encouraging him not to go to Panda's so frequently. He'd been spending a lot of time with her, and yet she had kept him away from the coffeehouse even more by telling him he needed to stay home and not go to work so often.

Had she, in a roundabout way, caused this problem with her misguided interference in his life?

As if he were reading her mind, Jake said, "I don't know if it would have mattered if I'd been there or not. This kind of writing is tabloid trash at best, full of half-baked truth that's more fiction than reality."

He had a point there, and she felt her heart lighten, although her stomach was still in turmoil.

"Still, he shouldn't have run the story without checking it out. And he never asked me anything," she said proudly.

She picked up the paper again and reread the article, forcing herself to go through it slowly. "I guess we can't sue him for slander or libel or anything like that since it's all sort of true in a basic sense. Besides it's not a signed article. It's just in that Shop Talk column, which is really no better than some tabloid coverage of the town's merchants."

"I could easily find out who wrote it," Jake said, "but I'm debating that. My mom always told me, 'Least said, soonest healed,' or something like that. I might just leave it alone and see if it blows over." He tried to smile. "So, kiddo, do you still want me as a neighbor? I'm probably *persona non grata* in my own neighborhood. They'd no doubt be glad to see me go now."

She dropped the paper and hugged him. "Anyone would be lucky to have you."

He hugged her back, but she could tell his heart wasn't in it. "I'm a member of the Community and Business Organization in the End. This was a terrible way to let them know I was thinking about leaving them, having to read it in the paper, especially in a column like this."

"You're starting to back down now, aren't you?" she asked quietly, holding his hand in hers.

He looked miserable. "I've always prided myself on being civic-minded and a good boss and a caring person. Think how many people feel betrayed this morning, reading this in the paper. I feel lower than a snake's belly."

He stood up and walked over to the window, shoving his hands in his pockets. "So Reverend Barnes wants us to prioritize what we want this week, does he? Why didn't he add the warning: 'Be careful what you wish for—you might get it'?"

She didn't know what to say, if in fact there was anything she could say. With all her being, she wanted to take his pain away, but right now it seemed beyond her power. She felt limp and weak as her helplessness overwhelmed her.

She started in the only way she knew. Silently she began to pray: *Dear Lord, help us pass through this time of trial. Guide us and heal his hurting soul. Take us through this valley of—*

"Are you praying?" His words rang out sharply. "Is that what you're doing? Praying?"

"Yes."

"Well, don't bother."

She stared as his sudden burst of anger contorted his face. "Don't you get this, Tess? This isn't about anything God can help with. He can't take those words off that newspaper page. He can't take them out of the minds of the folks who have read the article. It's done. It's all over. Every bit of it. And don't tell me prayer will help anything. It can't."

He snatched up his coat. "Because if there is a God, He sure has it in for me. How can I believe in a God who doesn't believe in me?"

With a slam of the door he was gone. And with him he took her heart.

She proceeded through the day numbly, smiling mechanically at her customers as she rang up their sales. Her sales didn't seem to have dropped, and she couldn't see any difference in the way people acted today from the way they'd acted all week long.

No one seemed to have noticed the article, and she took courage from that.

That is, until late in the day when the door swung open and Mayor Lindstrom strode into Angel's Roost.

She was wearing her trademark bright yellow wool coat and brilliant red boots, a burst of sunlight in the white of winter. At the commission meetings she had often said she was going to visit Angel's Roost, but this was her first time in the store. Somehow Tess didn't think she was there Christmas shopping.

At first Tess thought her worries were for naught as the mayor commented favorably on the store and the inventory. But then she launched into a discussion of the mayor's commission.

"I've appreciated everything you've done for us. You've been a tireless worker and a valuable asset to the commission. But we're looking at restructuring the committee now." Mayor Lindstrom straightened a rack of bookmarks cut out in the shape of angels, with Bible verses printed on the wings.

"You want me to leave," Tess said flatly.

"No. I don't. And that's why I'm here." The mayor was known and admired—or hated—for her way of speaking directly. "But the question of your way of operating is going to come up." She picked up a ceramic birth angel and studied it casually. "Pretty. You saw the paper, I gather. Did you influence him?"

Tess decided to answer as honestly as she could. "Jake and I have known each other for a very short time. He asked what I thought about whether he should move Panda's downtown, and I admit I was encouraging. But I was not the one to suggest it, nor did I in any way bribe or finagle him into this decision. As a matter of fact, it was a total surprise to me. I learned it by reading it in the paper this morning."

"Tess, it's not quite as simple as it might appear. The End is part of the city, too, and if Panda's moves, that'll have an impact on the End's economy just as it will on downtown's." The tension in the mayor's voice was sharp enough to snap.

"I never thought of that," Tess said. She felt like a schoolgirl being called on the carpet by the principal.

Mayor Lindstrom examined a wind chime made of shells carved into the shapes of angels. "The worst part of this situation is that reading about it in the morning paper is a rotten way to let people know. I've had phone calls from the End's CBO members, from Panda's regular customers, from the families of Jake Cameron's employees. It's not as simple as it seems."

Tess agreed with her, and the mayor turned to face her straight-on.

"Then why did he choose that way to let us all know? Why didn't he tell us first?"

"He didn't have any control over the story."

"Balderdash," the mayor said bluntly. "He talked to the reporter, didn't he?"

"Actually, no, he didn't." Tess began the explanation, detailing what Jake had told her earlier. When Tess had finished, Mayor Lindstrom was clearly angry. Her face had grown pale with a bright spot of red on each cheek.

When she spoke, each word shot out as if it had been bitten off. "I've never liked that business column to begin with. The use of unsubstantiated rumor and insinuation is irresponsible at best, but this is it. I've reached the end of my patience with that column."

As the mayor swung out of the store, Tess was certain she saw sparks flying from her heels.

Chapter 12

Tess watched the mayor stride down the front walk of Angel's Roost and step into her car.

She certainly didn't want to be the editor of the paper when Mayor Lindstrom arrived, although the snoopy part of her would have loved to be a fly on the wall.

The newspaper was only a few blocks from Angel's Roost, not time enough for the mayor to cool down if she headed straight there from the store. And Tess thought she probably would.

Tess knew the editor would get a piece of the mayor's mind when she arrived. As much as Tess was a nonconfrontational person and dreaded conflict, she was glad Mayor Lindstrom had stepped in. There were lines in ethics that needed to be drawn, and the mayor was the person to do it.

She picked up the phone and called Panda's. When she asked for Jake, the young woman on the other end said, "Um, he's, um, like not here—I don't think. He's, um, in a meeting. . .or something. I could, um, like, take a message if you want."

It did Tess's heart good to hear someone who was so obviously ill at ease with lying.

"He's there, isn't he?" she asked gently.

"Um, I, um, no, not really." The young woman's hedging was getting worse.

"Would you please tell him Tess called and that it's very important I speak with him?"

"Sure. Um, wait a sec, okay?"

The woman must have put her hand over the speaker part of the receiver because the background noise became muted. She could hear some mumbled conversation; then Jake came on the phone.

"Tess, I'm really busy." He sounded tired again and harassed.

"Is your staff fielding your calls?" Tess asked.

"Yes. It was their idea, but I gave in. It's easier this way."

"Phone's been ringing off the hook, huh?"

"Endlessly. People congratulating me on making a good decision. People ready to kill me. People wanting to know who this woman is who influenced me. People suggesting I do all sorts of interesting things I have no inclination for, nor are any of them physically possible—thank you very much."

"Then screening your calls is a good idea," she said.

"What about you?" he asked. "Has there been a lot of backlash at you?"

"I must not be as high profile as you," she said ruefully, "because I don't think anyone recognized who I am. Oh, wait. One person did. Mayor Lindstrom."

"Whaaat?" he asked in astonishment. She had his complete attention.

"Yes, indeedy. The mayor finally found the time to stop by Angel's Roost." She was unable to resist voicing what had bothered her since the mayor's visit— that she hadn't found the time to stop by Angel's Roost until there was trouble. She knew the mayor was busy, but Tess didn't like hollow promises.

"And did she buy anything?" he inquired.

"Are you checking into the mayor's purchasing habits, or do you want to know what happened?" An edge of testiness crept into her words, and Tess fought to keep the snappishness away.

"I want to know what happened. Can you tell me?" His voice filled with anxiety and a sprig of hope that seemed to bloom in the winter.

"Not on the phone. I'll tell you tonight," she said.

"Tonight? I can't wait that long. Please tell me now," he pleaded.

"Can't. Won't. Actually I don't know myself that anything happened. You know the mayor. She doesn't abide foolishness, at least not with her town."

"What does that mean?" he asked, thoroughly confused now.

She grinned into the telephone receiver. "Come by around five. By then it may all be old news. And, by the way, bring food." She hung up before he could say more.

She turned to Cora, who had been watching the telephone cord dangle, apparently trying to decide if it was worth her while to get up, cross the room, and try to catch it. Idleness must have won out because the cat hadn't moved at all.

"I hope I'm not getting him over here under false pretenses," she said to Cora, who yawned. "But I've been so concerned about him this week. First he's so tired, almost to the point of exhaustion, and now this. Body and soul can bear only so much, sweet pea, and I'm worried. Really worried."

She felt that she needed to be there for him, but what words could she say that would bring comfort, let alone advice? What kind of wisdom did she have, or could she call upon, that would lead her into the right way to address the situations he was facing?

The shop was empty of customers, so she left Cora guarding the store while she popped into the back of the house.

One place she could count on for finding an answer. It was a book that had been her guide for many years now, and it had never let her down.

Just holding her grandmother's Bible brought her an immediate sense of calm. Tess brought it close to her heart and let it soothe her more.

She took it to the store and sat on the chair behind the counter. As she did so, something fluttered to the ground.

It was a thin sheet of paper. The handwriting on it was familiar; she'd seen it a hundred times when her grandmother was alive. She'd never seen this paper, though, and she read it eagerly. It was a list of Bible verses appropriate to certain needs, and her eyes focused on one in particular: "For speaking wisely, read Colossians 4:6."

Quickly she turned to the verse: "Let your speech be alway with grace, seasoned with salt, that ye may know how ye ought to answer every man."

A snapshot memory of her grandmother appeared in her mind: She was standing by the old stove in the kitchen, stirring something warm and spicy and listening to Tess's tearful confession about a teenage spat. Tess had said something about one of her friends, words that had come back to haunt her, and her grandmother had advised her on that long-ago day, "Tess, make sure your words are seasoned with salt, as you may have to eat them." At the time it had seemed a curiously old-fashioned thing to say, but now it made sense. How like her grandmother to turn to the Bible for wisdom!

She read it again, just the verse, and then in context. How she wished she could have met Paul! "Walk in wisdom," he said in a nearby line. That was her goal.

She recalled Reverend Barnes's words. She needed to start making her wish list. At the top of it would be those words: "Walk in wisdom."

Jake burst through the door, balancing three take-out trays, a plastic bowl covered with foil, and a drink carrier. "I'm here," he announced breathlessly. "I know I'm early. So shoot me. Have I got news for you."

She flipped the sign on the front door to Closed and motioned him toward the back. Cora roused herself from her slumber and, at the sight of the take-out cartons, came to life with amazing alacrity.

The three of them marched into Tess's small dining room. Tess pushed aside the week's accumulation of mail she would get to, someday, and cleared a spot for them to eat.

Cora wound herself in and out of Jake's legs in a frantic figure eight, punctuating her movement with plaintive meows.

He reached down and absently patted her head with his hand, but it had nothing in it to eat. Cora's massive disappointment was clear. Fortunately Tess saw the look and captured Cora's attention with Meow Meals before the cat could snack on Jake's fingers. She'd seen that expression before and knew exactly what it meant. It did not bode well for him.

As she was saving his hand from certain attack, she noticed he seemed almost chipper. The more she watched him, the surer she was. He must have good news.

The take-out containers held a variety of sandwiches and salads, and the bowl was filled with wild rice and cheese soup. Her mouth began to water as she helped him set the food on plates.

The drinks were Italian sodas, and she poured them into clear glass tumblers so they could enjoy the bright colors.

Before he took a bite, she covered his hand with hers. "I've always done this silently, so maybe you don't know I do it, but I say grace before each meal. May I say it aloud this time?"

She dared not breathe as she awaited his answer. He had been so angry at God before, so opposed to her praying, at least for his plight. She had been hoping it was a temporary snap of anger with God and not a revelation of his true feelings. How would Jake react now? Would he let her pray?

"Tess, I must apologize for my angry outburst. There is no excuse for it. I wouldn't blame you if you could not forgive me." He looked down in misery.

"Not forgive you?" She gripped his hand. "How could I not forgive you? Think what Jesus forgave. They killed Him, Jake, and He forgave them. How could I hold this against you? Is your sin worse? No, it isn't. It is up to Him to forgive you, and I think He already has."

"Thank you, Tess." He looked up and smiled shyly at her. "I needed to hear that. And there's more I need to hear. I need to hear you pray. Yes, please, offer grace." He bowed his head in reverence.

She breathed a sigh of relief, and then she began.

"Heavenly Lord, bless this food which You have given us. We ask so much of You, and in return You provide. Thank You, dearest Lord, in the name of Your Son, Jesus Christ, who is indeed the greatest gift of Christmas. Amen."

"Amen." Jake joined with her in response.

Their eyes met, and for a moment Tess saw the oneness she had been seeking.

The mood was shattered as Cora meowed loudly, indicating it was dinnertime.

"What's your news?" Tess asked Jake as she passed him the plate of sandwiches.

"What's yours?" he countered.

"I don't want to get into one of those who-goes-first battles," she said, "so I'll start since mine is first in line chronologically."

She told him about Mayor Lindstrom's visit, and when she ended her narrative, he leaned back and nodded thoughtfully.

"That goes a long way to explaining my news," he said at last. "I had a call from the editor of the paper, apologizing. The entire situation is bizarre. Here's the story.

"The writer of Shop Talk had written the story before checking with me because his wife was due for a heart transplant, and he was working ahead to be ready. He had written the copy but hadn't intended it to go in yet, pending verification of the story. He'd heard about it from someone who'd heard about it from someone who'd heard about it—one of those long, convoluted stories you can never get to the bottom of.

"Then his wife got the call—there was a donor heart—so they packed up quickly and left for Rochester, where the transplant is being done. Unfortunately he left the copy on his desk as a way to remind him to call me and check out the story when he got back. And his replacement saw it, thought it indicated he wanted the story to run, and used it."

"Oh, wow," she breathed. "What an incredible story! Who ever would have thought it would be something like that? How's his wife?"

He stood and hugged her. "Only you, Tess Mahoney, would ask that question right off the bat. You really do care about other people, don't you?"

"Well, how is she?" she persisted. "Heart transplants are more common now, but a grave element of danger is still involved. Is she doing okay?"

He nodded. "So far, so good. She just underwent surgery, so it's early yet. But she's a fighter, they say."

She sent a quick silent prayer heavenward for the woman's safety.

"You know," she commented, "it tells me a lot that you knew the answer. That means you must have inquired about her health."

"I can't imagine," he said softly, "how it feels to know you must risk your life in order to live. And what those around you who love you must go through at the same time. How can they deal with the uncertainty, the not knowing?"

"It's called faith."

"Maybe someday I'll understand." He looked at her, his deep brown eyes liquid with hope.

The light over the table cast severe shadows on his face, and she was once again struck by how tired and worn down he was. It seemed as if the silver threading through his hair was more abundant now, but that had to be a trick of the light.

"Jake, it's there. You just have to reach out with your heart and accept it."

"I want to—I really want to," he said, "but there's this ironclad part of me that wants proof. And what can I do? Despite all your avowals how can you prove it to me? How can I prove it to myself? Is it even possible, or am I asking the impossible?"

"It is kind of a looping theory," she admitted. "You need to have faith in order to believe in faith or even to understand what it is."

"How did you come to have faith?" he asked. "I really need to hear this."

"I was raised in a family that went to church every Sunday, but more than that, they absolutely believed in Jesus and in God. It was as much a part of our lives as, say, electricity."

"No power failures?" His lopsided smile didn't cover the deep concern she heard in his voice.

"God doesn't have power failures," she stated firmly. "None. At one time when I was a teenager I tried to outrun God. I couldn't do it. My grandparents wouldn't let me, He wouldn't let me, and when it came right down to it, I wouldn't let me."

"You? You seem as if you've never doubted God at all."

"Wait a minute," she protested. "I never doubted Him. I was a teenager, sure that I knew more than anybody. God was in my life, but I had my priorities jumbled up. Grandma and Grandpa were rock-steady, and with their help I pulled through adolescence with few scars. One of the most important things I learned from my grandparents was that I had to have my own faith, not just a general 'I believe in God,' but a strong current that runs through every hour of my life. My faith is a commitment to Him. I made that pledge when my rowdy time, short-lived though it was, ended. I had the foundation from my family, but when it came right down to it I had to make a personal decision to give my life back to Him."

"I believe in God—I truly do—but I'm beginning to wonder if I have faith," he confessed. "I mean, I look at you, and you have this wonderful trust and assurance that it's all working out fine. While I'm a basket case waiting for the men in white coats to come and take me away to a place with pillows on the walls."

"What's interesting," she said, "is that all the worry in the world isn't going to make the situation better for you. As a matter of fact, it can only make it worse because it robs you of sleep, causes you to neglect your eating habits, and generally makes you a crabby person."

"Have I been crabby?"

"You've had your moments."

He grinned. "I certainly didn't mean to snap at you."

"That's my point. It's not what you intend to do, but it's what you do. How can worry possibly be good for you? Grandma used to say, 'Idle hands are the devil's workshop,' but Grandpa would correct her and say, 'A worrying mind is the devil's workshop.'"

"I wish I could have met them," he said wistfully. "They must have been great people."

"They were. Not a day goes by that I don't thank God for having given them to me, and I miss them. But they're with Him now, and I know their pains are gone, and their happiness is fulfilled."

Cora jumped up on her lap, and Tess buried her fingers in the soft longish fur around the cat's neck. "And Grandma has her cat the color of pussy willows, and so do I. Right, Cora?"

Cora sniffed meaningfully at the plate where uneaten remnants of Tess's sandwich were.

"I think she smells the seafood salad," Jake said. "It has crab and shrimp in it and some kind of whitefish."

"Definitely more appealing than Giblet Niblets," Tess said, scraping the sandwich filling onto Cora's plate. "And, I hope, a little more conducive to sweeter bedtime breath. That stuff lingered way beyond the normal span. If only they could make perfume that potent and long-lasting!"

"In the kitty world it's probably the equivalent of expensive French perfume. You know, if you rubbed some of it behind your ears, Cora would undoubtedly think you smelled heavenly!"

"I could just go roll in the garbage," she suggested cheerfully. "Maybe that would work instead!"

They chatted a bit longer until Jake said he had to go home.

"Home?" she repeated. "Are you serious? Even after all this, you're not going back to Panda's?"

He shook his head. "You've converted me to this thing called sleep. I sometimes have a little problem convincing my body it's okay to sleep, but I've been using your suggestion of a glass of milk, and it's working great. Last night I added a turkey sandwich and could barely stay awake enough to brush my teeth afterward."

"Oh, yeah, turkey has that stuff in it that makes you sleepy. At least, that's what Grandpa said whenever he slept in the living room after a big turkey dinner. Claimed he couldn't help it; it was nature's way of giving him a well-deserved nap." The old memory brought a smile to her lips.

She walked with him to the door. Cora trailed behind but backed away quickly when she felt the icy draft from under the door.

"The wind is blowing so hard it's coming right through the door frame," he said, putting his hand out to feel the air move. "That's one of the problems with old houses. The wood dries and shrinks a bit, and you get gaps. I can even hear the wind whistling through the cracks."

She patted the wall fondly. "Yes, this old house whistles and creaks and groans, but so will I when I'm this old, I suspect."

"I could seal the cracks and make it stop—in the house, I mean. You're on your own with your personal noises, I'm afraid. It wouldn't take long for me to straighten this right up for you, and I suspect it would save you considerably on your heating bill this winter. Right now you're trying to heat part of the outside, but with this wind it's just getting blown off to who knows where."

"So my leaky house is responsible for global warming?" she teased. "Actually, if you can fix these places where the heat is escaping, I'd very much appreciate it."

"No problem. I used to work for a construction firm specializing in renovating old houses, so I do know my way around homes like this and the problems they have. If it's warm enough tomorrow, I can hang your lights, too, if you have any."

"If I have lights, he says. Of course I have lights. And they're shaped like—?"

"Angels?" he guessed.

"Right!"

With promises to see each other the next day, he slid his arms around her.

Before she fell into the embrace, she saw Cora look up from her station near the heating vent.

She must have been mistaken. It wasn't possible.

The cat looked absolutely smug.

Chapter 13

The controversy over Jake's moving Panda's downtown blew over with the ease of a prairie wind. When the newspaper published the clarification that it was still tentative and explained the error in the column, the townspeople accepted it.

The Enders thought Panda's would, of course, stay put, whereas the downtowners were sure Panda's was joining them. But each side was so sure it was right that the issue never arose again, much to Jake's relief.

The newspaper even waited an appropriate amount of time for the Shop Talk column to be forgotten and then ran a full interview with Tess about Angel's Roost and what it was like to own and operate a downtown business.

Sales soared, and Jake began to tease her about how she was going to have to hire someone. And to think she'd once worried about how to advertise Angel's Roost.

Jake had fixed the leaking door frame and hung her precious angel-shaped lights that Grandpa had made. They were an intriguing set of small lights set on metal forms he'd fashioned himself. They gave the appearance of a host of glowing angels surrounding her house.

This was the first year Tess was involved with planning the Christmas Eve service at Nativity. As she explained to Jake, her part was simple. She told people, "Stand here and don't move. Now move." And that was it.

She had been placed in charge of the silhouette stable. A large sheet— she wondered where they had managed to get such a huge piece of seamless cloth—was hung across the front of the church. Behind it were the figures from the manger scene: Mary, Joseph, the baby in the manger, plus three shepherds and an assortment of farm animals.

The animals were shapes cut out of plywood, but Mary, Joseph, and the shepherds were portrayed by high school students. The entire scene was subtly lit so that the figures cast large shadows on the cloth.

The students had discussed trying to borrow a real baby to use, but they'd quickly discovered the disadvantages far outweighed the advantages. The youngest one they could find was eleven-month-old Andrew Tyler, a charming child with the lungs of an air horn.

As they explained to his slightly miffed parents, Andrew was a bit too large to be a newborn. In addition to his astonishing lungs, he was already the size of the average two-year-old.

So instead they borrowed Andrew's sister's Baby Snoozie, which didn't look at all real, but which they hoped would cast a realistic shadow. At least she wouldn't cry.

Andrew's sister, Katie, had given Tess very detailed instructions on how to make the baby snore, but Tess furtively removed the doll's battery pack. She'd replace it after the program before anyone realized it was missing. All they needed was for Jesus to start snoring during "Away in a Manger."

That was the only time anyone moved. The song was Mary's cue to put the baby in the manger. Tess hoped she would remember but was thankful it didn't matter if she forgot.

Two days before Christmas Jake stopped by the store for some last-minute employee gifts. Tess realized he'd never said what his plans were for Christmas Eve.

"If it's okay, I'll tag along with you and go to the service at Nativity," he said.

"You know you're more than welcome to come with me to church. Always. I'll have to leave during the shadows tableau scene, but other than that we can sit together the entire time."

"What are your plans after that?" he asked. "Are you going somewhere special?"

"Sure. I'm coming back home, and Cora and I will watch *It's a Wonderful Life* and open our presents to each other." She looked at him carefully. He seemed to be waiting for her to say something. "Would you like to join us?"

"I adore *It's a Wonderful Life*. It has to be the Christmas classic of all times. Is it on television?"

"Ha. Cora and I take no chances with our traditions. We own a copy."

After he left, Tess pondered what had just happened. Bringing someone into a tradition was risky, but leaving him out was not even a consideration.

He had quickly become part of her life.

The day before Christmas was wild at Angel's Roost. Customers swarmed through her store, buying last-minute gifts by the basketful. She ran out of bags by noon and had to dart back into her kitchen and grab some old grocery sacks.

She had promised herself she'd close the store at noon, but it was almost half past two by the time the last customer was gone and she was able to flip the door sign over to CLOSED. The store looked positively picked over, with gaping spots where entire displays had been purchased by the day's spree-shoppers.

She paused by the sunlit spot that Faith, the crazy angel, had once occupied, and she felt a twinge in the region of her heart. She missed the zany angel with the tilted halo.

More than anything she wanted to collapse on the couch with Cora and put her feet up, but she had something else to do first.

It was embarrassing, but she didn't have anything to give Jake for

Christmas yet. She hadn't been able to decide what would be an appropriate present.

A sweater seemed too impersonal. A robe, on the other hand, was too personal. Aftershave implied he could smell better than he did.

She strolled through Angel's Roost, rearranging the remaining inventory to fill the gaps left by the day's sales. What could she get him?

Her mind ran through an endless list of no-goes. A gift certificate. A catcher's mitt. A cassette deck. A fountain pen. A calendar. All her ideas were blah, blah, blah.

Her fingers absently straightened the remaining items left on a far shelf. As she touched one, it made a slight sound.

It was a sterling-silver bell, similar to the one Reverend Barnes had bought, but much less ornate. The only decoration was the set of angel wings etched into the body of the bell.

An idea occurred to her. It might work. It had to work.

She gift-wrapped the bell in the remnants of the store's angel-themed paper and scrawled a few words on a card. She proofread it once, paused, and then taped the card to the package and put it under the tree.

She barely had time to get herself ready for the evening.

Jake was prompt. Her breath caught as she saw him outlined by moon-light in the snow. His face had begun to relax and the tension fade. He looked ten years younger and, if it was possible, even more good-looking than he had before.

About two inches of fresh light snow had fallen that afternoon, and the air had turned wonderfully mild, so they decided to walk to church. The town was silent. What few cars had ventured out were muted by the new snow not yet packed on the streets.

The sky had cleared, and overhead the stars were bright and plentiful.

"Did you know some scientists have come up with an explanation of the Christmas star?" Jake asked. "Apparently there was a—"

She laid her mittened hand over his lips. "Stop. I believe in the star. I believe in the birth. Nothing you can tell me will make it any less of a miracle."

"But this article proves it existed," Jake argued. "Wouldn't you like to know for sure the Christmas story is real?"

"I do know it."

"I mean as a fact."

She stopped walking. She'd been through this argument before with other people, and it was a debate she didn't enjoy. The only way to win it was for the other person to allow change into their lives and to quit resisting the pull of faith.

"Proof. It all comes back to proof for you, doesn't it?" she asked. "There are all kinds of proof; yet you recognize only a few. Jake, I cannot make you believe. I cannot give you faith. All I can give you is my witness that it exists and it works. Beyond that you're on your own."

"I don't mean to bicker with you, especially on Christmas Eve," he said.

"Then let's not discuss it anymore. First we'll have a moving hour of deep religious significance for me. You can take it however you want in your heart, but let me enjoy this. It rekindles me for the next year."

She tried to quell the anger that was burning in her. This was Christmas Eve, the time when Jesus' life saga began anew. It always filled her soul, and she carried that with her into the next year.

He tried to interrupt, but she held up her hand. "Then we'll go back to my house and have a great time, opening our presents and watching Cora explode with happiness over all the things you bought her. Then I'll indulge myself with my annual dive into sentimentality with the movie. That's the way I do Christmas. You are welcome to come with me, but you may not change a thing about it. I need this."

There. She had said it. And now the evening wasn't going at all the way she'd envisioned it. Instead she felt crabby and out of sorts, and he was now probably going to be distant and not at all receptive to the renewing hour ahead of him.

They trudged along in silence, lost in their own thoughts, until they reached the walk leading to Nativity's inviting front door.

Jake took her hand in his and walked with her to the door. "If the animals can speak at midnight on this blessed night," he said softly, "I can try to keep silent."

"You don't have to keep quiet." She couldn't hold back the shakiness from her voice. "I just don't want to get into one of those 'discussions' that force me to say what I believe again and again. You know I give my testimony freely, but once in a while I like to have some time to reflect upon it."

"Isn't there a line in—help me here, my Bible knowledge is a little rusty—Ecclesiastes, maybe, about 'a time to keep silence, and a time to speak'?"

She nodded. "It's a beautiful passage. It begins, 'To everything there is a season.'"

"Maybe it's my time to be still, to let events unfold as they are meant to." His eyes rested upon her with incredible gentleness.

"You know," she said softly, "it's in the deepest silence that truth is heard most clearly. Maybe instead of analyzing truth and belief and proof and faith, you need to sit back and let it come to you. Let it tell you what you need to know. Maybe faith has proof. Why don't you let it prove itself to you?"

He was about to answer when the door swung open. The merry sounds of laughter rolled out into the night like a golden wave.

"There you are!" One voice detached itself from the others. It belonged to Lena, the young woman who played Mary in the silhouette stable.

Lena flitted down the steps, brushing off Tess's scoldings about not wearing a coat or hat or mittens. "Oh, shoo. I'll only be out here for a sec. Just long enough to tell you that Katie Tyler is screaming mad because she went to show her friends Baby Snoozie, and the stupid doll wouldn't snore."

"Uh-oh," Tess muttered. "Guess I got caught red-handed."

Lena looked confused for a moment but didn't stop. "So she's going around telling everyone you broke Baby Snoozie, and to top it off she's pulling the dumb doll from the play."

"I'd better go in and see what I can do," Tess said. She didn't look forward to it. Katie Tyler was a beautiful but spoiled child and as stubborn as a cat.

"I told her I didn't need her raggedy old doll. I'd just wad up a bunch of towels and use those instead," Lena continued.

"Oh no!" Tess groaned.

"And then she said, 'Where are you going to get towels, Miss Smarty Pants?' Can you believe it? She actually called me Miss Smarty Pants! So I told her I'd use her coat when she changed into her costume for the kids' play, and now she won't take off her coat, and her costume won't fit, but she won't take off her coat, and she's the star so she has to be in the show, and the choir director's about ready to kill both her and you!" Lena's exciting narrative came to a triumphant and breathless finish.

"And a merry Christmas to you, too," Tess said under her breath as she mentally girded her loins to go into the church and do battle with one Katie Tyler over Baby Snoozie's missing snore box.

Katie took one look at Tess's face and, without a word, stuck her arms behind her parka-covered back, protecting Baby Snoozie from the marauding clutches of Tess.

Tess motioned for Katie to follow her, and Katie did, mesmerized by Tess's silence. Neither one of them spoke as they went into the Sunday school room and sat in the minuscule chairs.

It was Katie who broke the wordless standoff. "You killed Baby Snoozie."

Tess pondered how to rectify the situation and do it quickly. She sent up a quick prayer for help and began.

"Katie, I'm sorry I took the battery pack out without telling you. I did it simply because I didn't want the doll to start snoring during the show. Just like you're pretending to be a star tonight, Baby Snoozie is pretending to be Baby Jesus. Think of it, Katie. Your doll is an actor, just like you!"

Tess was sure she saw the girl soften.

"I'll replace the battery pack as soon as the show is over. I promise." Tess leaned forward earnestly. "I promise."

The girl narrowed her eyes and studied Tess. "Okay," she said, shoving the doll into Tess's arms.

"Now please scurry into your star costume."

"Okay."

"Wow, that was fast," Jake said when Tess emerged with Baby Snoozie in tow. "How did you do that?"

"I tried something unheard of today. I told her the truth." Tess grinned at him. "Now I have to return this doll to Lena before she rips Katie's coat off her. Go ahead and find a seat and save one for me. I'll only be a minute."

Lena had calmed down considerably, enough to manage one last sarcastic comment about the doll's face: "If I have to look at the grotesque doll all evening long, I'm going to turn it upside down so I'll be looking at its feet instead."

The tableau was scheduled to be the last presentation of the show. Tess made a mental note to slip out a few minutes before its start.

She had just eased into the seat Jake had saved for her, ignoring the fond glances the rest of the congregation gave them, when Mrs. Smalley switched from the meditative introductory music. The organ notes swelled into the magnificent opening chords of "O Come, All Ye Faithful."

Everyone stood and joined in, most singing the words from memory. It was one of her favorite Christmas carols, so exuberant that it brought the wild joy of Jesus' birth even closer.

Reverend Barnes began straight-out with the reading from Luke: " 'And it came to pass in those days. . . .' " As many times as she heard it and read it, Tess could never tire of the words. So simple, so meaningful.

As he read through the story, he paused while the children presented a skit or sang a song. Katie Tyler, Tess saw with satisfaction, portrayed the Christmas star with a brilliance.

She couldn't help stealing a glance at Jake during Katie's play—was he, too, thinking back to their discussion on the way to church?

The stars moved offstage to allow the next heavenly host: the angels. The youngest children looked beatific in their short white robes that belled around them. Someone had gone to great lengths with their costumes. The wings were snowy puffs of feathers that made them look as if they could truly take off and return to heaven at any moment.

Tess almost missed her cue so enraptured was she with the little ones. But she slipped off just in time to corral the teenagers and hustle them behind the curtain, with Baby Snoozie in an upright position.

As she pulled the cords opening the curtain and revealing the sheet, she flipped on the lights. The congregation voiced a unison "Ooooh." Even from the side of the stage it looked impressive. Lena apparently was moved to new thespian heights and gazed at Baby Snoozie with rapture as the children around her sang "Away in a Manger."

Tess stole back to her seat by Jake in time to watch the angels flock to the front of the sheet. One of them kicked a light on the floor, but miraculously it didn't tip over. The angels fluttered around the silhouetted scene as the congregation joined them in "Hark, the Herald Angels Sing."

Then the lights were dimmed, and ushers distributed candles. One by one, the light was passed from person to person while they sang "Silent Night."

The sanctuary at Nativity was small, but in the light of all the candles it looked endless, like a scene of eternity.

Reverend Barnes invited them to keep the light of Jesus burning in their hearts throughout the year and to remember that one little candle can light a world of darkness. As the candles were extinguished and the lights brought up, he smiled at them. "He is born!"

Mrs. Smalley launched into "Joy to the World!" and the churchgoers sang with gusto.

Tess felt tears of happiness and renewal spring to her eyes. As she dug her handkerchief out of her coat pocket, she noticed Jake smiling at her through eyes that were a bit bright, too.

"Merry Christmas," he whispered to her as the last notes of the organ sounded.

"And to you," she responded.

She saw Lena signaling madly to her. "Excuse me for a moment," she said to Jake. "I promised Katie I'd reinstall the battery pack on her doll."

"Take this ugly thing away from me," Lena said, her stage piety totally evaporated. She pressed the doll into Tess's hands. "I don't even want to be in the same room with it anymore. It gives me the creeps."

She spun around on her heel and was several feet away before she stopped and called, "And Merry Christmas, Tess!"

"Merry Christmas, Lena," she answered back. "You were a splendid Mary."

Katie was surrounded by doting relatives, and from the way she was smirking and simpering Tess was fairly sure she'd forgotten about Baby Snoozie. She slipped back into the Sunday school room and reinstalled the doll's battery pack.

Immediately the doll began a chorus of snores that would have made Tess's grandfather proud. A small sound at the door turned her head.

"What on earth is that?" Jake asked.

"This is Baby Snoozie, the source of the earlier battle," she explained. "She belongs to Katie Tyler, the star of the program, no pun intended."

He picked it up and held it at arm's length. "This is possibly the ugliest doll I've ever seen. What's the big deal with her, other than that obnoxious snore?"

"This, my friend, was the best actor of the evening. You hold in your hand tonight's Baby Jesus."

"This thing? You've got to be kidding me!"

"Nope. Baby Snoozie played Baby Jesus. I took her battery pack out in advance, and she did just fine."

Katie arrived with relatives in tow to claim her doll, and Tess was more than glad to hand it over.

As they left the room, Jake bent close to Tess's ear and murmured, "Next time I start to get too mouthy, like tonight, just take out my battery pack, okay?"

Chapter 14

Cora met them impatiently at the door, letting them know that once again they had inconvenienced her. Her plate was nearly empty, and she led them to it. Their arrival had once more narrowly averted the near-catastrophe of her starvation.

"That cat is obsessed with food," Jake marveled as Tess put more Meow Meals on Cora's plate. "She can't possibly be this hungry all the time."

Tess cooed to Cora and stood up. "Cats overeat for a lot of reasons. Frequently it's because they're bored, which is a major problem with people who overeat, too. With Cora, though, I think it's something else."

He watched Cora as she hunched over her dish and ate. "Why do you think she chows down so much?"

"I think something happened to her before she got here. Maybe she was abandoned or a street cat or whatever. The way she acts, sometimes I think her life before she arrived here wasn't good. Remember—I've only had her three years, and she's much older than that. How old, I don't know. I'm guessing she must be around eight or nine, and the vet agrees."

The kinds of things Cora must have experienced always bothered her. Would it be better to know what her earlier life had been like? Or would that be too much to bear, if it were bad?

"Well, she is a precious cat, whatever. When you told me the story about her being here when you moved in, and your grandmother saying there'd be a cat the color of pussy willows waiting for her in heaven, well, I have to confess, I got goose bumps." He rubbed his arms as if experiencing them again.

"Tell me about it. I nearly passed out when I walked in and saw her. I thought for sure it was a sign that Grandma was in heaven. It was definitely a sign that God recognized I needed a little comfort." She smiled at the cat, who was chasing a last nugget of Meow Meals around the plate. "And what a comfort she has been. She is like a rock. A complaining, domineering rock, but a rock just the same."

"I need to run out to my car and get the Rock's presents. I'll be right back."

Cora had captured the last bit of food and watched him leave, too full to be more than vaguely curious. Tess picked her up and fondly buried her face in the soft gray fur. The cat's side vibrated as her purrs reached full throttle.

"Are you going to speak at midnight, Cora?" Tess asked, reminded suddenly of the legend Jake had referred to earlier. "And what would you say?"

Jake was back in before she could finish.

"Wow, that was quick!" she said as he dropped a large sack on the floor beside him.

"It's way too cold to dawdle. I ran," he panted, clutching his chest. "I hope you know CPR—or at least mouth-to-mouth." He leered at her teasingly.

"Cora does the mouth-to-mouth around here," Tess said, "but only after she's had a bag or two of Giblet Niblets. If that won't put air back in your lungs, I don't know what will."

"Ha! It'd probably kill me. So did I interrupt a conversation between you and Cora?"

"We were just discussing if she was going to speak at midnight and what she would say."

"Interesting concept." He shed his mittens and coat and tried to keep Cora away from the bag as he balanced on one leg and then the other, while pulling off his snow boots. "And what did she say?"

"Nothing, silly. It's not midnight."

"Oh well, of course."

"Although," Tess conceded, "this is a fascinating theory. If you could speak only once a year, what would you say?"

He looked at Cora thoughtfully. "I don't know. How long do I get to speak?"

She shrugged. "I don't know. Let's say you have five minutes."

"Five minutes for a whole year? Hmm. Let me think."

"I'll bet all the petty, whiny things wouldn't make it. Like who forgot to buy milk or who left the cap off the toothpaste or even carping about the guy at work who borrows your pens and never returns them. Things we spend so much time going on and on about and which are really nothing of importance."

He nodded. "You've got a point. So what would you say?"

"Point of clarification, please," she said. "Who am I talking to?"

"Oh, me, I suppose. And Cora. Yes, let's include Cora."

"And I haven't spoken all year, right?"

"Right."

"This is hard," she protested. "You and I have known each other for only a month."

"Try it."

"You know, if I were an animal, I'd have a whole year to think about it before my big moment came. It's not quite fair to put me on the spot like this." She smiled at him.

"I agree. This would take more consideration than we've given it. Let's come back to it later, okay?"

They moved into the living room where the tree stood. The blue spruce was large and full, and it filled most of one corner.

He crossed to examine the ornaments. "I'm surprised this isn't decorated in angels," he said as he touched a small red knit stocking.

"Decorated by angels," she said. "Most of these ornaments were made by my grandmother and grandfather, and the others came from my parents' collection. Grandma knit that stocking, for example. Grandpa carved that woodcut stable scene. And the blown-glass bulbs, like that one, are from a collection my parents started when they were first married."

He walked around the tree, examining each decoration.

"The tree topper was a difficult decision for me. Star or angel? My parents had an exquisite golden star, and my grandparents had a porcelain angel."

He looked up to see her choice and laughed.

At the top of the tree, an angel triumphantly held a star aloft.

Cora, who had followed them into the living room, plopped down under the tree, as if proclaiming herself the best present of all.

He opened the bag he'd brought and spread the colorfully gift-wrapped contents out under the lower boughs. Then, in silent accord, he and Tess waited and watched.

Cora's nose twitched once. Then twice. She rose, her nose now in constant use, and ambled over to the nearest package.

She eyed it from all angles. With a furry paw she batted it tentatively, then with more assurance. Finally she grabbed it with her teeth and front paws and tore at it madly with her hind legs, shredding the paper and most of the container with her powerful claws.

Cora rolled over and over with the catnip mouse, chewing and kicking the toy.

"So much for my cat's snooty decorum," Tess said. "She's absolutely nuts!"

One by one, Cora opened her packages with increasing fervor, until at last she collapsed in a satisfied heap with her catnip mouse tucked in her paws.

"For all the world she looks like a little kid holding a teddy bear," Tess said fondly.

"I think she enjoyed it."

"I'm ready for the movie now," Tess said. "Shall I make popcorn?"

"But I have a present for you," he objected.

"And I have one for you. But right now I want to revel in the memory of Cora's unbridled happiness and get good and teary with *It's a Wonderful Life.*"

As she popped the popcorn, she reviewed the gift she'd chosen for him. Was it appropriate? Would he think it was silly?

"Mmm." Jake tasted the top kernels from the bowl. "This is great popcorn!"

"I made it the old-fashioned way, with a popper and melted butter and loads of salt." She sat down beside him, balancing the bowl in her lap.

Cora's nose snuffled her awake from sleep, and she sprang from her spot in the middle of the floor, abandoned her catnip mouse, and leaped up onto the couch beside Tess. Tess offered a few of the popped kernels, and Cora sniffed at them.

Apparently even Cora had her food limits. She licked the butter from the kernels and gave up, curling herself into a warm ball beside Tess.

Tess clicked the remote control and started the video. Within minutes she was in Bedford Falls, and the dissension between downtown and the End, faith and proof, and anything else evaporated as she lost herself in the classic movie.

By the end of the video she was leaning against Jake, sniffling openly.

"I love this movie!" she exclaimed. "Love it, love it, love it!"

He agreed with her. "It's timeless. No matter how often I watch it, I still enjoy it. And it doesn't seem to age, either. I'm sure I'll never see this movie as old-fashioned or out-of-date."

She sighed. "Well, we're out of popcorn. I can't believe we ate that whole bowl by ourselves. And we can't blame any of it on Cora. She must be totally wiped out—she not only slept through the movie, but she was too tuckered to do more than lick the popcorn."

"She did make a valiant effort, though," he pointed out.

"True."

After putting the empty popcorn bowl in the kitchen, they returned to the living room. Cora had sprawled even more across the couch, her body occupying one entire cushion and her outstretched feet and head encroaching upon the others.

"I think we've been bumped," Jake said to her, his arm sliding around her shoulder. "Shall we sit in front of the tree instead to open our presents to each other?"

They hadn't turned the lights back on after the movie, and the living room was lit with only the glow of the bulbs on the Christmas tree.

"Christmas music?" he asked, motioning toward the stereo.

"Lovely."

He turned the stereo on, and soon mellow carols filled the air. "I love the music of Christmas," he said as he joined her in front of the tree. "It's hard to decide which carol is my favorite. I'll think I know, and then I'll hear another one, and I'll tell myself, 'Oh no, that one is my favorite,' and it is—until I hear the next one. And so it goes, on and on."

"I know what you mean. I have never been able to decide, although I like 'O Come, All Ye Faithful.' And 'He Is Born.' And, oh yeah, 'O Come, O Come, Emmanuel.' And that one about the rose. And. . ." She caught his expression and laughed. "I should quit before I run through the list of every carol I've ever heard. Maybe it'd be quicker to list the ones we don't like."

"Can't. I love them all."

"Me, too," she agreed. "Oh, listen! It's 'The Little Drummer Boy.'"

They sang along, helping each other with the words when one stumbled.

She loved Christmas. Something about it made people be at their best. She couldn't imagine anyone actually arguing at Christmas.

She handed him her present to him. He carefully undid the tape on the end of the box.

"You do that any more, and I will scream," she warned him.

"What? What did I do?" He raised his eyes to her in alarm. "I didn't say anything, and I haven't moved except to start opening this."

"Then open it!" She pretended to strangle herself. "I'm too antsy to open a present that slowly."

"Oh," he said, nodding. "Okay, here goes." And he ripped the paper open with an abandon that rivaled Cora's.

"This is wonderful!" he exclaimed as he took the bell from its wrapping and examined it.

"There's a note, too," she prompted, willing her stomach to quit roiling. Of course he'd like the gift, she told herself. It was a terrific present. And with the note she hoped she captured what she meant by it.

He read it aloud: " ' "It is a wonderful life." ' I'll always remember tonight, especially watching the movie with you—and Cora, of course—snuggled up with me. Thank you, Tess.' "

He rang the bell and grinned. "Giving an angel a boost."

She smiled at him, relieved that he understood the meaning of the bell. "I'm glad you like it."

He leaned toward her and dropped a sweet kiss on her lips. "It's perfect."

He handed her his present, a small gold-wrapped box with lacy ribbon. Under the wrapping was a box with a well-known jeweler's name emblazoned across it in gilt script, and she held her breath as she opened it.

It was a necklace. The fine gold chain held a cross that not only was a cross but, she realized as she examined it carefully, was also an angel. The two symbols were cleverly merged to form one shape.

His gaze did not leave her face.

"Like it?" he asked at last.

"I don't know what to say. It's way beyond anything I ever. . . I can't. . ." She looked at him. "I don't like it. I love it. Please put it on me."

She turned so he could fasten the necklace around her neck. The cross caught the varicolored lights of the tree and flashed an entire paint box of colors.

From her vantage point on the couch, Cora snored softly in time to the music.

They leaned back and admired the tree, until Tess remembered something.

"Every year I add a new ornament to the tree, chosen to symbolize something about the year that I want to remember. And I hang it on the tree on Christmas Eve. I haven't done that yet."

She stood up and pointed to a cat angel. "This is for the year Cora came to live here. This apple represents the year I planted the tree in the back. And this easel symbolizes the year I took painting lessons. You'll notice none of my paintings is displayed. I had fun but discovered I have absolutely no talent for painting."

She took a white box from the mantel and opened it carefully.

"What is this year's ornament?" he asked, craning his neck to peek inside the box.

"Just wait, Mr. Nosey-Parker."

She carefully lifted the new decoration from the cotton batting that lined the box and held it for him to see.

He squinted his eyes. "I can't quite make out what it is."

She held the flat brass ornament toward the light of the tree.

"It's the skyline of downtown. See? Here's the courthouse, and here's Saint Agatha's, and this, I think, is the bank. An artist on Third Street made it. I couldn't pass it up, since I became a member of the mayor's commission this year."

He was silent for a moment. "I thought we'd avoid that topic tonight."

She paused in the act of hanging the ornament on the tree. "Avoid what topic?"

"Well," he said, just a bit peevishly, "if I can't talk about scientific proof, I don't think it's fair that you talk about the downtown thing."

"Oh Jake. It's not the same at— No. You're right. It sort of is, isn't it? But I didn't mean it that way."

She finished placing the ornament on the tree and sat back down. "Maybe for you, being active in the community is easy. For me it was extraordinarily difficult. I didn't wait to be asked. I volunteered."

She could tell by his expression that he didn't understand why it had been such a major step for her.

"I'm not a naturally outgoing person." As she said it, she remembered what an effort it had been for her to put her name on the list of applicants for the commission.

She continued, "It took an incredible amount of gathering my courage and putting my self-esteem on the line. What if the mayor said no? It wasn't like I'm a financial big shot in town. I'm sure most people said, 'Tess who?' and 'Angel's what?' So this symbolizes not so much the commission, but the step forward I took in getting there."

He smiled. "I understand. That's a great tradition. Do you mind if I borrow it?"

"Not at all, but don't you think the decorations are going to be pretty well picked over at this late date?" she asked.

"Well, you may not be a financial wizard, but I sure am. On December 26 I'll be able to shop for my ornament at half price!"

The grandfather clock reminded them time was passing quickly.

They walked to the back door, and she watched as he put on his boots and coat. He motioned her to him, and she went gladly.

"I can't go without my Christmas kiss, now can I?" he asked.

She didn't answer but raised her lips to his.

His arms stayed around her long after their lips had parted. His voice was almost a whisper when at last he spoke. "Have you given any more thought to what you might say if you could speak only on Christmas Eve?"

She nodded. "Have you?"

"Yes," he said huskily. "I would say you are quickly becoming very special to me, and I want you near me throughout the year."

She smiled drowsily. It was so warm and comfortable in the circle of his arms that she could stay there a day, a month, a year.

"So what would you say to me?" he prompted.

"I'd say, 'Kiss me.'"

And he did.

Chapter 15

The delicious smells of turkey roasting in the oven sent Cora into near fits of ecstasy. She wound herself around Tess's legs again and again, stopping only to meow plaintively.

"Yes, yes, Sweetie-Cat," Tess crooned. "You will have a big chunk of this turkey all to yourself. But right now it has to cook. Be patient."

Patient was a word totally alien to Cora's vocabulary. She meowed even louder, and Tess looked around the kitchen frantically to find something that might appease the cat until dinnertime.

Evaporated milk might work. She had made fudge earlier in the day, and, as always, a bit of milk was left over. Cora inhaled it and begged for more.

Luckily Tess had bought two cans so she brought down the spare from the cupboard. "Okay, Cora, my dear. Drink up, and please, please, please go sleep by the register and leave me alone!"

Thus bribed, Cora wandered off to her spot by the floor heating register where she had the added bonus of mid-morning sunshine flowing in through the window.

Tess smiled benevolently at her cat. "Heat below, heat above. And a full tummy to boot, with the promise of turkey forthcoming. You lead a tough life, Cora-Cat."

She studied the recipe for truffles, her next Christmas expedition into cooking. She'd gotten the recipe from a lady at church who had since moved away. Although her version would never rival the chocolate truffle elegance she'd been served at Whispering Winds, it was impressive enough to have become her signature piece at Christmas gatherings.

Plus it was breathtakingly easy.

She had just combined the ingredients, shaped the chocolate mixture into balls, and begun rolling them in ground nuts when the phone rang.

"Merry Christmas." Jake's voice was a warm embrace on a cold day.

"Merry Christmas to you, too," she answered. "Did you sleep well?"

"Like the proverbial log." He chuckled. "Guess that would be the Yule log, huh?"

She smiled. His good humor was one of his best attributes. Suddenly she wanted him there very much.

"When are you coming over?" she asked.

"Soon. I just have to—"

"Where are you?" she asked, as a terrible suspicion surfaced in her mind.

"Um, well, I, um—"

His hedging didn't deter her. "You're at Panda's, aren't you?"

"Tess, honey." His voice was soft with suppressed laughter. "I stopped by to pick up some coffee for our dinner. You didn't expect me to drink that washy bilgewater you call coffee, did you?"

How could she have thought he'd be at work on a glorious day like Christmas? "I'm sorry," she said, truly apologetic she had doubted him. "But can you pick up a mild blend, please? I don't want to be awake until New Year's Day!"

"Wimp," he bantered back. He ended by saying he'd be at her house in thirty minutes.

Tess took one look around her kitchen where a major war had apparently just been fought. Used dishes were piled in the sink and trailed across the counter.

"Thirty minutes!" she said to herself, pushing her hair back with a hand that was, she realized too late, sticky with chocolate.

"I need a shower and the kitchen needs a—well, I guess it needs a power wash, but vanity wins. Into the shower it is," she said to a snoring Cora, who could have cared less what the kitchen looked like, as long as it produced a turkey at some point in the day.

Her hair was still in damp tendrils when Jake arrived, his arms full of bundles. "Cute," he said, pulling on an escaping curl from behind her ear. "New hairdo?"

"The wet look," she explained, taking the packages from him. "What do you have in all of these, by the way? You know I do have a turkey basting away in the oven."

"Better than wasting away, I guess," he responded, kissing her lightly on the nose. "These boxes are filled with Christmas cookies that will lose their seasonal oomph if we don't eat them sometime soon, so they're my contribution to the day's festivities."

The aroma of the turkey beckoned them back to the kitchen. Jake gave a low whistle at the sight that met his eyes.

"Is this classic or what?"

"What do you mean?" she asked, reminded of the impeccability of Panda's kitchen area.

"Whenever my mom and grandma and aunts and whoever else gathered in the kitchen, they cooked like crazy. There were always a lot of cooks, and none of them, not a one of them, would wash a dish."

"So what did they do, throw them away?" It was a curious idea, but as she glanced around her chaotic kitchen it gained ground as a possibility.

He shook his head. "No. Mom always said if you eat, you clean up." He rolled up the sleeves of his deep turquoise sweater in readiness.

"Oh no, really, you don't have to," she objected, but not too strenuously as he quickly assumed his post at the sink. She'd always resisted an automatic dishwasher, telling herself it was a useless expense when the only mouths fed there were hers and Cora's. But now it seemed as if it would probably be worth every penny of its cost.

He was remarkably fast, and soon he had the kitchen restored to rights.

The table was laid with an embroidered cloth that had been her great-grandparents', and the china was also three generations old. She felt a sacredness about sitting down to a table thus arrayed, and she identified every piece of table service, every bit of linen, for Jake.

"It's an honor to be seated here," he said reverently as his long fingers smoothed a napkin decorated with fine threads outlining a silhouetted Bethlehem.

He surprised her. He took her hand in his and asked, "Would you say grace?"

"Of course." She smiled, then bowed her head. "Dearest Lord, on this happy day of Your birth we celebrate the gifts of Christmas. First is the greatest gift of all—the gift of life. A baby's arrival is always a time of excitement and anticipation, and it is with shining eyes that we see the gift in the manger. We welcome You, Lord, into our hearts again. Make us as new as Yourself, free to see with eyes that do not know hatred but look ahead only with expectation. Lord, we thank You for the gift of each other, for friendship, for fellowship, and for love. Happy birthday, Lord, and welcome! Amen!"

"Amen." He raised his head and looked at her, his deep chocolate-hued eyes warm with emotion. "And I also want to thank you for inviting me over today. I'm afraid it would have been a very lonely day for me without this."

"And for me," Tess agreed softly. "Sometimes I rattle around in here by myself—"

Cora meowed loudly from beneath the table, and Tess and Jake both laughed.

"Well, maybe not by myself," Tess corrected herself. "By myself and supervised at all times by my watch cat, the incomparable Cora."

Cora demanded—and received—her allotment of turkey, and after Tess nixed the idea of clearing the dishes, let alone washing them, the three of them plopped onto the couch in the living room.

"There are probably some television programs on that would be good to watch," Jake said.

"Probably. Do you know of any?" Tess asked, too lazy and stuffed with turkey and other goodies to get up and check the television schedule that lay three inches from her grasp.

"Dunno," came the answer from the other end of the couch. "Do you know, Cora?"

The cat gave a perfectly timed sigh, followed by gentle, even snoring.

"She sounds happy," Jake said, still motionless on his end of the couch.

"Why shouldn't she be? She's transformed us into her idea of perfection. Look at us—we've become cats." She patted her full tummy.

"You're right. I can't move. And I don't care." He groaned.

"Meow." Tess's eyes began to drift shut.

He flung his hand out. "Okay. I'll assert my right as the reigning male here. Give me the remote control."

Jake set the television to a station that was showing *A Christmas Carol* and meandered out to the kitchen to make some coffee.

"Mild," Tess reminded him as she trailed after him. "I want to wake up now, but eventually I do plan to sleep again."

She arranged the cookies he'd brought on a tray and added her truffles. "I don't know why I'm doing this," she said as they took the tray and the coffee into the living room. "I don't have any more room in my stomach."

"I know what you mean," Jake said, nibbling on a sugar cookie. "I'm so stuffed I couldn't eat another bite." He popped one of her truffles in his mouth. "Wow! Where did these come from? These are great!"

"I made them," she said proudly.

"Can I have the recipe for the restaurant?" he asked eagerly. "They'd be a great seller."

She demurred as gently as possible. How could she tell him they were made from canned frosting and a few other common ingredients?

Fortunately his attention was diverted by the television, where the Ghost of Jacob Marley was rattling his chains at a terrified Ebenezer Scrooge.

"I can remember this movie from when I was a kid," Jake said. "I thought it was the scariest thing I'd ever seen."

"Really?" she replied, her mouth full of a delightful Christmas cookie.

"I understood the moral of the story, about appreciating your life, and every time I watched it I'd vow to take more time to remember the past, heed the present, and prepare for the future."

"Wow! That's some heavy thinking for a child," she said, reaching for another cookie. "I was more afraid of the spirits, but I have to be honest and tell you I didn't get the point until I was a teenager, and by then I'd figured out the spirits weren't ghosts as such. Guess I was a slow learner, huh?"

Jake laughed. "You sound like you were a typical teen."

"Probably. I hope I've learned from the story. The only sticky part is that I hope I'm not doing my good deeds now only because I'm selfish enough to want heaven for my future—as if all my actions are an insurance policy of sorts. They're not. I have to believe it in my heart."

"There's the rub," Jake commented. "How do you know if you're doing it right and if you're going to heaven?"

She smiled. "Jesus tells us. A lawyer asked Him what he had to do to have eternal life. And Jesus asked him back what the Scriptures said. The lawyer said, 'Thou shalt love the Lord thy God with all thy heart, and with all thy soul, and with all thy strength, and with all thy mind; and thy neighbour as thyself.'"

"I remember that. Jesus said that was the right answer, didn't He?"

"Yes, He did. So maybe the answer is to do those things, and good works and good deeds will follow as naturally as night follows day."

Jake fell silent. "I wish I had your convictions, Tess. Your faith is so solid and true. I believe—I truly do—but I don't have it as completely as you do. I wish I did."

Her heart opened, and the words flowed out. "Just wanting it is the first step. Let yourself be open to God, Jake. He's there, waiting for you. He's been there all along, in the past, in the present, and He'll be there in the future, too. He's never left you, and He will always be at your side. Let yourself be open to Him. Let yourself see Him."

"If only I had proof, it'd be easier to believe."

"Maybe. But would it be in your heart? Or would it be because you don't see another choice?"

"Good point," Jake said. "I don't know what I'd do if I had real proof."

"Actually, Jake, if you want proof, it's there. Look in the face of a newborn baby. It's there. Look in the face of an older person. It's there. I can even see it in Cora's face. God makes beautiful creations. And each one is a gift of proof."

She touched his hand. "The proof was there in the manger, and it was there in the empty tomb. Faith is an amazing thing. It is its own proof, even as it denies proof. I can't explain faith, but I know it is there."

She fell silent. His eyes were focused on hers, searching and seeking for this elusive thing they called faith.

"I need it, especially as I think about the possibility of moving Panda's," he said, breaking the quiet at last. "Maybe it's not the same thing, but I have an intensive need for proof. Give me charts. Give me graphs. Give me statistics."

"Did you build Panda's from a blueprint?" she asked.

He laughed. "Sort of. The conflict between the contractor and the architect gave it its distinctive rose brick and gray smoked-glass look, but basically, yes, we had a blueprint. Why do you ask? Is it really that bizarre looking?"

"No, no!" she demurred. "It's just that you've already invested heavily in faith. When you built Panda's, you did so on a promise—that the building would replicate what the blueprint proposed. Right?"

"Right."

"And did it?"

"Yes."

"But the blueprint didn't have the personality of Panda's. It didn't include all the little details like the cooking, the roaster, even the personnel. Like Todd." She couldn't resist asking. "Todd wasn't in the blueprints, was he?"

"No," Jake admitted, "though he probably should have been. He knows everyone and can keep the place running like a top, unless you want the till to balance."

"And you definitely had a role in it. Your enthusiasm and dedication to Panda's show. My point is that these little things make the entire place come alive."

A slow smile crossed Jake's face. "You know what else wasn't in the blueprints?"

She shook her head. "What?"

"Faith. A crazy angel whose halo will not stay straight. And Faith, Tess Mahoney, is making all the difference in the world. Without Faith I'd never have met you."

She didn't know what to say. And she didn't have to. He said it for her.

"Faith has brought us together. And I'm hoping—no, I'm praying—that Faith will keep us together."

Chapter 16

Tess grimaced at her reflection. She felt like a sausage, her body snugly encased in a set of thickly knit long johns, a long-sleeved turtleneck, a heavy sweat suit in a bizarre chartreuse she'd never had the nerve to wear before, heavy woolen socks, a bright green parka, her military olive snow-shoveling boots, an emerald and yellow patterned muffler, and an orange hunting hat topped with a fluorescent lime-colored pompom.

Jake's greeting confirmed what she feared: that she looked like an inflated and somewhat eccentric elf.

"I don't want to be cold," she said defensively. It was difficult to be assertive about what she was wearing when underneath it she was sweating like mad.

"Honey, you'd have to be in the Arctic before you got cold in that getup." He batted the pom-pom on her cap playfully.

"But most of First Night is outside," she objected. "It's freezing!"

"It's only eleven below." He grinned at her.

She looked one more time in the mirror. Chartreuse! What an odd color and definitely not for her. Whatever had possessed her to purchase it from the mail-order catalog? She knew the answer, though. The model had looked stunning in it, and the color hadn't been quite so, well, so chartreuse.

"I'll be right back," she said and ducked upstairs to change into jeans and her new sweatshirt that had been her Christmas present to herself. Its snowy white background was crusted with pink rhinestones that spelled out the words *flutter*flutter*flutter* across an outline of angel wings.

"I feel ten pounds lighter," she said as she came back downstairs. "And I probably look it, too. After a month of hanging around with you, I need all the help I can get, thanks to your insistence upon feeding me all sorts of gourmet treats."

Cora sashayed into the room and meowed loudly.

"Speaking of gourmet treats,"Tess commented, "Cora's girth has increased, too. She has a definite bulge now, and the old gal wiggles when she walks."

"Both of you get lovelier every day," he said, dropping a kiss on Tess's head and scratching behind Cora's furry ears. The cat lifted her gray head and drooled blissfully.

Jake watched as Cora waddled off to her spot by the heat register, apparently having had enough attention for the moment.

"That is a splendid cat," he whispered to Tess. "Absolutely splendid."

The First Night festivities were easily within walking distance, and they made their way quickly to the city center. In the town square a tent had been set up as a nuclear gathering spot.

Tess and Jake stopped there first. As Jake gathered the list of locations and events from the table, Tess warmed her hands by the kerosene heater that was almost unnecessary with all the people clustered in there.

"Where do you want to start?" he asked as he rejoined her.

"Ice sculptures, of course!"

Circling the frozen pond in the square was a fantasy display of statues carved of shimmering ice. They glistened in the reflected light of the street lamps like sculpted diamonds and crystals.

"The theme this year is the Winter Garden," she commented as they strolled through the array of sparkling images. "Look! Here's a hyacinth, I think, and over there—oh, I can't believe the detail! It's a prairie rose!"

Jake bent over the cards and read each one aloud. "Yup, once again they're all done by local artists. I keep thinking that some year they'll have to farm this out to a bigger city, but our art community sure can produce some astonishing works! Check out this one: Jack Frost as a master gardener!"

"And each one is carved from a single block of ice," Tess marveled aloud. "With my luck I'd be right at the end, and my little hammer thing or whatever they use would slip just a teensy bit, and, blammo, my statue would be minus an arm. What steady hands they must have!"

They decided to check out the local library's exhibit next. They climbed the stone steps with a host of other revelers.

"Sure are a lot of people out tonight," Jake said, turning back to gaze over the square from the top step of the library. "Look at that!"

The sea of humanity was impressive.

"A lot of people are like us," Tess said. "They don't want to see the New Year in by getting sloshed, and yet they want to celebrate without risking getting killed by someone who's been drinking and driving. That's one of the things I like the most about First Night—that I don't have to drive anywhere. It's all set up within walking distance of the downtown parking lots for those who don't live down here. And for the rest of us it's great to be able to stroll on over!"

More people surged up the steps, and Tess and Jake found themselves propelled into the library.

For the next half hour they were entertained by a team of storytellers from the town, including the children's librarian, a man who wrote poetry, and the mayor herself, who waved at them. The room was filled to capacity, and the temperature soared.

Tess wiped a band of sweat from her brow. It was a good thing she'd changed out of her earlier outfit; she would have been roasting in all those layers. Jake nudged her and indicated the door. They stole out together and stood at the top of the stairs, letting the cold air wash over their heated faces.

"That feels tremendous," he said. "Whew, it was hot in there!"

"Why isn't the sweat freezing on my forehead?" Tess asked. "Scientifically it should, right?"

He shook his head. "Beats me. It must have sizzled off when we came outside. It was blazing in that room with all those people crunched together like that."

He consulted the schedule. "Hey, if we hustle over to the police station, we might catch a ride on a horse-drawn wagon. Does that interest you?"

"Sounds like fun!"

The line at the police station extended the length of the block and wrapped around the corner. "There'll be a thirty-minute wait," the woman overseeing the rides told them.

"Want to wait?" Jake asked Tess.

"Sure. Look—a guy is selling hot apple cider and doughnuts!" She pointed to a man behind a red-and-gold painted pushcart, which was mostly hidden by the people hunkered around his source of heat—an open fire in an old oilcan.

Jake grinned at her. "Are you always hungry?"

She tried not to be embarrassed. "Well, it's been awhile since dinner, and doesn't that sound good—hot apple cider and fresh doughnuts?"

Jake admitted it did, and they agreed she would hold their place in line while he bought them some food from the vendor.

"There's something special about food served in open air like this," she murmured, gratefully biting into the doughnut. "It seems to taste a whole lot better than it does inside."

"Remind me to transfer all the tables out of Panda's then. At the very least, it'll keep them moving. No one will want to sit very long when it's fifteen below."

The line moved quickly, and they were soon climbing into the wagon. Jake made room for her on the straw bundle closest to the horse and created a circle of warmth around her with his arm. She leaned against him, enjoying the heat his body generated, but mostly reveling in being close to him.

First Night had never been so much fun.

It was only a tickle at first, then a little more, and it quickly mushroomed into a full-fledged itch. She tried to ignore it, but she eventually had to scratch her leg. And then her hip. And her leg again.

"Problem?" Jake asked her, his mouth tilted with amusement.

"I seem to be allergic to hay," she answered, trying gracefully to reach her hip again. "Or something. Whatever it is, I think this will be my last trip."

The ride seemed to take an eternity. Around the town square the wagon went, up the hill to the high school, around the water treatment plant, alongside the river, over the little footbridge, and back down past the post office to stop again in front of the police station.

She couldn't hop off quickly enough. She scratched and clawed, uncomfortably aware that Jake was finding her actions amusing.

"Do you need to go back home and maybe shower?" he suggested.

Tess pulled herself up to her full height and tried to regain her decorum. "No, I'm quite"—*scratch, scratch*—"fine. I can do that"—*scrape, claw*—"later. Right now let's just enjoy the"—*scratch*—"evening."

They went to an exhibit at the police station about drugs and how to recognize them, examined a display of historic photographs at City Hall, and stopped at the school to listen to the junior-senior choir sing hits from the major musicals.

By the end her itching had fairly well abated.

"I love downtown," she mused aloud, giving her hip one final scratch. "For one thing it's a comfortable place to be—well, except for when we have to sit on straw."

"It's nice, but I still don't know my way around here very well, so I can't feel totally at ease yet." He pulled out the schedule again and squinted at a street sign. "Is this Fifth? Or Fourth?"

"It's Perth, and you need glasses," she teased. "You probably feel the same way here that I do when I have to go to the End. I don't know the names of the streets or even what businesses are where. Like the Animal Kingdom. That place is heaven on earth for cats, but I've never been there since it's in the End. And this town isn't all that big. We probably use it as an excuse."

She couldn't believe that she, Tess Mahoney, was saying that. She was an ardent supporter of downtown growth and an adamant opponent of anything having to do with the End. How had she mellowed so quickly? Had she lost her edge? Or maybe her mind?

As she turned to say something else to Jake, she realized the little lines had reappeared around his eyes and mouth, the road map of tension.

Stupid, stupid! she berated herself. *He was finally relaxing, and you've tightened him right back up.*

She sent a prayer upward, so immediate that its words weren't formed, its ideas weren't clear to her, but its focus was true. Jake. He needed the freedom to come to his decision as she had needed the freedom to give away her precious Bible.

And with the prayer she felt her own self lightening, and she realized she had given herself freedom, too—the freedom to move away from the old patterns of thinking, the old ways of seeing, and into the new.

So new that she wasn't prepared for what happened next.

An idea roared into her mind with the strength of a tidal wave.

"Come on," she said, tugging on his coat sleeve.

"What? There's nothing down that street," he responded, consulting the now-bedraggled flyer he'd picked up in the tent.

"Maybe there is. Come on," she urged.

"What? What is it?"

She stopped and crossed her arms over her chest. "You are so stubborn sometimes, Jake Cameron."

"What do you mean?" He frowned at her.

"Always wanting to know it all, not trusting that the future might hold something you don't know about and yet you might want or need."

He sighed. "Tess, it's just a street."

"No, it's not 'just a street,' Jake. Have faith. Trust me. Walk down this street with me."

He shrugged. "Okay, but—"

She laid a mittened hand over his mouth. "Sssh. Faith. Trust."

They walked down the darkened street in silence.

Suddenly Tess stopped and pointed. "There. What do you think?"

"Of what?"

"Of that." She waved her hand toward a windowless hulk of a building that was shadowed beyond the streetlight's reach.

"What is it?" He peered at it.

Tess took his hand. "Come on. Take a look."

She pulled him up the unshoveled walk to the front door. "It's locked, of course, but I think this is it. Check out the back."

"This is what?"

She headed around the corner and threw the word back at him. "Panda's."

He hadn't followed her yet, and she had to wait for him to catch up with her. "Panda's? What? I haven't decided to move Panda's down here, and when I do—if I do—I will choose the location according to demographics, tax base, traffic patterns—those sorts of things."

"You want a good reason? Look at this back door," she said, flinging her arm toward the rear of the building.

A large wooden and metal door, nearly half the size of the building itself, opened onto an area cleared of trees and bushes.

"Under all this snow," Tess said, stamping on the ground to make her point, "is a large concrete slab. Imagine tables and chairs back here and deep green umbrellas. Flowers, maybe geraniums—yes, red geraniums—in terracotta pots scattered around. A white wrought-iron fence surrounding the patio. And it all overlooks the river."

She couldn't keep the enthusiasm from bubbling up in her voice. She knew she was in severe danger of overstating it and driving him away, but she was caught up in the wonder of her idea, and, as she looked at him, she realized he was, too.

He walked evenly around the building, as if pacing off the square footage, while Tess trailed hopefully behind, trying to step in the prints his feet made in the still-drifted snow.

She could see it—she could actually see it. If only he could, too!

"I'd have to take a look at the inside, of course," he said at last, stopping so suddenly that Tess, her head tucked down as she tried to match her footprints to his, crashed right into his back. "And check the city code. This might not be zoned for a coffeehouse. What did this used to be—do you know?"

"It's been called the River Exchange for a long time. It was originally used as a place where the barges and merchant shipping vessels could unload and take on new cargo."

He rubbed his chin thoughtfully. "How long has it been empty?"

"Quite awhile," she admitted. "I couldn't tell you the exact date—this was just a spur-of-the-moment inspiration. I hadn't planned on bringing you here—I hadn't even thought about this building as a possible location until God put it in my mind."

"God put it in your mind?" His voice brimmed with disbelief.

"He did."

For a moment he looked at her, not saying anything. Then he asked, "Why? Why would He do a thing like that? Don't you think He has other priorities, like war and famine and crime? Do you really think He's worried about whether a little coffeehouse like Panda's moves downtown?"

It was a common question, and she had heard the meat of it before. But this time it hurt, coming from him.

The answer came forth with a surprising ease. "God cares about you. You are not at war. You are not starving. You are not in the clutches of crime. Yes, for people who are at war, are starving, or are victims of crime, those are His priorities. And I don't pretend to know why God does everything He does. He doesn't answer to me. I answer to Him."

"But why are you saying He gave you the idea and led you down this street? Give yourself some credit here, Tess. It was probably in the back of your mind, and you weren't even aware you were thinking about it. Your subconscious solved it."

"God did it," she insisted. "Because God answers prayer."

He smiled. "Sure. I admit that. But who on earth was praying about this?"

"I was."

His eyes held hers. "You prayed for this? You want me downtown enough that you prayed to God to find me a place for Panda's?"

"Don't be ridiculous. That's not what I prayed for." She tried to look away, but his gaze was arresting.

"Then what did you pray for?"

"Prayer is private communication," she hedged.

He stared hard at her for a moment, then looked away, but not before she saw the expression on his face. It was part annoyance, part anger, and part disappointment.

Reverend Barnes had told her she would have a chance to share her faith. Perhaps this was it.

"I prayed that you'd find a resolution to your dilemma soon, that you could settle your heart about what to do with Panda's. Move here or stay in the End. At this stage all I know is that I care more about you than I do about the downtown commission or any growth statistics about recovering the lost merchantability of the heart of the city. I just want you to be happy."

He turned back, and his face was shining. "You goose. That wasn't your prayer He answered. It was mine."

A curious sensation arose in her chest, and it took a moment to identify it. Yes, it was indeed possible: Her heart was singing.

"You are a very sweet, wonderful man, Jake Cameron. You are kind and considerate and absolutely blessed, and I think you are terrific."

A deep red stain began to creep over the top of his collar and edged up his neck. He was blushing!

At that moment Tess fell deeply and totally in love.

Chapter 17

Their last stop was Nativity, where an array of brightly twinkling lights led First Night revelers to the door of the church.

The downstairs had been transformed into a children's craft fair. The dining room was filled with the chatter of children busily constructing masks of canvas, feathers, and glitter.

In the Sunday school area, preschoolers spread large swaths of paint across squares of muslin, happily dripping the plastic-covered flooring with wild splotches of red, green, blue, yellow, and purple.

Reverend Barnes's reedy figure separated itself from the horde and loped over to join them. He greeted Jake with a hearty "Good to see you again, friend!" and Tess with a "We need you—now. Somebody has to set up a secondary project area, because. . ."

His words blurred into the general noise as they left for the resource room. Tess looked over her shoulder and mouthed, "I'll be back in a minute," and Jake waved his acknowledgment.

The room was a delight for Tess. It was filled with orderly shelves lined with paper in a rainbow of colors, woolly pipe cleaners in clear plastic bags, cartons of glue sticks, baskets of scissors, and covered boxes her fingers itched to explore.

"We have more children coming than we can attend to right now. Could you possibly cobble together some other projects for some of them to do? You can set it up in the nursery—I'll dash up and get things arranged there. Thanks, Tess—you're a gem. And so's your young man."

"He's not my young man," she protested, but her heart was not in it.

"Sure, Tess. Give me a holler if there's anything else you need. I'm running up to the nursery now."

Running was undoubtedly the right word, Tess thought as he spun out of the room like a whirlwind. He had more energy than she had ever imagined a man his age could possess.

She shrugged out of her jacket and mittens and dug into the cupboard.

The boxes were a storehouse of wonderful things. She quickly pulled out several sheets of colored tissue paper, some cellophane pieces, construction paper, scissors, and glue sticks. She dumped her treasure trove into an empty box she found neatly stashed in a corner and headed upstairs to the nursery.

Reverend Barnes was just pulling the last chair into place around the table and looked up in surprise as she walked in.

"Are you ready this soon?" he asked.

She nodded and began displaying her treasures on the table. "We'll make stained-glass windows. First we'll cut out shapes from the construction paper and back the holes with tissue or cellophane."

"I remember those," he mused. "Great idea, Tess. I knew I could count on you!"

"Say, where's Jake?" she asked as she divided the materials.

"I don't know. He wasn't in the dining room, and I got only a peep in the Sunday school room."

A group of five children burst into the room, and Tess's career as a craftswoman began.

She had only stolen moments to think about Jake and wonder where he might have gone. There was a steady stream of children for the next hour.

At last Reverend Barnes poked his head in. "I think you can shut down now. It's almost fireworks time, and everybody's abandoning us."

She flexed her fingers, stiff from cutting countless pieces of paper, and tried to flick the dried-on crust of glue off her fingernails. Her pale pink polish was chipped, and what was left was hidden under the glue remnants.

She gathered up the pieces of paper and put them in a stack. She'd come in sometime during the week and straighten up the room with more attention to detail.

The dining room crafts center was closing down, and the Sunday school room had shut entirely. No one she asked had seen Jake, and she wandered back upstairs.

Where could he have gone? Surely he hadn't left already.

At the top of the stairs she could see into the sanctuary. Outlined in one of the middle pews was the shape of a man, not bent in prayer, but facing the large cross suspended behind the pulpit.

Could it be—?

She tiptoed around the side aisle, trying to be as inconspicuous as possible, but the floor creaked and gave her presence away.

Jake turned to her, and when he did, her heart sparked anew.

What she saw was a man transformed.

His eyes shone with a gentle radiance that could mean only one thing. "It makes perfect sense. I have the proof."

She slid into the pew next to him. "Do you want to tell me?" she asked softly, not taking her gaze from his face.

He nodded. "I wandered up here. It was dark so I was fumbling around, looking for the switch to turn on the lights. I remembered what you said about electricity and faith. That started me thinking. I have no proof electricity exists, other than the fact that my coffeemaker works and the lights come on at my house. And, of course, the monumental bill I get every month. But it could be squirrels in little wheels powering the utilities, for all I know. I've never seen what makes my microwave work. It just does. And when I put my nachos in there, I trust it'll work and the cheese will melt, whether or not I understand why it does. That melted cheese is proof enough of electricity's existence. I don't need more."

"Jake, I am 100 percent, completely, totally lost. What do squirrels and nachos and electricity have to do with God?"

"I've always believed in God. Always. But I've prayed for a faith that goes beyond just belief. What I needed was trust, the trust that would let me allow Him into my life. Didn't it make sense that I should trust God at least as much as I trust the power company?"

He turned to her and took her hand. "That's the step I didn't have before. I didn't trust Him, and without trust there really can't be faith. I'm still working it through, and I'm not sure yet that it's making any sense."

"Oh, it is," she whispered.

"I remembered your story about giving away your Bible, and suddenly I understood. I had to come to the point where I was willing to say, 'I believe, and more than that I trust.'"

He shook his head. "It was the hardest thing I've ever had to do—to give myself over completely to Someone I can't see, but who I do know exists. And it was the easiest thing, once it was done. I feel so different—refreshed, healthy, whole."

"Praise the Lord." Her words were barely spoken, but he heard them.

"Yes," Jake said. "Yes."

The song in her soul soared. He was home—she could hear it in his voice, see it in his eyes, feel it in the way his hand gripped hers.

They sat silently, hand in hand, relishing the glory together.

The noise level of the revelers outside increased, and Jake glanced at his watch. "We'd better get outside. It's almost midnight!"

A fresh vigor possessed her as they walked out, side by side, from the sanctuary and into the air that was so cold it snapped.

New faith. What was more beautiful than that, except perhaps the patina of old faith? She pondered this until the blare of a horn startled her back into the present. Whistles clanged, people shouted, and somewhere a band struck up the traditional New Year's Eve song "Auld Lang Syne."

Jake faced her, tilted her chin upward, and said softly, "Happy New Year, sweetheart."

With lips as gentle as a prayer he kissed her.

The world exploded into a stunning display of golden and purple glitter, streams of brilliant orange and yellow, a spray of red and silver.

And the earth moved to make room for heaven.

At last his lips left hers, and she opened her eyes. Behind his head a fountain of blue stars shot into the sky far above the horizon, and she laughed shakily.

"Fireworks," she explained. "The city display is on. I thought we were—I mean, when you kissed me, I saw—oh Jake. . ." Her words trailed off, and she was grateful the dark hid her heated cheeks from his scrutiny.

In the splashes of light that cut through the darkness, she saw him smiling. "I saw them, too—the fireworks. Both sets."

For not speaking much they were saying volumes, and the image of Reverend Barnes and his wife flashed into her mind. She remembered looking at them on Thanksgiving and wanting the same closeness of silent language they had. And now, apparently, she had it.

Her heart was full.

"Happy New Year," she said to him, reaching up to touch his cheek with her mittened hand. "It's going to be a great year!"

Especially for someone who had just committed his life to Jesus Christ, she added silently. Jake knew who walked with him every step of his life's way, who had been with him all along, and now was revealed.

The church doors were still open, and the voices of Reverend Barnes, his wife, and some of the First Night team from Nativity floated up from downstairs.

"I'm falling in love with you, Tess. I'm declaring it in front of God Himself because, if you feel the same way, I want His blessing and His guidance on us as we go forward."

Feel the same way? She could only nod, mute with the happiness that flooded her entire being.

It was a wonderful way to end the year and to start a new one.

~

Jake swung his head back and forth in amazement. "I can't get over that. You don't strike me as the kind of person to watch a football game at all, especially on New Year's Day."

He was pouring pretzels and chips into a bowl.

"Word of warning," she said, laughing at his expression. "I don't know a thing about football except that if the guy runs the ball to the end of the court—"

"Field," he corrected.

"Field, that it's worth more than if he kicks it down there. If there's logic in that, well, I'll eat a Giblet Niblet."

He grinned. "A Giblet Niblet, huh? That alone would make it worth my time to find out."

"If you want to see me be sick and die, yes, it'd be very entertaining. But to get back to football, the only reason I watch it is so I can sit on the couch and not think except to wonder where the pretzels are."

"Here they are," he said, carrying the bowl to the living room. "I've never been a pretzel fan, so you can have the whole bowl to yourself."

"Nothing like a pretzel when the ball hits the twenty-foot line."

"Yard line. Twenty-yard line. And you probably don't want to hit it, you want to—hey, you really don't know anything about football, do you?"

"Nope," she answered cheerfully. "And I like it that way, so don't even bother trying to explain it to me. My eyes and my ears both will glaze over, and I'll be as catatonic as, well, my cat."

He shook his head. "You are an amazing woman. Truly amazing. So when does the game start?"

"Two."

"When's that?"

"After one and before three."

"Funny woman. Which team are you rooting for?" he asked. Then, noticing her face, he winced. "You're not rooting for a team, are you?"

"No. I have no idea about either one of them. I just shout and yell and hoot and holler and have a ripsnorting good time."

He leaned back and looked at her. "I'm still finding this a total contradiction in you. How can you be so wild about a game you know nothing about?"

"My grandparents had a tradition like the one we're following. I asked Grandma one time why she let Grandpa watch the game and why she sat in with him the entire time, usually doing some sort of needlework. She said her mind wandered all over the place during the game. Even back to when she met Grandpa, after a football game when he was in his uniform and she was selling apples." She smiled at the memory.

"She was a romantic, was she?" Jake edged down the couch, past a sleepily objecting Cora, to put his arm around Tess. "I like that."

"She loved Grandpa, that's for sure," Tess said. "And that, my dear man, is the story of how Tess Mahoney came to her New Year's Day tradition."

The football game took all afternoon. Jake claimed he still couldn't see how Tess could possibly enjoy the game without knowing the rules of play. She knew all she needed to know, she told him.

"There's a football," she said, pointing at the screen. "That guy with the amazing shoulders has it, and everybody else who's wearing different colors wants it."

"They're on the other team," Jake offered helpfully, but he received a withering glance in return.

"I know that. And I also know those aren't the guy's real shoulders, that they're pads and not really paddy pads but big plastic jobbers that'd probably jar your teeth out if you ran into him face-on, which is why the other guy's wearing a cage on his head."

"Helmet," Jake said helplessly.

"And that one end of the, um, the big football place—"

"Field."

"Belongs to one side, and the other belongs to the other side, and the players want to kick the ball and make a goal."

"Touchdown." His voice was weak.

She shrugged. "So what's the big deal with rules? What I don't understand is why they run right into each other and pile on top of one guy. I mean, it's clear he's not going to slither out from under this heap of, what, nearly a ton of sweaty men, right?"

"A ton?" Jake looked confused.

"Well, there are ten of them, right?"

"Um, no, well, yeah, sure. There are ten. Close enough."

"And each one weighs what, two hundred pounds?"

He tried unsuccessfully not to laugh.

She glared at him, and he controlled himself. "You bet. Two hundred pounds."

"So ten of them would weigh two thousand pounds, which is pretty close to a ton in my book," she ended triumphantly.

He stopped and stared at her. "Through all that convoluted logic you've come to what has to be an absolutely correct answer. Amazing."

She smiled happily. "And that, Jake Cameron, is why I love football."

Later, when the team with the green and white uniforms beat the team with the gold and blue ones, as Tess explained it, they sat with the living room illuminated with only the lights from the Christmas tree.

"We need to take that thing down," he said. "It's flinging its needles off with abandon."

"But it's so pretty," she objected. "I like to keep it up until Epiphany."

He stared at her. "Isn't that January 6?"

"Sure is. What's wrong with that?"

"That tree will be nothing but a stem and some twigs by then. You'll have to take it down sometime this week, sorry to say."

"Um-hum," she responded lazily, leaning against him. "Cora's finally used to having her very own tree in the house. You expect me to justify taking it down with the thin excuse that it's dropping needles and it's so dry it's a fire hazard?"

"Take it down while she's sleeping and put a bag of Giblet Niblets in its place. She'll think the Tree Fairy came."

Tess snorted. "Giblet Niblets indeed. I'll send her over to breathe in your face—thank you very much."

Their conversation turned to the events of the night before.

"How many people do you suppose turned out for First Night?" he asked.

"I don't know, but we have a commission meeting next week; so if the paper doesn't have the count, I'll probably find out then." She stretched languidly. "The committee's been on hiatus during the holidays, and I still don't expect there to be much business to report on. So we'll undoubtedly hear every detail about how the New Year's celebration went."

"Next year maybe Panda's will participate in First Night," he said, absently tracing one of her auburn curls with his fingertip.

"Sure! You could have a stand somewhere and probably bring in a ton of money."

A yawn overtook her, and she nearly missed his next words.

"Setting the halo straight."

At least that's what she thought he said. It didn't make any sense, and she was too sleepy to figure out what he meant.

"You're tired, and I need to get home. Happy New Year, dear Tess," he whispered. "I'll lock the door on my way out."

She pulled Cora's warm body up and nestled her cheek against the soft fur and let the Christmas lights blur into dreams.

Chapter 18

Cora was not impressed with the swirl of red taffeta Tess proudly displayed.
"You don't like it, Cora?"

Tess held it up against herself and swished the dress around her legs. That caught Cora's immediate attention, and a gray ball of fur shot off the bed and attacked the hem of the dress.

"No, no, Cora! You'll rip it!" Tess gently disengaged Cora's extended claws from the fabric and grinned at the expression on her cat's face. "I suppose I shouldn't have teased you with it like that. Sorry, Sweetie-Cat." She rubbed Cora's nose, but the cat glared at her and stalked out of the room.

Tess didn't know for sure where she and Jake were going this Valentine's night. From his hints she assumed it was Whispering Winds. Her mouth watered at the memory of the elegant chocolate dessert she'd tasted there.

As she dressed, she thought about how she and Jake had both changed during the time they'd been together. In such a short period they'd come to know and understand each other.

Since making the step from belief to faith, Jake had grown both spiritually and personally. He attended Nativity regularly and had even joined the choir, much to Mrs. Smalley's delight.

Tess had seen the way his face had relaxed, the way the lines around his eyes and mouth had softened, the easy way he moved, since he'd let Jesus fully into his life. Now that he knew he no longer walked alone, that his burden was shared, he could allow the harmony of being in spiritual balance back into his life.

A glance at the clock told her she had better hurry. He was due to arrive soon.

"Wow!" Jake added a low whistle as she showed off her new red dress. "You look like a Valentine yourself in that!"

He knelt down to greet Cora, who had padded out to the kitchen to see if by any chance Jake had remembered to bring her some treats.

"Happy Valentine's Day, Cora," he said to the cat, who was already sniffing around the coat pocket he had reached into.

"Those had better not be Giblet Niblets," Tess threatened.

He laughed and took the bag out to prove they weren't. "No, these are plain old Tuna Buddies. See? They're shaped like little fishies, and they even smell like them."

Tess nodded. "So I notice—from way over here. But at least they're not as awful as the dreaded Giblet Niblets. Go ahead. She can have them."

The last words were unnecessary as Cora snatched the bag away from Jake. With one powerful swipe of her claws she had torn it open and was eating the treats before Tess could finish her sentence.

"Now's the time to make our getaway," he whispered to Tess, "while she's still wrapped up in the Tuna Buddies."

She had been right about their destination. They were headed toward Whispering Winds.

The night was cloudless, and the moon was bright. It was a perfect evening, even if it was seven below.

He pulled the car over to the side of the road at a familiar spot. "Do you remember when we first came out here?"

She nodded. How could she forget? The kiss had changed her life.

"And we looked at the stars?"

They had! He had shown her the patterns in the sky, but no shine was as great as the one in her heart that night.

"Well," he continued, "there's a nova I want you to see."

He unfastened his seat belt. "Come on. Let me show it to you."

They stood at the edge of the road. She shivered against him, and he wrapped his arms around her.

"Do you know what a nova is?" he asked.

"Sort of. Fill me in."

"It's a new star being born. I suppose it happens all the time—for angels, it's probably an everyday occurrence," he said, grinning at her. "But for us mortals, seeing a nova is rare."

The sky, away from the glare of the town's lights, glittered with thousands and thousands of stars.

"Each one of those was once a nova," he said. "Even the old stars."

"What does the nova look like? Where is it?" she asked, her eyes scanning the sky. "I can't see it."

"It's here."

"Where?"

"In my hand."

She looked down, startled.

Open in his hand was a jeweler's box with a ring nestled inside it. The diamond caught the reflected light of the stars and glittered wildly.

"Tess Mahoney, I love you. I love you completely, totally, and madly. I think I fell in love with you the minute I walked into Angel's Roost that first day and saw you standing there, looking as if you'd just alighted from heaven yourself."

She tried to speak, but something had happened to her voice. No words came out.

The verse from Ecclesiastes Jake had mentioned on Christmas Eve returned to her: "A time to keep silence." She understood and listened.

He continued. "I come to you as a Christian who has given himself to Jesus, but I need to know one more thing."

Right there, on the edge of County Road Four, Jake Cameron knelt in the snow. "Tess, will you share my life with me? Will you marry me?"

" 'It is not good that the man should be alone,'" she quoted softly, regaining her voice. "Nor is it good that the woman should be alone. Yes. Yes!"

He put the ring on her finger. Overhead the stars, both old and new, danced joyfully as the nova of love twinkled on her hand.

❧

Could an evening ever be more extraordinary? Tess pondered the question over a dinner she barely tasted.

He loved her! That much she had come to know, bit by bit, throughout the time they'd been together. But to hear him say it and to have him commit to her for life—she kept turning it over and over in her mind. No matter how she looked at it, it was spectacular.

"Where should we live?" he asked. "I feel as if your house is more like home to me, but if you'd prefer we can move to the Pines."

"Oh please, can we stay at Angel's Roost? After all, that's where we met."

"And," he said, his fingers pleating and unpleating his napkin, "it'll be closer for me."

"Closer for what?" she asked idly.

"Work."

She sat up straight. "How can you say that? Panda's is in the End!"

"Panda's South is. But Panda's Downtown is much closer." He looked up and smiled.

She couldn't stop the grin that spread across her face. "Panda's South and Panda's Downtown! It's the perfect solution, but can you do it?"

He nodded. "The River Exchange, the building you chose—the building God chose—is historic, and I'm getting a financial break in the restoration because I've promised to keep it as true to its original glory as possible."

He pulled some papers from inside his coat pocket and unfolded them on the table. "See? Here are some pictures of what it used to look like. I've been working with the county museum, with the special collections department at the library, and with the state historical society to re-create both the interior and the exterior accurately. I want to keep the integrity of that building, but the modern touches will all be removable, should we need to take them out at some time."

She studied the drawings. "Why didn't I know about it?"

"I wanted to keep it a surprise."

"I'm surprised—and so happy, Jake!"

He signaled to the server and whispered in his ear. The server nodded, smiling, and soon returned with a familiar foil-wrapped package.

"For Cora?" Tess asked.

"I need to ask her for your hand in marriage," he said, "and I'm just smoothing the way."

"I think she'll give her consent. If that has what I think it has in it—salmon?—she'd probably let you rob us blind."

"Oh, I think she's more discerning than that," Jake said. "After all, she chose you."

"And she has been a shameless matchmaker ever since she met you," she reminded him. "I'm pretty blessed by that furry girl."

"I have a question I've been meaning to ask," he continued, holding her hand as they left Whispering Winds. "Why is your store called Angel's Roost?"

"I hope it's a place where angels can stop and rest for a while before they go on to serve." She smiled. "After all, some of those guardian angels probably need a good rest now and again."

"Speaking of resting," he said as they stood outside the restaurant. "I'd like to bring Faith back home."

"But she's so perfect in Panda's!" Tess said.

"I think a certain cat the color of pussy willows would like her friend back."

"Maybe now Faith's halo will stay on straight," Tess commented.

"I hope not." Jake laughed, and Tess remembered his words on New Year's Eve. "I want her there, reminding us how wild and crazy the journey of faith is, and how much fun it's going to be, when we walk along the path with love."

He bent to kiss her, and as his lips touched hers Tess was sure she heard the fluttering of wings.

TESS'S CELESTIAL TRUFFLES

1 12-oz. package semisweet chocolate chips
1 can dark chocolate frosting
¼ cup ice cream topping, such as caramel or butterscotch
1 tsp. cold coffee
Ground nuts

Melt the chocolate chips. Stir in the frosting. Add the topping and the coffee. Chill until the mixture begins to set. Shape into balls (or drop with spoon, if mixture is very sticky, into the ground nuts) and roll in the nuts until the chocolate is covered.

Refrigerate. The truffles firm up when cold.

Note from Tess: If for some unfathomable reason you don't want chocolate, you can try different flavors and combinations of chips, frostings, and toppings with some interesting results. Be creative!

In the Cool
of the Evening

Dedication

In 1997, my community was evacuated as the river rose up over its banks and came into our homes. We were gone for six weeks, and we came back to houses that were devastated. There was so much to do; the task ahead seemed impossible. Plus we had to endure even more heartbreak as we threw out family heirlooms that had been destroyed by the flood. I remember holding my daughter's baby pictures, covered with sewage and mud, and crying as I dumped them into a garbage bag.

But through it all, we found that people everywhere cared. Strangers donated food, clothing, and personal care items. They came in teams to help rebuild this town they hadn't even heard of before. And above all, they gave us their prayers.

This book was written through tears and smiles, and is dedicated with love and gratitude to those wonderful folks who were so kind to us. I can never thank you enough.

Chapter 1

The Wild West barbecue was in full swing. Lily Chamberlain didn't have to search for the area where it was being held. Huge clouds of aromatic smoke drifted from the common area outside the dining room, and the happy shouts of young campers filled the air.

Her son tugged on her arm. "Mom, walk faster."

Her body ached. She didn't want to walk at all, let alone speed up. She and Todd had done the three-legged race, scooted on their stomachs through a cardboard maze, jumped rope, leaped over hurdles made of hay bales, and climbed an artificial wall. She'd be lucky if she could even move the next day.

"Look, it's Ric!" Todd broke loose and ran toward the serving line, his hair gleaming golden red in the late afternoon sun.

She hobbled painfully after him, vainly calling, "Wait! Todd William Chamberlain, get back here!"

One of the servers zipped around the table and caught her son in a bear hug. "Gotcha!" he said. "You're supposed to listen to your mom, young fellow." He set Todd down and held out his hand. "I'm Ric Jensen. I have Todd in my arts and crafts class."

His bright blue eyes sparkled under a thatch of summer blond hair that was now wind strewn. Charcoal was smeared across one cheekbone, and a spot of barbecue sauce had dried on his chin. She couldn't help but like him immediately.

"Pleased to meet you," she said. "I'm Lily. I hope Todd's doing well."

"He's the best five-year-old painter I've got!" Ric declared. "He's been working on his Noah's ark quite diligently."

"It's purple," Todd added.

"Yes, it is indeed." Ric grinned at Lily. "I'm glad to meet you. Todd talks a lot about you."

"Ah." She didn't dare ask what he said. Todd had an unusual knack for sharing the most interesting tidbits about her life. "Well, I believe we need to get in line here, Todd. It sure smells good."

"Usually you'd begin down at that end," Ric said, motioning to his right where grills were sizzling and steam was billowing from large open vats. "But since you're here, let's start."

He handed them two plates from under the table. "Make sure you sample all the sauces. As you can see by my apron, I've tried them all!" His body was swathed with a white apron that was stained with sauces of many varieties and colors.

"This splotch is Pastor Jack's southwestern marinade. Packs a kick, so you might want to be cautious. This mustardy bit is from a legendary concoction straight out of Fargo. And this," he said, pointing to another, "well, I don't know what it is. But it was mighty tasty. Yup, this apron tells a story all right. A story of gluttony and greed."

"It looks like an artist's apron," Todd said, somewhat in awe of the messy garment.

"Hey, I like that! I'm the Van Gogh of the barbecue world!" Ric spun his tongs with a flourish. "But today, corn is my canvas. May I interest you in trying some?"

He plopped an ear of corn on each of their plates, then he spooned a yellowish glob on, too. "My specially seasoned butter," he announced. "It makes plain old corn on the cob a gourmet delight."

"What's in it?" Todd asked suspiciously.

"Family secret, young man. Family secret." He winked at Lily as Todd examined the dollop of butter. "Say, if you two don't already have a place to sit, I've got a spot marked over by the teeter-totter. I'm just finishing up here, and I'd love some company."

It was blissfully close. After getting a hamburger for herself and a hot dog for Todd, she added brownies to each of their plates and picked up paper cups of lemonade. She gave Todd his plate and lemonade, which he promptly spilled down his shirt. "We'll just share mine," she explained to the young woman pouring the lemonade. "It's safest. And cleanest."

She limped over to the picnic table and sank down gratefully. There wasn't a part of her body that didn't throb, sting, or pound with pain. Todd, though, joyfully leaped past the slide and sandbox and headed toward the teeter-totter, the food on his plate in severe jeopardy of falling off. He circled the teeter-totter, dodged the swings, crossed the merry-go-round, and returned to her, out of breath.

"Isn't this the greatest place ever?" he asked as he took a bite of his hot dog.

"Don't talk with your mouth full," she said automatically. "And yes, it is the greatest place ever."

"Why?"

"Well, because it's got a lake and a church and a playground—"

"No, I mean why can't I talk with my mouth full? It saves a lot of time. I can chew and talk at the same time. Watch."

He provided a vivid demonstration.

"That's dreadful, Todd. Nobody wants to see chewed-up food."

He wasn't convinced. "It's not *that* gross."

"Gross enough. Just don't do it." She tapped him lightly on the nose and leaned over to hug him, but he wriggled out of her grasp. "Cooties!" he said with pretend disgust.

She shook her head. He came up with the strangest things.

Any conversation with Todd was interesting, but she didn't object when he abandoned his plate of food to accept another little boy's invitation to play on the teeter-totter. It gave her one of those brief moments of respite that were so rare with a five-year-old.

It wasn't easy raising Todd by herself, but they'd managed. Out of the heartbreak of early widowhood, God had sent the blessing of a baby, and she had been able to move through her grief.

Todd was bundled energy, but he kept her focused on what was real and important in life.

Who knew it would be so complicated? For the millionth time, she revisited the choice she'd made in Chicago. Which was more important: one man's ethics—or lack thereof—or the survival of a program that would benefit many women? Had she been wrong to leave? Should she have reported the wrongdoing and jeopardized the Nanny Group's existence?

The image resurfaced of the head of the Nanny Group smiling as he voiced threats so veiled that she'd often wondered if she had, in fact, understood him correctly. *Everything goes forward without any problem,* he'd said, *and all will be fine. Nothing is ever to get in my way. But you understand that, don't you, Lily? You know the importance of silence.*

In the back of her head, she could hear her mother's voice: *Nothing happens by accident; it's all part of God's plan.*

"Mom, look! I'm the king of the camp!" She looked up just in time to see Todd standing on top of the monkey bars, waving his arms at her. Before her heart could completely stop, he slithered down the metal railing to safety.

The child had to be part monkey. That, or he had a guardian angel working overtime.

❧

Ric knew Lily was worried about something. Almost all the parents at Shiloh Family Camp had come here because they had burdens of some kind or another. If she wanted to share, she would, but he knew that took time. He would be here when she was ready.

He had seen the way her eyes glowed when she watched her exuberant son at play and the twinkle they took on during the exchange about talking with his mouth full. Her love for her son was clear.

"Todd's a great kid," he said, sliding in beside her at the picnic bench. "We're having a super time in class. He does like purple, doesn't he?"

Lily laughed. "It's his favorite color. Is he really painting Noah's ark purple?"

Ric nodded. "He is. Mrs. Noah is purple, too."

"Probably not historically accurate, is it?"

"But infinitely more interesting than brown." He tore off a piece of bread. "Are you from North Dakota?"

She nodded, her light brown hair swirling around her shoulders. "I'm a returnee. I've been working in Chicago for the past couple of years, but I'm back now." She looked down as she spoke, hiding eyes that were so dark blue they were nearly indigo.

"Chicago? This must be quite a change for you. What did you do in Chicago?"

Lily swirled the lemonade in her cup as she answered. "I was a case administrator for a nonprofit organization."

"She worked with babies." Todd had joined them, and Ric watched with a smile as she wiped a smudge of dirt from his forehead.

"Really?" Ric asked. "What kind of work did you do at this place?"

"It was a child-care program for single parents. I'm a single parent myself, so I was especially committed to seeing it succeed."

"Sounds interesting. How did it work?"

"It was actually two programs that dovetailed. One was supplying day care for single parents who were being trained for careers, and the other was training people to be nannies and day care providers. So one program served the other."

Did he hear a slight break in her voice? Perhaps he'd imagined it because she looked at him and smiled. "It's a lifesaver for many women who otherwise would be stuck in a life of welfare."

In the back of his mind a plan started to grow. Maybe—

"What a great idea!" he said as he started to dream of the possibilities. "Well, we'll get you back to them nice and relaxed, ready to face a whole new group of people who need your help."

"We're not going back," Todd interjected. "We don't know where we're going. Maybe Gran's. Mom doesn't have a job anymore. We're almost poor."

"Is that true?" Perhaps this was what was weighing on her heart.

She looked trapped, and he quickly added, "You don't have to tell me anything you don't want to. But if you need some help, that's what we're here for. Shiloh Family Camp is a place for families to relax in a supportive Christian environment, and that means unsnarling the snarls that occur in any family's life."

Lily laughed. "You sound like the brochure."

He grinned a bit sheepishly. "I wrote it."

He could hear children laughing on the playground, and below the sound, the steady murmur of adult voices. He loved his time at Shiloh. It was a stress reliever for him, too.

"People come here for many reasons," he continued. "We don't ask that you reveal any more than you feel is necessary, but I do want you to know that we are here if at any time your burden becomes too great, and you want a friendly ear to listen, a friendly shoulder to cry on, or a friendly spirit to pray with you. Take it at your own pace."

Before she could respond, he knelt beside Todd. "I'd better go make sure we have enough purple to finish Mrs. Noah tomorrow, and I'm on cleanup duty, too. See you both tomorrow, I hope." He ruffled Todd's reddish gold hair and straightened up. "Don't forget there's a trail ride after church. And then the rodeo!"

Did he actually hear her groan?

❧

"Todd, hurry up." She knelt to tie his shoes and winced. There wasn't a muscle in her body that wasn't protesting loudly. No way was she going on a trail ride after church. Just the thought of getting onto the horse's back made her cringe.

She'd rather spend the day resting in the sunshine with a book and a glass of lemonade, like any sane woman.

"Church is going to start soon, buddy. Let's get going."

As they followed the path to the chapel, Todd sang a song. "God is my friend, I'm God's friend, you're God's friend. God likes dogs, God likes cats, God likes hamsters. God made potatoes, God made carrots, God made pudding."

"That's an interesting song," she said at last.

"Yes," he told her proudly. "I wrote it myself."

"Ah. It's lovely."

"Thank you." He continued, "God loves purple, God loves red, God loves blue. God can hear, God can see, God can talk."

He stopped so suddenly that she almost fell over him. "He can, right? He can talk?"

"Sure He can. We just have to listen. Now, let's go into church and see if we can hear Him."

The chapel was almost full, and they took the last seats available. She felt herself relax as the service began with the call to worship.

Her priority now was getting back in tune with what was real and eternal in life and reaffirming her priorities. She had it all figured out: God would do it. He could fix anything. She needed to focus on Todd.

Todd, like any five-year-old, had a mixed view of church services. He was enthusiastic the first five minutes, and then his interest waned as his attention span faltered.

Lily pulled the illustrated children's Bible from the bag she always carried to church. Experience told her this would occupy him for another five minutes or, if she were lucky, ten.

Pastor Jack asked them to join him in silent prayer.

And that was when the meeting of woman and Lord became unavoidable.

She started to pray but found instead that she was listening as her soul poured itself out.

It wasn't fair that Douglas Newton had managed to get into her life—just as she was straightening it out—and once again destroy it.

She'd loved her job, and she'd taken great satisfaction from knowing she was helping others in a situation like she'd been in herself. She'd tried to see it with his rationalizing explanation, but no matter how she'd turned and twisted it, what he had done—using the Nanny Group as his personal babysitting service—was wrong.

What scared her the most was the look he had given her when she quit. She had never seen anything quite so cold—and so menacing—in her life.

He scared her. There was something about him that made her wary, that set every cell in her body on edge.

He had revealed himself to be ruthless, as if he would let nothing get in the way of what he wanted. She'd seen the way he'd treated anyone he considered to be beneath him.

His impatience was legendary among service staff. She'd seen it herself, and what she hadn't seen, she'd heard about. Waitresses at the high-priced restaurant where he enjoyed lunches dreaded having him sit at one of their assigned tables. If he considered anything on his plate not up to the quality he expected, he created a scene that often ended with the server being fired or quitting.

They'd had a secretary at the Nanny Group for a while—actually, they'd had several secretaries—but he'd demanded so much of them that they usually quit within a day or two. The employment service they'd tried had finally quit sending applicants over.

Even the old woman who had cleaned the office at the Nanny Group had met with his wrath. When he'd deemed that the poor woman, her back twisted with arthritis, hadn't cleaned under his desk well enough, he'd thrown a pencil at her and dumped a potted plant onto the floor and told her to clean the soil and shattered crockery from the carpet. When she had finished, he fired her.

She had seen enough to make her very careful around him, but when she became the focus of his anger, she'd taken special care. Not only did she have to worry about herself and her job, but she had a little boy that God had entrusted her with, and she would walk over hot coals, crawl through broken glass, whatever it took, to keep him safe.

Maybe she was being melodramatic, but she couldn't shake the feeling that Douglas Newton would do whatever it took to keep her quiet about what she knew.

Why had God sent this wretched person into her life? How many trials and tribulations must she endure—must Todd endure, too?

First, the loss of her husband after only three weeks of marriage, a victim of a drunk driver, had nearly destroyed her. The total emptiness and the eerie sensation of being adrift, like a boat that had escaped its mooring, had haunted those first blind days of grief.

Then she discovered she was pregnant. That little life inside her had saved her, and now Todd was everything to her.

"Amen."

She raised her head as Pastor Jack pronounced an end to prayer. Guiltily she realized that she hadn't even prayed. She'd relived her problems again, without getting one step closer to a solution.

Maybe there wasn't a solution. Maybe God—

A sharp elbow in her ribs brought her back to the present. "Mom! Get up!" Todd whispered loudly.

People were standing again, singing a familiar old hymn, "Rock of Ages." As she sang, she paid attention to the words of the opening verse. If only she *could* hide in the Rock.

Pastor Jack's sermon was brief, about the partnership God offers His creation. He encouraged those attending to be an active partner, not a silent partner, in their relationship with the Lord.

Prayer, he said, was the most effective and dynamic when you offered yourself as a participant.

The service ended with a brief moment of silence. Here was her time to redeem herself, to pray honestly.

God, guide me. Please, I need a little help here. And then, although she'd been trained not to do this, not to tell God what to do, Lily couldn't resist adding, *You used to send angels as your messengers. Send me a sign. It doesn't have to be an angel, but I would like a sign. Please, God, I need some help.*

"God answers prayers." Her head spun around as Ric spoke beside her.

Her confusion must have shown on her face because he laughed easily. "I prayed that I'd get a chance to talk to you this morning. Do you have a minute?"

Before she could answer, he continued. "Here's the deal. If you really are looking for a job, I have one that needs you as badly as you need it. Want to help me set up an emergency day care in a flooded community?"

Lily could only stand there, astonished. Todd tugged on the hem of her shirt, but she ignored him.

Well, it was true that God answers prayers. But somehow she'd never thought a response would be this quick or that her angel would be wearing a neon green T-shirt that read Shiloh Family Camp, Where Playing and Praying Meet.

❧

"I can't go." The sunshine glinted in Lily's eyes as they walked toward the playground area where Todd could play while she and Ric talked.

Ric tilted his head and studied her for a moment before saying, "You don't have to commit now. You can think about it."

"I have thought about it." As soon as the words were out of her mouth, she knew they weren't true. Her response had been automatic.

Ric didn't respond. He simply continued to walk until he came to the swing set. He caught one of the rope-and-metal swings and sat down on it.

He began to swing silently, first slowly and then with continuing speed. She could feel herself frowning against the sunshine as she watched him progress higher and higher into the sky while she stood to the side, one hand lightly touching the frame of the swing set.

It seemed like a metaphor to her. Somehow she had to make sense of it all, bring it into focus.

She felt the need to speak. "I can't do something like that. I have Todd. I can't just pick up and go."

Her son tugged at her sleeve. "Where, Mom? Where?"

"Where what?" she asked almost absentmindedly as she ruffled his reddish gold hair. "You're supposed to be playing."

"Where are we going?"

"We're not going anywhere, honey."

"But I just heard Ric say—"

"Todd, we can't just pick up and move."

"Are we going to live with Gran then?"

The reminder of her situation rose in Lily's mind like a gigantic monolith, unavoidable now. Where were they going, anyway? She loved her mother, but she couldn't stay with her.

"No, no, Todd. We're not going to live with Gran." She knew anxiety had crept into her voice, but she couldn't keep it away.

"Then where are we going to live?" Todd insisted.

"Somewhere, sweetheart, somewhere. I just don't know where." Inside her chest the claw of tension tightened.

Ric spoke quietly. "Think about this job. These people could use you and your skills. Right now they have nothing. And what you have—knowledge, caring, and time to work—will help them more than you could ever know." He smiled at Todd. "Disasters are bad enough, but they shouldn't happen to children."

"Are we going to live in a tent?" Todd asked. "We don't have a tent, do we, Mom? If we don't live with Gran, then where are we going? Are we going back to Chicago? I thought you said—"

"That's enough, Todd." Her words shot out like bullets, and she instantly regretted her tone. She knelt beside him and ran her finger down the bridge of his nose. "We're going to be okay. You know that."

She sensed him closing up. Suddenly everything in her melted, and she clutched him to her in a near-desperate hug. "Honey, please don't worry. Leave that to me."

Something inside her began to move, like a glacier edging its way onward. But as quickly as it began, it stopped. She wasn't ready.

"We could go where Ric says." Todd's voice was muffled against her shoulder.

The block of ice jolted away from her heart a bit, just enough for the pain to penetrate briefly. He was so little, so defenseless against a world that had been totally unfair.

"I will take care of both of us," she promised him softly in his ear. "God will be with us, like He always has been. He will not leave us."

"I want to go home." Her son's words were so quiet that she wasn't sure he'd spoken at all until she felt the tears moistening her blouse. "I want to go home, but I don't know where that is anymore."

The glacier lurched inside her, nearly ripping her heart from its moorings. She looked up at Ric. "Let's talk about that job."

Chapter 2

Ric pulled a map from a manila envelope and pushed it across the table. The dining hall was deserted while the children were on a nature hike and the parents were swimming.

Lily looked where his finger pointed. "That's Wildwood," he said to her. "It's a lovely little town—at least it was until the Rock River left its boundaries and affected 98 percent of the town. Houses, businesses, schools—you name it—they're gone or at least damaged."

On the map, roads and highways intersected in red and black lines. An occasional blue squiggle indicated a river, and it was to one of these that he was drawing her attention.

It looked so innocuous, this unassuming curve of blue that wound past the dot marked WILDWOOD.

"What happened?"

"There was more snow than usual this year. This part of the state is very flat, and the snowmelt had nowhere to go except to the river. That's a lot of water, more than the river could hold within its banks."

"So one day the water just came up?" She'd heard about it on the news, how all the smaller tributaries had flooded, too, but because it had been at the same time as the situation at the Nanny Group was coming to a head, she'd let it slip past her.

"Along the river's edge, roads were washed out, and basements took water. Many highways between towns were closed, and the county roads began to go under until many farmsteads and smaller towns were isolated. Then one day in Wildwood, the lift stations failed, and the street sewers couldn't function any longer, and that was all it took. Wildwood flooded."

"With all that damage, wouldn't it be better to just abandon this place? Let the river say it won?"

He shook his head. "And where would they go?"

"I don't know. Somewhere. Anywhere."

"That's just it. There isn't any place for them to go. They can't just pick up and leave everything and make their town reappear magically in another location."

"I understand that. But doesn't it come to a point where you say, 'That's it. This and no more'?"

"Possibly. But not in this case. The flooding didn't take out the town, just inundated it. Most houses are structurally all right but need some internal

144

help. Basements need to be fixed up. People need furniture. Clothing. Help reorganizing their lives. How can I explain to you how damaged they are—not only their homes but their emotional and spiritual selves?"

He reached inside the manila envelope and pulled out a handful of photographs. With one quick motion, he spread them across the tabletop.

She couldn't lift her eyes from the tableau he had laid in front of her.

The houses were clean, and the lawns were evenly green. Overhead a lapis blue sky sparkled. But along the streets were piles of rubble. Bits of drywall. Furniture soaked and stained. Clothing that was nearly unrecognizable after two weeks of being submerged in floodwaters.

"And this doesn't even begin to capture the smell," he added.

She stroked one photograph that particularly caught her attention: a once-pink bear, now darkened to a patchy gray, perched in a discarded child's rocking chair. One runner was missing from the chair, and it balanced precariously atop the heap.

"Our job," Ric said, "is helping them clean and repair so they can get on with the business of living."

"Sure. This is all just stuff anyway."

She felt Ric stir uneasily. "'Stuff'? I don't know if I agree with that. What went with the river was often priceless, unless the family was able to salvage it, which is unlikely. Family photographs. Baby pictures. Scrapbooks. The things that can't be replaced at any cost."

The back of her throat felt dry. Papery. Her stomach twisted. Lily turned back to the photographs and the graphic display of devastation that was scattered in front of her.

She studied the single photograph that had held her attention. Inside her chest, a small invisible hand clutched her heart.

She realized why the picture took her by emotional storm. This could be Todd's bear. Only the color was different. His was brown, a rich chestnut brown. She'd bought it two years before as part of a department store promotion. It had originally sported a red plaid bow and a tiny green vest, but those had disappeared within days.

Nevertheless, the bear stayed with him. It was in their cabin at Shiloh now.

And there was more beyond the bear. The owner could have been Todd. And certainly the loss was physically a teddy bear and a rocking chair, but how much more had been taken by the river?

"It's going to be difficult," Ric said, interrupting her thoughts. "These folks have been through a lot, and their stories will tear your heart out."

"I'm tough." *No you're not*, the silent voice inside her soul answered. *You are ready to fall apart. You are in absolutely no condition to go into a place that is as hurt as this place, where people are struggling with despair, when your own battles are not fought and certainly not won.*

"Are you saying you'll take the job?" Ric leaned across the table and clutched her fingers eagerly.

The photograph fell to the table. The answer was on her lips before he finished. And when she answered, her heart spoke.

"Yes."

❧

The trees whispered among themselves, and Ric sat on the grounded end of the teeter-totter, letting the cool June breeze wash over him.

"God, I think we did it."

He spoke softly, although no one was out this late. He hadn't been able to sleep, thinking of what awaited him in Wildwood.

The congregation at Resurrection had insisted he fulfill his commitment to Shiloh, made before the flooding had occurred. As the youth minister who worked with children from the time they were infants until they graduated from high school, he'd been torn between his responsibility at the church and his promise to work at Shiloh, but Pastor Mike, the head clergyman at the church, had encouraged him.

"You need a break," he'd told Ric.

It was probably true.

The flood had crept in, slowly at first—a few inches in this basement, low-lying yards taking on water. At last the Rock River had been overwhelmed and left its banks entirely.

Wildwood had just under 30,000 residents, and it hadn't garnered the attention recent flooding had in larger cities, like New Orleans or Nashville.

As a smaller community, Wildwood was at a disadvantage in recovery. The folks who drove the refuse trucks, the electricians who had to replace each electrical box, the technicians for the cable company—all were struggling in their own homes, trying to get them back to normal.

His second-floor apartment hadn't been damaged, but the lower level had been affected. He'd worked day and night, not just in his building but wherever residents had needed help.

The chore seemed endless. Even in his dreams, he hauled out damaged belongings, power-washed basements, and swabbed walls with bleach. Perhaps more important was the task of keeping the children of Wildwood occupied while their parents toiled on, trying to balance post-flood cleaning with attending to their day jobs.

There was so much work.

And yet each day still had only twenty-four hours, and every human body needed sleep.

He lay back and rested his head on the red-painted board of the teeter-totter. The enamel was flaking off, a sign of its heavy use this summer. When he stood up, his back, he knew, would be covered with crimson flecks.

"You are good, God," he said aloud as he surveyed the sky above him.

Without city lights to challenge the brightness of the stars and the moon, the glow overhead was astonishingly reaffirming.

The same sky covered them all—from the greatest cities of the world to this little camp in the plains of North Dakota.

He'd felt guilty enjoying his time at Shiloh while his flock toiled on, but now he could return with the promise of help.

He would come back with hope.

It was in short supply lately in Wildwood. People were getting tired, and the full impact of what they'd lost was finally gnawing its way into their hearts.

Plus there was so much to do. The day before he'd left for Shiloh, he'd met with the Parenting with Christ study group in the church. Once the most vibrant class in Resurrection's offerings, its membership had dwindled to only a few couples.

"It's just so hard," one of the young women said with a sigh. "I want to do this, but we need—my children need. . ." Her words had trailed off as she'd fought tears.

It always seemed to circle back to this. Did they do this? Or that? What got short shrift? Life was now unbelievably complex.

But Lily, even though she undoubtedly didn't realize it, would take much of the burden from their shoulders. Just knowing their children would have a safe, secure place to go would be one less worry as they labored through rebuilding everything that made their lives.

Right now she had, understandably, no idea of the scope of the job ahead of her. But he had seen her expression when she saw the teddy bear, bedraggled by the floodwaters.

Her heart had spoken so loudly that he heard it.

He smiled at the stars sprinkled overhead, a vast array of silver white lights in a black velvet sky.

Whatever God had planned for him was making him very happy.

And it was tied in with a young woman whose eyes, when she forgot her own worry, sparkled like the very stars above him now.

"Thank You," he said to the One who had created the celestial display, the curtain of heaven itself. "Thank You."

Todd crowed with delight when Lily told him they were moving to Wildwood. "There'll be boys there," he said with assurance. "Boys who will be my friends."

That hand on her heart squeezed again. Her son needed friends.

"There'll be boys there." Lily stroked his reddish gold hair. "And they'll be needing friends. You'll be just the ticket."

"Just the thing God ordered, huh?"

Out of the mouths of babes, she thought. But ordered for whom? For her? For Todd? For the children of Wildwood?

"Time for bed," she said, standing up.

For once Todd didn't argue. "I know exactly what I'll dream about," he told her as he pulled on his pajamas. "I'll dream about Wildwood and all my new friends there, especially Ric. He's way cool, Mom."

"He's very nice," she commented, steering him toward the sink. "Now brush your teeth and then into bed with you, young man. Busy day ahead!"

Within minutes Lily was tucking in her son. "Say your prayers," she reminded him.

"I already did." He beamed at her.

"You did? When?"

"I've been praying a lot since I got here. Ric says any time I want to talk to God, I just have to pray."

Lily smiled at her son. "I'm sure God is glad to hear your voice."

"He is! Ric said so. Oh, guess what else? He also says that God is my friend. So I think that I should be God's friend, too."

"I guess the way to be His friend is to help His other friends, right? Maybe even those who don't know about Him?" She smoothed a stray lock of hair off his forehead.

A broad smile brightened his face. "And that's why we're going to Wildwood, right? To help God's friends?"

Once again the wonder of it all swept over her. Why was she asking God to send her an angel when she had this gift of her son?

She nodded and spoke with difficulty over the tears in her throat. "Yes, honey. That's it."

And she understood why her heart had spoken so clearly about accepting the call to Wildwood.

There was something about Ric, too—something that made her worn-out heart dare to hope. What it was, she couldn't identify, but it was an interesting feeling. Yes, that was it.

It was interesting.

❧

Somehow the mechanics of moving Lily and Todd to Wildwood were done, and within two weeks they were on their way to their new home. Her few belongings had been transported to a storage unit near her mother's house in Mandan. Ric had engineered the myriad of details so that all she had to do was put Todd in the car with her and drive the four hours to Wildwood.

Lily loved the North Dakotan landscape. From the flat lands to the gently rolling low hills and on to the Badlands, it reminded her of her childhood; of times that were calmer and less threatening. To her, it would always be a place of refuge from the irrational ways of the world she had come to know.

She had spoken to her mother before leaving Shiloh, and her mother's words echoed in her ears: "Chicago isn't everywhere, and Douglas Newton isn't every man. There are good places and good people all over the world. Don't let one bad experience spoil your enjoyment of life."

The gradual rises of the grasses and the cultivated fields nearing ripe heights lulled her further into the serenity she'd felt at times at Shiloh, and the reason for her trip fell from her thoughts as she let her eyes soak in the vista of green and gold that surrounded her.

Until a sign announced the turn for Wildwood. Within moments, she was there.

The main street was heavily populated with cars near what seemed to be a hardware and building supplies store. A truck parked in front of it was being loaded with pallets of drywall.

Not all the stores were open. Some were closed, and a grayish white film on the bottom two or three or even four feet of the plate-glass windows mutely told the story of the fate of their interiors.

A parking lot had been turned into a makeshift mobile home park, and she remembered what she had learned in preparing for the move—that these had come from the Federal Emergency Management Agency. FEMA had brought them in for families whose homes needed extensive repair or, in a few cases, had been too damaged to be fixed.

Lily slowed and checked the map Ric had drawn for her. According to his directions, if she stayed on this street and then turned left at the park, she should soon be at Resurrection, the church where she'd be working. Barring that, she was to follow the white steeple that towered over the abundant elms that seemed to grow everywhere in Wildwood.

The turn took her through a residential area. And nothing, absolutely nothing—not even the full panoply of photographs that Ric had laid out before her that day in Shiloh—had prepared her for this.

It wasn't so much the devastation that she saw—in fact, there was little to see immediately—it was the total sparkling cleanliness of the neighborhoods contrasted with the piles of rubble and debris that lined the road.

In house after house, people carted out wheelbarrows full of unrecognizable materials and dumped the ruins on the already crowded berms.

She was prepared for this—somewhat. The townspeople were still taking care of the damaged materials in their houses. Ric had given her a report that had explained it.

The flood had come in the middle of April, and the residents had been forced to leave. They'd been out of their homes until mid-May or later. Before they could move back in, they had needed to pump the water out of their basements and remove not only the items that had been soaked, but furniture and appliances that had been flooded and carry them to the curb. Toys, clothing, games. Chairs, couches, and tables. Furnaces, washers and dryers, freezers. Drenched carpeting and drywall had to be torn out and dragged to the streets' edges.

The infrastructure of the city had to be back into place before the debris pickup could begin. Trash removal had just begun in some parts of the town earlier in the week.

All services had been affected. Even electricity, usually taken for granted, had become a luxury as each inundated home's electrical box had to be replaced. It was too much to take in.

What happened, though, brought unstoppable tears to her eyes.

Each of them looked up at her car as it crept down the street. And then, pausing in their work, they squinted against the sunlight toward her and smiled and waved.

How could they? How could they possibly be so cheerful and happy when their lives were on the edges of the streets, soaked with floodwaters?

The church was easy to find, thanks to Ric's instructions. The white clapboard building was topped with a spire that seemed to point directly to heaven, although, as Lily reminded herself, that was precisely the reason for making it that way.

Resurrection, like the houses she'd seen, was spotlessly white—and finally it dawned on her. Many of the houses and businesses she'd seen looked so bright and fresh because they'd just been painted. The insides, however, were torn apart and damaged.

If she was looking for metaphor, she was certainly in the right place.

"Mom?" Todd's sleepy voice jolted her back to reality. "Are we there yet?"

"Yes, tiger, we're here."

She turned off the car's engine and leaned over the seat. "Are you awake?"

It was a silly question. Todd had the most amazing ability to require only thirty seconds to bring himself from a deep sleep to full wakefulness. It was a quality she'd envied since his babyhood.

"What does it look like? Is that it? Where are we going to live? I thought it was a trailer. That's not a trailer. That's a church. Are we going to live in a church? What's that smell?"

"Whoa!" she said, laughing. "Okay, Question Man, let's take them one at a time—not that I remember them all, but let's see how I do. First of all, this is a church, and I doubt we're living here. You're right, Ric said we would live in a trailer, although I think 'mobile home' is the preferred term."

She opened the car door, and a breeze carried in the faint waft of something she vaguely remembered.

Todd wrinkled his nose. "Yuck. Something stinks."

"Well, let's not say anything about it quite yet. Why don't we go inside and see if Ric is there?"

The lure of seeing his friend from Shiloh did the trick. Todd dropped the subject of the rogue smell and bounded to the door of the church.

Lily saw him stop suddenly, and when he turned, his face was squeezed in disgust.

She joined him and, at the open door, understood. The smell was nearly overpowering. Although the windows in the narthex were all open and fans were blowing air outside, the smell was pervasive.

"That's what a flood smells like." Ric spoke behind them, and Todd turned to him with a grin and propelled his little body into Ric's welcoming arms.

"What is it?"

He looked at her directly. "Sewage. The drains didn't work for obvious reasons, and sewage backed up into homes, businesses, churches, on the streets—you name it."

"What's sewage?" Todd asked.

"You don't want to know," Lily said smoothly. "Or we'll talk about it later. Take your pick."

He nodded. "Okeydokey. But it sure does smell stinky."

"I agree," Ric said. "Later this afternoon I'll give you the grand tour of Wildwood. First let me show you your new home and give you a chance to get your bearings."

"Sounds good. Should I follow you in my car?" Lily asked.

"You don't have to. We can walk. It's right back here." He motioned for them to follow him.

They walked through the area behind the sanctuary and back out into the bright sunlight. He led them around to the area behind the building.

"There it is. Hope you like it."

A mobile home was set up in a small clearing beside the parking area. Next to it was a small recreational area with swings, a slide, and a merry-go-round.

"From FEMA?" she asked, thinking of the homes she'd seen in the parking lot near downtown.

"No, this belongs to the denomination. The district brought it in for us to use. Is it all right?" Ric asked.

Two thoughts came to her simultaneously. The first was how small the home was, but when she quickly calculated the size, she realized it was about the same as her apartment in Chicago.

Her second was to notice the trees that sheltered the small home. She hadn't known how hungry she was to live next to trees or plants of any kind again after spending those years in the large apartment complex that had been their home in Chicago. There had been a single anemic tree in the courtyard and some carefully cultivated plants, but nothing natural.

Todd raced toward the playground and jumped on one of the swings. "Is this for me?" he yelled at Ric.

"It's for you and for any other children who want to use it," Ric answered. "It belongs to the church."

"I love it," she said simply.

"But you haven't seen the inside. Come on. Let's take a look at it."

The interior was clean and plain. There were no heavy draperies on the windows, only light yellow cotton curtains that billowed in the faint afternoon breeze. The furniture was utilitarian, not stylish but workable. And instead of lush carpeting, slightly worn throw rugs covered the linoleum.

"It's not much, I know," Ric began to apologize, "but it's—"

"Perfect. Absolutely perfect."

"It's not what you had in Chicago, I know."

She ran her hand over the scarred gray dinette table. "And that's why I like it, Ric."

He didn't say anything, but she sensed that easy acceptance that was so much a part of Ric.

"I'm not ready to talk about it." The answer to his unspoken question seemed to blurt itself out in the warm summer air.

"I understand. And I want you to know that if you decide you need to talk about it, and you want to talk to me, I'll listen."

Lily shook her head. "I don't know if I'll ever talk about it. This isn't. . . Oh, I don't know how to say it."

"Have you talked to God about it?" Ric's question was soft.

"He knows." Her voice sounded bitter, and she instantly regretted it. "I didn't mean it that way. I talked to God so much while I was in Chicago that I'm sure He got sick and tired of hearing from me: 'Oh, there she is again. What's her problem today?'"

"You don't mean that." Laughter edged its way into his words.

"No, I don't. Not really. But we're not here to talk about me anyway. We're here to help God's friends."

Ric tilted his head. " 'God's friends'?"

Her smile came back as she looked out the window at Todd gleefully zipping down the slide. "That came from Todd. According to him, we're all God's friends. He said he learned it from you at Shiloh."

Ric joined her at the window. "He learned it from me? Oh no. I learned it from him. I learned it from him and from every child I've ever come in contact with. And each day I learn it again."

He turned to her and smiled, and once again Lily saw the warm blue of the North Dakota sky in his eyes. "I'm glad to have you here. . .friend."

Lily felt the welcome all the way into her heart.

Chapter 3

Ric watched from the back door of the church as Lily cranked open the windows of the little trailer. He'd helped unpack her car and then left her alone to get settled. Todd raced back and forth between the swing set, the slide, and the door that Lily had propped ajar.

The refrigerator there had been filled with food earlier in the day, and the cupboards were stocked. He had even put shampoo and soap in the miniature bathroom, trying to make the old trailer as much like their home as possible.

With Todd beside her, she stepped out of the trailer and began to cross the short distance to the church. Suddenly she stopped and knelt, drawing Todd to her side.

What was she doing?

He chuckled as he realized what was going on. She lifted up a finger, and although he couldn't see what was on it, he recognized the stance.

She and Todd stared at her fingertip and then watched something as it flew away. They looked at each other and smiled as they stood up.

"We found a ladybug," she said when they reached the door of the church.

"You'll see lots of them here," a voice behind him said as a stout middle-aged woman joined him.

He grinned. "Lily, this is Marnie Rygg."

"Marnie, it's good to meet you. This is Todd, my son."

"I don't know anyone named Marnie," Todd said.

"Now you do," Marnie answered. "And you know what? Until thirty seconds ago, I didn't know anyone named Todd. But now I do!"

"Really? That's cool!" Todd was clearly delighted with this information.

"Marnie is the church secretary, organist, choir director, organizer of weddings, baptisms, and funerals—usually in that order—and just generally our jill-of-all-trades," Ric said. "Her husband, Sam, is the jack-of-all-trades here. He does about anything that requires pounding a nail or sawing some wood. I'm afraid Pastor Mike and I are not very good at that kind of thing, so we rely on him. The three of you will be working together to get the day care set up."

"I'm really glad you two are here," the older woman said.

"Let's go upstairs," Ric said. "Say, Marnie, any word from Pastor Mike yet?"

"The last I heard, nothing had changed," Marnie said, her face saddening.

"Pastor Mike is the senior minister here," Ric explained to Lily. "His mother's been gravely ill, so he's been spending as much time as he can in Fargo with her. He's been trying to commute and get back here for Sunday services, but I don't know if he'll be able to keep that up."

Ric said a quick prayer for both the senior minister and his mother. His own parents lived in Florida, so he didn't see them as often as he'd like, but he knew how distraught he'd feel if either of them were ill.

"I was going to take Lily and Todd inside and show them around the church a little later on," Ric said to Marnie.

"I'm ready now," Lily said. "Actually, I'd like to get started as soon as possible."

The church office was a small room off the main entrance. Boxes spilled out from it into the hallway, and Ric noted Lily's questioning face.

"Donations. Folks from all over the world have poured their hearts into helping us. We've got volunteers sorting through those cartons."

A breeze blew in through the open window, stirring the leaves on the plants along the side of the desk.

"My poor babies," Marnie said. "These plants are straggling back to life. They didn't get watered during the flood since no one was here, naturally, but they're coming back, even though they look like green string right now." She lifted the thin leaves of the nearest plant and cooed at it sympathetically. "My darlings. But we're back now, and they'll get super care and grow up big and strong."

Ric's eyes met Lily's over Marnie's head, and they both grinned.

"I imagine they'll thrive," Lily said, "considering the love and care you give them."

"I don't think they have any choice," Ric said. "Once they're in Marnie's care, they have no choice except to live. Ladies, let's continue the grand tour. The headquarters of the day care operation is in the education wing. I set up an office there for you."

The room he led them to was even smaller than the office, and it was occupied by two gray folding chairs and a stack of files and a pencil and paper on a scratched brown metal table. He watched her as she glanced around what would be her work home.

He began to explain. "We got our power restored early, thanks to a church member who's an electrician. And I should explain that the part of the church where we have a day care set up didn't take water, since it's raised up a bit, so don't worry about the sewage. It didn't get there. And any lingering smell will be gone as soon as we do one more round of bleach."

"All because of the flood," she said, her voice low. "I just thought it was water in the houses, but everything is affected, isn't it?"

"It pretty well leveled all the services in town," Ric admitted.

"But the people I've seen so far—I mean, admittedly I only saw them in their yards—they were all so happy and open and friendly. How can they be like that?" She looked at him, her eyes pooling with tears.

Ric exchanged a quick glance with Marnie, who laid her hand on Lily's arm. "Lots of reasons. They're in the stages of grief right now, and they're on that 'we'll rise above this' level. It's a fantastic stage, when people are almost euphoric and banded together to achieve the goal of recovery."

"So it'll all vanish in a few weeks?"

"No, not necessarily," Ric responded quickly. "But other aspects will become superimposed and take precedence. They'll have to go through frustration and anger yet. Those are the ones that are difficult for the relief workers to deal with."

"Let's look at the day care, or what will soon be a day care. Right now it's basically a babysitting service," Marnie said. "It's just down the hall. You'll love it. It's wonderful."

Lily's face brightened when Ric opened the door of the day care.

It was a big, cheerfully decorated room filled with toys and games—and children. Todd's eyes lit up with delight. "Am I going to play here?"

"You sure are," Ric answered, and the boy ran to meet his new playmates.

A woman waved at them as she read a story to a circle of children. "That's Eileen."

"Will she stay on?" Lily asked.

"I hope so," Ric said, avoiding the question in his own heart: *Will Lily stay on?*

"The day care is housed here now," Marnie said. "This is technically our nursery, but it's making do. After the lower level dries out—and the smell is gone—we'll move it downstairs. It's a bit crowded in here, and it's too far away from the playground for our tastes."

"We can go down there later," said Ric. "It's still pretty messy on the lower level."

"I don't understand. Why would you put a day care in a basement?" Lily asked.

"It's not really a basement," he responded. "It's kind of a garden-level arrangement. It's in the little addition behind the original church, which is where we're standing now."

Her confusion showed on her face, and both Marnie and Ric laughed. "This old church has been through many renovations and additions in its lifetime," Marnie explained. "Luckily it's never been big enough to become a monstrosity."

"I think it's charming," Lily said. "I'd like to look through the files and get started right away, if it's okay with you."

Ric almost laughed. Nothing had ever been more okay with him!

❧

Lily straightened her back and rubbed the nape of her neck. One look at the clock told her why she was so stiff. She'd been bent over the files for nearly three hours.

The stories she'd seen there were the same odd mixture she'd seen at the Nanny Group. The heart-wrenching personal histories sat right next to, or sometimes were embedded into, the impersonal government documents that were nearly clinical in their language.

She inclined her head one more time and buried her face in her hands. What had she agreed to do? What did she know?

So many people were depending on her, and she had in front of her such a monstrously large task that she could easily fail. Did she have what it would take to do this job and see it through to the end?

"Dear Lord. . . ," she said aloud. She couldn't form the words to finish the prayer.

She realized after a moment that she was not alone in the room. She glanced up in surprise and saw Ric standing there.

"My mama taught me never to disturb a praying woman," he said.

He came into the room and perched on the edge of the table.

"Oh, looking through the files, huh? That bad?" He picked one up and leafed through it idly. "This project seems to have come to us gift-wrapped in red tape. If you can make your way through it, more power to you."

"It looks like the initial okay came through fairly quickly," she said.

"Well, it was because of the flood that we got permission to open so quickly. Let's face it: This place would never pass inspection, and even if it could, we don't know a thing about running a day care center."

"I'm not clear on one thing," she said. "Do you intend to keep this open on a permanent basis?"

He shrugged. "Right now we're living one day at a time, not out of choice but out of necessity. We've been toying with the idea, but to be honest, we haven't come to anything conclusive. Right now we're just concerned with getting up and running as legitimately as we can and as quickly as we can. We can operate on this emergency basis only so long. And we want to be able to provide the parents—and the children—with some kind of stability. Heaven knows they deserve some after everything they've been through."

A wry smile twisted the corners of his mouth. "Well, I get a bit passionate about this, in case you can't tell. It's just that my frustration level with bureaucracy goes sky-high."

"They do make you jump through a lot of hoops, I know that," Lily said.

"Sometimes I can't help but think they do it only to see if you'll jump," he said, a surprising edge of bitterness scraping his words.

She shook her head. "It seems like that, but I don't think that's it. You know, whenever I'd get frustrated while I was at the Nanny Group, I'd remind myself who and what was at stake: the children. And then everything puts itself right into perspective. I'd rather they made everyone jump through the hoops and then turn around and jump again, if that's what it took to ensure a good environment for the children."

He looked at her with those eyes as clear blue as a summer sky. "I hadn't thought of that," he acknowledged. "I really hadn't. But put that way, I have to admit it makes sense."

Lily toyed with her pen reflectively. "You do what you need to do to get through the day."

"Excuse me?"

She realized what she had said—and how much she had almost given away. "Nothing. Nothing. It didn't mean anything."

Ric eyed her speculatively. "If you say so. Well, what I'm here for is not to discuss governmental policies and regulatory practices. Say, you and Todd haven't had a chance to settle into your new home yet. Do you want to go to dinner tonight?"

"Yes! Yes!" Todd's voice answered enthusiastically from the door. "Let's go! Where are we going?"

"There aren't any restaurants open in town yet," Ric said. "So we'll have to drive about half an hour to get to anything. Star City has a great steak house, a pizza place that's good, and a little café that serves terrific hot beef sandwiches. Take your pick."

She looked at Todd, who was fairly bursting at the seams with impatience. "Hmmm. Which to choose, which to choose."

"Pizza! Pizza!" he shouted, jumping up and down.

She smiled at her son and then at Ric. "We'd be delighted to have pizza with you tonight."

～

And a delight it was. Pizza Wonderama was clean, the food was good, and above all, Todd was on his best behavior.

Ric grinned at her. "Don't you ever feed this boy?" he asked as Todd reached for his fourth large slice of pizza. "He hasn't even slowed down yet."

Lily ruffled her son's hair. "Feed him? What a novel idea. I could, I suppose. But that'll wreak havoc with my budget."

"Put him to work," Ric suggested, pretending to size Todd up and squeezing the boy's biceps. "He's pretty strong. He could probably build houses or something and bring in some extra cash."

Todd looked first at his mother, then at Ric, and back at his mother. "I'm too little to do that," he protested. "I can't work. I'm just a kid."

"We're teasing, tiger," Lily explained. "I'd never let you go to work building houses." She glanced at Ric and winked. "For one thing, you don't have a contractor's license."

"What's a contractor's license?" Todd asked, taking another bite of his pizza.

"It's a paper you need to build houses," she explained. "And since you don't have one, you'll just have to stay with me until school starts this fall. I'm sorry, son, but working is out."

He shook his head as if to say "Grown-ups!" and bent over his pizza again.

It seemed so natural, the three of them sitting there together. It was as if they'd always been together.

Lily thought more about it on the ride back to Wildwood in the evening twilight.

She'd occasionally worried about whether Todd missed having a father around. He'd never mentioned it, and it was true that with people she knew through work and church, he'd known many men who'd treasured him and treated him well.

But none of them, she reasoned, had the commitment that being a father would bring to the relationship. Did Todd miss it?

She wondered if there was a way to explore his mind a bit more and see if he was happy without a father. Although, she had to admit, there wasn't a lot she could do about it.

It wasn't like daddies—and husbands—grew on trees.

"Penny for your thoughts," Ric said as he pulled his car into the parking lot behind the church. Summer evenings stayed light long, and sunlight still washed across the trees.

She didn't dare tell him. Instead she said, "A penny? That's all?"

He chuckled. "Well, it is the going rate."

"I'll take the penny," Todd chimed in from the backseat, and they laughed.

"I'd better get this guy into a tub," Lily said. "Thanks, Ric. We had a great time."

Half an hour later, his bath taken, his pajamas on, they went into his new bedroom.

"Wow! Look at this!" Lily pulled down the cover on Todd's bed. "Race-car sheets!"

"Cool!" Todd jumped onto the bed and bounced experimentally. "I like this bed. I wonder who picked out the sheets. Ric, probably."

"Probably," she agreed. "Do you want me to listen to your prayers?"

"Nah," Todd answered. "I'm into saying them in my head now."

She ducked her head to hide her smile. "That's fine. Now go to sleep and have sweet dreams about all your new friends here in Wildwood."

She'd just turned off the light when he spoke again. "Mom?"

"Yes, sweetie?"

"Do you like Ric?"

She stopped, her hand frozen on the light switch. "Yes, Todd. I think he's very nice."

"Nice enough to kiss him?"

Her hand jerked, and the light came back on. "What on earth—?"

He grinned at her. "Just checking. I know you wouldn't kiss him. And he wouldn't kiss you either. No matter what."

Her heart flipped. "Why do you say that, Todd?"

His answer was short and to the point: "Cooties."

Chapter 4

She managed a brief laugh and said something meaningless that apparently satisfied her son because he settled into a quick sleep.

Kissing Ric? What on earth would he come up with next?

She couldn't make herself settle down. Too much had happened in such a short time, and through it all ran the image of Ric kissing her.

It was silly. She barely knew him.

But you were willing to totally change your life because of him, a little part of her mind pointed out, and she had to acknowledge that it was true. There was something about him that made her trust him—but that wasn't the same as wanting to kiss him.

The mobile home was comfortable, but the days at Shiloh had spoiled her. She hadn't realized before how much she missed the feel of fresh air on her skin. Now she was almost addicted to it.

Marnie had left a pair of canvas-backed chairs and a small table on the patch of dirt and scrubby grass by the door to the mobile home, and Lily transferred herself out there.

A breeze whispered through the deep green leaves of the elms that arched overhead. Lily had never heard anything as beautiful as that soughing sound. It was a balm on her heart, a heart that was beginning to come back to life once again.

This was the cool of the evening. The early summer warmth of the afternoon had given way to the soft comfort of a gentle zephyr that lifted her hair from her neck and invited her to relax. It was her favorite time of day.

"Mind if I join you?" Ric materialized from the gathering darkness.

"No, not at all. I'd welcome the company." She motioned toward the twin of the chair she occupied. "Working late tonight?"

He ran his hand through his hair. "Tonight and every night, to be honest. I don't know how being gone for one week to Shiloh can put me back three weeks here. That just doesn't fit into the time-space continuum I've always known and trusted."

The trees cast moving shadows across Ric's face, drawing her attention to the dark hollows under his eyes. He was clearly exhausted.

"It is one of the universe's greatest mysteries, I agree," she said lightly.

Ric smiled. "I may be stepping into dangerous waters here, but how do you like Wildwood so far? At least as much as you've seen of it?"

"I haven't seen much," she acknowledged. "Just basically the church, my

new home here, and Pizza Wonderama, but I'm enjoying all three of them."
A thought occurred to her that made her chuckle, and she shared it with Ric.
"Of course, for Todd that pretty well covers his basic needs. Church, home,
and pizza."

"He's a neat kid," Ric said.

They settled into a companionable silence, listening to the leaves rustle
overhead, the far-off sound of children's voices raised in late play, the faint
sounds of someone's radio.

"I like Wildwood," Ric said at last. "It's the kind of place a guy can settle
into, buy a house, raise a family. There's not much crime here either."

"I wonder why there seems to be so much crime in big cities and not
much in small towns," she mused. "Do you suppose it's just a matter of population? That per capita, it's the same?"

"I don't know. Could be. People are people wherever you go, that's for sure.
I suppose your chance of meeting a bad apple is just greater in a bigger barrel."

Well, Lily thought, *if there's a bad apple in* this *barrel, I'll manage to come across*
him. Although her logical side reminded her that simply because she'd had the
miserable luck to become involved with an apple that was rotten to the core in
Chicago didn't mean she was a bad-apple magnet. It was an unfortunate set of
circumstances, that was all.

But she summed it all up in a single noncommittal word: "Maybe."

"Are you planning to go back to Chicago eventually?" Ric asked.

"No!" The word shot out with more vehemence than she intended. "I
mean, I doubt it. For a while, anyway. Todd and I are enjoying not living in
the rat race."

He seemed to accept her unresponsive answer. She decided to snoop a bit
into his life. "So tell me, are you from Wildwood? I get the feeling this isn't
your original home."

"It isn't. I came to Wildwood about a year and a half ago."

"Really? Where were you before that?" Maybe she was a snoop at heart,
but Lily loved to hear people's life stories. And her instincts told her this
would be a very interesting story.

"Central America," he said. "And—"

The cellular phone attached to his belt buzzed into action, and after a
short conversation with the caller, Ric clipped it back into place and turned to
her apologetically. "That was a call from the hospital. Since Pastor Mike's not
here, I'd better go."

"Not bad news, I hope." She slid to the edge of her chair.

"No, not at all." He smiled. "Joy and Linus Alfson have just given birth to
two healthy baby boys. I call that very good news indeed."

He stood up and stretched. "It's a beautiful evening. Look! A firefly!"

It was all she could do not to clap her hands in wonder. She hadn't seen a
firefly since she was a child.

Ric paused and watched it flit around in the advancing darkness under the shelter of the trees, its light blinking off and on. "You know," he said at last, "when I was a child, I believed that fireflies were angels."

Lily laughed. "I can understand that. They're so incredible that having them be angels is the only good explanation."

"I'd also wonder what they were doing. After all, an angel is supposed to have a message, I thought, and it occurred to me one evening that if I could just discover what they were up to, I'd have it all figured out. Break their code and all that."

"Did it work?" She couldn't resist asking him the question.

"Only partially."

"Really? Partially? What did you learn?"

"That fireflies talk to fireflies and not to Ric Jensen. It was a massive let-down at the time, but I lived through it."

"I'm surprised you didn't become a scientist," Lily commented.

"I did in a way, I guess. Only now I look at the universe and marvel at it openly." He flashed a grin at her. "Don't get me started on snowflakes, or I'll talk your ears clean off your body."

"I'll remember that when winter comes."

"Speaking of snow, Wildwood in winter is beautiful. I hope you'll still be here then," he said, sounding almost bashful.

"We'll see when winter comes," she said, but she had to admit that if there were a place for her to put down roots and build a future for Todd, this was probably as close to the perfect spot as anything she'd ever find. She'd only been in Wildwood a day and already it was home.

"Come winter, you'll have plenty of snow," he said. "But I'd better not say any more for fear of scaring you away."

"I'm from North Dakota, you know," she answered. "I grew up in Mandan, and my mother still lives there."

"Mandan, huh? Right next to Bismarck."

"They're both wonderful places. And both quite snowy in the winter."

"That's true. Well, I need to visit the Alfson twins. There's nothing like holding a baby to make a day end well. Two babies, actually. The only bad part is, I have to give them back."

"You don't have children, I gather." She pulled a blade of grass from the ground at her feet and twisted it into a knot.

"No, I don't. No wife, no children. Not even a goldfish. Someday the Lord will lead me to them, but I suspect He might start with the goldfish."

He left, but Lily made no motion to go inside. It was so pleasant to sit out here and let the breeze play across her face.

She shut her eyes and thought about what lay ahead of her. What she'd seen in the files was enough to galvanize her into action.

Day care seemed to be at the basis of so many lives, especially now. People couldn't work if they couldn't leave their children in reliable hands, and without work there was no income.

Where would she start? Where *could* she start?

Lord, I need Your help again. Please guide me through these uncharted waters.

She didn't want to let these wounded people down. They were relying on her, and she had to see it through to the end.

Her prayer came to an end. She couldn't put words around the idea. But He would know, wouldn't He, what was in her heart?

She opened her eyes, and as she stood to go into the mobile home and try to get some sleep, she looked down.

There, on her dress over her heart, was a firefly twinkling out a message. Maybe she wasn't a scientist, but she knew what the message was.

Prayer heard.

Lily watched the firefly as it paused a moment longer before taking flight. As it flew higher and higher into the trees, she smiled.

God was probably glad that she was trying to help His friends. Todd was right about that.

Her soul felt much lighter as she got ready for bed, and in those moments before sleep overtakes wakefulness entirely, one last thought floated through, uncensored.

What would it take to convince Ric that she didn't have cooties?

❧

Ric leaned against the elevator as it took him from the maternity floor to the lobby. He was tired beyond belief—but the babies were beautiful, and the parents were glowing with happiness.

There was something about babies that sang of possibility and hope. It was the promise of the future, the golden cord that pulled them through each day into the next.

One day he'd be guiding these two children through confirmation classes, taking them on mission trips, and praying them through the first tentative steps of adolescence.

His heart spoke to him, delivering a message he'd been suppressing for months—no, for years. It wasn't what he wanted to hear, but in this moment of exhaustion, the unspoken words poured through, undeniable, unstoppable.

He wanted a child. He wanted to be a father.

But first things came first. That was the way it was. The first thing was to find a woman, fall in love, and get married. Or was that three things? His mind was so blurred that he couldn't make sense of it.

It had begun with the last mission trip he'd taken before coming to Wildwood. A Central American orphanage, where poverty, hunger, and need were reflected in the luminous eyes of the children, had etched itself firmly into his heart.

He'd committed himself to not letting those faces leave his soul.

One day, he'd promised himself, he would give one of those children a home where *want* wasn't on the menu every day. One day. . .one day.

Fast-forward from the orphanage to a woman kneeling in the parking lot, a small boy at her side, and holding a ladybug on her fingertip so it could fly away home—the image came to him and would not leave.

For the moment, the youth of Resurrection had to be his major concern, his only concern.

He rubbed his hands over his face. He needed sleep. But could anything protect him from his dreams?

ᕈ

"Is your afternoon free?" Marnie asked Lily.

Lily flipped her appointment calendar open. She had been in Wildwood almost a week, and each of those days had been satisfyingly busy.

"At this point, it sure is. Just paperwork, paperwork, and more paperwork," she answered cheerfully. "Why? What's up?"

"Victoria Campbell will be in later today." Marnie's demeanor had changed somehow, but Lily couldn't put her finger on exactly what it was. "Can you possibly see her?"

"I suppose I can," Lily replied. "Who is Victoria Campbell?"

Marnie's posture told her this was important, so Lily closed the file and gave the older woman her full attention.

"Victoria Campbell owns Wedding Belles," Marnie said, fairly bristling now with disapproval.

Lily nodded. "I'm sorry. You've got me at a disadvantage here. What is Wedding Belles?"

"Oh, I'm sorry." Marnie came into the room and perched on the edge of Lily's desk. "Wedding Belles is where everybody who's anybody goes when they're fixing to get married. It's very hoity-toity, very posh."

"In other words, very expensive?" Lily asked.

"Oh, yes indeedy." Marnie's face began to redden with indignation. "I can't believe she'd come here and ask for our help. Her, of all people."

"What kind of help?"

"Day care. Her little darling, Edgar, needs a place to go while Victoria redoes her suite."

"Redoes?" Lily felt like a duck pouncing on a June bug. "What do you mean? Did she have flood damage?"

"Well, I'm sure she did. We all did. There isn't a house or business in this town, except those way out on that new northeast side development, that didn't take water."

"So what's the problem, Marnie? What am I not seeing here?" She spoke slowly and carefully. From what she'd seen of Marnie, she wasn't the kind of person to go off on a wild whim. No, there was some reason under all this that was making Marnie upset.

Marnie straightened her back. "It borders on gossip, Lily. I'm not sure what I should tell you about what she did to us here."

"Does it have anything to do with the day care?" Lily asked.

Marnie shook her head with determination. "No. Absolutely not."

Lily rubbed her forehead. This was not an auspicious start. "Perhaps this is one time when I should be left in the dark."

The church secretary seemed to weigh Lily's words, and at last she nodded. "That makes sense. If you do decide you need some gaps filled in, though, I'll help you." She stopped and bit her lip before continuing. "I will say this, however. There's no love lost between that woman and me, not after the shenanigans she pulled here, so don't be surprised if I'm not her biggest cheerleader."

Lily patted the woman's hand. "I understand. I've known people like that. But if I'm going to make this day care succeed in the spirit we intend for it to, I need to not let those kinds of things bother me."

Marnie sighed. "I know. But it's hard, this always trying to be like Jesus." She stood up and walked out the door, pausing to grumble. "Though personally, I think if He'd known Victoria Campbell, even His patience might have been tried."

Oh, Lily thought, *it's going to be an interesting day!*

She turned back to the file and was soon immersed in the paper trail of objectives and permissions.

But soon something wonderful wafted toward her office and into her senses. Before she could form the idea of what exactly the source of the delicious smell was, Ric poked his head in the door.

"Hungry?"

He held in his hands a familiar red-and-white-striped bucket from which emanated the aroma of fried chicken. Her mouth immediately began watering, and she nodded.

"Then follow me," Ric invited and led her back into the church office where Marnie had set up a folding table and laid out the plastic forks and paper napkins.

The three of them sat down, and Ric blessed the food with a familiar grace that Lily recognized as being the same one they'd used for dinners at Shiloh.

As they dug into the fried chicken, they discussed the morning's events. Ric told of the twins he'd seen the night she'd arrived, and then again this morning. "Joy says the doctor says they're perfectly healthy, even if they are a bit smaller than usual."

"How much did they weigh?" Marnie asked, wiping her face with a napkin. "This is great chicken."

"How much did the chicken weigh or the twins?" Ric teased. "Well, to be honest, she told me, but I don't remember. But they're little, about, oh, this size." He held up his hands first six inches apart, then ten, then eight, and then gave up. "They're little."

Marnie shook her head. "Honestly, Ric."

"Sorry," he said, looking sheepish. "So, in an obvious attempt to change the subject, Lily, how's it going?"

"I'm beginning to get a picture of the history of the day care," Lily reported. "It looks like everything is in order, at least as near as I can tell at this point. I've got a call in to the fellow who's overseeing this in Bismarck, and when he gets back to me, I can start to move along faster."

"Sounds great!" Marnie said.

"How's our enrollment?" Ric asked.

"Well, we're at max," the secretary reported. "And that's looking to be a problem down the line. Very shortly down the line, as a matter of fact."

Ric laid down the piece of chicken he was eating and looked at Marnie. "What do you mean?" he asked her. "What kind of problem?"

"People still need day care. Some need it on a part-time basis, some on a full-time basis. So far I've been juggling it, offering one person half a week and another person half a week, so at least they have something, but that's always been a temporary fix. Folks need to get back to their jobs." Marnie looked as if she might break into tears. "I don't know what else I can do."

"Why don't you let me work with it?" Lily asked. "I can call Bismarck and see if we can get a temporary raise in the number of children we can tend."

Ric turned and looked at her. She had his total attention. "Do you think they'll let you do that? Can we take in more children?"

"I don't know," she confessed. "I'd like to say yes, but the fact is, they're concerned about the children's well-being and their safety, and that does mean a lower ratio of children to provider."

"What if we could offer more providers?" He looked at Marnie. "We've got Eileen, but we probably could get some of the church members to help out."

"Well," Lily said, "possibly. But it keeps circling back to whether they think that would be in the children's best interests. And in this case, maybe yes, maybe no. We'd just have to see."

"How soon would you be able to find out?" he asked eagerly.

"I'm not sure who the person is that I'd talk to," she said. "I suppose if I can talk to the right person, we could know this afternoon."

Ric leaned back and smiled. "That would be utterly fantastic!"

"But"—she held up a warning finger—"that is just spoken permission. I'd like us to wait for the written okay unless the official gives the go-ahead to take more children without that."

"And how long would that take?"

"A couple of days."

"It'd better be soon," Marnie said. "I don't know how much longer Lily can wait on this."

"Oh, surely a couple of days would be all right," Ric said easily. "What harm could be in that?"

"What harm? What harm?" Marnie pushed her chair back with such vehemence that it screeched across the wooden floor. "Do you know who called this morning looking for day care? Do you know? You don't know, do you! It's that woman, that awful, awful woman."

Ric shook his head in confusion. "Who are you talking about?"

A waft of aromatic and clearly expensive perfume joined that of the fried chicken. And from the door of the office a throaty voice answered, "I believe she's talking about me."

Chapter 5

The group of three froze for an instant and then whirled in unison to gape at the speaker who stood in the doorway to the office, her back erect and her chin held high with just a hint of haughtiness.

"Victoria, welcome," Ric said, leaping to his feet and pulling out a folding chair. "Come join us."

She managed a polite smile before shaking her head slightly. "I don't believe so, but thank you for asking me."

Lily tried not to stare at the woman. She was a vision in white and gold, two colors that had always appealed to Lily as the epitome of wealth, more so after Todd was born and anything white became a luxury.

Especially when the white was white linen. Lily had owned only one linen thing in her entire life—a tan A-line dress—and it had the most amazing property of wrinkling when she was standing still. If she were to sit in it, or even wear it while driving, the slightest wrinkle became a deep, abiding crease. She'd always felt as if she looked like she had just crawled out of a laundry bag when she wore it.

But Victoria's white linen suit was unwrinkled. The gold accents at her neck, ears, and wrists looked real. Her matching golden hair, however, Lily was sure was not. At least the color wasn't. Perhaps the hair was.

She was pretty, in a brittle sort of way. Underneath the thick application of black mascara that weighed down her eyelashes were eyes the color of rich chocolate. Lily stood up and walked over to the door. "I'm Lily Chamberlain," she said. "It's nice to meet you. I believe we had an appointment this afternoon, and if you'll let me tidy myself up a bit, we can get right down to it."

Victoria's eyes flashed uneasily from Lily to Ric and then Marnie. "Are we meeting in here?"

"No, I have an office closer to the day care. Why don't you come with me, and we can talk down there?" Lily tried not to look at Ric and Marnie, although she knew their expressions would be telling.

Victoria's impression of Lily's office was clear from her expression. She obviously had been expecting it to be something on a grander scale, but she graciously took a seat in the folding chair Lily offered.

"What can I help you with?" she asked the woman who sat poised on the folding chair.

"I need day care for my son."

"That's what we're here for." Lily opened the drawer on her desk and withdrew a file from which she took a paper. "First we need to have you fill out this application. Here's a pen—"

Victoria Campbell shoved the pen and the application away and smiled winningly at Lily. "Do I really need to go through all this paperwork? Surely not. Can't I just bring Edgar in?"

"Edgar is your son?"

Victoria nodded, and briefly the mask of sophistication fell from her face. Lily saw there pure love for her little boy. "He's six. And no trouble at all."

"I'm sure he isn't," Lily responded. "But the fact is that the state requires these papers to be filled out."

"Oh, it'll be fine. I'll bring Edgar around nine tomorrow morning." Victoria started to pick up her purse.

"Edgar can't stay here without the paperwork," Lily said. "It'll only take you a few minutes to fill it out. I'll help you."

The blond woman picked up the application and put it in her purse. "I'll take it with me and fill it out at home tonight. Then tomorrow when I drop off Edgar, I'll leave this application, too."

"Mrs. Campbell—" Lily began, but the woman interrupted her.

"Please call me Victoria. Everyone else does."

"Victoria, I cannot stress to you enough how important this particular sheet is." Lily tapped the file folder. "We can't take every child who needs day care, unfortunately, and we use this as a screening device."

"Screening? How?" Victoria edged closer to Lily's desk.

"We have to establish a hierarchy of need. For example, if a person might lose her job because she needs to go back to work and her prior day care is closed, that would give her priority. Or if there's a health concern while a home is being sanitized. Income is also a factor in determining who we select."

"Income? How?" Victoria leaned forward toward Lily even more.

"Well, if the parents' bank account is fairly well depleted, then they clearly don't have the resources to hire private care. But if there's a regular income that's not been affected by the disaster, then we have to take that into consideration."

Victoria seemed to consider what Lily had said. Then she said, "How public is this information? No one sees it except you?"

"I can't promise that. If there is an investigation of some kind by a governmental body, such as a licensing board, then our records would be opened to them. But even so, they are not supposed to share the information they find there. Does that answer your question?"

Victoria shrugged. Even that little motion seemed so elegant when she did it. "Locally, though, how private is this information?"

"Again, no one would see it except those involved with the operation of the day care, and even then, not the actual providers, aside from basic necessary information, such as contact phones, medical data, and so on."

"What about here?"

"Here?" Clearly Victoria was searching for something specific, but Lily wasn't sure what it was.

"Here. In the church. Who would see it here?"

"Oh!" Suddenly light dawned. She was checking on how secure the financial and personal data was being kept here.

"Again, no one unconnected with the day care would know."

"What about Marnie? And Ric? Would they have access to my application?"

"I don't see why they would. The only reason they might be able to see it would be if, say, I were ill and one of them had to review it. Other than that, no, I can't say that they would. But nevertheless, even if they saw the application, they would not share the information on it with anyone else."

"Would not or could not?"

"I'm sorry. I don't see where this is going." This conversation was getting way out of hand. "If you want to have Edgar come to the day care, you have to fill out one of these applications. That's the bottom line."

Victoria's eyes became hooded. "I can't do that. I need this to be off the record."

A flash of anger rose in Lily's chest. She would not compromise her standards. Especially not after what she had been through in Chicago.

"No application, no day care," was Lily's blunt answer. "No ifs, ands, or buts. That's it. I don't care if you're the empress of China, you don't get day care here unless you fill out the application."

"Okay, I'll do it." Victoria snatched up the application. "I'll fill the stupid thing out. Anything to get Edgar in a day care."

"Well, we have a second problem," Lily said. "The day care is full. I'm hoping—"

Victoria slammed the pen down on the desk so hard it rolled across the surface and onto the wooden floor and kept rolling until it came to rest under a baseboard heater. "They got to you, didn't they?"

"Who got to me?"

"Marnie. And Ric. I don't trust either one of them. They told you the whole story, didn't they? Well, it's *not* the whole story. Not by a long shot. But I'm not going to tell you any of the story because I'm sick of it."

She stood up and walked to the door, but not before Lily stopped her.

"Wait a minute. I don't know what you're talking about. All I know is that you own the wedding place in town, and that's it. Even if there were some kind of history between you and Marnie and Ric, that's between the three of you. It doesn't have anything to do with me, and unless it has something to do with the day care, I don't give a rip about what happened in the past."

Victoria Campbell stood there, motionless, as if pondering something important. For a moment, neither woman spoke. And then Victoria turned and looked at Lily with tears pooled in her eyes. "I wish I could believe that. I want to believe that. But—"

And with those enigmatic words, she spun around and walked out the door.

Lily stared at the now-vacant doorway. What on earth had that been all about?

She recovered the pen that had disappeared under the heater and sat back down at the desk. Obviously Victoria had something on her mind, something of major importance to her. But Lily had no idea what that might be.

Ric knocked on the jamb of her open door. Although he looked at her curiously, he didn't pursue the situation with Victoria. Instead, he handed her a pile of envelopes. "Mail call."

She leafed through them. One of them bore her name, and she opened it. Her stomach tightened as she read it.

"Bad news?" Ric asked, his forehead wrinkling with concern.

How could she explain it? How could she tell him why this single letter renewed her anxiety without telling him the whole tawdry story about the Nanny Group?

"It's a letter from the state licensing board. They want a copy of my résumé, plus this application filled out and returned. And I need three references, too." She stared at the paper. The black letters swam in and out of focus.

"So?" Ric shrugged. "That should be a no-brainer for you. Is it a deadline problem? Mail's been a bit erratic since the flood, but it hasn't been too wildly slow. Is that the problem?"

She shook her head. "No. It's nothing, really." She looked up at him and tried to smile. "Nothing to worry about."

"Good." Ric stood up. "Want to join me for dinner again tonight?"

Her smile trembled and almost refused to stay put. "I think we'll pass. Todd and I need to get settled in tonight, so I think we'll eat at home."

Home. It had such a comforting ring to it. Even if her home was a little mobile home parked outside a church in a flood-ravaged community.

But she knew that all she had to have was her son and her Lord with her, and wherever she was, she was home.

That's what her heart told her. If only her brain could believe it.

❧

Ric stood at the stove in his apartment, mindlessly stirring the chili he'd taken from the refrigerator.

Victoria Campbell's appearance had put a crimp in his day, that was for sure. In a town the size of Wildwood, it was nearly impossible to stay invisible, so he'd certainly seen her in the past year.

The woman had caused more dissatisfaction among the congregation than anyone he'd ever known. He wasn't totally sure what had happened, or why, although he'd heard variations on a single theme: She had, in some way, created problems within the church. Whatever it was had come before his arrival in Wildwood.

Marnie knew the story, and he was sure that if he ever had to hear a straightforward version of it, he could ask her. But the situation seemed to have resolved itself—or at least subsided into ancient history—until today when it had reappeared.

Lily hadn't told him what had happened, but she seemed to have dealt with it. Should he have said something to her? What would he have said?

Besides, Victoria Campbell seemed to come with her own variation of a flashing red light on her head, signaling *warning*. Some people simply had the ability to make others not like them—and aggressively so.

Victoria was one of those women.

She had quit coming to Resurrection shortly after he'd arrived. As the youth minister, he'd tried to contact her about her son, Edgar, and to ask her to keep Edgar at Resurrection if she chose not to have another church home, but she had refused his calls.

Now she was back.

Lily seemed up to the task of dealing with Victoria, but he needed to be ready to support her if necessary. He didn't know Victoria well, just enough to be aware that she had a strong personality.

Well, if Lily needed him, he would definitely be at her side.

He stood over the pan, spoon in hand, lost in that thought, until the sound of the chili furiously simmering interrupted his reverie.

He frowned at the bubbling concoction on the stove, and he turned off the burner. If he planned to eat the chili soon, he'd better not have it boiling.

Pay attention, Jensen, or you'll have the place on fire.

The last thing he needed was to burn down his apartment.

He took the pan off the heat and ladled steaming chili into a green and white bowl. Yes, he had to focus on the other issues at hand. And there were many.

❧

After dinner Todd settled down with a handheld game, and she sat at the kitchen table and studied what the agency was asking of her.

A résumé. She could do that. And, she supposed, she'd have to include the Nanny Group on it. It was, after all, what had enabled her to get this position in Wildwood and start a new life.

How could anything be such a bane and a blessing at the same time? It was through the Nanny Group that she had discovered how she wanted to proceed through her life.

Her parents had raised her with the strong principle that she should live her life as a form of service. This, they had taught her, was the highest form of praise, returning to the Maker what He had given you with more.

God had given her an intense love of caring for children. It was, she had known from her own childhood, what she was meant to do in life.

With a sigh, she turned back to the materials she needed to fill out.

The employment history was going to be the most difficult. *Reason for leaving.* What would she say?

"Discovered massive wrongdoing"? "Identified top-level illegal activities"? "Ran for my life"?

Lily frowned at the form. She opted for a noncommittal "Career realignment." That was the truth. It was vague and very true, and she hoped it would satisfy whoever examined the applications.

If asked, she could explain that Chicago was not the environment she wanted to raise her son in. That was true. She'd already seen him blossoming under the care Resurrection offered, and tonight at dinner he'd chattered happily about his new friends.

Plus the advantage of having him in the same building where she worked was a blessing. Ric and Marnie had managed to save a place for him when one child's family moved away from Wildwood, so the transition to his new home was smooth and seamless.

The next question brought her up hard against the cold reality of what she'd left in Chicago. *May we contact this employer?*

Was Douglas Newton aware of her knowledge of the situation at the Nanny Group? That was a big unknown. She hadn't said anything to him about it. And, on the record, she'd simply left to return to North Dakota to be near her mother.

But he'd suspected something. She could tell by the way he studied her when he thought she wasn't watching. And she knew he'd rifled through her papers one evening after she'd gone because the next day her "to-do" pile was mixed with her "to-file" pile. She was meticulous about those things, the result of not having her own secretary, and it was obvious he'd been looking for something.

She'd been foolish in not duplicating or saving incriminating documents on a jump drive, but she'd been so anxious to get out of there that she had simply given her two weeks' notice and tried to work ahead far enough that the agency was not impaired by her loss.

He'd watched her like a hawk at work, and even at home she didn't feel safe. Sometimes in her home, the faintest waft of cigarette smoke would materialize and vanish just as quickly, as if someone who smoked heavily had been there.

Only now did she piece together that part of the puzzle.

Newton always smelled like cigarettes, the victim of his habit. He'd never be so foolish as to smoke in her house, but the smell was there, perhaps the residue of old smoke from his clothes.

Had he been in her condo in Chicago? The thought made her skin creep. She was safe here in Wildwood, she told herself. For one thing, she lived in the shadow of a church. What could be safer? A bed in the police station?

Ric's image floated in front of her tired eyes. She could feel herself being drawn to him. Was this part of God's plan for her, too? A part of her almost begged for the answer to be yes. He was a good man, she could tell that.

But she had to resist the urge to let that relationship develop. She had to work through the problems left by her encounter with the Nanny Group. At the very least, she owed it to whomever she might begin a lifetime relationship with. It wasn't fair to go into a new life together with the specter of that hanging over her head.

The Nanny Group had to be put into the past, where it belonged. And maybe, just maybe, this was her opportunity to do something about taking care of it. Maybe this application that was giving her fits was a way of taking her through the trauma and into the light.

Nevertheless, before she turned off the lights for the evening, the application still lying unfinished on the table, she tiptoed into Todd's room.

He sprawled across the bed, one arm thrown across his bear. His mouth was open slightly, and as she leaned closer, she could hear the steady rhythm of a faint, even snore.

Lily smoothed back his hair and smiled. Whatever else had happened in her life, this was the one immutable fact of God's existence, right here before her.

She kissed him, and he stirred slightly.

"Thank You, God," she whispered. "Thank You."

Chapter 6

"Did you get that application figured out?" Ric asked her cheerily the next morning.

Lily smiled and waved. Actually, she hadn't finished it. It was back inside her briefcase, right on top, a pen clipped to it, ready to go. She had it all set so she could start on it as soon as she went into her office and sat down.

Maybe a change in environment would help.

She'd even gotten up early and sat down at the table with a cup of freshly brewed coffee, intending to finish the application. But she couldn't make herself fill it out. Answering the questions seemed about as easy as climbing Mount Everest in high heels.

Marnie called out a hello to her as she walked with great efficiency down to her office. Yes indeed, nothing would stop her once she got there.

Nothing except everything. She couldn't do it. The application still lay on her desk, the same blanks still unanswered, when Ric came to get her for lunch. She shoved it into her top drawer and turned her attention to him.

"I thought we'd have lunch with the day care today," Ric said. "That way you can get a good idea of what's going on in there, both as a mother and as coordinator of the child-care site."

Eileen, the child-care provider, greeted them when they walked in. Every night, Todd came home with happy stories about Eileen, who knew more finger plays than any other human being.

"Go ahead and have a seat at those tables over there," Eileen said. "We'll be eating in—whoa!"

Todd ran into the group of adults at full speed. "Mom! Mom! Hey, everybody, this is my mom!"

Lily found herself surrounded by a cluster of small children, all looking at her curiously.

Lily knelt down to eye level with the children, who moved in even closer. "Hello, everyone! My name is Lily."

A young blond girl touched Lily's hair. "I like that name. Lily. Are you named after the Easter flowers? We have them in church every Easter." She frowned. "Except maybe this one, on account of the flood. We missed Easter, sort of."

"No, we didn't," interrupted another child. "The flood wasn't until after Easter."

The little girl smiled shyly at Lily. "Then maybe we didn't miss it, and I just forgot about it. I think I maybe remember it now. I had a new pink dress with a swirly thing in my hair."

Lily hugged the girl. "I bet you looked very pretty. I'd like to see that dress sometime."

Her smile evaporated. "I don't have the dress anymore. It went away with the flood."

"My mom will make you a new dress," Todd volunteered. "And a swirly thing for your hair, too."

Lily laughed out loud. "Todd, you nut. I can't sew anything. I'm not a seamstress, I'm a seam-less. Don't offer me up for anything more complicated than sewing a button back on!"

She turned back to the girl. "What's your name, honey?"

"Corie."

"Corie, I'm very sorry you lost your dress in the flood. It sounds beautiful, right down to the swirly thing for your hair. Next Easter I'm sure you'll have a dress that is just as pretty, and you know why?"

Corie shook her head.

"Because you'll be inside it. No matter what your dress will look like, you will make it beautiful."

Corie smiled and turned to Todd. "I like your mommy. She's really nice."

Eileen returned with lunch trays, which she wheeled in on a cart. "Okay, everybody, have a seat. Yes, Todd, you may sit by your mother."

The food was delicious. Lily and Ric got larger portions of the meatballs and vegetables, although Todd warned them not to expect extra desserts. "Eileen lets us have more of everything except dessert," he said in a loud whisper. "And today it's cherry bubbles, so I know we won't get seconds."

"What's cherry bubbles?" she asked.

"I don't know," he said. "But it's good and don't ask for more."

"Is Ric your daddy?" the little boy across the table from Todd asked.

Todd shrugged innocently and continued to chase a meatball around his plate. "Not yet."

Ric's eyes flashed over to meet Lily's, and she almost laughed at the cornered expression on his face.

Eileen intervened again with the arrival of the dessert Todd had been anxiously awaiting. Lily was relieved to see that "cherry bubbles" when translated into adult English meant "cherry cobbler."

The much-loved "cherry bubbles" diverted the children's attention, but it didn't do much to settle her heart.

❦

Ric walked back to the office with Lily.

"I think I need to apologize for Taylor," he said. "He's the kind of kid who thinks something and then says it."

"Taylor is the one who asked if you were going to be Todd's dad, I gather."

Just the thought of it made his breath catch in his chest, but he pushed it aside. The time had come to broach the question that had been nagging at him. It wasn't any of his business, but he wanted to know. He needed to know. "Todd has a father, of course."

"Well, Todd *had* a father. He died before I even knew I was pregnant." Her face was unreadable.

"Oh, I'm sorry," he said, automatically reaching out to touch her arm.

She smiled at him, and it was like the sun breaking through clouds. "I appreciate it. If he gets too clingy, just let me know and I'll try to pry him off you."

He laughed. "Oh, I don't think that would be a problem."

"If you heard how often your name comes up in his conversations—Ric says this, Ric said that—you wouldn't dismiss this so blithely. He really thinks the world of you."

His heart beat a bit faster. "I'm honored, really I am."

"As a youth minister, you're probably used to it though, aren't you?"

"Well, I don't exactly have a fan club, but so far none of them have started an I-Hate-Ric group—at least not that I know of."

Lily leaned a bit closer and in a conspiratorial whisper asked him, "So do you think we were wise to be seen in public, having lunch together? In front of the children?"

"What were we thinking?" He made light of it, but he knew what he'd been thinking—his thoughts were filled with what a loving mother she was, how her voice was low and melodic, and how her perfume smelled so good, like flowers and clean clothes and vanilla cake.

Lily leaned even closer so that her hair brushed against his cheek. "We were thinking of cherry bubbles."

"Ah," he said. "That explains it all."

After she went to her tiny office, he stood in the hallway then headed into the sanctuary. He sank onto his knees, his head on his folded hands, and poured out his heart to his Lord.

When he rose several minutes later, he knew he had to slow his heart. Lily was a wonderful woman, and Todd was a charming child, but he was an ordinary man whose days and nights were given to the Lord's service. Maybe in time it would come, but for now the message he had received told him to move carefully.

Again. The message was the same as it had been at the orphanage: Not now. Not yet.

There would be time for love, if it came to that end. But for now the answer was no.

❧

At last it was done. Lily stood at the mailbox, the sealed envelope in her hand,

and she simply opened the slot and dropped the application in.

After much thought, prayer, and an incredibly long sleepless night, she had summoned all her courage and checked YES, giving the agency permission to check her references.

After all, she realized, this would give her the answer she'd been agonizing over. If Douglas Newton stood in her way, at least she knew what she was up against and could take appropriate steps, whatever those might be. At the moment, she didn't want to think about it.

On the other hand, her worries might be for naught. He may have simply considered her nothing more than a fly speck on the ledger.

Life became too busy for her to think about much of anything else except the day care and Todd. Even Ric was delegated to a tiny corner of her mind, pushed far into the back where he wouldn't be any trouble to her as she concentrated on what she was doing at the moment.

Ric continued to stop by her office—although that was strictly business, she told herself. He hadn't asked for her and Todd to join him for dinner again—perhaps he was being cautious now that she had told him about how Todd had elevated him in his mind.

Whatever she wrote on the application seemed to have worked. Approval was returned immediately, and she felt herself relax, even allowing herself to go up and sit with Marnie for a coffee break.

Pastor Mike was back weekly for short visits, and she felt comfortable with the portly minister immediately. He was jovial, and Lily's heart went out to him as she realized what a burden he was bearing at the moment, yet willing to take the time to make her feel comfortable.

July sped past in a flurry of fireworks on the banks of the now-tamed river, picnics in the park, and files and more files on her desk. Late one August night, Lily and Todd drove through Wildwood's residential streets. The rubbish heaps were long gone, and the grass had grown back in places where the debris had been piled. Inside the houses, the bare basement walls, stripped of the flood-damaged drywall, had dried enough to begin reconstruction. Homeowners had been advised to wait several weeks to let the walls and floors dry out completely before rebuilding, and a number of the houses were done already.

"Look, Mom!" Todd pointed to a small brick house with a FOR SALE sign on it. "Let's buy it!"

"Oh Todd, we can't buy a house." Her mouth spoke the words, but her heart agreed with her son. She'd never fallen in love with a house quite as quickly as this.

"Why not?"

"Well, because we're not here forever. Just long enough to do our work."

"And then what, Mom?"

His question brought her back to reality. And then what?

"I don't know." She looked at his face and saw the uncertainty settle back in again. She relented and pulled over to the side of the road. "Let's get out and take a look."

The house was empty, and through the curtainless windows, she saw a fireplace with a mantel, perfect for placing those family photographs that she treasured. And the bedrooms were large enough for their needs, and the kitchen was spacious and airy.

She knew she couldn't leave it without learning more. She wrote down the Realtor's name.

"I'm not promising anything, Todd," she said, "because there are lots of reasons we wouldn't buy it. It might be too expensive, or it might have some major problems we can't see from out here, like a bad foundation. And I don't know—"

A swing. There was a swing in the backyard. Not one of those little aluminum jobs, but a full-bore, heavy-duty thing, like the one at Shiloh. Her mind re-created the image from the camp, and she realized that in the swing she was picturing Ric.

As she got back into the car and drove back to the mobile home, listening with only half her mind to Todd's chattering, she realized there was one part of her that was coming to life again.

It was the part that imagined, that thought about the future, that spun hopes into dreams.

She'd gone to Chicago with dreams. She could help these young mothers, she knew it. She felt it in her bones and in her blood, and it pulled her and pushed her through days when she thought she couldn't go any further but she did.

And those dreams had flourished, and she had felt good about herself. Then one day, it all came down around her head like a house of cards.

She'd gone into Douglas's office, looking for a file that perhaps he'd taken from her desk, and when she opened it and saw what he had done, it was as if all the oxygen was taken from her body. She'd had to sit down to avoid falling.

The file was that of a young woman whose schooling required her to be at the college at night twice a week. Because the woman's daughter was so young, Lily had asked for and received permission to qualify the woman for an additional night of assistance so she could go to the library and leave her daughter with a well-qualified babysitter.

The woman had only used the extra night of service once, but in front of her Lily saw vouchers dating back six or seven weeks—and all with the initials L.C. on them.

Yet she hadn't even seen these vouchers. They certainly hadn't been in the file when she'd had it on her desk earlier in the day.

With shaking hands, she'd replaced the file and checked the other ones. And in each case, there were vouchers, all apparently initialed by her and filled out in her handwriting.

There was only one possibility. Douglas Newton was forging them. She and Douglas were the only people in the office. No one else had access to the files.

She'd checked the paper trail of the payments and found that the checks had been issued to a single babysitter, someone named Tammy Novak. Yet in her care-providers file, there was no one by that name.

When Douglas came back, he looked at her curiously. Her face must have given something away because he went into his office and shut the door. When he emerged a short while later, he asked if anything had happened while he was out.

Oh, not much except for the world caving in, she'd thought, but instead she'd just said, "No."

"Mom? Mom?" Todd was shaking her elbow. "Can we? Please?"

"Can we what, honey?"

"Can we get some ice cream at the Bright Spot?" He looked at her pleadingly.

The Bright Spot was owned by Marnie's husband, Sam, and Todd adored him as much as he did Marnie. It had reopened just in time for the late summer heat to bring in a raft of customers.

"Sure. An ice cream cone sure would feel good on a hot night like this."

Both Sam and Marnie were at the Bright Spot, and Todd rushed to them with open arms for hugs.

"Guess what! Guess what!" he shouted at them. "We're going to buy a house, and it's got a big gigantic swing set, like at Shiloh, and there's a fireplace, and a yard big enough to plant carrots in and everything!"

Marnie looked at her with delight. "That's wonderful news, Lily! Where is the house?"

Lily quickly tried to correct what her son had said, but she found herself getting excited as she told Marnie about the house. "I like it, Marnie. Of course I haven't seen the inside yet, and I don't have a clue how much it'd cost, but I do like it."

Marnie had her explain where the house was, and then she nodded. "Oh, that's the Martinson house. You should be able to get it for a song. The Martinson kids—Darcy and Ned—have been gone for years and have been renting it out, but I've heard they're tired of it and want to unload it as soon as possible."

Sam rubbed his chin. "If you want to see what it looks like inside, I know a really good real estate agent, sings bass in the choir, so maybe you've seen him, Wilson Jones, who could show it to you."

"Let's not jump the gun," Lily said. "I don't even know how long my job lasts here."

"You're kidding me." Marnie looked at her, aghast. "Hasn't Ric told you?"

"Told me what?"

"Well, dearie, I don't want to steal any of his thunder, but I don't think you have to worry about this job being temporary."

"What?" Lily resisted the urge to shake the words out of the other woman. "What do you know?"

But Marnie drew an *X* over her mouth with her forefinger. "My lips are sealed. If Ric hasn't told you anything by tomorrow night, then let me know and I'll make him tell you."

Todd had totally lost interest in the conversation, and Lily had to look for him. She found him deep in conversation with another little boy who looked to be about the same age.

"Yup," Todd was saying, "we're buying a house here that has a fireplace and a swing and a garden, and we're going to live here forever and ever and ever."

His new friend grinned. "Cool. Where's the new house?"

"Um, over by some trees."

His friend considered that and then nodded. "I know where it is. I think it's by my house. We have trees at our house. And one has a tree house. Do you have a tree house?"

"Not yet," Todd said, clearly mulling that over. "But there are some trees that'll make great tree houses. Ric and I could make a tree house in one of them. Ric could do it. He can do anything."

"Who's Ric?" The boy pushed his ice cream back on top of the cone with a grubby finger, and Lily winced.

"Ric is cool. Very cool." Todd's small chest swelled with pride.

"Is he your brother?"

Todd shook his head.

"Your dad?" guessed the boy.

"Pretty soon," Todd said.

Lily rushed in and grabbed her son by the hand. "Hi, nice to meet you." She sped through the introduction that Todd tried to give her.

She pulled her son back to the car and quickly buckled him inside.

"Todd, you are a walking, talking garden of misinformation."

"What does that mean?" he asked.

"It means that we are not necessarily buying the house. It depends on a lot of things, like the interior of the house, the furnace, the plumbing. And whether or not I even have a job after the town's recovered from the flood. Oh, and the price. I don't know if we'll be able to afford it."

His face crumpled. "Are we poor again?"

"We were never poor. No, we'll be fine. But I don't know how much longer this job lasts. Before we can decide to buy that house, or any house, we have to know a lot more than whether it has a fireplace and a swing set and a place to grow carrots. Tomorrow I'll talk to Ric about the job, and I'll talk to the real estate guy that Sam referred me to, and then we'll see."

He visibly relaxed, and his eyes got that daydreamy look that she'd come to know all too well. "And before you start planning who all's going to live in that house, you might want to consult with me. There's no way that Ric is going to be there, too. We're not getting married, tiger. We work together, that's all."

Todd shook his head slowly. "You'll get married to him, Mom."

She sighed in exasperation. "What makes you think so, Todd?"

He beamed at her. "I heard Marnie and Eileen talking about it."

She added one more item to her mental list of things to do: Gag Marnie and Eileen.

Chapter 7

Ric sat in front of his computer in his office, staring at it. On the monitor, a screen saver of a family of ducks wearing sailor hats swam back and forth, back and forth, but he didn't pay any attention to them.

He had other things on his mind. What if she said no? What if she said she didn't want to stay? What if—

"So do you like it?"

Marnie leaned against the doorjamb, watching him.

"Like what?"

"The screen saver."

"The what?"

She sighed and crossed the room. "This," she said, jabbing her finger at the computer monitor. "The ducks."

"Ducks? Why on earth would you—and why are they wearing sailor hats?"

"Ah, just noticed, did you? I thought they were cute. And definitely more interesting than that dot thing you had on there before."

"They weren't dots. They were stars."

"And you're going to tell me that was more interesting than ducks wearing sailor hats?"

He sighed. Past experience told him that he'd have to get used to the ducks. If he removed them from his computer, she'd probably put flying snails or horses in sneakers in their place.

"You're worried she might say no, aren't you?"

"I'm not worried—," he began, but she shook her head. "Okay, I am worried. A bit. I do know that God has this all in His control, and whatever He has planned is for the best. I guess I'm hoping that He and I are on the same page here."

"Been advising Him again?" she asked with a sympathetic tilt of her head.

"Constantly."

The sound of Todd's voice echoed down the hallway, and Marnie laughed. "I'll take Mr. Todd to the day care and leave you to discuss the deal with Lily."

Discuss the deal. He wanted a cup of coffee, but he was so nervous that more caffeine would probably jangle his nerves so much he could play "Jingle Bells" without an instrument.

He could hear Todd's words still going as Marnie led him to the playroom, and Lily stuck her head in.

"Marnie said you wanted to talk to me?"

Suddenly he realized that his announcement needed grander surroundings.

He stood up and, with a nervousness that took him by surprise, cleared his throat.

"I'd like to take you and Todd out to dinner tonight," he said. "Wildwood Inn is open again. It's kind of a legend in the area since it's so old."

"Oh, I've heard of it!" she said. "The food is supposed to be terrific."

"They're known for their walleye. Plus, the Inn has quite a history, and many of the original furnishings are still there. It's quite a showcase."

She smiled. "I'd love to go."

⌒

"I don't want to go." Todd stood in the living room and crossed his arms over his chest stubbornly.

"I'm not going to argue with you. We're going." Lily stood her ground firmly, too.

"But I hate those places. And I hate getting in my nice clothes. They itch. I'll have to sit there all evening and eat icky food and itch." His lower lip came out.

"Todd—"

The phone rang, and she reluctantly left the argument to answer it.

It was Marnie. "Lily, my grandson is visiting for the evening, and we're going to a movie. Would Todd like to come?"

She glanced at her son, still pouting in the center of the room. "We're going to the Wildwood Inn with Ric."

Marnie hooted. "That's no place to take a boy. I'll run by and pick him up in five minutes. We're just going to stop by the Burger Beat and grab a snack, and then it's off to the show."

Todd's mood was getting darker by the minute. She hated to relent, but taking him to dinner in the mood he was in was inviting trouble. "Thanks, Marnie. I'll have him waiting."

"Well, tiger," she said as she hung up the phone, "you've just received a reprieve."

"What's that?" Todd asked sulkily.

"That was Marnie, and she's going to pick you up in five minutes and take you and her grandson to Burger Beat for dinner and then to a movie."

The joy on her son's face told her she'd made the right decision. As he quickly changed into a clean T-shirt, he babbled about the fun he would have.

She'd just handed off her now-changed son into Marnie's capable care when she realized she had only moments to get herself ready.

She tore out of her work clothes and into a long black knit shift. It was classically simple enough that no matter what the dress code was at the Wildwood Inn, she should be fine.

A quick comb through her hair, a last dusting of powder and pink lipstick, a light gossamer sweater thrown over her arm in case the Inn was overly air-conditioned, and she was ready to go.

"Where's Todd?" Ric asked when he arrived.

Lily told him, and he smiled. "Hope he has fun."

She couldn't tell if he was sorry or not that Todd wouldn't be going with them.

The Wildwood Inn was a beautiful old house not too far from the river. Ric explained to her that it had belonged to a steamboat captain at the turn of the century, and the gracious building had been turned into an inn in the twenties.

Her reservations about it just being the two of them quickly dissipated as Ric chatted easily, drawing her into conversation and making her feel at ease. Part of the problem, she knew, was that she didn't know if this was a date or if it was just two friends having a nice dinner together.

Until she knew, she'd consider it the latter. It was safer.

But still, a date would be nice.

"How are you liking Wildwood so far?" Ric asked.

"Oh, I love it! It's the kind of place I'd like to have Todd grow up in." Then the entire story about the house poured out. "It's my dream house, Ric. Of course, I haven't seen the inside, so maybe I'm being foolish, but both Todd and I lost our hearts to it. I'm seeing it tomorrow after work. A real estate agent that Sam knows is going to show it to us."

"Tell me about it," he prompted her.

"Well, I've only seen the outside, and I know it's probably had flood damage. I mean, what house hasn't? But it's a little brick house, and it has a swing set, and a fireplace, and Todd has decided he wants to grow carrots in the backyard."

"Carrots?"

She grinned. "Well, that's today. Tomorrow it may be corn, and the next day the garden may be out of the plans entirely and he'll be building a fort there. But I'd love to have a garden. Fresh tomatoes! Think of it. Fresh tomatoes! Fresh corn! Everything, right from my own backyard!"

"You're glowing. You should get the house."

"It's a good dream," she said. "But the fact is, I don't know if I can afford it."

"Maybe this can help you as you make your decision." He cleared his throat. "You know that the flood has fast-tracked a lot of things that would, in a normal, unflooded world, be tied up in administrative red tape for months on end. The day care is an example."

She nodded.

"Lily," he continued, "we've received permission from the district to offer you the position of child-care coordinator on a permanent basis."

"Forever?"

"Forever—or as long as you want," he said. "Do you want the job?"

"Do I want the job? Of course I do! I love it here. I love Wildwood." There was more, but she left it unsaid.

This job meant everything to her. She couldn't bear to think about leaving Wildwood and Resurrection and Marnie, and even Ric. Yes, the vision of life without Ric in it was almost too terrible to consider.

"There are a few changes to your job description," Ric said, and he proceeded to explain them to her.

The duties were somewhat expanded from what they were now, which made sense. The day care right now was an emergency setup, but in the future it would have to operate under different circumstances.

The inherent challenge was exciting. The district wanted her to upgrade the facility while keeping it within the confines of the church. She was to keep an eye on possible expansion if the need presented itself, which it might if more day cares didn't reopen.

She had the authority to apply for any grants that might enhance the day care. At the Nanny Group, she'd written a successful proposal that had funded a special project, so that was good.

But what was especially appealing was the salary. It was generous, far beyond whatever expectations she might have secretly harbored.

When she'd talked to the real estate agent in the morning, he'd told her the asking price of the house. Maybe she would be able to afford to buy it now, if she was careful with her money.

"Still sound good to you?" Ric asked, his blue eyes twinkling like azure stars.

She nodded. "I want this job, Ric. I want to stay here, and Todd wants to stay here. I feel I can do some good here in Wildwood and live my life of service."

"It may not be as directly related as the ministry," Ric said, "but it is the Lord's work."

"Theirs is the kingdom of God," she said almost to herself.

The server arrived with their food, and before they ate, Ric looked at her. "Shall we say grace?"

They bowed their heads, and his hands covered hers in a warm grip. "Blessed Lord, we thank You for this food and for the company of our friends. We ask always to stay mindful of You and to live in Your service. In the name of the Most Precious One. Amen."

Dinner was wonderful, the kind of food that Lily liked but never seemed to have the time to prepare at home. And, to be honest, even if she had the time, Todd wouldn't have cared for the herbed crème sauce on the baked walleye, or the cheese-flavored potatoes, or the crusty crab cakes that came as a side dish. For him, the best food was a pile of chicken strips and french fries served in a plastic basket at the Burger Beat.

Lily gave in to temptation and let Ric order dessert, some horribly calorie-filled concoction called Chocolat a Deux, a rich fudgy mousse with bittersweet chocolate drizzled on the top and tart raspberries on clouds of whipped cream around the edge.

The server brought them two spoons. "It's a bit much for one person," he explained. "That's why it's called Chocolat a Deux, which is sort of French for 'Chocolate for Two.'"

After the waiter left, Ric looked at her with raised eyebrows. "Sort of French?"

Lily shook her head and dipped her spoon into the dessert. "That way he's covered, in case it's really sort of Italian."

She took a bite of the rich dessert and closed her eyes. "I know what they serve in heaven. This is absolutely incredible! It's drenched in calories, I know that, but wow!"

Even with both of them working on it, they couldn't finish the dessert, and at last they sadly laid down their spoons in defeat.

"I can't eat another bite," she confessed.

"Nor can I." He groaned. "And I can't move anymore. We still have a major hurdle ahead of us. We've got to get to the car."

"Just pull up to the front door, and I'll roll out to meet you. I couldn't walk for anything."

The server returned with the check, and while Ric settled the bill, Lily fought the increasing urge to fall asleep.

"They're going to kick us out unless we go of our own volition," Ric said.

She glanced at her watch and suddenly came back to life. "It's after nine! I have to pick up Todd. He needs to go to bed."

They were both too stuffed to do much talking on the way to Marnie's house to pick up Todd. The even movement of the car's rhythm on the road was like a lullaby, and she fought to stay awake.

As Ric pulled up in front of the secretary's house, he turned off the car's engine and faced her.

"I had a good time tonight, Lily."

"So did I." Somewhere in her mind the message peeped through that he was going to say something of importance, but she was too lulled by the evening to comprehend.

"I'd like to see you more. Can you give that some thought?"

She nodded sleepily. More than anything, she wanted to curl up beside him, put her head on his shoulder, maybe let him wrap his arm around her, and go to sleep.

But it was not to be. The car door flew open, and Todd launched himself into her lap. "Mommy, Mommy!" he shouted in her ear. "I met Andy, and now he's my bestest, bestest friend in the whole-wide world that doesn't live here. He's got this game, too. You hold it in your hand, and it beeps and shakes, and he got it at that store with the big Z on the front. Can we go now and get it?"

She struggled to make sense of his words, and over her son's shoulder, she saw Ric watching them. She couldn't quite decipher his expression, but in there she could have sworn she saw sadness.

That evening, after Todd was settled and asleep, she lay in bed and thought through the events of the day. Her life had suddenly taken a change that she'd never expected it to.

Obviously God had something in His plan for her to do, and maybe the trouble at the Nanny Group was just a way of preparing her to do her major service here in Wildwood. It was a possible answer to the question she'd been asking herself for so long.

And now that she had the answer, she could attend to other parts of her life. Like Ric.

She'd been sleepy tonight—and maybe she'd misunderstood what he was saying—but he seemed to want to take their relationship beyond the world of work. At least that was the impression she had gotten.

And she didn't have to ask herself how she felt about it. She knew. Just the thought of him, the sight of him, made her smile.

And now, without the awful image of the Nanny Group hanging over her head, she was free to let all those thoughts she'd tucked into the back of her mind come to the forefront.

Who would have imagined that out of the catastrophe at the Nanny Group, and out of the disaster in Wildwood, something as wonderful as love might grow?

It never paid to second-guess God, she'd learned. But when He made His ways known, it was sweet, so sweet.

Lily was singing as she got ready for work the next day. Song after song poured out of her, and when she ran out of songs she knew, she made up some more.

Even Todd's grumpiness, the result of his late bedtime, didn't faze her.

"Why are you so happy?" he asked her as he struggled into his clothes.

"Lots of reasons, tiger. We're going to stay in Wildwood, I've got a good job, we're going to look at the house tonight where we can have a carrot garden for you, little guy. And above all"—she plunked a kiss on the bridge of his nose—"God's in His heaven, and all's right with the world."

She threw open the curtains in the living room and smiled at the outside world of the parking lot. "Isn't it a beautiful day?"

Todd frowned. "It's raining."

"And a beautiful rain it is. Here, put on your slicker and boots, and I'll put mine on, too, and we'll run through the puddles."

"On purpose?"

"On purpose."

"You'll get mad."

"No I won't."

"How come you're so happy?" he asked her again, pulling on his bright red rubber boots. He smiled impishly. "Did you kiss Ric?"

"You shush!" she reprimanded him. "No, I didn't kiss Ric, and you shouldn't talk that way. I'm just in a really great mood today because life is good. This morning, nothing can upset me. Nothing at all."

But when they got to the church and Todd joined his friends in the day care, Marnie handed her a registered letter.

And Lily's world caved in.

Chapter 8

Dimly, Lily heard Marnie asking her if she was okay. She probably responded, but what she said, she had no idea at all.

The envelope's return address was the state licensing agency for child cares, and the letter itself was short and to the point, like a dagger.

> *Regarding your employment at the Chicago organization the Nanny Group, certain irregularities have come to our attention.*
>
> *We will be looking into them, and we will keep you informed of our progress.*
>
> *Your location's petition for an emergency-licensing override to allow more children at your facility will not be processed until this issue has been resolved. Recognizing the disaster Wildwood has experienced, however, we are allowing your day care to stay open at its current capacity.*
>
> *Your status as a nonprofit child-care operator has been changed back to provisional, pending the outcome of our examination of pertinent documents and records.*
>
> *We will be contacting you to discuss this matter. We would appreciate your total cooperation.*

Lily was too devastated to even cry. The pain welled up inside her like an erupting volcano.

How dare he? How dare he? Douglas Newton had successfully pulled her into his web of deceit and fraud, and now she was put in the awful position of having to defend herself against a barrage of untruths, half-truths, and out-and-out lies.

Beside the anger grew the urge to run. More than anything, she wanted to run to the day care, grab Todd, and leave Wildwood—to run away from all of this.

But she knew she couldn't run. No matter where she went, she would be pursued by the evil deeds of Douglas Newton. And now, more than ever, she had to resist the urge to flee. Too many other people were dependent on her, on this day care.

Her stomach twisted and knotted itself.

"Excuse me," she mumbled to Marnie. Blindly she pushed her way out of the office and into the ladies' room where she threw up.

She rocked back and let her head rest against the cool metal of the stall.

How could she ever have thought he would have set it up so the wrong-doing would follow him instead of her? He was sleazy, despicable, low, contemptible.

But calling him names, while it vented her immediate anger, did nothing more than focus her energy on him when she needed to bring it back to focus on herself.

She cleaned up as best she could and flew into the sanctuary.

She went right to the altar and knelt before it, not even bothering to wipe away the tears that ran freely down her cheeks.

"Lord, tell me why You are doing this to me. How can this be in Your service? Am I fighting the great battle here alone?"

The silence was overwhelming. She waited for the relief she'd come to expect from the cross, but she was too tight with anger and fear to let it seep into her heart and into her soul.

She knew it, but she couldn't let go of the hostility that surfaced and demanded to be dealt with, and with great sadness, she put her head on the altar railing and wept before her Lord.

It wasn't fair. She hadn't done anything—except flee. Was God punishing her for that? What had He expected her to do? How could she have fought a snake like Newton?

Even as she asked the question, she knew the answer. God was not punishing her. God's ways were mysterious, and there were some things she just had to take on faith. She knew that.

But why was He putting her—and Todd—through this? Why didn't He let her be done with what had happened in Chicago? Didn't He realize that having this surface here in Wildwood was going to jeopardize Resurrection's child-care facility?

Even as she asked the question of herself, she knew it was foolish. God realized everything. She was the one who was confused.

At last her tears abated. But she continued to stay in the cool of the sanctuary, where life was calm and there was only the cross and her. A relative peace descended upon her, and she finally stood up. She'd have to talk to Ric about this and show him the letter.

He was standing in the office with Marnie, and both of them broke off their conversation when she entered. "Are you all right?" Ric asked. "Marnie said something upset you."

She had intended to talk it over with Ric in private, but Marnie's kind and concerned face changed her mind. "I need to talk to you about the Nanny Group. And this letter."

❦

Ric read the letter, read it again, and read it a third time. With each reading, the words did not become any clearer. He knew what they said, but what did they mean? The letter might as well have been in Greek. He passed it to Marnie, whose immediate reaction was one of denial.

"It's all a mistake. It has to be. What could be wrong? A good Christian woman like Lily? What irregularities? Of all the nerve—" She sputtered until she ran out of words to say.

Ric didn't speak but studied Lily's face. Then he said quietly, "Let's sit down. Do you know what this letter's about?"

"Yes," she said as they sat at the small round table. She fidgeted with the centerpiece, a basket of fresh daisies.

"Start whenever you're ready." He tried to keep his voice gentle and kind. She looked terrified.

Slowly at first, and then with increasing intensity, she let the story pour out. As she told of finding the altered vouchers, Marnie nearly rose out of her chair with indignation, but Ric silenced her before she could go further than a single, "That scalawag!"

"And so I ran," she finished. "Ran to Shiloh, and then when you offered me this temporary job, Ric, it seemed like an answer to my prayers. But now, I can't think this is good for the day care, so maybe I should leave."

The thought of her leaving shot through him like an arrow. He shook his head firmly. "No way are you leaving. We need you here."

The phone rang, and Marnie answered it. As she listened, her forehead wrinkled, and she motioned at last for Ric. "It's for you. I'll transfer it into your office."

Ric took a seat in his office and, with a quick prayer for clarity, took the call.

The caller was Carl Palmer from the state licensing agency. With straightforward sentences, he explained the situation. Rick pulled a notepad over and began to scribble furiously as he listened, his heart growing heavier as he understood what was being said.

At last the call ended, and Ric leaned back in his chair, covering his forehead with his hands.

How could this all unravel so quickly—and so badly?

He had trusted Lily—he still did—but the evidence was mountainous. Nevertheless, he'd heard in the investigator's voice something he couldn't quite identify. Perhaps it was some sign that he wasn't accepting the story he was telling Ric?

Or maybe, Ric reminded himself, he was clutching at straws. *Might as well*, he thought. *At least then I have something to hang on to.*

That wasn't true. There was much more to hang on to.

Matthew 10:16 was a verse he'd turned to again and again when life had sent him trouble. *Behold, I send you forth as sheep in the midst of wolves: be ye therefore wise as serpents, and harmless as doves.*

He'd always called it the menagerie verse. Sheep, wolves, serpents, and doves. The Bible counseled that it was a dangerous world and Christians were to be wary.

No matter what his feelings for Lily were growing to be, he had to remember the families of Resurrection. He had to be cautious. They, especially the children, were the "sheep in the midst of wolves."

But the Bible also exhorted him to be harmless. It wasn't modified: He had to be careful not to hurt anyone.

The sound of the coffeemaker and the ticktock of the porcelain clock were the only sounds Ric heard when he emerged from his office. His stomach wrenched when he saw Lily clutching Marnie's hand.

Wise and harmless. That was his duty.

She stood up. "What is it, Ric?"

"You'd better sit down. Both of you."

When the three of them were seated again, he began to speak. "That was Carl Palmer from the licensing agency. Yes, he's the man who signed your letter, and he's been assigned to investigate the situation."

"What did he say?" Marnie burst out. "He said it was all a mistake, right?"

Ric shook his head and turned to Lily. "Lily, it gets worse. I'm sorry. Marnie, did you just make coffee? Maybe we should have some—"

"No," Lily whispered. "Just tell me."

"It's about those vouchers. The way you saw them was not the way they ended up."

"That horrible man tore them up, didn't he?" Marnie asked.

"No, he didn't, Marnie. He changed them. There is a paper trail, but now it leads to you, Lily."

The blood drained from Lily's face. "What do you mean, Ric?"

"I mean the vouchers look as if you used the system to care for Todd."

She began to protest, and he nodded. "I know, Lily. It's got to be untrue. We'll piece together your time in Chicago and see if we can't prove those vouchers are faked."

"How," she asked, "can I prove I *haven't* done something? How does a person have evidence of something they didn't do?" She sagged back into her chair.

"I don't know," he said. "I truly don't know."

"There's more, isn't there?" she asked with the dead voice of certainty.

He nodded. "There is. I wish there were some way I could soften the blow, but I guess I'll have to come out and say it. Now it looks as if the reimbursements were made to you."

"Oh, now that's the limit!" Lily exploded, slamming her hand down on the table so hard that a daisy fell out of the vase. "I did *not* use the service, and I certainly never paid myself!"

Marnie reached out a hand to soothe her, but Lily shook it off. "This time I am not going to run. I'm going to stay and fight it, and if I have to hang

Douglas Newton from the steeple here, I'll do it!"

"Lily!" Marnie's voice was shocked, and Lily realized she'd gone too far.

"I'm sorry, Marnie. That was my anger speaking. I shouldn't have said that. I'm truly, truly sorry. But I will fight him with every breath in my body!"

Ric forced a smile he did not feel. "I'm glad to hear that you're not going to take this lying down, and I want you to know that you have all the support in the world from us. We know this is a pack of lies—"

"Indeed!" interjected Marnie.

"And we'll do whatever we can to clear your name. One thing I did learn from the discussion with Mr. Palmer is that Newton knows how to manipulate the system. He knows how things work, and it sounds to me like he's cagey enough to use it to his advantage."

"Mr. Palmer said that?" Lily asked. "Then he must suspect something isn't on the up-and-up with the Nanny Group, right?"

"I don't know if he suspects that or not. But from what he said about Newton and his position at the Nanny Group, I could figure it out. Newton is not a stupid man, and we can't underestimate him."

Marnie was staring at the bowl of daisies, and at last she returned the stray one to the others. "But how," she asked slowly, "did the irregularities come to light? Did Newton say something?"

Ric rubbed his chin. "That's interesting, Marnie. I didn't think about that. I don't know."

Lily leaned forward. "But isn't that crucial? If Douglas is sabotaging me, why? That doesn't make sense, does it?"

Ric nodded as the stream of hope returned to his soul.

"He wouldn't say anything," Lily continued, "because then I'd be put in the position of having to defend myself and I'd have no choice except to lay the whole thing out in public to clear my name. So he'd be better off keeping quiet and not drawing suspicion to himself. But if there were an audit or something, well, that's when the whole issue would come to light."

"And—?" Ric prompted.

"So the question is why the audit, and, yeah, now that I think about it, it had to be an audit. It wouldn't get this far if it were limited to the board of directors at the Nanny Group looking into it—at least I don't think so. Anyway, even if they suspected something, they'd hire an independent auditor." Her smile was shaky. "Sorry if I'm less than coherent. I'm thinking out loud."

"Go ahead. I think we're getting somewhere," Ric encouraged.

"So, something has made somebody suspicious, or maybe it's come about as part of an IRS audit, or a random audit? I don't know. But I'm becoming more and more sure that it's not a matter of Douglas Newton coming after me."

"On the other hand," Ric reminded her, "he's the one who laid the trail that led to you. He's a pretty nasty character. We can't let that out of our sights. If Lily's right and the Nanny Group was audited, and the audit highlighted some irregularities, he's going to be very edgy. Especially if it's an IRS audit."

"And," Lily added, "if the vouchers are looked at closely enough to prove they're faked."

Ric thought about that for a moment. "True, but I don't think we can pin our hopes on that too much. Newton sounds like he knows the ins and outs of deception too well."

"A handwriting analyst!" Marnie said excitedly. "We could get one and prove that Lily didn't write those vouchers."

"It's a good idea," Lily said slowly. "I don't know if it would stand up in court, but—"

Ric sighed. "He got smarter. Apparently the questionable vouchers that are in the files now were typed on Lily's typewriter."

"I don't have a typewriter!" she objected.

"Mr. Palmer said the type matches that of the typewriter in the Nanny Group office."

Lily sighed. "Oh, that old thing. It hopped and skipped around, and the ribbon would stick and then jump. I hated it so much that I hardly ever used it. I used the laptop instead."

"We could get the typewriter checked for fingerprints," Marnie suggested.

Lily shook her head. "That wouldn't work. I did use it once or twice for preprinted forms. So my fingerprints are on there anyway."

"He's clever," Ric said. "Very clever. He's made sure that he covered his tracks as completely as possible. So far we haven't uncovered a single hole in his method. That's scary."

"What can we do?" Marnie asked.

"One thing I'm *not* going to do is give in." Lily sat straight up. "I will fight this until the whole shebang is taken care of and my name is cleared. I refuse to live like this any longer!"

Marnie applauded. "You go, girl! Todd will be so proud of his mother."

Lily clapped her hand over her mouth. "Todd! He can't be here now. I can't expose him to this."

"Can your mother take him for a while?" Ric asked.

"Sure. Mom would love to see him. But what about the day care? It's all well and good for us to think about how I'm going to take on Goliath, but what about those little children down the hall? What's going to happen to them? We're not going to have to close down the day care, are we?"

"Mr. Palmer said it was all right for us to continue operation. He said under usual circumstances he would probably suggest that you be put on a paid leave of absence, but in the current situation, he realizes that's not a viable option, so he said it would be all right for you to stay here." Ric's fingers twisted together. "But you're not to handle any money transactions. All of that will have to be done through this office."

The phone rang again, and Marnie struggled to her feet. "Dumb arthritis. Worst part of rainy days. That and the worms on the sidewalks. Hello?"

She handed the phone to Lily. "It's for you."

Lily took the receiver with trepidation. What would this call bring?

"Hello?" she asked tentatively.

Ric held his breath as she listened, and then he released it with a sigh when she raised her chin and nodded.

"Yes," she said firmly. "Tuesday at seven thirty would be fine. Yes, I'm still interested in the house."

She hung up the phone and smiled at Marnie's and Ric's astonished faces.

"It's called an act of faith, my friends. Faith that good will overcome bad. Good *will* rule."

And with those words, she left the room.

Marnie cleared her thoat as Ric poured himself another cup of coffee. "You know that if you drink much more of that, you'll never sleep," she said.

Ric stared at the cup. "This is my second cup of the day."

She snorted. "Second pot of the day, maybe."

She walked across the room and took the cup from him and set it on the file cabinet. "Sit down, shut your eyes, and breathe in and out for a while."

"I don't have time for a nap."

"As if." Marnie pointed to the cup of now-cooling coffee she'd taken from him. "I don't know how long the half-life of the caffeine molecule is, but you've got so many of them rolling around in your bloodstream that it'll be days before you get to dreamland."

"It doesn't bother me," he protested.

"Sure. That's why your leg hasn't stopped jiggling all morning. You're going to drive yourself nuts, Ric."

"I have things to do." He knew he sounded petulant, but he couldn't help himself. She was right. He hadn't slept at all the night before and only sporadically for the past three evenings.

Worry was not something a Christian should do, he knew that. But it was easier said than done, at least when the night's darkness stole over the day's hours and shadowed clarity with doubt. Things that were minor in the daytime took on monstrous proportions after midnight.

Life was filled with uncertainty—as a pastor he saw his share of its surprises—but the flood had put a whole new layer of it into everyone's lives. The life of the congregation itself and the situation at the day care gave him extra areas of concern. Plus he couldn't ignore the fact that a young woman and a little boy had moved into his heart completely, and he wanted their complete happiness.

So he hadn't slept, and the longer he went without sleep, the harder it was to sleep. He was exhausted, even more than in the initial days after the flood had come, but the crazy paradox was that he was too tired to sleep.

"No more coffee," Marnie said. "Let your brain stop working overtime. Give God some time to work."

"It's just so—" He stopped. He didn't know how to finish the sentence.

"It is." Marnie's voice was warm with sympathy.

He put his hands over his eyes. "She's planning to buy the house, you know."

"So?"

"What if—I mean, she could—they could—" He broke off.

"Well, she could and they could," Marnie said. "But we won't."

He dropped his fingers from his eyelids and gaped at her. "What are you talking about?"

"I have no idea," Marnie said cheerfully. "And neither do you."

Chapter 9

Lily's mother was delighted at the suggestion that Todd spend some time with her in Mandan. But her maternal instinct must have told her that something more was afoot because she immediately launched into a barrage of questions: "What's the problem? Is it with work? Is it a man? You've found a man, haven't you? Or maybe, wait, it's your health. Are you okay? Have you seen a doctor? Do you want to see mine?"

"No, Mom, I'm fine." Lily laughingly reassured her mother and forestalled her next question. "And Todd is fine, too. I sure can tell where Todd got his Question Man gene from."

"Well, you'll soon learn that you have to ask questions in order to get answers, you know."

Lily grinned at the phone. Her mother had a way of talking in what seemed to be truisms, but she knew they were all original, or basically original, with her mother. "Todd never gives me time to get an answer out before he's on to the next question."

"The child is inquisitive. It's a good trait. You should encourage it."

"Well, can you encourage it for a while in Mandan? I know he's been wanting to see you," Lily said. "I could bring him tomorrow."

"Tomorrow?"

"Unless that doesn't work for you. Mom, I don't want to interfere with your life. If you have other plans, or if it flat-out isn't a good idea for him to come now, please say so. I won't have my feelings hurt."

She grinned as she listened to her mother switch to the defensive. "No, no," her mother protested. "I want him to come here. I'm just concerned about what—"

"It works out best for me to bring him tomorrow and drop him off at your place. I have to be back the day after tomorrow, so I'd better drive home tomorrow night."

It wasn't totally untrue, but she realized that one of her major hurdles lay ahead of her: making it through tomorrow without letting her mother get wise to the situation with the Nanny Group. Trying to hide something from her mother had never been successful. She'd never make it through an entire weekend.

Lily didn't hold much with psychics, but when it came to her mother, she had to admit that her mother had an uncanny ability to zero right in on the unspoken. "Any word yet on the Nanny Group thing, Lily?"

Sometimes the woman was downright eerie. Lily opted for a hedge on the truth. "Mom, I want to put that whole rotten incident behind me."

There was the briefest of pauses, and then her mother said, "Good. That's where it should be. Behind you. Now, when can I expect to see you tomorrow?"

If Lily had any illusions that she had put something over on her mother with her brief trip around the truth, they came to an end when her mother said before she hung up, "You fix up whatever that trouble is with the Nanny Group, and don't worry about your boy. He'll be fine with me."

Lily hung up the phone, chuckling. One of the things she liked most about her mother was that she knew when she shouldn't pry further.

"Thank You, God, for giving me such a tremendous mother, and make me more like her. Amen." That was her quick prayer before calling Todd in from the park, where he was happily sloshing through the mud from the morning's rain, to tell him he was going to visit his grandmother in Mandan the next day.

"Wa-hooooo!" he shouted happily. "Gran is the coolest."

"I'm sure you'll have lots of fun with her, but don't get too crazy," she warned him.

"I know." He nodded seriously. "She's older than I am, and she doesn't bend where I do."

"That's true, but I meant don't use up all your crazies on her 'cause I'll want some when you come back home!" She caught him up in her arms and hugged him.

Holding him close like that, she nearly changed her mind. It was going to be torture not just to defend herself against the false charges, but coming home to an empty house afterward—well, it was almost too much for her to even think about.

She buried her face in his neck. "I'm going to miss you, tiger."

"I'll miss you, too," he said.

"I'll miss snuggling with you and hugging you and kissing you."

Todd pulled back and said impishly, "You can do that to Ric!"

He ran off before she could stop him, and she could hear him in his bedroom giggling over his joke.

She couldn't take it too seriously. For him it was just fun, all tied in with his concept of girl cooties, which were the most dreadful of all afflictions, according to him.

As long as he didn't say it at the wrong time to the wrong person. . . like Ric.

Lily sighed and pushed Ric once again back into the corner of her mind. It seemed as if whenever she allowed herself the luxury of doing some cleaning in the far reaches back there, something happened that caused it to fill up again. Kind of like her hall closet.

Her stomach tightened as she recalled what was ahead for her. She knew she was up against an able and talented adversary in Douglas Newton. He would do anything to prevent himself from being tied in with diverting the money from the Nanny Group.

She almost gasped as another rogue thought slipped into her mind. What he had done was—what was the word? Every time she tried to put a name on it, it would turn elusive and slip beyond her mental grasp.

Lily stood up and got the suitcase from under her bed and began to pack it from the laundry basket. Luckily she'd just washed and dried Todd's clothes, so he had plenty to wear when—

Embezzlement. The ugly word sprang into her brain. That's what Douglas had done. It wasn't just immoral; it was a crime. He had embezzled money from the organization. How much, she didn't know.

He'd committed a crime. She shook her head sadly and began to place Todd's folded T-shirts and shorts into the suitcase. Douglas was a sleaze.

Her breath froze in her throat. Douglas. She knew what he had done, and he knew what he had done, but everyone else thought she had done it.

To the rest of the world, she was the embezzler.

Her stomach coiled itself into a tight spring. She hadn't put it in this perspective before.

She slammed the clothes into the suitcase.

Enough was enough.

God, I've tried to be patient about this. First You put me into the Nanny Group, and I thought I was going into Your service, but I don't think so, God. How can You have meant this for me? Once, I could see—maybe it was an oversight on Your part. But twice? And to label me a criminal? And what about Todd? Did You forget about him, God? Huh? Did You?

She cracked open one eye, half expecting to see a long flash of lightning headed her way, but she was met with only the happy twittering of birds, delighted over the bumper crop of earthworms because of the rain.

"Yeah, easy for you to be cheerful about it," she grumbled to the birds outside her window. "But ask the earthworm how *he* feels. Things aren't so chirpy happy for him, are they?"

"Who are you talking to?" Todd asked as he came into her room and hopped onto the bed. She kissed him on his forehead.

"I was talking to God," she said. She hadn't even been aware that she was speaking out loud.

"Were you asking Him for something?"

She considered his question. "I suppose so. I think that's pretty much what prayer is all about, don't you, tiger?"

"No. At Shiloh we learned that you shouldn't ask God for things like bicycles." Todd stopped and looked at her speculatively. "Were you asking God for a bicycle?"

"No, I wasn't asking for a bicycle." She managed not to smile. "It was a bit more serious than that."

"Oh. Well, if it's a car, you still can't ask God for a car. It's the same thing as a bicycle, I think. Why do you want a new car, anyway?"

"I don't want a new car. I was talking to God about something else."

"Did God answer you?"

She was ready to say no when she stopped. Just at the point that she'd expected to be zapped with a lightning bolt, Todd had torn into the room.

She thought back to what the end of her prayer had been.

God had clearly not forgotten Todd. In fact, now that she ran it all through her mind again, perhaps He'd sent the little boy flying into the room as an answer.

"Yes, tiger, I think God did answer my prayer."

"That's good," Todd responded. "I usually don't get answers that quick. I think sometimes I don't get answers at all, but Ric said that we had to learn to listen to how God speaks since He maybe isn't using English. Like words. Not Spanish either."

To anyone else, Todd's sentences may not have made sense, but to Lily, they were direct and real. She couldn't expect God to simply holler out an answer to her question. Instead, she had to let herself be open to His response whenever and however it might arrive.

And, no matter what Todd's hopes were, she didn't think God's answer was going to be a bicycle.

The drive to Mandan was interesting, as any ride with Todd was. He chattered and sang the entire way. Usually his patience expired about half an hour into any trip, but not this time. He was apparently too excited about seeing his grandmother.

Although there was a part of her that wanted to stay with her mother and pour out the story, she stoically unloaded Todd's bags, made sure he knew where his bear was, took a quick break at the condo for a glass of lemonade and a sandwich, and then, pleading a need to take care of some urgent cases at the day care, kissed them both good-bye and headed back to Wildwood, fighting tears the entire way.

She'd pulled her car into Resurrection's darkened parking lot when she noticed a car parked in the shadows. Someone moved in the car, and she nearly passed out when the door opened and a figure emerged and approached her.

The scream died in her throat when she recognized Victoria Campbell. Her relief must have been obvious as Victoria's face crumpled with concern.

"I didn't mean to scare you," she said hastily. "I wanted to talk to you, and you weren't in—and please don't think ill of me. I know it looks bad, but I wasn't lurking in the lot here just waiting for you to come home. I really wasn't."

"That's fine," Lily said as the desire to reassure the woman grew to be nearly overwhelming. "No problem at all. Would you like to come in and have some iced tea or something?"

Victoria paused and then nodded. "Thanks. I think I will."

She turned and headed toward the church, but Lily stopped her. "Let's go into my home here."

"Are you sure?" Victoria seemed stunned by Lily's invitation.

"Absolutely. Please join me." As Lily unlocked the door of the mobile home, she continued to talk, hoping the flow of everyday conversation would ease the other woman's obvious tension. "I drove to Mandan and back today, so I'm grateful for the chance to sit down and put my feet up. Come on in."

Victoria's uneasiness dissipated only slightly in Lily's living room. She walked around the perimeter of the small room, examining the photographs and knickknacks until she apparently realized that she shouldn't be because she suddenly sat down.

Lily handed her a glass of iced tea that was already beaded with moisture.

"Whew, it's hot!" Lily exclaimed as she sank onto the recliner. "The only change I would make in this place would be to add an air conditioner."

"Is it yours?" Victoria asked. "I've often wondered what it was doing here."

"It's here temporarily until the need for flood relief is gone. It's like the FEMA mobile homes, but it belongs to the district office of the church. I'll be moving out of it before winter, I think."

Victoria motioned toward Lily's wedding photograph. "Is he your husband?" Then she laughed, a tight, brittle laugh. "Of course he's your husband. You're wearing a wedding dress, he's wearing a tuxedo, and you're standing together in front of an altar holding hands. Who did I think he was? The washing machine repairman?"

"Yes," Lily said softly. "That's Barry. He died not too long after that in an accident."

"Oh, I'm so sorry," her guest said. "That's why I like to wear nice shoes since my feet are always firmly in my mouth."

Lily stroked the edge of the frame. "I used to feel as if God had cheated me, taking Barry from me so quickly, but He gave me Todd. Barry didn't even know I was pregnant, but I know he would have been delighted."

"Do you miss him?" Victoria asked, her voice smoothing out.

"Yes. Every day it gets easier, and sometimes it's almost as if it was all a dream. But I look in Todd's eyes, and I know it wasn't a dream. It was real. And I thank God for giving me the chance to live that dream, even if it was only for such a short time."

"How can you be so accepting of this?" Victoria asked wonderingly. "Life has come up to you and kicked you hard, but you still welcome it, and look at you, you're smiling all the time!"

"Well, not all the time. But one of the things that losing Barry taught me is that each day is a gift. You have to live each day to its fullest. And you know, I'd heard that over and over again, but it didn't really settle into my heart until Barry died. What I would have given for one more day with him. . . ."

"Sometimes it seems like it would just be peachy keen if it *would* end," Victoria said darkly. Then she hastily added, "Oh, don't get me wrong. I'm not thinking of jumping off a bridge or anything like that. I mean that sometimes getting through it all, day by day, seems like I'm slogging through a bog. And I've been watching you. Here you are, with a little boy, taking on this job and all. How do you do it and stay so incredibly cheerful?"

The irony of this conversation hit Lily. Here she was, on the verge of losing everything and possibly being charged with a crime, all because of someone else's greed, and she was being asked how she stayed so cheerful?

She pulled together a smile that, remarkably enough, appeared easily. Maybe she was cheerful after all.

"I have faith," she said. "Faith that God is taking me where He wants me to go, where I need to go in order to know Him better."

"But wouldn't you know God better, wouldn't it be easier to believe in Him if He took you to places that were pretty and happy and good? Why does He take you to despair and loss?" Victoria objected. "It doesn't make any sense to me."

"Well," said Lily, "I'm not all that well trained in theology, but it does strike me that you learn more when you are challenged. Besides, if God only took you to wonderful places, how could that help you grow? You'd only know what you knew before, that you liked pretty and pleasant places. And that's a no-brainer. We all like them. We learn from what makes us think and question."

As she spoke, Lily had the increasing sensation that she was speaking to herself as much as to Victoria. Increasingly, she began to feel her soul rise to the challenge ahead of her, understanding a bit more why God had put this in her way.

But she still didn't understand why God had put this on Todd. That she couldn't reason her way through at all. He was just a child.

"I acted like a jerk that day in your office." Victoria's abrupt change of subject threw Lily's thought processes off.

"Excuse me?"

"That day. In your office. I was overbearing and horrid, and I'm sorry." Victoria's apology came out almost as an accusation, and she immediately shook her head. "No, no. Ignore that. I didn't mean for it to sound that way. You've been very nice to me, and I don't want to alienate you, too. You must think I'm awful. You must have thought I was awful then, especially with everything I did before then."

Lily leaned forward. "Please, Victoria, don't do this to yourself. I don't know what happened in the past, and I probably wouldn't care anyway. What's done is done. I know people say that all the time, but I really mean it. I don't hold the past against the present."

"You really don't know?" Victoria seemed unable to keep the astonishment from her voice.

"No, I don't. Does it have anything to do with your son and his need for day care?"

Victoria shook her head. "No."

"Then I don't care."

The other woman paused, as if weighing Lily's response. "I think I should tell you anyway. It's all tied together."

"You need to tell me only if you want to, and only if it's applicable to getting your son in day care," Lily reminded her.

"Okay."

Victoria put her head in her hands for a moment and then began. "I grew up very poor. And I do mean 'poor.' I lived with eight brothers in a house that was made of bits and pieces of other houses basically nailed together. I was the only girl."

She stopped, and Lily waited as the blond woman took a breath. "Sorry," Victoria said. "I have such bitterness over it all. I keep trying to ignore it and pretend it didn't happen, but it did, and to be honest, that's what really hurts."

"Do you want to stop?" Lily asked gently. "You don't have to continue."

"No. I want to tell it all. Maybe bringing it out into the open will make it cleaner, make it go away."

Lily's heart swelled with worry. She not only had more than enough on her own plate, but now she was about to hear something that had obviously prevented this woman from living fully.

Lord, help me as she needs me. It was the only prayer she had time for.

"I suppose lots of kids wear hand-me-downs," Victoria went on, "but I had to wear them from my brothers. Mom tried to make them a little more feminine, but let's face it—overalls are overalls. And patches are patches. It's not chic when it's from necessity."

Lily nodded. "I understand."

"So as soon as I could, I got out of there and didn't look back. I got married and got out of that, too, with a nice big settlement and Edgar. I feel the same way about him that you do about Todd."

"Of course," Lily murmured.

"I started Wedding Belles before I got divorced, though, and it took off. I was making money hand over fist, and I loved it. I wore nice clothes. I lived in a big house. I drove a big car. Life was good, really good, I thought. And then my husband and I split up."

Victoria stood up and walked around the room, her hands busy on Lily's display of photographs. "Sorry, I'm a bit nervous," she apologized as she sat down again. "Anyway, I liked having all this money. And I especially liked having people know that I had money. So when the time came to expand the church, I volunteered to pay for it. All of it. Crazy, huh? Pastor Mike tried to talk me out of it, but I wanted to be the great woman, the current-day saint who saved Resurrection."

Lily felt as if she were being held back in her chair by centrifugal force. This was an amazing story.

"And it was about that time that the money from the divorce settlement came to an end, and there I was, left with only what I had from the store. I thought there wouldn't be a problem—it had always done well—but sales dropped off. Business slowed to a crawl."

Victoria lifted a now tear-streaked face to Lily. "I'm broke. Totally broke."

"And the addition to the church?" Lily prompted gently, fearing the answer.

"I couldn't pay. But the worst part is that I couldn't say why. My stupid pride wouldn't let me. The same way it wouldn't let me fill out those papers. Lily, if you saw how much I made now, you'd be horrified."

"So the people in church don't know *why* you wouldn't pay for the addition?"

"No. They think I wouldn't do it because it wasn't done to my satisfaction or because it wasn't named after me, depending on who you talk to, but the upshot of it all is that I never told anybody the real reason. I couldn't bear to."

Her pain washed across the room like a wave, so strong it was nearly tangible. Lily got up and crossed the room. She sat beside Victoria on the couch and put her arm around her. "That little girl in the hand-me-downs still hurts, doesn't she?"

Victoria nodded, the tears returning again.

"Let's pray for her," Lily said, her voice barely above a whisper. "Dearest Lord, we need Your help. Take the pain of the past away from Victoria and hold her in Your hands and open her eyes to a future that is bright because it is made by You. Guard her, Lord, from self-doubt, from fear, and from uncertainty. We know You can do it, and we trust in Your power. We ask it in the name of Your Son, the ultimate gift of Love. Amen."

And, as she prayed for Victoria, Lily knew she prayed for herself.

"I feel better already," Victoria said at last. "It's like a weight has been lifted from my chest. I can breathe."

Lily patted her hand. "That's good. You shouldn't carry this burden around with you. It's not good for your heart and your soul, and above all, it's not good for Edgar."

Victoria looked at her watch and gasped. "I'd better get home. He's with a sitter, and I know he's already asleep, but I've got to kiss him good night anyway. Thanks again, Lily. You are so kind and forgiving. How can I ever thank you?"

"I didn't have anything to forgive," Lily demurred. "But I do think you'll feel better if you clear the situation with the church."

"They'll hate me!" Victoria said, and Lily could hear the panic in her voice.

"It's got to be an improvement over the way it is now," Lily pointed out.

"How do you want to do it? Do you want to talk to Ric, or do you want me to?"

"It'd be easier if you did it," Victoria answered. "But I think I should do it. I'll come in tomorrow morning and get this whole thing straightened out."

"And we'll see about getting Edgar settled in, too," Lily promised.

Victoria looked at her in amazement. "I thought it was full!"

"Well," Lily said, "we can get him in for at least two weeks. He can take Todd's place. Todd's visiting his grandmother and won't be back for a couple of weeks, so Edgar can use his slot."

"Two weeks?" Victoria wondered. "How are you going to bear it?"

A wave of loneliness washed over Lily. She knew it was just the first of many. "I don't know," she answered honestly. "I really don't know."

As she closed the door behind Victoria, Lily glanced at the church. A light glimmered from a window. Ric was at work.

Ric. Along with so much else, she put him at the back of her mind, too. There was no time for love when you were fighting for your life.

Chapter 10

The initial chords of the processional were beginning, but Ric was on his knees, not in front of the altar but in front of a sink, a wrench in his hands.

The faucet in the men's bathroom had been dripping, and his fumbling attempt to fix it had resulted in a cascade that had soaked the floor—and him. Luckily he'd been able to crawl under the sink, and after wrestling with a recalcitrant valve, he'd managed to get the water turned off.

He backed out from under the sink and wiped his forehead, then he groaned as he stood up and surveyed the damage. Not only was there water all over the floor, but there was water all over him.

The water on the floor was easily remedied—there was a mop in the janitor's closet just outside the door—but how was he going to deal with the soggy trousers?

He mopped up the floor and swabbed his pants as dry as possible with handfuls of brown paper towels that seemed to do nothing except add a thin layer of tan lint to the wet cloth. He glanced down at his trousers and shook his head. Now he not only was waterlogged—he also looked as if he were covered in dust.

In other words, he was a mess.

If only he had time to put his clothes in the dryer that was part of the day care! He chuckled as he thought of what the members of the congregation would think to see their youth minister running through the hall pantsless.

Too bad he didn't have a pastoral robe like some ministers did. It would cover this quite nicely.

There was nothing to do but go into the church, wet trousers and all. He was lucky it was August, when the heat would dry the material quickly.

The service was well underway. The congregation was standing for a hymn, and no one noticed the condition of his slacks.

He saw Lily at the end of a pew on the side, and he tapped her on the shoulder. She moved down to let him in beside her.

She looked at him inquiringly. "Everything okay?" she asked under cover of the anthem.

"Plumbing problem," he whispered. "It's all fixed now."

"Good," she mouthed back to him.

The song ended, and they sat, so close that her perfume drifted over to him. She was wearing a dress the color of red roses, and the sun through the

206

stained glass made dancing designs on the fabric.

This was God's hour, though, not Lily's, and he needed to focus on worshiping the Lord. He spread his hands over the wettest parts of his attire and turned his wandering attention to the front of the church where Pastor Mike was beginning his sermon.

"Why do bad things happen to good people? We often ask ourselves this question, and I wish I had an answer to give a grieving mother or to share with patients who have just heard the word 'malignant,' but I often find myself stammering and trying vainly to find the words of comfort.

"It often seems as if it's personal, as if God has some kind of vendetta. It often seems as if that's the only possible answer. And that's why I've called today's sermon, 'Why Me, God?'"

Ric sneaked a look at Lily, but her gaze was steadfastly on the minister.

He had told Pastor Mike what was going on with the day care and Lily. Although his own family problems had called him away during the week, he was still the head of this church and had the right to know what was going on.

Of course, the sermon could be about the senior minister's own situation, having to deal with a flooded community and the life-threatening illness of his elderly mother in a town five hours away.

The topic could be about any of them, Ric realized, looking around the sanctuary. The man in the third row was battling depression. The couple behind him was struggling through a rocky patch in their marriage. The teenagers clustered together on the side had talked to him about their own difficulties with peer pressure. The older woman in the back of the room had near-constant headaches, and the young man across from her had confided in Ric that his brother had been charged with theft in Arizona.

Truly, the sermon's topic touched them all.

He turned his attention back to the words Pastor Mike was delivering.

"—and so we ask for His understanding as we question whether we have been forsaken, and we find comfort and heart's ease as we realize that we are never alone. We are always with the One who watched His Son die, and we know that He, truly, is the One who understands. Amen."

Well, that was swell. He had managed to miss the entire sermon, but he had heard enough to give him something to think about through the day.

At least his pants were dry. That was one thing to be thankful for as he and Lily stood at the benediction.

"Lily—," he began, but a touch on his arm interrupted him.

"Sorry to break in to your conversation here," Marnie said, "but apparently there's no water in the men's room. Do you think you could take a look?"

He laughed ruefully. "I already did. That's why there's no water there now."

"It sounds like you're needed elsewhere," Lily said with a smile.

"That's the life of the youth minister," he said. "Always being called to the restroom!"

Lily went to the narthex where the coffee line was set up. It was her turn to serve.

Pastor Mike approached her in the line, and she began in a voice barely above a whisper, "I think you and I should visit. I need to tell you—"

The gentle minister held up his hand. "Is it about your problem with the organization in Chicago?"

Fear washed over her. "Yes."

"Ric has already filled me in. He tells me that he believes you and so does Marnie. So, until I learn otherwise, so do I."

"But you barely know me!" she protested.

"I know Ric, and I know Marnie. And"—he lowered his voice—"I have also talked to someone this morning who has told me that you provided her with some very wise counsel last night, and to my way of thinking, anyone who resolved that long-standing issue is blessed by the Lord indeed. Thank you."

Before she had the chance to recover from her astonishment, he left. She saw him greet a few other congregants and then slip into his coat and leave.

What a burden he must be bearing, she thought. The pressures of his own family illnesses combined with the needs of a disaster-stricken church would be overwhelming for most people, but he seemed to be bearing up well under the strain. That must have been the source of his sermon.

A movement to her side caught her attention, and she saw Marnie hug Victoria. Over her shoulder, Victoria caught Lily's eye and gave her the thumbs-up signal.

Lily smiled.

God was good.

She cleaned the kitchenette and put the coffeepot away for the next week's service and went to say good-bye to Ric.

Ric was doing some last-minute straightening of the sanctuary, picking up the stray papers that were left and putting hymnals back into their holders. He stood up and smiled when he saw her.

"Would you like to join me for lunch?" he asked. "I understand Todd's gone, so we could go someplace where you don't get a toy with your dinner." He smiled winningly, and she almost gave in.

"I don't think I'd better," she said, not daring to look at him as she spoke.

"Can I ask why?" His voice was guarded.

"I—until this, um, matter is settled, I don't think I should. . ." Her voice trailed off.

He took her by the arm and led her to a pew. "Let's talk a minute. Do you know how I feel about you?"

She nodded then shook her head. "Yes. No. I mean, I hope I know how you feel, but I don't really know. I can guess, somewhat that is, but it's just—"

Her words broke off, and she looked at him. "I'm babbling, aren't I?" she asked ruefully.

"Let me put it this way: I have my answer," he said. "So, to dispel any doubts, let me tell you how I feel, right here, in front of God." He motioned toward the altar. "I really like you. My feelings are getting stronger every day."

"But until—"

He laid a finger over her lips. "Shhh. Tell me, are your feelings like mine?"

She nodded. "Yes." Her voice was barely above a whisper. "But—"

He shook his head. "That's all that we need to say now. We can put the rest of this on hold until your heart is clear to go ahead. Just as long as I know and you know that there is a possibility, that we share this kooky feeling."

Why did she feel so miserable when he had just declared what she had wanted to hear? Life was so strange.

"And now, let's go to lunch." When she started to object, he interrupted. "As friends."

"Okay," she said at last. "As friends."

It was good to have a friend like Ric. She hadn't realized until they were at lunch how lonely it was going to be to go on with life as normal without Todd there.

She mentioned it to Ric while they were seated again in Star City, this time at the little café crowded with after-church diners.

"Todd told me that at Shiloh you taught we're all God's friends, and as such we have a kind of network obligation to God's other friends," she explained to him as they waited for their sandwiches and coffee.

"I said that?"

"Well, it's gone through the filter of Todd's mind; I interpreted it, sent it through the filter of *my* mind and out of my mouth. Let's go with you said something like that."

"I'll take credit, although I don't think it's all rightly mine. Todd's a good kid."

"He is," Lily said. "And I miss him already. I don't know how I'm going to get through two weeks without him. He's been my anchor for so long."

"You said his dad died." The sentence fell into the conversation a bit awkwardly, and Ric immediately apologized. "I'm sorry. It's none of my business, I know. I'm sorry."

"No, no, that's all right. It's just strange because Victoria asked about him last night." She immediately clapped her hand over her mouth in an involuntary motion. She hadn't meant to tell anyone about their conversation.

"She told me about it," Ric said reassuringly. "She thinks the sun rises and sets on your happy little face now, I hope you know."

Lily rolled her eyes. "All I did was listen. And pray with her. I just did what anybody would have done."

"But no one *had* done," Ric pointed out. "She'd held herself off for so long that we'd all given her up as virtually untouchable, but she said you made her realize the church would welcome her back, that we were in the business of forgiveness. You accepted her and welcomed her. We'd kind of missed the boat on that one, and I personally don't feel really good about it."

They'd moved away from the subject of Todd's father, and though Lily was tempted to leave it there, there was nothing to be gained by not telling Ric.

"You wanted to know about Todd's father. His name was Barry, and I loved him intensely. He was killed in an accident shortly after we were married." She smiled as she thought of something. "We hadn't even been married long enough to have our first big argument. And certainly not long enough for him to know that a piece of him was living inside me. He died before he found out I was pregnant with Todd."

"Does it hurt to talk about him?" Ric asked. "You don't have to, you know."

"No, it's okay. There used to be this pain that stabbed deep into my heart whenever I thought of him. It was so real that it felt like a knife slashing right into my chest." She winced at the memory. "For a while after he died, I went to the emergency room with regularity, convinced I was having a heart attack."

"It was that bad, huh?" Ric's voice was kind and concerned.

"Yes. But finally one ER doctor took me aside and said, 'Yes, there's something wrong with your heart; it's broken.' He held me while I cried."

Tears gathered in her eyes as she recalled that evening in the hospital, surrounded by the hustle of emergency care, while this doctor took the time to heal her heart.

She wiped her eyes and continued. "Now the memory's faded, like a yellowed piece of paper, but it's still there. And to be honest, there are still times when I miss him so much I can barely stand it. Ric, no matter what happens between us, I have to keep that memory. Not only is he Todd's father, but I loved him."

She looked at Ric and saw tears pooling in those eyes that were as blue as the North Dakota sky.

And at that moment, she fell completely in love with him.

❧

Ric pushed the papers away from him, sliding them to the far side of the desk. More forms, more questions, more times he had to repeat the same sad statistics.

Ninety-eight percent of the community's residences suffered damage.

Almost every business was inoperable for at least two weeks, causing great economic loss.

Now, four months later, things were better, but there was so much more to be done. Buildings could be fixed quickly. People took longer.

He was so tired of the flood. The entire community of Wildwood had moved past the initial upbeat "we can beat this" attitude that followed the flood and was now deeply into wearied exhaustion.

They were short-tempered with each other. More than once, one of them had come to him and asked him flat-out, "How could God do this to us?"

The answers he'd learned in seminary that had seemed so easy to say weren't quite covering what he was encountering now. People were stretched to their limits. Money went only so far. Time went only so far. Patience went only so far.

One of the members of the Parenting with Christ group confessed that she had completely lost her temper with her children over a glass of juice that had spilled. And an older woman had come into his office, shaking because of a grocery-store incident in which angry words had collided.

Marriages were shaken as husbands and wives tried to balance too much. Jobs were precarious as what was called "economic recovery" wasn't progressing as well as it should, and layoffs were occurring to save businesses. Children, the emotional sponges of the community, absorbed everything that was going on, and Ric heard story after story of nightmares, food refusal, separation anxiety, headaches—the list went on and on.

He'd encouraged the congregation to cry.

Tears are God's overflow piping, he liked to tell them. *When you just can't take it, have a good cry. It releases the stuff that's stuck inside and lets it come out.*

Usually it was true, but now it wasn't enough.

They were past crying.

But they were never past praying.

Lily walked through the house again. It was as charming inside as it was outside. It had been kept in immaculate condition, and as near as she could tell, the basement only needed drywall, carpeting, and furniture.

When she said as much to the agent, he laughed. "Can you imagine yourself saying that, say, a year ago? 'Only needs drywall, carpeting, and furniture.' Then it was everything. Now it's nothing."

She wanted the house immediately, but she knew she'd have to wait for the outcome of the investigation, and she'd have to figure out what to do regarding the down payment. Lily took the information about the house that the agent offered her and promised to call him back.

"I won't be able to make a bid on it for a couple of weeks," she said without elaborating. "But I am interested."

"I'll be showing it to others," he warned, "and I can't guarantee that it'll still be on the market much longer. It's a sweet little house."

She frowned. That little corner bedroom with all the windows would be perfect for Todd.

"But," the agent continued, "the market is strange right now. Lots of people want to move, but they've got to sell before they can buy. Others want to sell and get out of Wildwood. Some are sick of renting and figure this is a good time to buy. Market's up and down and around the bend. Go figure."

"I'll have to wait," she said. "I love it, but I'm not in the position to make an offer yet."

He shrugged. "Don't wait forever. Sometimes a good thing just comes your way, and you're a fool not to pick it up."

She stared at him.

He was talking about a house. . .wasn't he?

❧

That night, sleep eluded her. The house was perfect, but could she even think about something like that now? Was she absolutely delusional to even consider it?

She tossed and turned in her narrow bed as questions crowded her mind. Why hadn't there been any progress on her case? How long would she have to wait before there was a response? And, above all, what would that response be?

It wasn't just about her and her job. If the day care were to fail, the entire community would feel the effects. They needed the day care so the businesses could stay open and people could continue to be employed.

She couldn't bear it any longer alone. And this had gotten to the point that even friends like Ric, while they were helpful, were not enough to share this burden with. It was too great.

So she approached Him.

Lily sat up and clutched her pillow to her chest. And then, with the same abandon and cleansing that she had experienced that night in the emergency room after Barry's death, she wept.

She wept for Barry. She wept for Todd. She wept for herself. And she even wept for Douglas Newton.

Chapter 11

Lily bounded into the church office bright and early. In her hands she held a plastic laundry basket filled with assorted containers and jars.

"Ta-da!" she cried triumphantly, placing the basket on the table with a flourish. "I bring you breakfast!"

Marnie helped her unload a small tray of crisply fried bacon, a jar of orange juice, three sliced grapefruit, a packet of still-warm toast, and a napkin-wrapped bowl of cinnamon rolls.

"I didn't bring any coffee, Marnie," she said, giving the woman a quick hug. "Hope you don't mind. Your coffee is the best anyway."

"No, I don't mind at all, but I have to admit this is all a bit overwhelming." Marnie looked at the array of food on the table.

Ric whistled from the doorway. "Where did all this come from?" He picked up a cinnamon roll and bit into it. "Mmmm. This is wonderful! Where on earth did you get rolls like these?"

"From my oven," Lily said proudly. "I made them myself this morning."

Ric's look questioned her, and she nodded.

"I feel 100 percent better, but I suppose I should after finally getting some sleep!" she bubbled happily. "I got up early and decided to bake some rolls, and, well, the whole thing just mushroomed. I guess I was hungry!"

They all sat down at the table, and after Ric offered a blessing, they dug in. When they'd eaten their fill and packed the leftovers into the basket, Marnie poured them each a cup of fresh coffee, and they sat in companionable silence.

Finally Lily spoke. "I've decided what to do," she announced.

"What?" Ric and Marnie chorused.

"I'm not going to let myself be held prisoner to Newton's unethical behavior and my own doubt. I'm moving forward on this."

"Hooray!" Marnie shouted. "It's about time to take some action."

"I've been giving advice," Lily continued, "and all the time I should have been listening to myself. Let go of the past and move forward. The past, when it's kept in the dark, is more troublesome than it is when it's let out into the open."

"I see what you mean," Ric said, and Marnie nodded in agreement. "It makes perfect sense."

"I'm not going to let the past mess up my present and ruin my future. It's the past, and I'm going to keep it there."

"How?" Ric's single-word question dropped in the air like a bomb, but she had an answer.

"I'm going back to Bismarck," Lily declared. "I'm going to see Mr. Palmer or whoever it is that I need to talk to, and I'm going to tell him everything I know about the Nanny Group and Douglas Newton and the vouchers, even the typewriter. Everything."

Her stomach turned once at the thought of what she was saying. Did she have the nerve to follow through on it? Was there any chance that doing this would bring Newton back into her life in an awful way?

"I have to do it," she explained, "because of Todd. He deserves a mother who isn't hiding from the past, especially something like this. I finally truly faced it last night. Folks, I didn't do anything wrong. Not at all. Newton is the snake in the grass. It is all his fault. Every bit of it."

"I knew that." Marnie, her staunch supporter, straightened her back angrily.

"But I didn't," Lily said. "I mean, in an abstract way I did, but I hadn't internalized it and made sense of it. And I had to do that in order for it to mean anything to me."

"How do you want to do this?" Ric asked. "And when do you want to do this?"

"Let's start now."

Lily walked over to the phone and stood there, feeling for all the world like a crusader for justice and truth. The only thing she lacked was a cape.

And the phone number.

❧

Fifteen minutes later, the phone number had been located, and both Ric and Lily had spoken to Mr. Palmer and set up an appointment for Friday.

Ric was already feeling a lightness of spirit. This was definitely a step in the right direction.

"This will work out well," Lily said. "I can pick Todd up on the way home, too."

"It'll be good to have him back," Marnie said. "It's a bit too quiet around here without that little guy."

"Absolutely," Ric agreed. "I've missed having cherry bubbles with him."

Marnie tilted her head questioningly. "Cherry bubbles? What is Eileen serving in there?"

" 'Cherry bubbles' is Todd's version of 'cherry cobbler,'" Ric explained. "I have to confess that I can't think of it without seeing bubbles—and I've never seen a cobbler in there, so his name for it makes complete sense."

Lily nodded. "I can't wait to see him again. I'll probably make a total fool out of myself and embarrass him."

She turned to Ric. "Speaking of embarrassing people, I should warn you about my mother. She'll take your very presence in the same car as an overt avowal of a serious relationship."

He laughed, hoping that its lightness hid the little flip his stomach did at the thought of such a thing. "Really?"

She winked at him. "Really. You should have seen her when I rode up one time in a taxi. I think she still sends that poor driver a Christmas card, just in case...."

"I'll keep that in mind in case she asks for my address," he responded. His eyes twinkled as he leaned over and said in a stage whisper, "Maybe I'll even give it to her."

"Don't you dare!" Lily shot back. "She'll have a heart attack first, and then she'll start calling reception halls from the ambulance."

"Cute, cute, cute," Marnie said, her voice showing her obvious satisfaction. "You two are absolutely darling together, did you know that?"

Lily whirled around. "Are you in cahoots with my mother?" she asked.

Marnie grinned. "She pays me big bucks for what I do, you know. I'm no amateur at this matchmaking business. I take pride in what I do."

Ric shook his head as Lily blushed. "Marnie, don't you have a letter to type or a song to practice or some pencils to sharpen?"

"Yes, boss," Marnie said with a twinkle in her eyes. "You want to be left alone. I get it."

Lily laughed as Marnie left.

It was so good to see Lily happy once more.

Ric broke the spell by pulling out a pad of paper. "We should start making notes so that by the time you sit down in front of Mr. Palmer, you'll have it all prepared. We'll make sure there won't be any questions that take you by surprise. Let's start with making a timeline. I think that's the most important, don't you?"

"I sure do, which is why I already started one." She opened her bag. "But two heads are better than one, so let's work on it together."

They focused on getting it done in detail that week, and every night they worked more on it, with Lily trying to add as much detail as she could remember.

"You know," she said as they got ready to leave Wildwood to drive to Bismarck, "the weirdest thing has happened. The more I've dug around in those memories, the less power they have over me. It's like bringing them into the sunshine of truth has chased away the shades of the lies."

"You'll do great. You're not nervous, are you?" He resisted the urge to pat her hand.

"I'm not, but tell me honestly. I don't look, well, too patriotic, do I?"

He laughed. "Patriotic? Oh, because you're wearing red, white, and blue. No, I think you're okay. I don't have any strong feelings to salute you and say the Pledge of Allegiance, if that's what you mean."

"A sailor. I look like a sailor." She pointed to her blue suit with the red and white accents critically. "Do you have the urge to say, 'Ahoy, mateys!'?"

Ric shook his head. "Not even that."

"Whew. Well, I chose the suit because I can wear my red shoes with it." She smiled down at her bright red shoes.

"I see," Ric said, although he didn't. "Red shoes."

"My mother always said you couldn't be down when you were wearing red shoes."

"Is that true? I've never worn red shoes, at least not in recent memory, so I don't know." He grinned.

"It seems to work. But it doesn't do a thing for nerves."

"Nonsense. You'll be great. You're prepared, you're confident—"

She snorted inelegantly.

"And you're telling the truth about Newton and the Nanny Group," he finished.

"I know that. You believe that. How am I going to get him to take my word on it?"

"He won't, not at first," Ric said thoughtfully. "But at least he'll look into it, and you'll have moved some of the pressure off you and onto the spot where it should be, right over Douglas Newton."

"That's true," she commented.

"And just from talking to Mr. Palmer, he doesn't sound like the kind of guy who's going to overlook the fact that besides embezzling the money, Newton set up a perfectly innocent person to take the blame. No, Mr. Palmer will have something to say about the punishment for that, too, I imagine."

"If there is punishment," she added darkly. "You don't know Douglas. He has a way of getting around almost everything."

"There will be punishment, I'm pretty sure of that. Embezzling is a serious crime, but embezzling from a nonprofit organization is smarmy, and I'm sure they won't let it pass."

"But they have to catch him first," she objected.

"They will. He's changed too much of the truth, and I'll wager that somewhere along the line he's goofed up, some i he didn't dot, some t he neglected to cross. You can't cast suspicion without ending up in the shade yourself."

"Maybe," Lily said. "It's almost too much to hope for."

"Nothing is too much to hope for," Ric said. "Nothing."

❧

It seemed to Lily that all too quickly they were being ushered into Mr. Palmer's office. Ric grabbed her hand and squeezed it. She squeezed back. They were going in.

The room was small, but the side that faced the street was mostly glass, so the sunshine streamed in. To Lily, it seemed like a good sign.

Mr. Palmer introduced himself to them. He was a short, balding man with expressive dark eyes that gleamed from behind wire-rimmed glasses.

"Sit down, please," Mr. Palmer said. "Would you like some coffee?"

"No thank you," they chimed together, and then all three laughed. It was a great way to break the ice, and when Mr. Palmer moved a thick file to the center of his desk, Lily was surprised at how calm she actually felt about it.

"You understand that some discrepancies have been discovered in the record keeping at the Nanny Group?" he asked.

Lily nodded.

"Do you know anything about it?"

A week ago she wouldn't have known how to answer that question. But thanks to Ric's coaching and guidance, she provided Mr. Palmer with a coherent answer.

Her words must have impressed him because throughout their discussion, he took copious notes, pausing occasionally to check a fact or an item in the file.

He withdrew a piece of paper from it and passed it to her. "Do you recognize this?"

"Yes. It's one of the vouchers the Nanny Group used to pay the day care providers."

"Are these your initials?"

"They are my initials, but I did not write them," she answered.

"How do you know?" he persisted.

"I worked closely with the people in this program. I had benefited myself from a similar program when I was in college and a new widow with a young child. I took a personal interest in each of the clients I worked with. And I can assure you that I never met Tammy Novak, the alleged babysitter."

"How can you be sure?"

"Aside from the fact that, as I said before, I worked closely with my clientele and took great interest in them, I also remember or at least recognize their names. This name would particularly ring a bell."

"And why is that?"

"I never wrote checks to shortened names. For example, Ric here would have had his checks issued to Richard Jensen. I felt it impressed upon the young women the seriousness of what we were all doing. With someone named Tammy, I would have asked if that was her given name or a nickname. May I have a piece of paper?"

Mr. Palmer looked puzzled but passed her a page from his notepad.

She wrote *Tamara* on it. "This is often the given name for Tammy. I find it a pretty name, but I have no idea how to pronounce it. I would have asked. To this date, I still don't know if the accent is on the first or second syllable."

"That hardly constitutes proof, Ms. Chamberlain," Mr. Palmer objected.

"No, it doesn't," she agreed. "But it does allow me to say with certainty that I did not have a client named Tammy Novak."

"We are going to subpoena your bank records," he said. "It's something we have to do to check the amounts of the transactions to see if something unusual is there."

"I have nothing to hide."

"We'll also check into Newton's accounts and the account that the Nanny Group had at State Federal," he added.

"State Federal?" Lily shook her head. "Not unless they've changed banks. Or closed an account or two."

Mr. Palmer suddenly looked wary, and he drew his pad of paper closer to him. "What do you mean?"

"We didn't use State Federal. That was way across town. In our building there was a smaller branch of, let me see, what was it called? First Security, that's it. First Security. We used that for the voucher disbursements. And another one, it was about two blocks away—oh, Illinois National. We used that for donated funds that were nonspecified. And the checks to the mothers in educational programs came from Lake Center."

She was aware that both Ric and Mr. Palmer were watching her closely. And it began to dawn on her what was going on.

"Which bank was your paycheck drawn on?" Mr. Palmer asked.

"You know, that I'm not sure. I used direct—oh no!" The impact of it was overwhelming. She had to remind herself to breathe. "I used direct deposit, so he could have manipulated all kinds of functions in my bank account, couldn't he?"

"You had two bank accounts, I believe," Mr. Palmer said, leafing through the papers in the file. "And both were at—"

"State Federal," she finished for him. "I had one account. I never had two."

He showed her the notations on the investigator's report. "See? Two accounts."

"I am telling you the truth. I did not have two accounts. I had one account, a checking account that had nothing more interesting than checks that were made out to the grocery store, the utility company, and the apartment manager."

Ric spoke for the first time. "How hard is it to track bank activity? Is there anything she can do to prove that the account is not hers?"

Mr. Palmer considered the question. "It's amazing what can be done, especially when the federal authorities are involved."

"Federal authorities?" Lily squeaked.

He turned his luminous eyes toward her, and Lily hoped that what she saw there was sympathy. "If you are telling me the truth, the best thing for you at this stage is to bring in the federal authorities. They may very well hound everyone to tears, but they have the ability to ferret out the most elusive of information."

"I'm telling you the truth," she assured him.

"Then may I ask you to sign the permission to begin investigating your banking activities?" Mr. Palmer asked her.

Lily nodded and, after reading it, signed the form Mr. Palmer gave her.

"This has been a very interesting conversation," he said, standing up and offering them each his hand. "I'll be in touch."

"Whew!" Lily breathed a sigh of relief as they left the office. "I think it went okay, but I don't know. What do you think?"

"You did a super job in there. I was really proud of you."

"I'm so glad you were with me," Lily said. "It meant so much to me."

"I didn't say much." Ric grinned. "I was too busy praying for you!"

"And it worked." She paused as she noted Rick patting his pockets, a concerned look on his face. "What's the matter?"

"I think I forgot my keys." A thought dawned on his face. "Oh wait. I think they're on Mr. Palmer's desk. Better go get them."

They returned to the office. As she raised her hand to knock on the door, she heard Mr. Palmer's voice: "Yes, Newton. Douglas Newton. Did you get the names of the banks? Good. It looks like this money taken from the nonprofit is piddly stuff compared to what's sitting on my desk now. Are you ready for this? I think this young lady has just stumbled across a money-laundering setup."

Lily and Ric's eyes met in shock.

What had they gotten into?

❧

"Are you going to knock?" Lily asked in a hushed voice.

"No." Ric couldn't imagine interrupting the conversation they'd just overheard.

"Then how are you going to get the keys?" She clutched at his elbow.

"I'm not. I'd rather buy a new car to drive home than break into *that* discussion."

"That'd be pricey." Lily's eyes danced with laughter.

"But worth it. Unless, of course, *you* want to pop in and snag the keys."

"Uh-uh. So what kind of car are we buying?"

They finally told one of the secretaries farther down the hall that they'd left the keys in Mr. Palmer's office, and she was able to retrieve them.

"Wow," Lily breathed when they were outside. "That's bizarre. Money laundering!"

"And beyond that, it's going to get even weirder. They don't launder money just because it's smudged. It's drug money or gambling profits or something illegal. This is big-league stuff."

"Ric, before we go pick up Todd, can we go somewhere and have a cup of coffee or something so my heart can start beating normally again? I don't want him to see me like this."

Within minutes, they were in the real-world environment of a brightly lit coffee shop.

"I'm still overwhelmed by it all," she said. "And I've got to admit, I'm getting worried. Do you think they'll do anything to us? I'm worried about Todd."

"I think Newton is probably more at risk than you are. I know practically nothing about crime, but I imagine he's not the big cheese of the operation.

He probably has to answer to others higher up. And I wouldn't want to be in his shoes in the next couple of months."

His heart was still pounding away wildly. The closest he'd ever gotten to this kind of criminal activity was late at night on his couch, a safe distance from the cops show on television.

Lily sipped her coffee. "I can't stand it," she burst out. "I know I said I didn't want Todd to see me until I'd calmed down, but at this rate, I won't see him for years. Can we go get him now?"

"Sure," Ric said easily. "Let's go."

Twenty-four minutes later, a tiny rocket named Todd propelled himself into Lily's arms while her mother beamed at Ric and asked him: "What's your address?"

Chapter 12

Ric grinned as he caught Lily's attention over her mother's shoulder. "Do you think I can trust her?" he asked Lily.

She shook her head. "I wouldn't count on it. You know, she's had offers to buy her mailing list from those junk mail distributors. But she does send out nice Christmas cards."

"Lily Marie Chamberlain!" her mother said. "You tell him the truth right now."

The sheer normalness of this conversation, this loving bicker between mother and daughter settled on her soul like the balm of Gilead.

She hugged her mother. "You are a wonderful, wonderful woman. I absolutely adore you."

"What's all this about?" her mother asked, but as Lily noticed the pleased smile that played across her face, she mentally resolved to tell her more frequently how much she loved her.

"Well, did you have a good time with Gran?" she asked Todd, who was buzzing around the group of adults like an excited bee.

"The best! We went to a couple of movies, and we ate lots and lots of ice cream, and we made cookies. I meant to save some for you, but I ate them on a accident."

"You ate them 'on a accident'?" she asked. "Is that compared to eating them 'on a purpose'?"

"I guess so. I was just standing there, and the cookies were on this plate, and we were waiting for you, and the next thing I knew, the cookies weren't on the plate, but they were in my tummy." He made an exaggerated expression of regret as he looked at his mother.

"That's okay, tiger. I can live without the cookies." She turned to Ric. "I suppose we should go now."

"Oh no, not so soon!" her mother objected. "Can't you stay tonight, too?"

Lily knew her mother had enjoyed having Todd stay with her, but she could see the exhaustion in her face. This time with Todd had been short, but it had been just on the edge of too much for her. She knew that as soon as they left, her mother would go in and take a nap.

"We'll be back next month, maybe during Labor Day. How does that sound?" she suggested when she saw her mother's tiredness battling with the urge to spend time with her daughter and grandson. "That's only a couple of weeks away."

Her mother nodded. "I'll be counting the days." Then she turned to Ric. "You're invited, too."

Lily started to say something, but Ric smoothly intercepted her remark with, "I'd be delighted to see you again."

When they were in the car and on their way back to Wildwood with Todd in the backseat happily playing with his new toys, courtesy of his indulgent grandmother, she mentioned it.

He looked at her, his blue eyes soft. "I was serious. If you don't mind, I'd kind of enjoy going with you and Todd. I like your mom."

"I like her, too," Todd piped up from the backseat. "She's really neat, and she knows how to play 'Chopsticks' on the piano, and she taught me how to play it, too. When we get back, I'll play it for you. And you know what else, when we were at the museum, we—"

The sun was warm, she was with Ric, and Todd was safely with her again. For just a while, she was able to push the worries of her life into the back of her mind and bring those things that had been in the back to the front. The switch was relaxing, and she felt herself smiling drowsily.

Ric broke into her reverie. "Thinking deep thoughts, Lily?"

"I'm not thinking. I'm simply enjoying being here with you and Todd and reveling in having spent some time with my kooky mother and pretending there is nothing, absolutely nothing else in the world."

"Sounds wonderful," he commented briefly. "I wasn't kidding about liking your mother. She's terrific. And I felt like I wasn't a stranger."

"You weren't," Todd contributed from behind them. "She already knew about you."

"Yes, Todd," Lily said. "We're all friends through God, right?"

"Not just that." He paused to put the wheel back on one of his toy cars. "I told her all about you, Ric. She liked to hear me talk about you, so I told her lots and lots and lots."

Ric looked at the boy in the rearview mirror. "And what did you tell your grandmother?" he asked, his voice casual.

"I told her that I liked you a lot, and that you were a good guy, and that Mommy liked you a lot, and that we were going to live in a brick house with a fireplace and a place to grow carrots."

"You told her about the house you and I are looking at?" Lily asked.

He nodded. "And I told her we were going to live there and maybe we would buy it if the basement wasn't cracked in half."

"And who all did you say was going to live there?" she asked warily.

"Four of us."

"Four?"

"You, me, Ric, and Snap."

Her concerns about having Ric included in the group evaporated upon the unexpected appearance of Snap in the group.

"Who," she asked cautiously, "is Snap?"

"I am me, you are you, Ric is Ric," Todd explained carefully, "and Snap is my dog."

For the remainder of the trip back to Wildwood, Todd entertained them with the adventures of his invisible dog, Snap, whom he had apparently found in a park in Mandan. More than ever, Lily promised herself, she would do all she could to settle them into a house where he could have a dog named Snap.

～

From the day care came the sounds of singing.

"Listen," Pastor Mike said. He stood at Ric's elbow, amusement in his voice as they listened to the children. "You know Corie, the little girl who Todd befriended? It turns out the girl has quite a voice, even if she doesn't always get the lyrics quite right."

"Jesus loves me, thistle snow!" Corie caroled out. "Forty Bibles tell me so!"

"Well, I'm not sure about the thistle snow, but she's got the forty Bibles right," the senior minister said. "Actually, I like her version even better. The more Bibles, the better!"

"Todd's really brought her out of her shell. He's quite a kid. I'll tell you, I missed him fiercely when he was visiting his grandmother. This place was entirely too quiet." Ric grinned as Corie took on more words to the song: "Little buds to Him be song. They wear wink, but He spells strong."

"Again," Pastor Mike noted, "I can't argue with the girl."

They walked down the hall toward the office. "We're still waiting for word about the day care situation, aren't we?" the older man asked.

"Yes, but there is hope breaking on the horizon. Let's go into your study, and I'll fill you in," Ric suggested.

Nearly an hour later, Ric leaned back in one of the green, overstuffed chairs in the minister's office, nearly spent after filling in Pastor Mike on the events in Bismarck. "So I think it'll all take care of itself eventually."

"It sounds to me like the scoundrel was counting on Lily to take the road of least resistance," Pastor Mike mused. "As long as she didn't say anything, his game was still alive. He could do anything. And once she left, he was free to do whatever he wanted with the records."

"And that's going to be his undoing," Ric said. "You know the Bible says in Proverbs 16: 'Pride goeth before destruction, and an haughty spirit before a fall.' The more Douglas Newton felt that he was unbreakable, the more he laid his own trap."

"It is one of the greatest learning lines in the Bible, isn't it?" Pastor Mike leaned forward and made a note on the pad on his desk. "I think I'll do a sermon about it. We often collapse the verse into the more modern interpretation of 'pride goeth before a fall,' and it certainly does, but there's more to this verse than that."

Ric tilted his head. This was one of his favorite parts of this job, talking about the Bible with such a wise man.

The senior pastor continued. "The verse says that pride takes us to destruction, not to just a fall. It's ruin. Now, sheer snootiness, that's a different story. You're snooty? You'll fall. Will you end up destroyed? Maybe. But the two are definitely separated in the Bible."

Ric's thoughts flew right to Victoria Campbell. She had definitely qualified as what Pastor Mike called "snooty," and she had fallen. Yet she wasn't defeated, and now she was back with a clean spirit and better intentions.

God was pleased. Ric knew that.

He was about to share his deep thoughts with his fellow minister, but the door flew open as Todd barreled in, a Styrofoam cup in his hand.

"This is for you, Pastor Mike," Todd said, leaning on tiptoe and sliding the cup across the polished wooden desk as little bits of soil escaped onto the sleek surface. "It's a plant. See? It's just a little guy. We grew it from a teeny-tiny seed. It's from us at the day care, all of us, although Miss Eileen planted it, but she let each of us poke our fingers in the dirt once. It's a Marry Gold. Are you married?"

"Well Todd, thank you, and it's wonderful, and yes, I'm married." Pastor Mike's eyes crinkled with laughter.

"Good. Otherwise I don't think it'd be a good idea for you to have a Marry Gold. You," Todd said, turning toward Ric, "don't get one, and I'm sorry because I kind of knocked it off the ledge where the books are. We have another one planted for you, but it hasn't popped out yet, so there's nothing to see, but you can come see it if you want to. Even though there isn't anything to see. It just looks like dirt, but you know what? There's a Marry Gold growing under it, and one day it'll pop out, and then you can see it."

Eileen's voice called from the hall. "Todd? Todd? You were supposed to wait. . . ."

"Bye," the little boy said, and as quickly as he'd appeared, he vanished.

"It just looks like dirt, but under it all, there's a seed growing," Ric said thoughtfully. "Sorry, Mike, but I'm taking that one for the children's sermon!"

❧

Lily had just arrived the next morning when Marnie hailed her from the office. "You have a call on line two. I think it's that Mr. Palmer. I'll transfer it to you."

Lily dashed down the hall and unlocked the door to her office with trembling fingers. What would he have to say to her?

"Ms. Chamberlain, this is Carl Palmer. I wanted to update you on your case."

Her voice sounded remarkably calm as she answered, "I appreciate it."

"We're examining the bank accounts in your name as well as those of the Nanny Group, and we're looking into the statement you made in my office. Now between you and me, those aspects of the current situation that you brought to my attention are serious, but I didn't hear you make any allegations or claims, and I will say so in a court of law if necessary."

"What does that mean?" Lily asked. He might as well have been speaking another language. She didn't understand a word he said.

There was a pause, and then he said, "In case Newton attempts to discredit you."

"He's already done that," Lily responded.

"Perhaps 'discredit' is too weak of a word. Maybe I should say in case he would try to charge you with defamation."

Defamation? He might charge her with defamation? Lily was almost surprised that she didn't react in anger. Instead, she closed her eyes and shook her head. "I wouldn't put it above him," she said to Mr. Palmer.

"It is a defense that is occasionally used, although it doesn't often go to court. Usually it's merely a way of trying to get the other person to back down." His voice was noncommittal, but she could sense an undercurrent in his words: *Be careful.*

"At any rate, you can expect a visit from two officers of the law who will take your statement formally, and there may be others as well from both state and federal agencies as this thing expands. I'm not sure at this stage who all will be involved."

"I understand."

"Ms. Chamberlain," he said, his voice lowering a bit, "ask for identification. Keep track of who you talk to, their names, agencies, everything you can. Don't get in a car with anyone to ride to an interview. Meet them there or offer to make your statement in your office. And if you know someone reliable, perhaps that young man who accompanied you to see me, have that person with you during the statement. And remember, you do have the right to legal counsel if things get too dicey. If you ask for it, they must stop interrogating you at that point. Actually, you might want to think about retaining counsel now."

The conversation ended with a few pleasantries that floated over and around her head, and at some point she hung up the phone.

She stood up and, on shaky feet, walked down the hall to Marnie's office, where she was talking to Victoria Campbell. Ric looked up through the open door of his office, and suddenly all was quiet.

"I need a lawyer."

Her words fell into the silence with the strength of a megaton blast.

Ric was at her side in a second, and soon all three were asking her questions at once.

She related the conversation, pausing occasionally to fill Victoria in on the gaps, and at the end Ric leaned back thoughtfully.

"I think it's a good sign," he said at last.

"Are you out of your mind?" Lily couldn't believe what he was saying.

"I think it means that he is convinced you're not guilty. Otherwise, I don't think the conversation would have gone the way you've relayed it to us. It would have been much more matter-of-fact, and I doubt he would have advised you to get a lawyer. He probably would have asked if you had a lawyer."

"But why do I need a lawyer if I'm not going to jail?" she wailed.

"You need a lawyer so you *don't* go to jail," Marnie said.

"My ex is a lawyer," Victoria said. "We had our problems when we were married, but as lousy as he was as a husband, he was a superb lawyer. And one thing I learned from him was that lawyers, among other things, protect the process of law, even though it may not seem that way to us. So you need a lawyer to make sure your rights aren't trampled on in the search for justice."

"What does that mean?" Marnie asked.

"I'll try to clarify," Victoria responded. "Heaven knows I heard the spiel enough times from him. The government is set up as a system of checks and balances, and one of the balances comes from lawyers, who make sure that when their clients enter the court system, all the rules are followed. That's why you hear about these awful people getting out on technicalities."

She motioned for them all to sit down. "Sorry. This takes awhile to go through. We're—all of us—given legal rights regarding searches and evidence and admissibility and that kind of stuff. For every single case, a good lawyer will make sure that those rights are preserved."

"Yeah, but that stinks when somebody gets out because something was wrong with the arrest!" Marnie said.

"I agree, but in the long run, it's a protection, because if it's ignored once, it can become precedent and become like a new regulation or law, and that's wrong." Victoria raised her eyebrows. "Wow. I usually don't give speeches. Maybe I was paying closer attention than I thought when Mr. Wonderful was talking."

"But how on earth am I going to get a lawyer?" Lily stood up and walked to the window. Outside the sky was blue, and she could hear a bird singing.

Victoria picked up the phone and dialed a number. "Max Campbell, please." She covered the mouthpiece with her hand. "Watch this. Max? This is Victoria. A friend of mine needs some legal backup, someone to be with her when she's questioned by the feds, and really, to make sure that whoever's doing the interrogation is legit."

She paused and smiled. "No, she's innocent. She really is. She's too good to do something like—yeah, it's her. Yes. You will? Great! I'll send her down, and smooches to you and the missus. Bye!"

She hung up the phone with a big grin. "You got a lawyer!"

"But I thought you and your ex weren't on good terms," Lily said slowly. "How did you. . . ?"

Victoria smiled. "After our talk, I called him, and he and I and his new wife sat down, and we talked the whole thing out, and while I still think she's a money-grubbing husband stealer, well, to put it nicely, it's a perfect match. We've come to a new understanding, and we're all happier, especially Edgar.

So Max is willing to give you a helping hand, no problem, in gratitude for all you've done for us."

"Wow." That was all Lily could say. That and, "Thank you!"

Max Campbell was quiet and as steady as a rock. He sat beside her through all the interrogations, occasionally interrupting to ask for clarification but generally listening and watching like a hawk.

She was relieved when, after the final interrogation, he took her into his office and gave her his opinion of what was occurring.

"It looks to me as if you're not under suspicion anymore. It appears that the interest seems to have shifted to Douglas Newton and away from you except as a witness. I have to explain, though, that it looks as if we're moving into federal territory with the bank question. Banks, you know, are controlled by federal law, and violations of banking regulations generally result in the FBI being called in."

"The FBI?" Lily breathed. "I can't believe it!"

"Believe it." He smiled at her, the first time he'd done so since meeting her. "You'll be able to say you have an FBI file."

"Swell. My claim to fame."

"Could be worse."

It didn't take a Ph.D. to figure out what he was referring to, and she nodded.

"So, I think you're okay at this point," Max finished. "But don't hesitate to give me a call if you have a question or if someone else shows up wanting to chat with you. Don't talk about this on the phone or on e-mail, and don't write or sign anything without letting me take a gander at it first. Deal?"

"Deal." She stood up and shook his hand. "I can't tell you how much this has taken a load off my mind, Max. I appreciate everything you've done for me."

"And I appreciate what you've done for Victoria and my family. I don't know what you said to her, but it sure changed her around. She says she's back at Resurrection, too."

"Yes, and we're glad to have her. She's a grand addition to everything we do."

"I've been thinking about Resurrection. I used to go there, you know, before Victoria and I split up. I kind of miss the place," he mused.

"You're always welcome back, you know."

"It might be awkward for Victoria and my wife, so I think we'll pass." But his voice sounded wistful, and Lily recognized the undercurrent of need.

"Do you have another church home?" she asked him gently.

"Another? No, no, I don't. I haven't been in a church since I left Resurrection except for funerals and weddings. Tiffani and I got married at the courthouse here." There was a note of regret in his words.

"I can understand your reluctance to come back to Resurrection," Lily said. "But God lives in many houses. I'm sure there are others that will suit your needs here in Wildwood or one of the other surrounding communities.

You could ask Ric. He'd know what would be compatible with our beliefs at Resurrection."

"I may do that."

He walked her to the door. "Do you realize what you've just done?" he asked her. "Not only did you bring Victoria back to the church, now you've got me thinking that Tiff and I might search for one to attend. Did you ever think about going into sales?"

❧

Ric came over that night to join Lily and Todd for a picnic in the playground area.

"We do this when it's hot," she explained. "It's more comfortable out here, and Todd likes the change of pace from the kitchen table. I love this time, what my mom always called 'the cool of the evening.'"

As they sat on the blanket they'd spread out, eating peanut butter and jelly sandwiches, Ric reflected on how much she and Todd had integrated themselves into his life and how much he'd come to expect Todd's cheerful voice and Lily's light humor every day.

Todd couldn't stop talking about kindergarten, which started next week. He was in the morning group, Lily explained, and since the school was only a block away, she planned to walk over each day at eleven thirty and bring him back to the church where he'd eat lunch and stay until she was finished for the day.

He and Lily had gone that afternoon for an orientation, and Todd was ready to spin off the planet with excitement.

"This weekend we have to buy crayons and a backpack and some pencils. You should see how many books there are! The teacher says we're going to read them all, every single one of them! And there are puppets and—"

"Todd, mouth closed," Lily said with a tolerant smile. "Eat, then talk, or vice versa. But not at the same time."

Todd popped the last of his sandwich in his mouth and zoomed to the playground.

"The child never walks. Ever." Lily smiled ruefully.

"Hey, Ric! Watch me!" Todd called from the top of the slide and then proceeded to launch himself down headfirst.

"That's quite a trick, but I think we'd all be much happier if you'd go feet first," Ric said with a chuckle.

"That's for babies," Todd called back. "Want to see me stand on top of the swing set? I think I can walk from one end to the other up there. Like a circus guy!"

He zoomed toward the swing set, but Ric leaped to his feet and intercepted him and brought him back to the blanket.

"When you are in the circus, then maybe, just maybe, your mom will let you do that, but don't count on it. Your mom is a chicken."

Todd made clucky sounds and then helped himself to another sandwich.

Ric had accompanied her to each of the interrogations and kept track of all that had been going on, but it had become more than that. He found himself there in ways totally unrelated to their jobs: helping Todd learn to shoot baskets with occasional accuracy, reaching the elusive jar from the high shelf in the kitchen, changing the oil in her car to save her a trip to the service station.

"Do you have any dreams for the future, Ric?" Lily asked.

"Me?"

"Yes, you. There's nobody else here named Ric. I'm just wondering. This has all been about me and about the people here who have been impacted by the flood, and through it all, you've been helping other people get on with their lives so they can allow themselves to dream. But does Ric allow himself to dream?"

"Of course I do."

"Just tell me to hush up if I'm being too pushy," Lily said, pushing her hair back self-consciously. "You don't have to tell me anything."

He lay on his side and propped himself up on his elbow. "I will tell you everything. What do you want to know?"

"Well, for one thing, why children's ministry?"

"I made a commitment almost two years ago. I stood in an orphanage in Central America, in the midst of the worst conditions I'd ever seen, and I promised God that I would do two things when I returned. I promised God I would look after His children here and that I would use His financial blessings to help the orphanage."

"I had no idea," she said softly.

"I send a check every month to a friend who is still there, and he makes sure it gets used wisely." His next words barely made it over the lump in his throat. "And one day I would like to adopt a child from there."

"That would be a very lucky child indeed." Lily reached over and touched his hand. "You'll be a great father."

Todd leaped over him and ran back to the playground.

Once the cloud of the Nanny Group fiasco was lifted, he was going to do it. He was going to let himself fall in love.

He looked over at Lily, cross-legged on the blanket and calling encouraging words to Todd, who was now trying to climb the rope ladder to the top. The late afternoon summer sunlight glinted across the scene, illuminating her with bright gold, and he knew it was too late.

He had already fallen.

✎

The verdict came in bit by bit, not in one glorious swash.

The vouchers, it had been determined by one of the auditors, did not belong to the group that had run through the formal auditing done earlier in the year.

Subtle differences in the paper identified those vouchers as counterfeit, and further, that they had been used as part of the embezzling scheme.

A handwriting analyst had filed an affidavit stating that the initials on the faked vouchers were likely not hers and further attested to the fact that major variances in the pressure exerted during typing indicated that Lily had not typed them, and that, in fact, a left-handed person had typed them.

"Douglas is left-handed," Lily said as Ric read the report over her shoulder late one October afternoon.

"I didn't know they could tell who did the typing, but maybe they can. It says 'major variances.' I wonder what that means," Ric said.

"Well, I've seen him type. You'd think it was a personal thing with him. He attacks the typewriter so hard that sometimes I'd come to use it and the keys would be all jammed together. It'd take me about fifteen or twenty minutes to untangle them. I've seen a couple get fixed together, but never as many as with him." She shuddered at the memory of his temper.

"Well, you're pretty well cleared on the vouchers," Ric said, sitting down in the visitor's chair in her office. "That's got to be a load off your mind."

"I cannot begin to tell you how I feel. There's more to come, I know, but I have to keep hope that if I've been cleared on that part of it, the rest has to follow soon, and I'll be fully cleared. I just know I will."

"I agree," he said. "It'll be nice to have you out from under this cloud. Do you, um, think that you're clear enough to consider, um. . ."

It was cute how he stammered his way through the sentence.

She took pity on him, but she couldn't resist teasing him. "Ric, can I ask you something? It's kind of personal, though."

"Personal? Um, well, sure. Go ahead."

"Ric, would you like to go out with me tonight?" At his look of surprise, she added, "Yes, sir, I'm asking you for a date."

She'd never seen anyone blush so deeply. And then he said yes.

Todd stayed with Marnie and Sam to "help" at the Bright Spot. Lily tried not to imagine what kind of "help" he would offer.

The evening was enchanting. They returned to the Wildwood Inn, and their dinner conversation was light and carefree, not about anything in particular but truly about everything that mattered, like what her favorite flower was, what kind of music he liked, what games she had played as a child.

After dinner they went for a walk along the river. The moon was full, and it glimmered on the now-tamed river in a shimmering golden orb, with red and orange and topaz leaves drifting around it.

"It's hard to believe that this river was once as wild as it was," she said as they strolled along its edge. "I look at it now, and I can't see it as something that would damage so many lives."

"It's taken awhile to get to the point where I trust it," Ric responded. "But now it's so calm and peaceful looking, it seems as if the flood never happened at all. It's almost easy to believe that."

"And I'm impressed at how people have come back after such a disaster. They have such strength."

She shivered, and Ric took off his jacket and wrapped her in it.

"We should go back to the car," he suggested, "before you get chilled."

She looked up at him.

Maybe it was the moon. Maybe it was the crisp smell of autumn fires on the wind. Maybe it was the splendor of the maple trees.

Or maybe it was love.

Chapter 13

Ric fell asleep with a smile on his face, and he woke up with one, too. He smiled through his morning coffee, the bowl of cold cereal, and all the other morning rituals.

Lily. It was all Lily.

Did everyone feel this way when they were in love? Did every single moment of their lives revolve around the beloved, the way the earth orbits the sun?

It was a wonderful, heady feeling, but he needed to pull it together and get some work done. There was more to being the youth minister than worrying about the future of the day care.

He had programs to organize, most notably a Christmas pageant. It would have to be something that didn't require great costuming efforts, since all their materials had ended up in sodden piles along the berm earlier in the year.

Maybe this would be the year to do a simple carol sing, along with Bible verses. The more he thought about it, the more he liked it. He recalled the intensity of some of the parents about who would be chosen as the stars of the shows—and who wouldn't be chosen.

God didn't choose some over the others. This might be a better way to celebrate His love, by having all the youngsters be stars. Shy or outgoing, every one of them would have the chance to shine in their own way.

The day care had grown more, thanks to a change in their licensing, and with more children—and thankfully, more helpers—there would be more balancing and juggling to include them, too.

Later today he'd have to get to the post office. A box of gifts was ready to be shipped to Central America.

This train of thought reminded him that the Parenting with Christ group was meeting in the afternoon, and he needed to prepare for that.

Being in love might be a glorious thing for poets, but it sure wreaked havoc on a minister's schedule.

&

Lily stood outside the door of the day care, listening. Eileen began each day with the Lord's Prayer, and although many of the words were beyond the children's vocabulary, she was helping them understand.

She had been headed for the kitchen to get a fresh cup of coffee for Ric, but she'd stopped upon hearing Eileen's voice.

Today Eileen was explaining to them what "trespasses" meant. Through the glass in the door, Lily could see that the day care leader had the line from the Lord's Prayer on the chalkboard: *Forgive us our trespasses, as we forgive those who trespass against us.*

Being Christlike, she was explaining, meant that we needed to forgive those who had done something bad to us.

Forgiveness. What a beautiful word.

Forgive the past. Forgive Douglas Newton. Forgive herself for ever doubting that God was in charge and that He was seeing her through this time of suffering and that He was always with her, as He always had been and always would be.

She ran into Ric's office. "It happens, it truly happens," she said in wonder as she sat in the chair next to him. "He takes away the pain."

Ric nodded.

All of her worries evaporated as she gave herself to God and renewed her commitment to a life of His service.

"I've prayed for this before, but somehow this time something was different. I don't know what it was. I wonder why God heard my prayer this time, but He didn't before."

"Oh, He heard it," Ric responded. "And He's been answering it, just as He's been answering my prayers, but we can't always discern His ways. We don't always understand."

"It's very complicated," she said, still feeling a bit overwhelmed.

It was almost too much to focus on at the moment, and she seized upon the first thing she noticed.

"Your coffee!" she said to Ric. "I forgot!"

She stood up and went into the kitchen, his cup in her hand.

Almost absentmindedly, she placed the cup on the counter, ignoring the splash on the white counter.

Why, she wondered, had God chosen to direct her life in this way? Surely she would have been serving His purpose in the Nanny Group had she stayed.

She picked up the empty coffeepot and looked out the window. She could see the trees that ringed the playground leaning toward each other, almost as if they were conferring with each other on this cool October evening. If she listened closely, she could hear their leafy whispers. What were they talking about? What were their secrets?

But that was just fancy. It was the wind bending the trees, and the soft murmurs were only the leaves as the autumn-night breeze snatched them from the trees and flung them into the sky for one last splendid flight before settling to the ground.

This was her favorite time of year, and she had nearly missed it entirely because she had been so caught up in her problems.

Time didn't stop for her. It marched right on, and she hadn't heard the lesson of the trees. *Move on, too*, the trees were saying to her. *Bend to His will as we do to the wind's.*

She had a clarity of vision now that she had never had before. The world was not as confusing as it had been, now that she could see it.

The Nanny Group—it all made sense.

Her mind worked it through, piece by piece.

She had been used as an arm of the truth. Through every bit of the circumstances of the Nanny Group, from the moment of that initial discovery of the altered voucher to the understanding she'd just received, the momentum had been toward the truth.

What had happened to her was almost incidental when seen in that light. Through the movement of her life, she had begun the long process of not only bringing Douglas Newton to justice, but stopping a destructive process that would eventually have killed a deserving organization, the Nanny Group. Now the Nanny Group, for all its difficulties, would be stronger and able to serve those in need even better.

And Ric—his faith had been tested again and again. Had he been found wanting in the Lord's eyes?

No. There had to be another reason, and it would not be hers to know. Ric was the one who had to understand it. Her role in it was to be beside him, as he was beside her, and stand when he was weak, comfort when he was weary, uphold when he faltered.

It wasn't hers to carry. It was God's.

The realization brightened her heart.

"He'll take it if I share it with Him," she mused out loud. "God is always ready."

Ric came into the kitchen. "Lily, did you say something?"

She turned to him, the still-empty coffeepot forgotten in her hands.

"Ric, I feel as if a load has been lifted from my soul. God has heard my prayer."

"It's going to be all right," he said. "I can feel it, too."

He took the coffeepot from her hands. "Here, I think I'd better do this."

As he found a filter and measured the grounds into the basket, he continued, "Just because we prayed and we have a good feeling about it, that doesn't mean God is going to make things go our way."

"A bicycle prayer," Lily said.

"A bicycle prayer? What does that mean?"

"Oh, that's from Todd, of course. He explained to me that I wasn't supposed to pray for a new bicycle because that isn't what prayer is all about."

A smile played over Ric's face. "Were you trying to pray for a bicycle?"

She shook her head and laughed. "If I were praying for transportation, I'd select something with a motor and four wheels and a heater, thank you very much. No, this was a bit more general than that."

"I remember the lesson. He must have gotten that from Shiloh," Ric said.

"It was one of those 'Which would you pray for?' exercises, and as I recall, a bicycle was one of the choices."

"Todd said no, I hope."

He grinned. "I think he had the right answer, sure. A few of the kids said no, they wouldn't pray for a bicycle, and just as I was feeling rather smug about having taught the lesson so well, I found out it was because they already had one."

"There's nothing to teach you humility like a child," Lily agreed.

"True. Anyway, we have to face the fact that at any moment we may get another surprise, and we need to remember to keep sharing it with God."

"And it's not going to go away overnight. Those memories are still there," she said. "And I don't know if I want them to go away entirely because they're there, in place, as a learning tool for me."

He nodded. "Good point. They do serve a purpose, although we may not like to acknowledge it."

He poured the water into the pot and switched on the brewer. Soon the warm aroma of coffee filled the small kitchen.

"I really do believe in the power of prayer," Ric said as the coffeemaker perked its way through its brewing cycle.

"Plus, think about what God has done with trouble in the world. Look at how He's reworked this—the flood, the problems rising from the Nanny Group, the situation with Victoria Campbell—somehow it's converged and become something wonderful: the day care."

Ric poured her a fresh cup of coffee, but she left it untouched on the counter.

"You know what else I realized tonight?" Lily went on. "I don't have to shoulder it alone any longer. I mean, I sort of knew it all along, but now I really know. With the cross, He took my burden. He carried all of that with Him to the hill."

He didn't answer at first. And somehow, Lily knew that more than one prayer had been answered.

"The burden is lighter when two or more share it," he said softly.

"Somehow, I think, it had to be you," she added thoughtfully. "Does it seem to you that our meeting was part of His plan?"

"Nothing happens by accident," he said. "Nothing. Not even this."

He took her in his arms, and there, in the church kitchen and in the glorious presence of God and all His angels, he kissed her.

Two lips pressing against each other. It was a simple act. There was nothing in it at all to account for the sudden weakness in Lily's knees, or her unexplained inability to stand up on her own power, or the singing that resounded in her ears.

Nothing, perhaps, except that it was so long awaited, this kiss, and it was so absolutely, so totally, so incredibly right.

There was promise implicit in this kiss. This man cherished her—she knew that—and he cherished her son. But above all, he cherished their Lord. He would never do anything to hurt her or Todd.

It was a precious point of contact, this kiss. She wanted it to last forever, into the eternity it held forth as a covenant.

They parted, and Lily smiled at Ric.

His blue eyes, as clear and bright as heaven itself, rested on her face as if memorizing it.

"I've been wanting to do that for a long time," he said, his voice husky with emotion.

"I've been waiting for you," she responded. "For a while I worried that it might never happen, that I would have to go through my entire life without a kiss from you."

He ran one finger over her lips. "Perish the thought. Whenever you want a kiss, Lily Chamberlain, all you have to do is ask."

"I'm asking."

Their lips met again, and the sweetness of it all renewed itself.

She leaned into him, and he into her, and for the moment they were one.

This love, and it was indeed love, was special, a sacred reward from God.

The love she had known with Barry was holy, too, and she would treasure it and its product, Todd, for as long as she lived. But it had been so terribly foreshortened with his accident, and all she had known was the first bloom of their love.

This love—this love would linger. It would be tested and grow stronger. It would stumble and maybe fall, but it would rise again and be whole. Nothing could stop them. Nothing at all.

Not even the voice of her son as he padded up behind them in his bare feet.

"Eeew," Todd said. "Cooties."

❧

Ric sat with the members of the Parenting with Christ group. There were four couples attending now, and earlier in the week he'd had inquiries from two more families who were interested in joining them.

"How are you all feeling?" he asked. "You know, as the seasons change and we head into winter, you'll probably have some unexpected emotions. You'll reach for the platter for the Thanksgiving turkey, and you'll remind yourself that it's gone. Christmas is going to be tough. Most of you, I'm sure, kept your ornaments and decorations downstairs."

The couples looked at each other and nodded.

"This is our first Christmas with the twins," Joy Alfson said. "So we're going to start fresh. New traditions for the new family members."

Another woman sighed. "I lost the little snowman my son Alex made me when he was three. It was so cute. He stuck together Ping-Pong balls and covered them with feathers. Why feathers, I don't know, but it was the cutest thing.

Of course the glue didn't stick, and the Ping-Pong balls came apart, and the feathers fell off, but putting it back together each year was a tradition I'll truly miss."

"You know," Ric said gently, "I don't have children. I'm not married. But I'm here to offer the children's side of this whole thing, if I can. Your son will mourn the loss of the snowman, that's true. But I know Alex, and I'd say he has his eyes firmly on the future. That's the way it is with children. They look forward."

"So what are you trying to say?" Linus Alfson asked.

"Keep the traditions," Rick said. "What you did together is more important than what you had. If you decorated the tree on Christmas Eve, then by all means, do it again. I have a suggestion here from a relief group that recommends each member of the family have an ornament especially for this year. It can be meaningful, or it can be simply appealing to them. But it should be theirs."

Joy reached over and covered her husband's hand with her own. "That's a good idea. We are all starting again, not just the twins, and the ornaments could be the symbol of that."

The group began to make plans to offer an ornament workshop the first week of Advent, and as their voices eagerly suggested the kinds of ornaments they could make and possible sponsors for the activity, Ric leaned back.

The healing had begun.

❧

"I knew it, I just knew it!" Marnie burst out when Lily entered the office and smiled at Ric. "I saw it in your faces from the moment you walked in here, Lily. 'Those two are meant for each other,' I told myself. Yessir, that's what I said, and that's what I meant."

Lily and Ric looked at each other and laughed.

"Marnie, I'd just stepped into the church and was dealing with a recalcitrant little boy who didn't want to walk into a stinky old church, no way, no how."

"I know." Marnie beamed at her in pleased satisfaction.

"You weren't there," Ric said. "It was just the three of us."

"I was watching from the window. I saw you get out of the car, Lily, and I looked down at Ric, and I saw this look of total meltdown on his face. He fell in love with you the first time he saw you."

"I think you're jumping the gun," Lily said. "We haven't even really dated yet, so bringing in, well, the L-word is, um, gee, premature," she finished in a rush, horribly aware that she was blushing and totally unable to stop it.

Marnie shrugged. "Love is love. Sometimes it creeps up on you, and sometimes it just comes up and slugs you a good one."

Ric looked at Lily. "I don't know, Lily. This love business sounds pretty grim."

She nodded. "All creeps and slugs. Yuck."

A sound at the door made them all turn around. Victoria Campbell stood there.

"Come on in," Lily said. "We're just chatting about love and slugs and other creeps."

"Really?" Victoria raised her eyebrows. "And why would you be talking about my ex-husband?"

"Oooh, low blow," Ric said.

She wrinkled her nose. "I'm teasing, of course. Max and I have an understanding now. I still don't like it, but I can live with it." She handed something to Ric. "This came in on my fax machine at Wedding Belles. I don't know why except that maybe the creep, oops, I mean Max, put down the store's fax number from habit when he was doing work for you all."

"What is it?" Marnie asked, crowding in closer to get a better look at it, but Ric took it into his office and shut the door.

"I don't know. I didn't read it. Well, okay, I'm in a church so I have to tell the truth. I did read it, sort of. Just enough to know it wasn't for me—it was for Lily."

"Victoria Campbell, I'm going to throttle you one of these days," Marnie threatened.

"Okay, okay. It's about that Nanny Group thing. It looks like they've proven that Douglas Newton has dirty, dirty hands."

"We knew it would work out," Marnie said, beaming happily. "Right, Lily?"

Lily nodded.

"Oh, by the way, the Lord giveth and He taketh away, also." Marnie handed Lily a message. "The mayor's office called. It looks like the grant for the day care center is a no-go."

Lily sagged. "Did the mayor say why?"

"I just talked to his secretary. She said the need seems to be decreasing, and that, oh dear, I can't remember the rest of what she said. You probably should call her and check."

"How can she say there's less need? There aren't enough day cares here in town yet. Even with our increased limits, I still have a list of people waiting to get their children in here."

Marnie held out a piece of paper. "Here's the number. Ask for Linda."

Lily walked down the hall to her office. The spring in her step was gone.

They needed the grant to expand enough to fill the need, even if it was temporary. They couldn't rely on the former day cares reopening.

Many of the providers that she'd talked to were caught in a double bind. They needed money. They needed jobs. But they couldn't do their jobs without having their houses rebuilt, which took money, which took jobs. . . .

The upshot of it all was that many had decided to take other jobs out of necessity. When, if ever, they'd return to providing day care was anyone's guess.

She called the mayor's office and talked to the secretary.

Linda was sympathetic and understanding as she presented the mayor's case. But it came down to one irrefutable fact. Like everywhere else in town, there was only a limited amount of money and many hands were reaching out. They needed to make the most effective use of the funds they had.

Lily understood the reasoning behind it. But how could she make them understand that the children were the community's most valuable resource?

She thanked the secretary and hung up the phone, trying not to feel despair.

Lily cradled her head in her hands and prayed. *Lead me along on this, Lord. There's so much at stake.*

Children should be happy. They should not hurt, and this flood had hurt them all badly. They deserved better. No child deserved to suffer, and no mother should have to choose between work and her children.

That had been one of her guiding principles at the Nanny Group, and she'd kept that firmly in mind as she worked through the cases. The files there had teemed with stories of deprivation and loss, those in which the mother had to make a decision based not upon her heart but upon her bank account.

The Nanny Group. In the far reaches of her mind, something glimmered. But try as she might, she could not get ahold of it.

Lily decided to go for a walk in the crisp autumn air to clear her mind. She put on her jacket and started out of her office.

She could hear the happy shouts of the day care, less crowded now that school was in session, and an idea blossomed in her head.

An hour later, she skipped back down the hall to the office.

"Don't ever give up hope," she said breathlessly as she flew in, interrupting a very startled Marnie in the act of sharpening a pencil. "God is good."

"What is this all about?" Ric asked, coming out of his office.

"God is good," she told him.

She caught a glimpse of herself in the glass of his office door. Her cheeks were bright, her collar was twisted, and her hair was sticking out in all directions, and she didn't care.

"Yes, God is good," he agreed, smiling at her, "but slow down."

"I can't. I've got an appointment at the mayor's office."

"I thought we didn't get the grant," Marnie said, taking the pencil out of the sharpener at last.

"We didn't. But we may get something much, much better. I'm off to find out. Pray!"

Within minutes she was seated in front of the mayor himself.

"I've heard a lot about you," he said as he took the papers she handed him. "You're quite an addition to our little community."

"Thank you," she said, still somewhat out of breath from her wild dash to his office. "And thank you for taking the time out of your busy schedule for me. I know it's a bit of a miracle getting in without an appointment like this, and I appreciate it."

"No problem. What did you want to talk about? The grant? Did Linda explain to you—"

She nodded, aware that she was interrupting him, but too impatient not to. "Yes, she did. But I've come to talk to you about something a bit different that may work better for Wildwood."

And she began her pitch.

She began by explaining about the Nanny Group, and how one population sector in need assisted another. As she spoke, she saw the realization settling on him and watched him gaining her excitement about the project she was proposing.

"We could be an incubator," she said. "Only we won't raise chicks, we'll raise children. And day care businesses."

He nodded enthusiastically. "It works like a business generator."

"Precisely, but with the concerns of the flood thrown in. Those who want to return to being day care providers can operate out of our building while reconstruction teams can work together to rebuild the day cares. There are many that still need help. They lost so much, not just structurally but with supplies and even assistants in some cases."

"Is there going to be enough space for everyone?" the mayor asked.

"I've been in contact with most of the people who had day cares before the flood," she answered. "And I think we have enough little rooms and a large enough kitchen to fulfill most of the need I've seen expressed so far."

"Eventually won't you put yourself out of business?" he pressed.

"I hope so." She grinned at him. "Although the fact is we probably won't. We'll slow down, but I think there'll always be the need for more child-care facilities."

The mayor leaned back in his chair and tapped his pen against his cheek. "I can't say yes and I can't say no, but what I can say is that I like the idea very much, and I'm going to propose that it be given a priority in the next round of funding requests. Can you put together a formal proposal for me, say, by next week?"

"No problem at all."

She left the mayor's office sedately, but inside she was whirling with delight.

It would work, it would work.

She spent the week laboring on a proposal to establish the incubation center, and when she hand-delivered it to the mayor's secretary the day before it was due, she felt gloriously free.

Linda scanned the proposal briefly, making sure everything was there.

"Looks good," she said at last. "Everything seems to be in its place. I'll pass it on to the mayor when he gets back from his meeting."

"Thanks," Lily said. "I appreciate it."

Linda smiled at Lily and added softly. "And good luck. Just between you and me and the stapler, I've seen all the proposals so far, and this one is by far the best. Unless something really wild comes up, I think you can count on something from the city."

The relief Lily felt was overwhelming, and she turned her attention back to those people who meant the most to her: Todd and Ric.

That evening, in celebration of getting the proposal done and submitted, they went to Pizza Wonderama.

The real estate agent was there, too, and when he saw Lily, he hailed her. "I've been meaning to call you. I talked to the owners, and they're willing to deal. Can we get together next week and talk turkey?"

Todd went with her as she set up a time with the agent to see the house again and discuss the price. He could barely contain his excitement at the thought that they might be moving into the little brick house, but something seemed to concern him.

When they returned to their table, she found out. Todd asked her, "Mom, why is that man coming to Thanksgiving dinner at our new house?"

"What?" Lily asked. "I don't follow you at all. What do you mean?"

"Why is that guy coming to our house for Thanksgiving?" Todd repeated. "You said you were going to talk turkey at the house. And we always have turkey at Thanksgiving. And stuffing."

Even as she explained to him what the term meant, she realized that Thanksgiving was only a few weeks away. With a bit of planning and some quick action. . .

She mentally totaled up the days. Yes, it was more than possible.

Maybe Todd would get an early Christmas present.

❧

Christmas started early at Resurrection. The Parenting with Christ group had taken the My Ornament project, as they called it, to heart and were gathering enough glass and plastic baubles and beads and ribbons to outfit a thousand trees. Ric hadn't seen them this happy, or this united in purpose, for a long time.

The children had taken to the revised Christmas program with glee. Ric was pleased to see the more outgoing children partnering with the shyer ones on their own, and they'd come up with a way that everyone would have a role.

Initially some of the children had resisted reciting the Bible verses from memory, and he understood that. Several children had stage fright even thinking about it. One poor little girl cried.

But the braver ones had stepped up to the task. He'd been delighted to hear Todd say to Penny, a girl who was so shy she hid behind her parents' legs all the time, "Penny, if you go up there with me, I'll feel brave. You can say,

'This is Todd,' and I'll say, 'Why, thank you, Penny,' and I'll say my Bible verse, and then you and I will bow like on that singing show on television, and we will be done, except maybe we will sing or something. We can stand together, okay, Penny?"

Ric had expected Penny to shake her head at the mention of singing, but instead she smiled and whispered, "Okay."

It seemed so early, but Ric knew if they didn't plan it now, they'd be crunched by the time Advent rolled around.

Had it really been—Ric had to stop to count—more than six months since the day the flood had taken over their lives?

In one month it would be Thanksgiving, and then a month after that, Christmas, and then New Years Day, and they would be done with this year.

It was amazing what they had lost—and how much more they had gained.

❧

Lily received a call from Linda at the mayor's office late on Friday afternoon. The decision on the funding would be announced late on Monday, so she would hear then about the success of her project.

She was on tenterhooks all weekend. It didn't seem possible for a Saturday to creep by as slowly as this one did. Even shopping and a trip to the Bright Spot for ice cream didn't move it along faster.

She and Ric went to a movie, leaving Todd with Marnie, but she couldn't concentrate on the plot.

And Sunday morning she heard the sermon only marginally. Everything revolved around this grant.

After church Ric took them to brunch at the café in Star City. As Todd contentedly colored in the new coloring book his Sunday school teacher had given him, Ric and Lily leafed through the Bismarck newspaper.

They were discussing the interesting things they found, such as the man who had a trained hedgehog ("Why would anyone want to?" Ric asked), when Lily sat up straight.

"Listen to this, Ric. 'Nanny Group Director Indicted.'"

"What? What does it say?"

"It's not much. It's just a short little bit. 'Douglas Newton, 43, director of Chicago's Nanny Group, was indicted earlier this week on charges of embezzlement, misappropriation of funds, and larceny, based upon an auditing of the nonprofit organization's records. Further charges are expected soon, but a source close to the organization said the investigation was focused solely on Newton.'"

"Wow. They got him." Ric laid down the sports section. "This means—"

"Yes. It means I'll probably be called to testify." Her chin rose just a bit. "I'm ready."

Ric didn't say anything else, but she knew he was worried—and what he was worried about.

This news might jeopardize the funding that was so necessary for the day care's survival at Resurrection. Just being associated with that kind of criminal activity might tar her with the same brush. She had to face that.

The timing couldn't be worse. She knew the mayor's office had to be careful with the money they distributed through these grants.

Would they yank whatever appropriation she might get in light of the bad publicity something like this might generate?

It was a very real possibility.

And it was an ugly one.

Chapter 14

She sat nervously by the phone on Monday, not daring to stir for lunch. Every time she had to step away, Marnie or Ric came down and listened for the ring that would tell them whether or not they'd gotten the money.

It was late in the day when the call finally came. Ric was in the hallway, and from her desk, Lily watched him sprint down the hall and stop at her door, shamelessly eavesdropping.

The call was short—and sweet. They'd been awarded the money.

Lily had been prepared for it to go either way. But what she wasn't prepared for was the explanation.

"We were a bit concerned about the recent bad press the Nanny Group director's been receiving, so we checked into it, and one of the findings that came back again and again is that you are as honest as the day is long," the mayor declared. "The primary investigator in Illinois said, as a matter of fact, that your records were the cleanest he'd found."

She couldn't believe her ears. All of the mistrust that the fiasco had generated in her, and all the worry, and it ended like this.

She felt as if the world had just hugged her.

"Furthermore," the mayor continued, "we understand that you are employed by Resurrection, but if in the future this program grows, we're prepared to offer you a job with the city of Wildwood overseeing this and potentially other similar programs."

As soon as she hung up the phone, she let loose with a whoop that brought Marnie at a run. "We got it! We got it!"

She shared the news with the others and then told them the additional news. "There's a new director at the Nanny Group, a fellow with impeccable credentials, so their work will go on." She looked at them. "I can't begin to tell you how much that means to me."

Lily looked at the framed picture of Todd on her desk. "Excuse me. As much as I adore you both, there's someone else who needs to hear this next bit of news first. I'll be back in a minute."

She raced down the hall to the day care center, where her son enjoyed playing after school.

Todd was back from kindergarten, and he looked up from the truck he was guiding through an obstacle course. "Mom! Is it time to go home?"

"Honey, what a good question. Come here." She sat in one of the tiny chairs and patted her lap. "I want to tell you something."

Todd eyed her questioningly but obligingly came over and sat on her lap.

"Todd, how would you like to stay here in Wildwood for a long time?"

His face lit up, but she could tell that he was withholding full enthusiasm. "That would be nice, but don't we have to leave after the flood is fixed?"

"How about if we could stay anyway?"

His grin could have lit the entire building. "Mom! Really?"

"Really. I was offered a great job with the city after this job ends, if it does. We can stay here. Forever and ever."

Her heart felt as if it were floating. Never, never had life seemed so good.

"Can we get the house?" Todd asked.

"Now that depends on the house, but if everything goes okay with it, I think so, tiger."

"Yea!" His shout of joy reverberated through the room and brought the rest of the children to his side.

"We are going to stay here and live in a house, and I'm going to grow carrots!" he announced. "You can all come over and eat carrots right out of my garden."

"Ick. I don't like carrots," one boy said.

"Won't there be dirt on the carrots if you take them right out of the garden?" another boy asked.

"Can I plant some beans? I like beans better," said the little blond girl who had so captured Lily's heart earlier.

Lily smiled. "If we get this house—and that's *if* we get this house—you can all come over and we'll plant the world's biggest garden. But I don't think it'll be real soon because look outside!"

The children clustered around the large window that brought sunlight into the room.

Huge, lazy snowflakes drifted down, melting almost as soon as they hit the earth.

Immediately all interest in Todd's garden was lost as the children clamored to go outside and play in the snow. The woman in charge of the day care that afternoon caught Lily's eye and winked. They understood the uniqueness of big, puffy snowflakes.

She left the playroom and followed the voices to the church office. Marnie and Ric stopped their conversation and turned to her in delighted anticipation.

"I'm so excited I can barely stand it," Marnie said. "Fill us in on everything."

When she was finished filling them in, Ric caught her up in his arms and twirled her around. "Is it true? You're staying?"

She smiled and nodded, too happy for words.

The clock struck five o'clock, and Marnie jumped. "I didn't realize it was so late. I've got to go pick up my hubby at work. His car's in the shop, so I'm his wheels today." She gave Lily a parting hug. "I can't tell you how happy I am today."

At last Ric and Lily were alone in the office.

"It's been an incredible day," Ric said to her. "I don't think I've ever heard as much good news as I have today."

"It's been an astonishing day," Lily agreed. "I don't know when I've ever been so happy. Except—"

"Except what?" he asked, his face lined with concern.

"This is going to sound crazy, but I feel sorry for Douglas Newton. I know, I know, his own actions brought this down on his head, but I can't help feeling bad about it all. It could have been avoided, all of it."

"That's true," Ric said thoughtfully. "Although I do wonder why you can find it in yourself to forgive him for what he's done to you."

"Ric, I came out of it okay. I'm a bit shopworn around the edges, but I'm okay. I've got to feel sorry for those who haven't found that living by God's laws is as easy, if not easier, than trying not to."

She chewed on her lip. There was one other thing. A note she had seen on the counter of the office. Maybe Marnie forgot to show it to her. Or maybe she didn't want to ruin Lily's day. The real estate agent had called with a short message: The house was no longer available.

It seemed so shallow, but there it was. She wanted that house. It had become the symbol of so much.

In low words she told Ric. "The house isn't mine. It's gone."

He didn't say anything. He just handed her her coat, and they silently began their way down to the day care center to pick up Todd.

She motioned to him to come with her.

They went into the darkened sanctuary, and she looked at the cross, silhouetted against the wall in the early winter twilight.

"Thank You," she said to the shadowed cross. "Thank You."

Ric squeezed her hand, and they stood there a moment or two.

God is good, Lily thought. If only she had learned earlier to let go and stop worrying so much!

" 'Consider the lilies of the field,' " Ric said softly, his voice resonant in the empty sanctuary. " 'How they grow; they toil not, neither do they spin.' "

"I've always thought the lilies were lazy, but they're not, are they?" she asked him.

A ray of light slanted through the stained glass and decorated his wheat-colored hair with a rainbow of colors.

"The lilies are doing exactly what lilies are meant to do, and we are meant to do exactly what human beings are meant to do. Our struggle is to find out what that might be."

Lily mulled that over. It wasn't an easily answered question. Certainly what *not* to do seemed often an easier option.

"I wonder what our lives will be like," she said. "After living in the shadows, what will it be like to live in the sunshine? What direction do we go in now?"

"This way," he said, taking her by the hand and leading her forward. "Shall we move toward the altar—together?"

Before she could answer, he knelt. "Do you remember that evening along the river when I lent you my jacket, and I said I wished I had something heavier for you?"

She nodded. "I will never forget that night."

"I'm sorry. I don't have anything heavier. But this is lighter, and maybe it will do."

He pulled a small square box from his pocket and handed it to her.

"A ring!" she breathed as she opened it.

But it wasn't a ring that met her eyes. It was a shiny new key.

"Lily Chamberlain, I can't promise you that you will not toil, although you may never spin—that part is up to you—but would you please consider becoming Lily Jensen and living with me in a little brick house with a fireplace and some land where Todd can grow carrots?"

She nodded.

Carrots were good.

Epilogue

Two years later

R ic came into the kitchen in a blast of cold air and dumped the day's mail on the kitchen counter. Red and green and white envelopes spilled in a colorful array of Christmas cards.

"Anything from your mom?" he teased.

She sorted through them. "Actually, there is." She tossed it to him. "Today's letter. She's been writing us every single day, even though we'll be seeing her this afternoon!"

He opened it and smiled as he scanned through the letter. "She's excited about coming to see us for Christmas. She says she found a great hearth box that will look perfect by the fireplace."

Lily laughed. "She's nuts about that fireplace."

"And she wants to see Todd play basketball while she's here." He looked at Lily. "I can't believe he's seven already."

"And that we're getting to be old married folks? Almost two years now?"

"How have we ever stood it?" He kissed the tip of her nose and returned to the letter. "And she says she's anxious to see her new granddaughter."

Lily's eyes got a faraway look. "I am, too. It's been so long, and I wonder what she'll be like. Rosie. It's a perfect name for her. Our daughter will be perfect, like a little budding rose."

"I'm anxious for her to get here." Ric took his wife in his arms and held her closely. "I'll have my very own flower garden, Lily and Rosie."

She nuzzled her face in his neck. "I'm getting nervous, Ric."

"The bag is ready. Her room is ready."

"Everything's ready except me," wailed Lily. "I can't believe how nervous I am!"

Ric hugged her even tighter. "It'll be okay. Our—"

Todd spun into the room at a furious pace and screeched to a halt when he saw them. "How long until Rosie gets here?"

She looked at the clock. "We could go any minute now. As soon as my mother gets here, we're going, no matter how long we have to wait once we get there."

Todd raced into the entryway to get his coat and mittens. "I'll wait outside," he told them as he struggled into his boots.

"Isn't it too early?" Ric asked her. "Rosie's not due for another couple of—"

"Shhh." She laid a finger over his lips. "I can't wait any longer. It's not every day that you get to see your daughter for the very first time." She paused. "Especially when she's coming on a plane all the way from Central America."

A little girl. She was going to have a little girl now to love also.

She touched the locket that she'd worn every day since they found out about the little girl. One side held Todd's portrait, and the other was the agency's photograph of Rosie.

Her big brown eyes had haunted her from the first time she'd seen the picture, and she knew that Rosie was meant to live with them.

A car pulled up outside.

"Mom's here," she said to Ric.

He kissed her. "This is a tremendous day. Have I told you in the last five minutes how incredibly in love I am with you?"

She smiled into his eyes, those bits of blue heaven. "I can never hear it enough. But scoot. Mom probably needs some help. She seems to have brought most of the mall with her. Rosie's already spoiled. And Todd is hopeless at this stage."

Some things, she thought to herself as she watched Ric hug her mother and give Todd—now waving a catcher's mitt overhead—a piggyback ride across the snowy yard, *are simply meant to be.*

Some things just are, like love.

SUNSHINE

Dedication

For Kacie, without whom there wouldn't be Sunshine, North Dakota. You are so good for my heart! (And you make the best gravy ever!)

For Greg, my fishing advisor. Leeches, lures, worms—you explained them all, and if you rolled your eyes and sighed, you didn't let me know, and for that, I am eternally grateful.

For Patty, who's been my steadfast friend down this bumpy road of life. How can I ever thank you enough?

For North Dakota, despite your crazy weather—which, to tell the truth, I actually kind of love—you will always be home to me.

> *"If people concentrated on the really important things in life,*
> *there'd be a shortage of fishing poles."*
> *Doug Larson*

Chapter 1

Sunshine, North Dakota
Population, including barn cats, chickens, and earthworms: 14
Form of government: Benevolent anarchy
Main industry: Fishing. Or thinking about fishing.
Recreational area: Little Starling River
where you might find a sunnie or two.
Entertainment venues: Chasing the cats that chase
the chickens that chase the earthworms.
Selling price: Make an offer. If we take it, that's the selling price.
If we don't take it, that's not it.

Livvy Moore leaned back in her chair and studied the advertisement again. It was charming, certainly a change from the usual text she wrote: "Move-in ready. 3 BRs, 2 bth, full bsmt." But there was something else about this ad.

Maybe, just maybe, this was what she'd been waiting for. This could be it. In fact, this *had* to be it. Why else would a newspaper from some small town in North Dakota have blown up against the tire of her car in downtown Boston? Neat freak that she was, she had tossed it into her car, intending to recycle it when she got to work. A broken-down panel truck had backed traffic up for blocks, and she was stuck with nothing to read. . .nothing except this newspaper, with this intriguing offer.

It had to be divinely given. Her ideas of God and Jesus and the whole church thing were vague and fuzzy and lovely, but she was willing to give credit where credit was due. God was in charge of the wind, right? God had put the newspaper right where she'd see it, knowing she'd feel compelled to recycle it.

She ran her fingers through her hair, knowing that it didn't do her hairstyle any good but beyond caring. Right now she had more important things to think about.

She loved Boston, she truly did. The hustle and bustle that had attracted her, though, was wearing her down. Her job paid well, but she never seemed to have the time to take advantage of the generous salary and do what she wanted, which was to travel. At the moment, her knowledge of the world was limited to what she saw on her regular drive to and from work, or what she viewed on the Travel Channel before she fell asleep each night.

There had to be more. China. Egypt. Zanzibar. Even North Dakota.

"Olivia, I need you to look over these bids again," her boss said, walking in without knocking. "They're too high for my taste. We can't offer that kind of money for those properties, and don't give me any of your sob stories about somebody's widow or ancient granny. We're not in the charity business, you know. I want them by tomorrow at the open of business, so I hope you don't have plans for the evening." He stopped to frown, obviously pretending that he cared.

"Actually," she said, lifting her chin, "I do have plans." From deep inside herself, she'd found a backbone. She'd never told Mr. Evans no before.

"You can cancel them, I'm sure."

Somewhere in the distance, she was sure she heard the soft swish of swords being drawn. "No, I really can't."

He lowered the papers and stared at her over his half glasses. That look had slain dragons, but it hadn't dealt with a woman holding an ad for Sunshine, North Dakota.

"Excuse me?"

A garden. The vision of a garden snapped into place. A garden with peas and corn and carrots, and a white-painted fence surrounding it. She wanted to feel the rich warmth of dirt on her fingers, and to hear the sharp *ping* of a hammer hitting a nail.

That was not going to happen in Evans Real Estate Management, unless she counted watering the skinny philodendron that trailed sadly along the edge of her desk as gardening, and smacking the broken heel of her shoe back into place as construction.

She stood up, folded the newspaper, and placed it in her bag. "I'm giving my notice."

He shook his head as if he didn't understand. "Notice? Notice of what?"

"I'm leaving."

He laughed, a cold humorless sound that was the cement in the fragile wall of her decision. "Do you have another position? You know we have a non-compete agreement. It had better not be another real estate management company you're going to."

"I'm leaving Massachusetts entirely," she said, reaching for her coat.

"You're going to New York, aren't you?" His eyes narrowed.

"No I'm not. I am going to North Dakota."

"North Dakota? Are you out of your mind? Why, there's nothing there except buffalo and snow."

"I like buffalo and snow." Snow she'd seen, but the closest she'd come to a buffalo was seeing one on an old nickel—and on Animal Planet.

He leaned against her desk and studied her. "You're serious. You're going."

"I am."

"You'll regret it."

"Not as much as I'd regret staying."

Occasionally one is presented with the opportunity to make a grand exit, and this was it, Livvy knew. With great style and panache, she swept out of the room and down the hall to the elevator, quite aware that he had followed her out a few steps and then stopped, his icy glare at her back.

Once she was in the elevator, she pushed the STOP button, leaned against the cold brass railing, and shook like an aspen leaf.

What had she done? *What had she done?*

৵

Hayden Greenwood threw the last piece of lumber onto the pile, swiped the Cooter's Hardware hat from his head, and mopped at the sweat that dripped from his forehead. He'd never perspired like this in his life, but then, he'd never had to do so much hard labor before.

He looked around him and sighed.

Apparently Gramps had never seen a slab of wood he didn't like, judging from the contents of the small blue building behind the café. Possibly the kindest thing to do—for him, anyway—would be to burn this thing to the ground, but he knew his grandfather would never allow that. So here he was, on a perfectly good June day when he could be out fishing, emptying yet another storeroom.

As near as he could figure, whenever Gramps ran out of storage space at the Sunshine Resort, he'd simply built another shed. They dotted the swathe of cleared land behind the café, some red, some yellow, some blue. Hayden had a suspicion that the purpose of this storehouse of lumber was, yes, to build more sheds.

"Grub!" Gramps ambled over to Hayden. His body was bent from years of working hard and falling harder. His back was twisted from the time he had a small accident with a blowtorch and a gas canister, when he'd ended up several feet away from where he'd begun. His left arm crooked at an awkward angle, the souvenir of an accident with a saw. His legs bowed as if he'd spent his life on horseback, when, in fact, Hayden knew that Gramps's stance was due to the beat-up cowboy boots he'd worn for at least twenty years, patched and repatched until little was left of the original shoes. No human could walk in them normally.

"Grub, you're not throwing anything away, are you?"

Only Gramps could get away with the childhood nickname. Anyone else trying to use the hated moniker got a quick poke in the stomach, at least when they were kids. Now that he was a grown-up, he hadn't had to enforce the no-Grub rule, but on the other hand, he didn't really have anyone to fight with.

Plus his fighting days were over. It was like the Bible said. You get to be a man, you put away childish things. And to his way of thinking, that included punching people who called him Grub.

"No, Gramps, I'm not throwing anything away. See these boards? They all came from inside this shed."

The elderly man peered at the stack with eyes that were bleary with age. "I recollect there were more."

"And there are." With Gramps, Hayden always managed to find a well of patience that he didn't really have with the rest of the world. "I'm not finished yet."

"Good thing we're selling this place." Gramps looked away and sniffed. He wiped the back of his hand across his nose before turning back to Hayden. "Too much work for an old codger like me, and not enough to keep the young blood like you here."

It was the end of an era. The CLOSED sign had been hanging on the canteen door for almost two years. The bait shop now held boxes of half-empty BB canisters and rusted fish hooks, left over from the Sunshine Resort's heyday.

There hadn't been much else to the resort. As long as the kids had a place to buy taffy and ice cream during the day and a cleared area for bonfires and marshmallow roasts at night, and the grown-ups had a pier to fish on and a jetty to launch their boats from, all had been good. There was no stress at the Sunshine Resort, not until the lure of places that included shopping as a recreation edged nearer. At the back of his closet, Hayden still had a T-shirt, once orange but now faded to a soft coral, emblazoned with the words: AT THE END OF THE DAY, THERE'S SUNSHINE.

His parents had died when he was ten, and Gramps and Gran had taken him into their hearts and home and provided everything the grieving boy had needed. He could never thank them enough.

He glanced at his grandfather, who seemed tinier than ever before, and his heart contracted painfully. Gramps's health had been steadily failing since Gran had died two years earlier, and he knew it wouldn't be long until God would call the old man home.

Hayden wanted to savor every moment with Gramps.

He cleared his throat. There was only one thing to do.

"Let's go fishing."

❧

Livvy moved the monitor of her computer so the last rays of the early summer sunlight didn't glare on it.

"Mom, it's all taken care of," she said to the screen.

"Can't you wait until your father and I can come and help you?" her mother said. "August would be good."

Livvy sighed. Her parents were in Sweden, teaching at a school there, and through the magic of a computer program, they were able to talk. They could even see each other's image as they did it.

It was a mixed blessing. Her father was quiet, the kind of man who listened and absorbed everything, and spoke rarely. Her mother made up for any of his silences. "It'll be fine. I'll be fine," Livvy assured her.

Mrs. Moore shook her head vigorously, the image flickering as the computer tried to keep up with the rapid motion. "Livvy, I can't think this is a good idea.

You've got a good job—"

"Had a good job," she interrupted.

"Had a good job," her mother continued. "Livvy, that reminds me. What did you do with the things from your office? If you just walked out—"

"What things from my office?"

"You know, like photos and mementos."

Livvy's laugh was cold. "Photos and mementos were not allowed. We could have one plant, which was replaced regularly because there wasn't enough light to keep anything alive. No, when I left, I think I left some pens, and maybe a sweater and my planner. Nothing too big."

Her mother persisted. "Your apartment is nice. What's going to happen with that? Don't you have a lease?"

Livvy smiled. "Not anymore. The apartment was re-rented by the end of the day. I just have to be out in two weeks."

"What about your furniture?"

"I'm putting some of it in storage. The rest I've donated to that thrift shop down the street. They even came and got it. You know the one—the sales support the homeless shelters."

"Do you see the irony in that?" Mrs. Moore frowned. "Homeless. You could be homeless."

"But I'm not, Mom. I will have a home, in North Dakota."

"Did you call, to see if it was available?"

"I'm waiting to hear."

Her mother sprang on the words, like a triumphant duck nabbing a fat beetle. "Waiting? Waiting for what? They haven't called you back?"

This was the problem with the visual part of this computer chat program. Her mother could see her expression, so Livvy faked a hearty smile. "It was an address."

"An address?"

Don't ask me any more questions, Livvy pleaded silently. If her mother found out it was a post office box number, she'd never hear the end of it.

"So how do you know—" Mrs. Moore began, but Livvy broke into the sentence.

"Mom, if this makes you feel better, I have enough in my savings to stay in a motel for months. I will not be homeless."

"So you're driving out there—you have your car insurance up to date?"

"Mom! I'm twenty-five years old! I know about car insurance."

Actually she had sold her car. It was good in the city, but it wasn't the kind of thing she'd want to drive across the country. Instead, in her purse right now were airplane tickets to North Dakota.

"Oh Livvy," her mother said, "you know your dad and I want the best for you, but we think you're being hasty. Please think this through."

"I know, Mom. I know."

"Be careful," her mother advised. "You know how we worry."

"I do."

Mercifully her mother's phone rang, and the conversation ended. Livvy turned off her computer and leaned back in her chair.

Had she convinced her mother that she was in control of this situation? More importantly, had she convinced herself?

It would have been so easy to stay in Boston, living this life that was split between two spots: behind her desk helping people fulfill their hearts' desires of a home, and in front of her television, vicariously dreaming of what was out in the world, just waiting for her, for someday. . . .

It was time to move away from the desk and the television, and to stretch, to explore, to find herself.

This may not have been the most conventional way, but it would work. She had it all set up. Everything was ready. She just had to go.

❧

It was the one thing Livvy hadn't thought of when throwing things together for her hurried flight to North Dakota—how to get to Sunshine from the last airport.

She was so tired. The only flight—make that the only flights—she could get with such short notice had hippity-hopped her all over the southern and midwestern United States. She'd always wanted to travel, but this was ridiculous. She'd been to Charleston, Baton Rouge, Oklahoma City, Indianapolis, over to Kansas City, up to Detroit, to Minneapolis, then to Bismarck, and finally a puddle jumper had brought her here, to Obsidian. It was so tiny it didn't even have a dot on the map.

Or a car rental agency.

But thanks to a young lad at the airport, who saw an enterprising way to make some money, she was seated behind the wheel of a pickup truck, rattling her way toward Sunshine.

She turned on the radio and smiled. The teenager had some priorities. The truck had satellite radio.

She hit a bump and the book on the seat beside her slid onto the floor. She'd bought it in the Indianapolis airport—or maybe it was Detroit—and read it eagerly. *The Complete Guide to Home Construction and Repair.* She'd had some doubts about how thoroughly the topic could be covered in 249 pages, but it had been enlightening.

Something alongside the road moved, and she slowed to a stop. A family of deer watched her curiously, and she spoke to them from inside the truck. "You're wondering what I'm doing here, aren't you? Well, so am I."

She wasn't the kind of person to be impetuous, but here she was, on a gravel road in North Dakota. Just two weeks ago, she'd been sitting in traffic in Boston, reaching for that stray newspaper. If it hadn't blown up against her car, if she hadn't picked it up, if she hadn't been stuck in traffic, if she hadn't lost her temper with Mr. Evans. . . It was an amazing chain of sequences.

She got out of the truck and stretched. The deer took one last look at her and bounded away, and she was alone, except for the warbling melody of a bird.

Along the western horizon, jagged peaks sprouted up. The colors were wild. Russet and brick with terra cotta and cinnamon. The Badlands.

Beside their wonder, under a sky that was the purest blue she'd ever seen, she felt suddenly a part of it all. A tiny part, but a part nevertheless.

Praying hadn't been something she'd done a lot of lately, unless she counted urging God to let her car start on a cold morning, or pleading with Him to let there not be a long line at the drive-up coffee place.

Now though, when it was just her, the deer, and the Badlands, it became important to recognize God's handiwork and to put herself in His mighty hands.

"God, I don't know what I'm doing here, but I'm going to need some help. You've put me here for some reason, I'm sure, and I want to thank You for choosing such a spectacular setting." She paused. "Amen."

She got back into the truck, and after several noisy tries, got it to start.

This was an amazing trip. Here she was, Livvy Moore, in North Dakota, on a gravel road in a pickup truck with a gun rack in the back, headed for a place she'd been drawn to by the sheer appeal of a windblown ad.

Amazing.

❧

"Ready for a break?" Hayden stopped sorting through the lumber pile and stood up, his back protesting vehemently.

"Yup." Gramps pulled his straw hat off, ran his hand over his nearly bald head, and stuck the hat back on again.

The two of them had tackled yet another outbuilding. This one held smaller pieces of wood, salvaged apparently from the old boathouse.

"Look, Gramps." Hayden handed him a sign that was in the heap. BUDDY SYSTEM SWIM—

"Remember that? You had the buddy system rule over at the swimming beach."

"Save it," his grandfather said, taking the sign and laying it aside. "We'll fix it and use it again."

"But there's no swimming beach anymore. Remember, Gramps?"

Gramps frowned a bit, and the veil came over his eyes that Hayden was seeing much too frequently. His grandfather got confused more and more, and details didn't stay with him.

Hayden put his arm around his grandfather's shoulders, trying to ignore the clutch of fear that assailed him whenever he felt how thin his grandfather had become. Under the red flannel shirt he could feel every angle of the old man's bones.

"Let's go inside and have a root beer," he said gently, guiding Gramps back to the house.

Once inside the cool kitchen, he uncapped two brown bottles of root beer. "Just like the old days, right, Gramps?" he asked as they took deep sips of the icy sweet drink. "Remember how we used to come into the canteen and buy root beer and those candy ropes? We'd eat them until we were sick."

Gramps laughed, his gaze bright and snappy again. "Everyone was covered with sand and the flies came in because you kids couldn't remember to shut the screen door."

"That screen door never shut anyway. Those were some good times, weren't they?"

"You know what was my favorite?" his grandfather asked. "The bonfire."

Hayden smiled, transported back to those summer evenings at the bonfire his grandfather built each night. The kids had their favorite marshmallow-roasting sticks, and dodging the sparks to get your marshmallow done perfectly was part of the fun. "Does anything taste better than a marshmallow cooked over a bonfire?" he asked. "So hot you can't eat it, and so gooey you can't help yourself. Of course, the best ones are the ones that catch fire and turn black. Yum!"

"And the vespers." Gramps leaned forward. "Remember the vespers?"

"Of course. Every bonfire ended with a prayer. It was the perfect ending to perfect days."

Gramps turned to him and wrapped his gnarled fingers around Hayden's hand. "Grub, we had good times here. But we can't keep Sunshine wrapped in a bubble. We've got to move on. You're a grown man now, teaching math, no less, to those high school kids. And me? I'm an old codger who gets his nows mixed up with his thens."

"You're doing fine, Gramps, and you're coming with me to live in Obsidian," Hayden reminded him. "You've got to make sure I don't do anything too goofy."

Gramps chuckled. "And vice versa."

A loud sound, like a gunshot report, broke the afternoon silence. "What was that?" Hayden asked, bounding out of his chair and reaching for the screen door.

A horn honked. And honked again. And again.

He tore out of the kitchen and across the yard. An old truck was parked there, with a woman trying to do something to the hood of it while the horn continued to honk.

"What are you doing?" he hollered at her.

"It won't stop!" she yelled back. "And I can't get this hood thing to open."

"There's a lever inside you pull first."

"I know." She held it up. "It came off in my hand."

Fortunately there was enough rust on the truck to make opening the hood fairly easy, and Hayden disconnected the horn.

"Sorry about that," the woman said, smiling at him. "And sorry about that bang. This thing backfires something fierce."

She reached her hand out to him. "I'm Livvy Moore, and I want to buy Sunshine."

Chapter 2

The two men stared at her, and Livvy's smile began to fade.

"This is Sunshine, isn't it? I have the advertisement right here on the front seat." She pulled the door of the truck open, and had to slam it twice to make it latch. "Sorry," she added. "It's not mine. A young fellow rented it to me."

"It's Trevor's truck," the older man said. "Boy has a fool's heart but an accountant's mind."

"Excuse me?" The conversation had just started and she was already lost.

The younger man stepped forward. "I'm Hayden Greenwood and this is my grandfather, Charlie Greenwood. Please excuse our manners. We don't get many folks visiting."

"I'm not visiting," she said. "Unless Sunshine is already sold?"

Behind Haywood, his grandfather grinned. "Nope."

"Gramps and I were just sitting down to a root beer in the kitchen. Would you like to join us? We'll be more comfortable in there, out of the sun," Hayden said.

For a breath of a moment, Livvy paused. In Boston, she would never have gone into a house with two men she didn't know, but on the other hand, she wasn't in Boston. These guys didn't look dangerous, and if they were, her fate was sealed anyway. What was she going to do? Leap into the rattletrap pickup truck that might or might not start?

Clutching the advertisement in her hand, she nodded and followed them. The house was a traditional two-storied home, plainly structured with no extra gingerbread features, slatted decorative shutters the only nod to adornment.

Why had she chosen open-toed shoes? The ground was a strange mixture of sand and tiny pebbles and loose red dirt, and it quickly worked its way inside her designer shoes where it ground away at the soles of her feet, and it certainly wasn't doing her hosiery any good either.

She hobbled behind the men, trying not to wince as the debris dug even deeper into her feet.

At the door of the house, she surreptitiously slipped her feet out of the open sandals and shook the soil and stones out, vowing never again to wear those torturous things here.

The inside of the house was welcoming. In the open windows, light yellow curtains lifted and billowed in the afternoon breeze. An old-fashioned oscillating fan whirred in the corner, keeping the air moving.

"This is such a comfortable home, Mr. Greenwood," she said as the older gentleman caught the screen door so it didn't slam behind them.

His face crinkled into a smile. "Do us all a favor and call me Gramps. You use city words like *Mr. Greenwood* here and nobody'll know who you mean. Right, Grub?"

"Grub?" she asked.

Hayden rubbed his grandfather's shoulder. "Only Gramps can call me Grub. The rest of the world is forced to call me Hayden."

She liked them already. The love between the two was clear.

She looked around the living room.

The floors were wooden—the original planks, she was sure, judging from the soft satiny patina and the slight dip in the floor leading from the front door to the kitchen, the worn path of many feet heading for a treat or a cup of coffee after coming from the outside.

A large braided rug, its edges curled and mended, had also held its place of honor in the middle of the living room for at least two generations. She'd noticed similar ones at auctions in Boston, going for quite a fine price as what the decorators called "vintage Americana."

A tabby cat, the biggest one Livvy had ever seen, was curled in the middle of the rug. It opened one eye and looked at Livvy with a deep golden gaze and then, apparently deciding that the newcomer was no one important, shut the eye again and began to snore.

"That's the only cat left here. Got the last of the barn cats—or resort cats, most rightly—adopted out a week ago. No, this is Martha Washington," Gramps said with a fond smile at the slumbering cat.

"Martha Washington?" she asked.

"She came pre-named." Hayden knelt and stroked the cat's back, but the animal was clearly unimpressed, and slept on. "We inherited her from a lady in Obsidian who let her granddaughter name her. Why she chose that is a mystery that is unsolved today. And the goofy cat doesn't answer to anything else."

"Critter doesn't answer to anything," Gramps said, shaking his head. "She has a brain the size of a peach pit."

"Now, now," Hayden said with a chuckle. "You love that cat."

Gramps harrumphed. "By the way, Miss Moore, the cat comes with Sunshine. Don't want her? That's a deal-breaker."

"Call me Livvy, and the cat is welcome."

"No changing your mind," Gramps warned. "But let's get back to those root beers and see if we can cool ourselves off a bit."

She followed the men into the kitchen, which was bigger than the living room. Cabinets lined three of the four walls, with breaks only for two large windows. The fourth wall was covered with framed photographs, plaques with mottos and Bible verses engraved on them, and a painting of the Last Supper.

"Root beer?" Hayden asked as Gramps pulled out her chair for her.

The table and chairs were from the early 1950s. The chairs were upholstered in red vinyl, patched and re-patched with tape, and the tabletop was a matching marbleized red plastic with a dented aluminum edge that ran around it.

"Root beer would be lovely."

"Back in the good old days," Gramps said as he stared at a photo on the wall, "we had a big cooler that we kept all different kinds of pop in. Green River, Yoo-hoo, grape Nehi—remember those, Grub? Your favorite was Green River. Or was that your dad's?"

"Dad's," Hayden answered. "I was always a root beer fellow myself, just like you, Gramps."

"Root beer is mighty good," the older man said, "especially when you drink it out of a Sunshine glass."

"Right you are," Hayden said. "Coming right up."

Soon they were pouring root beer into tall blue glasses with SUNSHINE, NORTH DAKOTA, on the side.

"We used to have these by the boxful," Hayden said. "Now we're down to just a few."

"You'd better order some more, then," his grandfather said.

"We don't need them," Hayden reminded him. "Sunshine closed as a resort two years ago."

"End of an era, end of an era." The old man sighed.

"So," Hayden said, looking directly at her with eyes that were an amazing light blue, "you're considering buying Sunshine, Miss Moore?"

"It's Livvy, please. If you'll sell it to me, I'll buy it."

She heard her own voice speaking the words, but it all seemed like a dream. This was so out of character—but maybe she didn't know what her own character was, having had it buried under the heavy thumb of Michael Evans for too many years.

"Why?" Gramps's question was direct.

"Because I—" She faltered. How could she explain the series of circumstances that had led her there?

She looked at the two men sitting across from her, and began. When she had finished telling the story of the windblown paper, she said, "I think it was one of those God things. Do you know what I mean?"

In the Boston agency, with the people she usually dealt with, the answer would have been a benevolent chuckle, but here the reaction was different. After a moment, both men nodded. "We do know," Hayden said.

"God works in mysterious ways," Gramps added. "Very mysterious. Sometimes I wish I knew what He had planned for us, but this life is one long voyage to our reward. He's given us a map, and we can stay on the road and enjoy the ultimate destination, or we can do like most of us do and meander all over the countryside, taking wrong turns and finding dead ends."

"So you believe that God led you here," Hayden said.

She swallowed. It sounded as if they had lived their lives as Christians. It wasn't that she hadn't, but she had taken many of those wrong turns.

"Maybe," she said slowly, "it's about time I listened to Him."

Hayden leaned back in his chair and ran his fingers through his straw-colored hair, bleached by the summer sun. "Sunshine was always run by His principles, you see. One of our favorites is: 'Therefore all things whatsoever ye would that men should do to you, do ye even so to them.'"

"That's the Golden Rule, kind of," she said.

He laughed. "You're right—kind of. We have it right up here in its traditional format, the one everybody learns as a kid. The Golden Rule isn't just something we have on the wall." He pointed to one of the many plaques displayed beside them. "Those words are the foundation of everything we've done here for three generations."

"*Do unto others,*" she said, and as she spoke the words, her stomach twisted. It was such a basic tenet of living—one she'd let herself forget.

"*As you would have others do unto you,*" Hayden finished. "I know that in some businesses, the rest of the line is *Before they do unto you,* but that's not the way we operated."

"Our customers were family. Some still are, but the fact is that there's not money to be made in this any longer," Gramps added. "The big vacation spots have advertising budgets that we just couldn't compete with."

There was no rancor in his words. It was evident that he had come to peace with the fact that Sunshine wasn't what it had been in the past.

"What do you plan to do with Sunshine?" Hayden asked.

The question brought her up short. It was the one part of her plan—if she could call her half-baked, spur-of-the-moment decision a "plan"—that she hadn't developed completely.

"I'm not sure," she said. "I just know that I want to be here."

"Because God sent you here?" Gramps asked, and his eyes, the same sky blue as his grandson's, but clouded, met hers squarely.

She nodded. "Yes."

"Maybe," Hayden suggested, "you'd like to see Sunshine before you decide. Drain those root beers and let's go out for a walk."

She groaned inwardly at the thought of walking even one more step outside with her sandals on but she smiled and stood up. "I'm game."

As if reading her mind, Hayden asked, "Do you have some sneakers you could put on? Those shoes don't look very comfortable."

She started to shake her head but then she remembered that in the borrowed truck was her suitcase, and in that suitcase was a pair of rubber-soled shoes that she'd tucked in at the last minute, in case there was an exercise facility at Sunshine. She almost laughed at how clueless she'd been.

Soon, with her feet in the shoes that had cost her a week's pay, she began the tour of Sunshine.

"Here's an outbuilding," Hayden said, "and there's another one, and there's another one, and there's another one."

"What are they all for?" she asked.

"For storing lumber from torn-down sheds in case we want to build more." He grinned at his grandfather.

"This larger one was once the canteen," Gramps said, ignoring the good-natured gibe. "That's where kids used to come in from swimming and buy taffy and pop."

"And the parents would gather in the late afternoon or evening for a rousing game of Monopoly or Clue," said Hayden. "In the evening, we'd grill hamburgers and hot dogs or serve some of Gran's famous tater tot hot dish. On rainy days, which were rare but they did happen, everyone would gather there and we'd play charades."

"Now it's a storeroom." Gramps opened the door and led them inside.

Boxes were piled haphazardly around the perimeter of the room. On one end, a counter divided a small kitchen from the rest of the building. Dust motes danced in the midafternoon sun, and Livvy thought that if she stood still and listened hard enough, she'd be able to hear the laughter of the years of customers.

"We had some good times here," Gramps said, running his hand over the back of a chair draped with what seemed to be an old curtain. "Do you remember, Grub?"

"I do."

The two men were lost in memories, touching the doorknob, the windowsill, the scattering of tables. With the kitchen and the bathrooms, now marked LADS and LASSIES in an old-style block print, it was easy to see what it had been.

Livvy walked around the room, her real estate training clicking into place. The canteen was a mess right now, but it had possibilities. For what, she wasn't sure, but it was there.

"Let's show her the swimming hole," Hayden said, breaking the silence.

They left the canteen and reentered the bright afternoon.

"This is beautiful," she said, looking at the vista that was so incredible it was almost overwhelming.

The Badlands, touched with coppery tones, surrounded them. Overhead, only one stray cloud drifted lazily, the sole break in the endless blue sky. In the distance, a bird trilled, its melody gracing the air with a song.

They passed a cluster of cabins, each one painted a different color that had probably once been bright but had faded to a softly muted hue. Each one sported a worn sign declaring its rather prosaic name: the GREEN CABIN, the YELLOW CABIN, the RED CABIN, the BLUE CABIN, and so on. She counted quickly: There were eleven of them.

A chicken, startled from its hunt for bugs in the dirt, flapped off in a great display of wings and feathers and screeching squawks that shattered the afternoon stillness.

The path to the small swimming area had been permanently etched in the ground by countless feet making their way to the water.

Hayden provided the narrative as they followed those long-gone footsteps.

"It's part of Little Starling, the river that goes through here. It makes a little bend here, and with the help of a tractor, a dredge, and some good old-fashioned elbow grease, that became Sunshine's version of a lake. Today it probably wouldn't be legal, but the river's adapted to it, so it's all good."

Around a straggling set of trees, the glistening water was a surprise in the dry landscape.

The pier, now weathered to a soft gray, was missing some of the boards, and it leaned to one side. A lifeguard station was near the sandy beach, but it was missing most of the steps to the top. Only a foolhardy soul would attempt to climb it.

Algae-laced waves lapped at the shore, and in the stillness, Livvy could hear more birds and the faint sound of insects buzzing along the water's edge.

"It needs some work," Gramps said.

"The whole thing needs work," Hayden said. "I don't know, of course, what you plan to do here, but the fact is that except for Gramps and me and our friends, no one comes here. Sunshine hasn't had any customers for two years now."

It was such a difference from the hustle of Boston. There were no car horns honking. No radios blaring. No one talking.

Livvy stood motionless, letting the nothingness of it all overtake her. She felt tiny and yet part of all creation. The soft breeze lifted and dropped her hair around her cheeks and forehead.

And, as she listened to the sounds of God Himself—the soft splash of the waves, the trill of the birds, the hum of the insects—she fell in love.

"I want it."

The words hung in the air. She saw the exchange of a glance between the two men, felt their sadness, and knew in her heart that with those three words, she had sealed all of their fates.

"Let's go back to the house," Hayden said at last.

She reluctantly tore herself from the idyllic scene and followed Hayden and his grandfather back up the path, past the odd assortment of outbuildings, and to the house with the ancient pickup truck parked in front of it.

Martha Washington acknowledged their return with the flick of an ear, but otherwise didn't stir as they walked through the living room and back into the kitchen.

"I don't suppose in Boston they do much business at the kitchen table," Hayden said as they sat at the red dinette set.

Livvy laughed. "Some. But you're right, usually I'd invite you to my office and we'd draw up the paperwork there."

"You're still interested? Even after seeing the rest of Sunshine?" His tanned forehead furrowed into a concerned frown.

"Especially after seeing the rest of it."

Gramps's fingers traced a groove in the tabletop. "This has been our life for many years. Decades, in fact. It's—" His voice broke, and Hayden covered his grandfather's hands as the old man gathered himself. "It's hard, letting this go into a stranger's possession. It was everything to Ellie and me. Now she's gone, and I'm going to lose Sunshine, too."

"Gramps—"Hayden began, but his grandfather shook off the interruption.

"I need to say this." He took a deep breath and exhaled. "I hope you understand that I want a few days to absorb this, to make sure that we're doing the right thing."

"It's our only choice," Hayden said gently. "We can't do this any longer. Not this way. We have to let it go."

Livvy fought back the tears that suddenly choked her. She'd arranged many sales of family homes, some of them foreclosures, and most of them had torn at her heart, but none of them had been as personal as this. She'd never been the buyer, the one who was taking the property.

She reminded herself that this was a business transaction. They would receive payment for it, and it would probably be enough to keep them solvent for years to come. It was their choice. They had put the property up for sale. They had done it. Not her. She was merely the one who had come to their aid.

So why did she feel so terrible?

"Gramps, tonight we will pray about it," Hayden said, and his grandfather nodded. Then the old man pushed his chair back and stood up.

"I'm very tired. I hope you'll excuse me, Livvy, but I need to lie down."

She nodded. "Of course."

Hayden's eyes followed his grandfather's steps as he left the room and went into the living room. Neither of them spoke as they listened to the man's heavy tread as he climbed the steps to the second floor.

"My grandfather means everything to me," Hayden said at last. "Everything. It's important to me that he is at ease about this. Before we make any agreements, I want to make sure he understands."

"Certainly."

"Plus I know you'd like to see the house, too." He glanced upstairs, as if he could see right through the ceiling and into what must have been his grandfather's room, judging from the footsteps that she could hear through the plaster. "That will have to wait until tomorrow."

"I understand."

They stood up, and together they left the kitchen. In the living room, Martha Washington had woken up and was following Gramps up the stairs.

"She's his cat. No matter what he says, she is his." Hayden watched the cat climb the steep staircase. "The other cats have been adopted out, so she's the only one left. Despite what he said earlier about her coming with the property, Gramps won't let her go—he can't let her go."

Livvy didn't know what to say. The entire thing—the decision to quit her job, put everything she owned into storage, and come to a state she knew nothing about—was overwhelming. Intensifying it all was seeing the interaction of the two men as they bid good-bye to a family treasure.

At the front door, he pulled a baseball cap from the coat tree there and shoved it on his head as soon as they stepped outside. She smiled as she read the printed words over the bill: COOTER'S HARDWARE.

Outside, he paused to move a chicken from in front of the doorway. It flapped its wings and objected strenuously as he placed it onto the ground. "We've managed to get our animals down to Martha Washington, who is about as much a barn cat as I am, and this hen. I suppose you could technically call her free-range, but it's mainly because she refuses to listen to us and stay in the coop area."

As if understanding exactly what Hayden was saying, the chicken glared at him with her beady eyes, clucked, and strutted right back onto the porch.

Livvy and Hayden looked at each other and laughed. "See what I mean?" he asked. "Not only has she made this entire place her home, she has attitude. At least she does go back to the coop to lay her eggs, although once in a while this old lady"—he pretended to scowl at the recalcitrant chicken—"she'll think she's funny and plop an egg in a lawn chair, so you'd be wise to check before you sit down out here."

"It'll be hard for you to part with Sunshine, won't it?" she asked.

He turned his head and studied the horizon, with the irregularly shaped buttes notching into the sky. "This has been part of life since I was an infant," he said at last. "Oh, I was born in Bismarck, and I went to college in Grand Forks on one end of the state and Williston on the other, but Sunshine was where my heart was. My grandparents ran this place from the time they were married, and the highlight of every summer was coming here. And then when my parents died, Gramps and Gran took me in and I moved to Sunshine permanently."

"It's part of your family," she said softly.

He tugged the baseball cap off and ran his hand over the top of his head. The sun caught his golden hair for just a moment before he slapped it back on and moved off to shoo the chicken away again.

"It is. Gran died two years ago, and Gramps lost his heart. He decided to close Sunshine then. He said he couldn't have one without the other."

Livvy wished she had her sunglasses with her to hide her eyes, which were once again filling with tears.

"One day," Hayden said, "one day I want to have what they did."

"Sunshine, you mean?"

"I mean their love. They not only finished each other's sentences, they often spoke together. I remember being a kid and watching them sit next to each other. They breathed in unison. My mom used to say that their hearts beat as one. When Gran died, Gramps. . ."

His words trailed off, and she put her hand on his arm. "It must have been really difficult."

He nodded. "He's gotten vague and forgetful now. It's for the best that we sell Sunshine. I can stay with him in the summer, but I teach in Obsidian in the winter, and I can't always get out here to check on him. It's a trek in the winter as you might imagine. The road gets pretty nasty when the snow comes, and I worry about him. He can't drive anymore. And with our winters here, somebody can't always get to him."

"It's the sensible thing to do," she said.

"Sensible—but horrendously painful." He straightened his back. "Well, as we know, we can want what we want, but that doesn't mean we can have it. Meanwhile, do you have lodging in Obsidian?"

"I'm going to be staying at the Badlands Vista Motel."

He winced. "You'll want to move out of there rather quickly. Lu and Ev, the owners, are as honest as the day is long, but they haven't upgraded anything there in at least twenty years, and that includes the mattresses, I've heard. How long are you planning to stay?"

Livvy leaned against the side of the house and studied the man in front of her. He really was amazingly good-looking—his face was tanned, his eyes were an astonishing bright blue, and his legs were long and rangy in the denims he was wearing—but had something gone wrong with his brain?

Hadn't they just spent most of the afternoon discussing her buying the old resort?

"I am planning to stay here," she said, her voice sounding, to her relief, sure and strong.

"Here? Oh no. No. No, that won't work." He looked quite distressed.

"Well, not *here*. Not right away, that is. You and your grandfather will need some time to find a place to stay, and I don't know how long you'll need because I'm not familiar with the housing situation in Obsidian, if that's where. . .you'll be. . .staying?" Her words faded away as he began to laugh.

" 'Housing situation'? Obsidian has one apartment building, which is where I live in the winter. It's got four units and is nearly as bad as the Badlands Vista Motel, but not quite. It's cleaner, for one thing. I don't know what we'll do."

"I have no intention of kicking you out of your home. There are still many dotted lines to sign on—inspections and assessments, transfers and titles—before the deed changes hands." She knew from her experience working for Mr. Evans that one could never plan definitively on moving in quickly. There was almost always some snag somewhere. Paperwork didn't arrive on time, floodplain issues appeared, a banker was on vacation—they'd all happened.

"This is really sudden," he said. "I have to say that when Gramps and I put the advertisement in the *Bismarck Tribune*, we never thought it would travel all the way to Boston, and certainly we hadn't even dreamed that someone would take us up on it. If you don't mind, I'd like to take a little time to consider this."

She clutched the edge of the railing that ran around the porch. He couldn't back out of it. The tumbledown resort, with its crazy assortment of colorful sheds and the rainbow of cabins and the dusty canteen, had taken root in her heart.

"We have no choice except to sell," Hayden continued, his voice so quiet that it seemed as if he were talking to himself. "We have no choice."

"I don't want to rush you, but—" She stopped before saying what was obvious to both of them, that he and his grandfather needed to sell, and she was a ready buyer. In any market, a decrepit, closed-down resort in the middle of nowhere would attract few buyers, and in this market, anyone showing even a faint glimmer of interest needed to be kept close to the deal.

He pulled the cap from his head and once again smoothed his hair and shoved the cap back on. "Tomorrow let's get you set up with a decent place to stay. I think this will all work out. If it's His will, it's my will."

She nodded. "I'll see you in the morning, then. Here? Or in Obsidian?"

"Meet me at Clara's Café, at eight?"

"I'll see you then."

She climbed back into the truck Trevor had rented to her, and she was aware that Hayden was watching her as she tried several times to start it. Just when she thought she'd certainly flooded the engine, it caught in a great blaze of muffler sounds and backfires, and she waved as she pulled away from the resort and onto the county road to Obsidian.

So this was Sunshine.

Her mind was spinning with the possibilities of what could happen with it. Given the proper amount of love and care, it could come to life again. She was sure of it.

An idea had started to take root. Maybe it wasn't possible, but maybe it was.

The vision of those little shacks scattered around the house poked at her mind, begging for her to pay attention to them. Could she do it?

Fishing.

Hayden hadn't mentioned it during the tour, but the advertisement had touted it. If the fishing was good, then maybe, just maybe, it would work.

The idea wandered around in her brain, picking up momentum as she began to see the possibilities.

A fishing resort. People loved to fish. On the Travel Channel, she'd seen shows about folks going deep-sea fishing to get marlins or some other huge fish. Of course, there wasn't a deep sea around here, but there had to be something swimming in that river.

It was good. It was. It would take a lot of work, but she wasn't above that. If she did most of it herself, it wouldn't cost a horrendous amount.

She'd never swung a hammer but just the thought of it sounded wonderful. Nailing boards into place, putting up drywall, even plumbing. None of it was too much for her.

Yes, she was headed into the construction business. She patted the book beside her. *The Complete Guide to Home Construction and Repair.* It would be her Bible.

Her Bible.

She remembered the faith she'd seen displayed. Hayden and Gramps hadn't said much, but their belief was clearly the cornerstone of their existence.

She'd gone to Sunday school and church when she was young, in the little town on the western edge of Massachusetts, but when she got to be a teenager, overnights and weekend getaways with her friends had taken precedence, and she'd never gotten back to it.

She pulled at last into the motel parking lot, and let herself into her room. She picked up the remote control for the television and clicked it, but nothing happened. The batteries were probably dead.

It was all right. She wasn't in the mood for watching television anyway. Instead, she sprawled across the bed, the pillows bunched under her, and opened her laptop. The motel, as old and decrepit as it was, managed to have a fairly good wireless signal, and soon she was connected with her mother.

"Hey, Mom. It's Livvy. You'll never guess where I am."

"Livvy! Are you all right? What happened? You're in North Dakota? What's it like?"

"It's incredible. It's just incredible. I don't know any other way to say it. It's incredible."

"And what's this place like? The place you want to buy?"

"Sunshine is incredible. The owners are incredible. Mom, am I saying *incredible* enough?"

Her mother laughed. "I'm just guessing, but I gather the place is incredible? I'd love to see it, and I wish your dad and I could get there to help you, but we're stuck here until December. I'm sorry, hon. I feel bad, but we're tied up with our teaching."

"I understand, Mom," she said.

"You're not in over your head, are you?" her mother asked, suddenly serious. "This isn't really like you. Usually you're such a quiet young woman. I expected you to be working for Mr. Evans forever."

"That's just it," Livvy said, noticing a water stain on the ceiling over the foot of the bed. Luckily it looked old. "I needed a change."

"There's a boy, isn't there?"

"A boy? Mom, I'm twenty-five years old!"

"Okay, a man. A young man. There's a young man involved with this, isn't there?"

Livvy thought of Hayden as he stood on the porch, his gaze fixed on the Badlands silhouetted against the sky, his hair as golden as reflected sun, and the tenderness in his voice as he talked about his grandfather.

She changed the subject. With mothers, it was the safest thing to do when young men were involved.

❧

Hayden sat on the porch, ignoring the chicken that pecked at his shoestring. This day, which had started out dealing with the endless supply of boards, had moved into the promise of fishing, and then ended with a flourish when Livvy Moore had driven up in Trevor's truck, which had more filler than original metal.

He shook his head. That truck—he'd have to have a talk with the young Trevor about putting a city woman into it and then sending her out on the county roads, some of which were so washboarded that you risked your teeth driving on them, you'd be so jarred by the unevenness. If the truck had broken down, what would she have done?

She probably had a fancy cell phone, but coverage was spotty out here, and only one company provided any service. If she wasn't with that provider, the only thing her phone would be good for was—well, he couldn't think of anything it would be good for.

He sat forward suddenly, startling the chicken so much that it squawked at him and flapped off to sit on the railing and watch him with a wary eye.

What bothered him, what he needed to know for once and for all, was why she was there, wanting to buy Sunshine.

She had told them the story of the windblown newspaper and he had no reason to doubt its veracity. But there were many unanswered questions. What was a Bismarck newspaper doing in Boston? Why did it blow up against Livvy's car? Why hers?

He stared at the chicken, which walked sideways along the railing while clucking to itself.

"Do you have any ideas, chicken?"

Apparently it didn't, for with a flap of wings, it propelled itself from its perch to the seat of the chaise longue on the other end of the porch.

"Don't even think about laying an egg there," he warned, but the chicken settled in, still keeping watch on him. He'd have to check the crease in the cushion later in the day.

The front door swung open, and his grandfather came out and joined him on the porch.

"I couldn't sleep," Gramps said. "Kept thinking about this whole thing, and then I thought Ellie was making a peach pie. It sure smelled good."

Hayden patted his grandfather's hand. He didn't trust himself to speak.

272

Gramps continued, "But then I remembered that she was gone, and you know, I guess maybe I was asleep and just dreaming, wasn't I?"

"Maybe."

"When you were just a little pup, Grub, you came to your grandmother and me and asked how we knew that this life wasn't just a dream."

"And what did you say?" Hayden knew the answer, but he loved to hear the story.

"I did what any sensible grandfather would have done. I yelled, 'Wake up!' at you as loud as I could."

Hayden laughed. "You nearly scared me into the next year!"

Gramps shrugged. "Made my point. If that didn't wake you up, it wasn't a dream."

Hayden let the afternoon breeze drift over him as he sat next to his grandfather. How often he had taken these moments for granted, but now each second seemed precious, measured as it was.

He was not only losing Sunshine, he was losing his grandfather.

A scratching at the door broke into his train of thought. He got up and let Martha Washington out. She waddled over to Gramps's feet, and he scooped her up and placed her in his lap.

She stretched out, draping herself across his thin and bent legs, and shoved her head under his hand so he would pet her. Her purr filled the air, and Hayden shut his eyes.

He wanted to savor this moment, a time of perfection, a—

It all happened at once. The cat screeched and tore across his arms and knees, claws out, while the chicken attacked it with beak and talons. Hayden reached into the skirmish and separated the two.

He got the chicken off the porch and the cat back into the house before rolling his eyes at his grandfather.

"Wow, that fray was a furious flapping and flurry of feathers," Gramps said with a twinkle in his eyes. "Hey, maybe I've got a second career as a poet!"

Hayden shook his head. "As they say in the movies, don't quit your day job, Gramps. Don't quit your day job."

"My day job, huh? You are a hoot and a half, Grub. My day job is making sure Martha Washington doesn't take out the chicken."

"Or that the chicken doesn't take out Martha Washington."

They settled back and looked out at the vast panorama.

"This is the end of it," Gramps said.

"Maybe. It's your call." Hayden glanced at his grandfather. "I don't want you to make a decision you're not comfortable with."

"I think she'll be all right, don't you?"

"Who? Gran?" Hayden's stomach twisted, as it always did when Gramps's mind slipped.

"No, you goof. Livvy."

"She doesn't have a clue what to do with it," Hayden said.

Gramps laughed. "You'll be here to advise her."

"Once Sunshine is hers, I won't have anything to say about it."

"Sure," his grandfather said. "Sure. You go ahead and think that."

Hayden thought of Livvy, the way her short dark hair was tossed in the gentle summer breeze as she stood by the swimming hole, her dark eyes, deep with sympathy, watching his grandfather. She was going to be good for Sunshine.

Chapter 3

Livvy stood in front of the mirror that was attached to the wall of the old motel. She brushed and rebrushed her hair, but no matter what she tried, it wouldn't lay flat. An early morning rain threatened, and her hair responded as it always did in high humidity. It became a dark brown curly mop.

Someone knocked at her door. It was probably the maid coming to straighten the room.

"Just a second," she called. "I'll be out in a minute."

"I can wait," a male voice answered, "although it's starting to sprinkle."

Hayden!

She gave her hair one last desperate swipe with the brush and shook her head in despair. It was not going to cooperate.

"I'm coming now."

She slipped on a zippered sweatshirt, pulled the hood over her wayward hair, and stepped outside.

He was hunched against the light sprinkle, his ever-present Cooter's Hardware cap on his head. "Ready for one of Clara's omelet specials?"

"I was going to meet you there, but I'm glad for the company on the walk over." She looked at the sky, which was dark with clouds. By the end of the day, she'd look like she had a small poodle sitting on her head. She pulled the string on her hoodie tighter.

"I've got an umbrella in the car, not that it does us any good in there," Hayden said, grinning through the mist. "Do you have one?"

"Somewhere. That's the problem with moving. Everything is somewhere, but I have no idea where it is. It might be at my old office in Boston, still hanging on the back of the door. Or in the storage unit with my couch. Or on its way here now, courtesy of We Really Move You."

"We Really Move You?" he repeated.

"It's a relocation service I used, consisting of three college students and a herd of old vans."

"Vans don't come in herds."

She laughed. "You couldn't look at this group of vehicles and call them a 'fleet,' not by any stretch of the imagination."

"I see," he said, grinning back at her. "You know, the café is about half a block away. Should we brave it? We should be fine, unless the skies follow through on their threat and completely open up."

"Let's go for it."

"Gran used to say that God made us washable so we'd go for walks in the rain. Gramps wasn't convinced."

"I can imagine."

They hurried through the light rain. A large pickup truck was parked in front of the café, and in the back of the cab, she could see a rifle rack.

This definitely wasn't Boston.

The warm aroma of bacon and toast and coffee and something lusciously cinnamon-scented drifted toward them as they approached the building with the sign swinging overhead, proclaiming that Clara's Café was the home of the best omelet in the Dakotas.

"Is that true?" she asked, pointing at the sign.

"Absolutely. Trust me on that," he said solemnly.

As soon as they stepped inside, Hayden took off his cap and ran his fingers through his hair.

Guys had it so good, she thought. That was all it took. They didn't even need an actual comb, just their fingers. Whereas she'd struggled with a comb, a brush, an electric straightener, gel, and spray, and she knew that as soon as she let the hood fall, that effort would be for naught.

Well, she might as well get it over with. She untied the string and with a quick shake of her head, let the hood drop.

"Hey!" he said, looking at her hair, which she could feel springing out in all directions even as she stood there. "I like your hair like that!"

"You do?" She couldn't resist reaching up and touching it to see how bad the damage was. It was worse than she'd thought. What didn't wave was curled, and what didn't curl was frizzed.

"You look real."

"Real what?" she asked cautiously.

A flush began at the base of his neck and climbed steadily to his face. "Real. Just real."

She was prevented from inquiring further by the arrival of a very tall, very thin woman who greeted Hayden with enthusiasm, flinging her arms around the man with abandon.

"This," he said to Livvy as soon as he was released from the pink cotton embrace, "is Clara herself. Clara, this is Livvy Moore."

"Glad to meet you," Clara said, grasping Livvy's hand and pumping it up and down as if it were the handle on a well. "Glad to meet you indeed! And honored to have you here today. Hayden, why don't you and your young lady sit right here?"

She led them to the corner table. "Sit here, and then you two little birdies can have all the privacy your little hearts desire!" Her gaunt hands flapped together happily. "I'll be right back with coffee."

Livvy knew that now she was the one who was blushing. She slid into the seat and picked up the menu that was leaned against the napkin holder.

"I'm sorry about that," Hayden said in an undertone. "Clara is, in Gramps's words, a frustrated Noah."

Livvy let the menu drop. "A frustrated Noah? What? She wants to build an ark?"

"No," he answered, laughing. "She wants everything living to be matched. She can't stand to see a guy without a girl."

"And that's the way it should be," Clara said, reappearing and pouring coffee into their cups. "By the way, I assume you want some of this, miss, but if you don't, the java hound you're with will finish it for you. And ignore his fresh mouth."

"Fresh mouth?" Livvy said, trying very hard not to snicker.

"Yes. Making fun of me. The natural order of things is in twos, that's my theory. Salt and pepper. Bacon and eggs. Steak and potatoes." Clara crossed her bony arms across her equally bony chest and glared at Hayden, but her lips twitched in what Livvy suspected was a suppressed smile.

"Miss Moore is here on business." Hayden's voice was serious but his eyes twinkled.

"There's business and then there's business," Clara shot back. "And speaking of business, I have one to tend to. You ready to order?"

"Clara, we just sat down. Give us a few, okay?"

As the woman turned and walked away, Livvy heard her mutter, "All this and I'll bet he orders the usual."

Hayden leaned across the table and said, in a conspiratorial whisper, "The sad thing is that she's right."

"What is the usual?" Livvy asked, glad to have the conversation on food rather than Clara's notion of pairing them up.

"An omelet, naturally, made with tomatoes and cheese. Hash browns and bacon, both extra crispy. Four slices of white toast with grape jelly. And, of course, coffee, without which I might very well cease to function."

With those words, he lifted his coffee cup in a mock salute and took a clearly grateful swallow. "Ah. Nobody, but nobody, can make coffee like Clara."

She took a sip and sighed. "This is truly extraordinary. She'd have people lining up for this in Boston."

Almost wraithlike, Clara appeared at their table again. "Did you have time to decide? The usual, right, Hayden? And for your lady?"

"I'm not his lady," Livvy objected, "and I'll have the same as Hayden."

"Sure. Whatever." Clara swept the menu from in front of Livvy and slid it back into place over the napkin holder.

Desperate to move the conversation in a different direction, Livvy broached the subject of the coffee. "What's your secret of this great coffee, Clara?"

"Waste not, want not."

"Excuse me?" Either Clara had misunderstood her, or vice versa.

"Waste not, want not," the woman repeated.

"Certainly." Livvy shot Hayden a *"Do you have any idea what she's talking about?"* look. Perhaps Clara was having moments of disconnecting from reality?

"How many eggs do you suppose I go through here every morning?" Clara asked, her dark eyes fixed on Livvy while her thin, lipstick-less mouth twisted in a wry smile.

"I have no idea." Livvy shrugged. "A couple dozen?"

Clara laughed. "A couple hundred is more like it. And I'll give you a hint that you can carry on into your household when you get married." She rolled her eyes in Hayden's direction, and Livvy sighed mentally.

"What is that?" Livvy asked, avoiding looking at Hayden.

Clara leaned in so close that Livvy could smell the woman's lily of the valley perfume over the scent of the griddle that permeated the entire café. "Eggs," she said in a stage whisper. "Eggshells, to be exact. You put those in your pot with the coffee grounds and whoo-ee, your java will taste like liquid gold."

Livvy smiled. She wasn't sure she wanted her coffee to taste like gold, but she understood the idea. "I've heard of that. Cowboys did that, right?"

Clara cackled. "I guess. In the big city, everybody only want lattes and cappuccinos. Here, though, you get coffee. Good coffee. No need for that fancy-schmancy stuff with the hoity-toity syrups and such. 'With whip,' I had a fellow say the other day. 'You want a whip?' I asked him. 'Why? You going to be the ringleader in a circus?'"

Hayden shook his head. "Clara, you are something else."

"Well," she said, lifting her chin proudly, "I'd rather be something else than just like everybody. Omelets are almost ready, by the way."

"But we just ordered—" Livvy began, and then stopped. "Ohhhh."

"Yup," Clara said, "had them going as soon as I saw young Hayden step in the door. Boy never varies. He's been eating the same thing since he was a sprig of a boy. Somehow I didn't think today would be the day he'd switch to something as exotic as French toast."

Within minutes, Clara was at their table, a large platter heaped with food in each hand. "Eat up and be healthy!"

"Be healthy?" Livvy said, looking at the mound in front of her. It was a display of artery-clogging delight. And it smelled delicious.

"Before we begin, may I ask the blessing?" Hayden said.

"Blessing? Oh, grace. Definitely."

This wasn't something she had seen in her day-to-day life in the city, but then most of her lunches had been a granola bar and a cup of coffee from the dispenser in the building and had been consumed at her desk over paperwork.

Some people, she knew, held hands while they prayed, but Hayden just lowered his head and shut his eyes. She followed suit as he prayed, simply,

"Lord, bless this food. Touch all of our actions with Your grace. We ask this in Your holy name. Amen."

She was surprised at how good the short prayer made her feel. It was refreshing.

"You ready to have the best of the best?" Hayden asked. "Dig in!"

Livvy took his advice and as soon as the first bite of the omelet hit her tongue, she knew that the advertising was well-deserved. The outside was just crispy enough, and inside, the omelet was fluffy and light. It truly was the best she'd ever had.

As she ate, the sheer incongruity of the situation she was in struck her. Here she was, sitting in a café in North Dakota, unemployed, with a man she'd just met across from her, and she was planning on investing her life savings in a resort that had been closed for two years—a resort in the middle of the Badlands.

She must be insane. That was the only answer. Or dreaming. What was she planning to do with it? At some point she would have to earn a living—and how would she do that?

Fishing, of course, came to mind, but the fact was that she knew nothing about it—or running a resort—or what a fishing resort did in the winter, although she had once seen a program on the Travel Channel about ice fishing. That show constituted the sum total of her knowledge about ice fishing, hardly enough of a foundation to build a successful business on.

But she could learn of course. Everybody had to learn at some time. Nobody was born knowing this stuff. The trick was looking like you had though.

This was all so out of character for her. She was a nice, normal young woman with a nice, normal job in Boston. Or she had been until she'd taken total leave of her senses and come to North Dakota.

There was still time to change her mind. Nothing had been signed. She could still back out. Maybe she couldn't get her job back from Mr. Evans—although with the appropriate amount of groveling, he'd probably hire her again—but it wasn't too late to undo everything.

But this just didn't feel like a misstep. It felt right.

She took another bite of the incredible omelet. It was the best she'd ever tasted, even if it did come served with a side of Clara's quirkiness.

"Gramps and I talked more last night," Hayden said. He nabbed a last bite of shredded potatoes and popped it into his mouth.

Livvy froze, her own fork stopped midway to her lips. This was what she had been waiting for. She leaned forward a bit, knowing that what he was about to say would tell her the direction her life would take.

These were her crossroads. The next words that Hayden uttered would change her life.

"If I wouldn't end up broke and the size of a barn, I'd eat Clara's breakfasts for every meal."

Her fork clattered to the plate. "Excuse me?"

"Good food." He wiped his mouth with a paper napkin.

"It is, but you said you and your grandfather talked last night? About selling Sunshine to me, I gather?"

"Yes, we did." He pushed the plate aside and leaned forward. "We're interested, to the point of saying yes, I might add, but we have a couple of questions we'd like answered."

"Shoot," she said, and then, remembering the truck they'd walked past with the rack in the back of the cab, doubled back on what she'd said. "Don't shoot. Just ask."

He grinned. "Okay, I won't shoot. But here are the questions." He reached into his shirt pocket and pulled out a list. "First, Gramps wants to know if you can keep the place from going back to nature."

"Back to nature?"

"Any building left unattended will eventually be reclaimed by nature. The wood will fall apart, and animals will move in. Once they're in there, it's nearly impossible to get the building back to its former glory."

"I won't let that happen."

He looked at her squarely. "How will you prevent that?"

"I'm going to live there."

As soon as the words were out of her mouth, a great peace descended on her. It was right.

"Alone?" he asked.

"Possibly. Probably. At the moment, yes."

"You're a woman."

"And you're observant."

"The Badlands can be aptly named, you know." A slight frown creased his tanned forehead.

"Listen," she said, suddenly a bit angry, "Boston has its moments, too. Every place does. I think I can handle it."

"Do you have a gun?"

She thought again of the truck with the rifle rack outside the café. "No, I don't, and I never will."

"How will you protect yourself?"

She shook her head. This was not going at all well. "I will protect myself by being careful and using the brains God gave me. I have never been in the practice of putting myself in bad situations, and it's usually served me well."

He nodded, his gaze never leaving her face. "That's good. But what if you find yourself staring down a rattlesnake?"

"A rattlesnake." She shrugged with an assurance she didn't feel. A rattlesnake had never been part of her plan. "The chances that I'd have a loaded gun at my fingertips and that I'd know how to use it without blasting off my own foot are pretty minimal—no, they're nonexistent. So I guess I'd have to say I would stand still and wait for him to go away on his own."

"That's the right answer."

"It's the only answer. Trust me, Hayden, if I went into the kitchen to get coffee one morning and there was a snake in there, I would be paralyzed with fright. I'd have no choice but to stand stock-still."

"You wouldn't have a rattlesnake in your house anyway. They'd be in the out-buildings and in the rocky parts on the edge of the grounds. They don't want to see you any more than you want to see them. Now, if you were a plump rabbit, that would be different."

"Ah. So I should probably ditch the fuzzy bunny slippers just in case, huh? It would be just my luck that I'd see Mr. Snake and he'd think I was wearing breakfast on my feet."

Hayden laughed. "Fuzzy bunny slippers? That's quite the image."

She pretended to fluff her hair. "We Bostonians are all about fashion. But back to the question. I see this as a challenge, one that I'm willing to take on. I've never backed down before when confronted with something that makes me work a little harder, learn a little more, dig a little deeper."

"Do you know anything at all about buildings?"

"I was in real estate management in Boston for several years. Actually, I was until a couple of weeks ago."

"Did you ever hammer a nail?"

She had to think fast. She'd hammered her fingernail one time with a can when she was trying to fix the edge of a countertop that had worked loose, but that was too far from the truth. She'd hung pictures, but that wasn't really hammering and they weren't really nails but tiny tacks. The heel of her shoe that was coming undone, the top of a can of touch-up paint for her apartment, the cabinet door that wouldn't quite close—she'd smacked a lot of things into place in her life, but hammering a nail?

"Not really. I mean, maybe years ago—but how hard can it be? You hit the nail with the hammer."

"I see. And have you ever used a saw?"

"No."

"A level?"

"No."

"A screwdriver?"

"Yes! I have!" She felt ridiculously happy about this. Finally, he mentioned a tool that she had used.

"What did you do with it?"

"I fixed my sunglasses. And my laptop. The little screw that holds the monitor on was coming out and I tightened it."

This was not coming out at all as she planned. She took a quick moment and regrouped her thoughts, drawing on the skills she'd learned from Mr. Evans. She could almost hear his voice: *"Never play defense. Always have the right of way. Steer the ship."*

He'd been quite the fellow for folksy adages, but he'd made her an effective agent for closing deals.

And his advice was apropos here. She took control of the conversation.

"I have years of experience in real estate. I know buildings. I know construction, even if I haven't done it myself. I know what has to be union-labor, and what can be done by handymen—or handywomen. The best contractor doesn't do it all. He or she knows when to call in help. And let's face it, Hayden—" She used a trick she'd employed many times in getting an unsure client to agree with her. She got closer, and dropped her voice. "All construction workers had to get in at the ground floor, no pun intended. Everybody starts somewhere."

"But they had skilled people training them. Who will train you?" Hayden asked. His logical query poked an immediate hole in her argument.

"I have resources to help me when I need help." It was true. . .sort of.

"Oh." He sagged in obvious relief. "You've got a crew?"

"I have resources," she repeated, although she could count them on two fingers of one hand: the book and the Internet.

"Super," he said, "because if you're relying on the Internet, good luck to you. There's no signal out at Sunshine."

No Internet. She tried not to choke.

"So the next question Gramps and I came up with," he said, referring to his list again, "is if you intend to live there while the remodeling is being done."

That one was easy.

"Yes."

"How soon do you need to move in?" he asked.

"As soon as possible, of course, but I know that you and your grandfather need some time to move out and get settled."

"I have a place here in town, and I'd be happy to have Gramps with me, but he says he won't."

"He's too independent, I gather?"

"That's part of it. He doesn't want to be a bother, that's what he says." Hayden stared sadly into his nearly empty coffee cup. "As if he could ever be a bother."

"One set of my grandparents lives in Arizona, and the other one lives in Maine." She chuckled. "My parents are always trying to get them to move closer to me, and I'd love it, too, but they have absolutely no interest in it."

"I would like Gramps to be close though. I'm hoping I can get him in at the senior living apartments, but you can guess what he says. 'They're for old people!'"

"I understand the need to get him settled, that it's a priority," she said. "Did you say you can help me find a place to live in Obsidian? Oh, wait. That's a lot to ask of you, since you need to deal with moving your grandpa, too."

"Actually, yours is easy. I hope you don't mind, but I think I have a place for you. This morning I dropped off some eggs—yes, we have the world's orneriest chicken but she does lay eggs, even if you do have to find where they left them—at Jeannie Baldwin's house, and got to talking with her. She said she had turned the garage into a guesthouse for her cousin, who, in Jeannie's words, 'up and married some fellow' and now wasn't going to use it. She's fretting because she spent a lot of money fixing it up."

"Maybe I could rent it!"

"You could. Knowing Jeannie, it'll be sparkling clean. The only thing that might be an issue is that she's taking off soon to go to Africa on a mission tour so you'd also have to watch her house."

"I can do that!" This was working out wonderfully, and a rush of relief coursed through her.

"And her dog. And her bird. And her fish. And her crab. The rabbit escaped or else you'd have to watch it, too."

"That's quite the menagerie," she said.

"It's a zoo, that's what it is. The only thing missing is a monkey and a zebra, and that's only because she hasn't thought of them yet, I'm sure." Hayden shook his head.

"She must like animals."

"That, my friend, is an understatement. I think we can get the bird and the fish moved to the church. I'm not sure about the crab. It's one of those that live in a painted shell. She saw it at a mall, at one of those kiosks, and felt sorry for it. So she bought it and carted it all the way back here to Obsidian."

Jeannie Baldwin was sounding like a fascinating woman.

"What kind of dog is it?"

He didn't answer at first. Then he said, slowly, "I have no idea. It's big. It's got a lot of fur and a lot of drool."

"It's friendly, right?" she asked, cautious about this beast. She had about as much experience with dogs as she did with hammers.

"Friendly? Oh yes. Friendly. Very friendly. He doesn't bite. The worst he would do is lick his enemy's face off, or maybe drown him in drool. But he will like you."

"And after six weeks, he goes back to Jeannie, and I go to Sunshine, right?" She ran the calendar in her head. Based upon her experience in the projects she'd managed in Boston, six weeks should be plenty of time.

Plus, as she had seen countless times on her favorite television shows about flipping houses—buying them, rapidly remodeling them, and selling them for a profit—six weeks would give her lots of wiggle room.

Fixing up Sunshine should take three weeks, tops, once she got in there and could work in a fairly empty place. She knew that much from the house remodeling programs she'd watched on television. The key was to have the place free of furniture and carpet, so time wouldn't be wasted cleaning during the renovation, but instead could be done in one great swoop—or sweep—at the end.

"Are there other questions on your list?" she asked.

"Just one. What are you going to do with Sunshine?"

The world, which had been spinning so merrily, came to a dead halt.

This was the one part of her plan she hadn't figured out, and it was the most important part. Without it, this was a journey without a destination.

She quickly weighed her options of how to respond to the question.

She could lie and come up with some scenario of investors and plans. That wasn't going to happen. Lying was never a good idea. It might get you past an immediate situation, but it had been her experience that lies had longer legs and greater staying power than she did, and they always caught up with her.

Plus she couldn't lie to Hayden and Gramps, even if she knew she'd never get tripped up on her own words. They were honest people. She could not imagine either of them telling a lie.

They deserved what she knew—and what she didn't know.

"Well," she hedged, "I haven't decided yet if I will do anything more than live there, at least for the time being. I was thinking about a fishing resort."

He shook his head. "I'm afraid that probably won't work. Folks here don't go to a resort anymore to fish. They've got their own boats."

"Whatever I do, I can assure you that I won't turn it into anything that would bring embarrassment to you or your grandfather. It won't be a bar or anything like that."

"There's not a lot you can do with that property," Hayden warned. "It's too far away from the interstate to be commercially appealing."

"So you're saying I can't make it into a discount mall?" she asked. "Or a twenty-plex movie theater? Or a fireworks warehouse?"

The horrified look on his face let her know that he didn't understand she was kidding, and she backtracked quickly. "I was just kidding. Just kidding!"

"Fireworks! You had me going there for a moment. At any rate, I think it'll all work out for both of us. How soon do you want to do this? Do you need more time to think?"

She probably did, but she didn't dare let herself think any more. She might talk herself out of it.

"No," she said. "No, I don't."

With those words, she felt as if she'd walked to the edge of a cliff—and taken one more step. She hadn't seen all of the house, she hadn't had an appraisal done on it, she hadn't looked at a plat map—she hadn't done anything she should have done.

"All right then. I'll talk to the real estate agent later today and get things started. Meanwhile, let's go look at Jeannie's guest house."

Clara waved them on past regarding the bill. "I'll put it on Charlie's tab.

Tell the old coot to come in and see me sometime. I'll make him a Charlie special."

"A Charlie special?" Livvy asked as they left the café.

"My grandfather invented it, or so he claims. Scrambled eggs, loaded with onions, garlic, jalapeños, and sausage. I make him stay on the other side of the house for twenty-four hours after he eats one. Those things are lethal."

The sun had come out, and the morning mist was drying quickly. "Good fishing weather," Hayden said.

"Really? That's one thing I've never done."

"Do you want to learn?" he asked, apparently not bothered that just moments before she had been planning to embark on a career dependent on fishing.

"I should if I'm going to be living at Sunshine, I suppose. Does it involve worms?"

"Not necessarily."

She shrugged and smiled. "Then let's do it. Can we see Jeannie's guest house and also the real estate agent this morning? They're not far away, are they?"

"Livvy, we're in Obsidian, not Boston. Nothing is far away. Jeannie's place is right up the block, and the real estate agent is next to the Badlands Vista Motel."

Jeannie was in her backyard at the clothesline, a basket of laundry at her feet. Her mouth was full of clothespins, and she stuck them on the sheet she was hanging up.

"I'm so glad the sun came out," she said, "or I'd have had wet sheets draped across my living room like some house of horrors."

Hayden laughed. "You could never have a house of horrors, Jeannie. This, by the way, is Livvy Moore. She's going to buy Sunshine."

Livvy immediately liked Jeannie. A mop of reddish-gold curls topped the middle-aged woman's head, and her ready grin took Livvy in as if they were old friends.

"I'm glad to hear that! It's a great place and we have wonderful memories, but it's time to let someone else have at it and begin their own," Jeannie said. "I just don't want to see Charlie out there one more winter alone. I know you go out and see him, Hayden, but he really needs to be in town."

"I agree," Hayden said. "It's still going to be difficult."

Jeannie straightened one edge of the sheet she'd just hung on the line. "After church last week, you'd gone to get some coffee, and I found him headed out toward the street. Now, he's not a two-year-old who has been warned about going into traffic—and I guess we all know that there really isn't anything like traffic here anyway—but what worried me was I asked him where he was headed, and he said he had to get the mail."

"The mail?" Hayden asked, clearly at a loss. "What did he mean by that?

It's delivered to Sunshine."

"That's what I asked," she said, "and he stopped for a moment, shook his head, and turned and went back into the church."

The pain on his face was clear. "It's the right thing," he said almost to himself. "It's the right thing."

"Well, let's see about getting you out of that nasty Badlands Vista Motel and into a more comfortable place. Hayden tells me you're from Boston—"

Jeannie's chatter covered the sadness of the moment with a layer of cheer as the three headed over to the guesthouse.

The garage door had been removed and the wall replaced so expertly that Livvy, even with her expertise in the housing world, couldn't tell that this had once been a garage. The faint fumes of gasoline that might have lingered had been erased by new flooring and paint.

It was basically a single room with a counter divider and built-in shelves and cabinets, and a stove and half-sized refrigerator tucked into the corner by a glistening white sink.

The furniture was new, and it was expertly coordinated in gentle tones of honey and ivory, creating a calming, restful atmosphere.

"I think it might work for what you need," Jeannie said. "The furnace and water heater are behind this divider, and the kitchen and bathroom are pretty small but functional. Upstairs is the loft, where you can sleep if you want. This is a futon though, so you could sleep down here, too."

"It's awfully small," Hayden said.

Livvy laughed. "I used to have an apartment in the city that was about two-thirds the size of this, and it didn't have a loft either. I suspect you're just used to the dimensions of Sunshine, which seem to be endless."

"Well, speaking of small, I think you need to meet Leonard." Jeannie beamed proudly. "I believe that Hayden told you about him? He's my puppy."

Hayden snorted. "Puppy? Hardly!"

"You hush," Jeannie said, taking Livvy by the elbow and leading her out of the guesthouse. As they got close to the house, a series of deep woofs greeted them.

"Careful now," she warned as she opened the door. "Leonard loves people."

"For lunch," Hayden muttered, but Livvy knew he was kidding. At least she hoped he was kidding.

A gigantic dog launched himself at Jeannie, and she grabbed him by his collar. "Leonard, best behavior now! We have company."

The dog stopped and turned to look at Livvy. With a look of absolute glee on his furry face, he ran toward her, stood up, put his paws on her shoulders, and slurped his gigantic tongue across her cheeks.

She tried not to shudder. Dog slobber.

"Down, Leonard. Down!" Jeannie laughed as the dog obeyed. "See? He's a good boy. I can't take him with me to Africa, obviously, so he's part of the deal.

You'd have to take care of him until I get back."

"I can do this," Livvy said, more to convince herself of it than to tell Jeannie. "I take him for a walk, I feed him. I can do this."

"He has to stay with you at night. He gets very nervous at night."

"He gets nervous at night," she repeated. "Excellent."

"That creature can't fit in there with her," Hayden objected.

Leonard looked up at Livvy adoringly, his head tilted to one side. She could have sworn the dog was smiling at her.

He really was quite cute, in a big dog sort of way. There was evidence of a terrier in his lineage, as evidenced by his short curly gray and brown hair and his long straight legs. A bit of Labrador retriever showed in his thick torso. The rest of him was bits and pieces of different breeds. All together, the dog was a mutt.

She didn't like dogs, not particularly. And certainly the thought of having one this size live with her inside the tiny little guesthouse was unappealing.

Then Leonard lifted one paw and placed it on her hand, very gently, very carefully, and her heart turned to mush.

"Okay," she said.

"Good!" Jeannie said, beaming at her. "Oh, look at you two. You're going to be best friends."

"Hayden and me?" Livvy asked, a bit taken aback.

"No. You and Leonard."

"He is a wonderful dog." Leonard gazed at her with liquid brown eyes, and she rubbed the soft spot behind his ears. "But my only worry is that I'll be out at Sunshine soon, that is, assuming that the moving is done and the renovations are complete."

Hayden cleared his throat. "Livvy, how long are you expecting all of this to take?"

She stood up, and Leonard came closer and leaned against her, nearly throwing her off-balance.

"I figure three weeks to get the place fixed up. I'll work on the outer buildings and the grounds and probably the swimming hole while you and your grandfather get resettled."

"Three weeks?" Hayden looked as if he had swallowed a toad. "Three weeks?"

"You can, of course, take as long as you need. My stuff is still on its way here, and it won't arrive for about a month, they told me at We Really Move You, since they have to pack everything up, too, so I don't have much to move in yet. You don't have to get everything moved out right away. I know there are many years of memories stored there, and I understand that."

It was amazing how well it was all working out. She congratulated herself on how quickly she had put it together in her head.

"How long are you giving yourself to fix up Sunshine, seriously?" he asked, his voice slow and even.

"Three weeks ought to be plenty."

He shook his head. "I think you need to back up on this. You haven't even seen the house except for the living room and the kitchen. For all you know, the rest of it could be a wreck."

"But it isn't, is it?" she asked stubbornly. She did not want to let go of this dream.

"I'm just saying—" He clapped his hand on his forehead and walked off.

"Honey," Jeannie said, her voice low enough that only Livvy could hear it, "this is a lot of money to invest. You need to be careful."

Livvy let her fingers trail across Leonard's ears and was rewarded with him rubbing his snout against her new black jersey slacks. She was sure that she now sported a line of dog goo across the fabric but she didn't care.

"I can trust them, can't I?" she asked, holding on as tightly as she could to the new life that Sunshine offered.

"Of course you can. But Gramps is old, and Hayden is a math teacher. Neither one is a carpenter or an electrician or a roofer. All they can do is chase after problems. You probably want to start over, tear out the plumbing, look at the wiring, investigate the heating system."

"I can do that."

"You can?" Jeannie's surprise was clear.

"Sure." Livvy watched Hayden pacing by the clothesline pole, clearly conflicted about something, and felt her resolution ebbing as totally as if someone had pulled the plug on it. Maybe hours of watching renovation shows on television hadn't prepared her after all. Her precious book, *The Complete Guide to Home Construction and Repair*, would help, but she knew it wasn't as complete as it proclaimed itself to be.

He pulled his Cooter's Hardware cap off, ran his fingers through his hair, and jammed the hat back on. And then he stalked over to Livvy and Jeannie.

"I never represented Sunshine as anything but an old run-down resort that has seen its time come and go, did I?"

"No," Livvy said in a little voice.

"And I never said it was in good shape, did I?"

"Well," she said, "you're living there with your grandfather, so I assumed it was livable."

"How are you going to get back and forth between Sunshine and Obsidian?"

"Trevor said—"

"Trevor wants an iPod more than anything. Keep that in mind whenever he's offering you a deal. That truck is held together with duct tape, putty, bubble gum, and a hot glue gun. Not to mention a whole lot of prayer—on the driver's part."

"I left my car at a lot to be sold before I left, but I can buy another one."

Jeannie coughed beside her as Hayden tore off his cap, ruffled his hair, and pulled it on again, this time with more vigor.

"When are you planning to do that?"

"Soon, I guess." She knew how bad this sounded, how unprepared she came across, but it was the truth.

"I don't know if I'd wait. That truck isn't going to make the trip between Sunshine and Obsidian too many more times before it becomes a permanent resident of the junkyard. That's where Trevor got the parts for it, I'm sure, so it'll be a homecoming of sorts."

She knew it was true. The truck made some pretty dire clacks and bangs, and she didn't even want to find out what shape the tires were in. She didn't have to wait—Hayden told her.

"And those tires—they're no better than balloons at this stage. Unsafe." He rubbed his chin thoughtfully. "Gramps has an old pickup out at Sunshine. It's not pretty but it's got four-wheel drive and it's a sight safer than Trevor's bucket of bolts. Let me make sure it's got good plates and registration. I think he kept it up but I want to be sure. If it's still good, we'll throw it in as part of the deal. I know Gramps doesn't drive it anymore, and I sure don't need it."

Four-wheel drive. She hadn't given much thought to the fact that she would probably be driving in winter.

As if reading her mind, Hayden continued, "You usually don't need four-wheel drive, but when you do, you're mighty glad you have it."

Jeannie nodded in agreement. "It's going to be a good idea, Livvy, especially if you plan to winter out there. That's a long, lonely road from Sunshine into Obsidian, and sometimes it drifts over pretty badly."

Livvy swallowed. Hard. This was more than she'd thought about.

She tried to dismiss it. Winter driving didn't faze her. She'd managed Boston traffic in snow, and she could certainly make her way just fine on these uncrowded streets during winter. It wouldn't be that bad, would it?

"You could drive Gramps's pickup for a while. Whether or not you want to keep what you have, well, that's up to you and how safe you feel," Hayden said.

Her car was cute, a bright yellow little import that zipped through the city and was easy on gasoline. She loved it—in Boston. And now it sat at Buster's AutoWorld on the edge of the city, unless it had been sold to someone else. She'd miss it, but it wasn't what she needed here.

The fact of the matter was that Hayden was right. She had to do something about transportation, and Trevor's truck wasn't the answer.

"Thanks for the offer. Honestly, I'm delighted to return Trevor's truck to him. At least he's somewhat closer to his iPod, even if I don't keep the truck any longer."

"Good. I'll check into it. Well, we'd better get on with our errands if we're going to get a fishing pole in your hands this afternoon," he said.

"You're going fishing? That's lovely," Jeannie said. "The sun's burning off most of the rain, and it'll be pleasant. Use sunscreen, dear," she added in an aside to Livvy. "You'll burn worse than one of Alvin's pizzas if you don't."

"Alvin's pizzas?" she asked blankly.

"Alvin Johannsen owns Pizza World. His pizzas are legendary—for being crispy," Hayden explained.

She nodded.

The day was heating up, now that the drizzle had stopped. Overhead a lone cloud, wispy and thin, was stalled over the Badlands. Nothing else interrupted the space between the sky and the earth, save for the tops of the elms that brushed the endless blue. The sun touched everything, chasing away the shadows and warming roofs and sidewalks.

Cooter's Hardware. Alvin's Pizza. Clara's Café. It was a different world, and she was loving every light-drenched moment of it.

❧

Hayden caught the door of the real estate office just before it slammed shut. Tom Clark, the agent, had assured him that the sale of Sunshine would be accomplished quite easily, and he'd draw up the papers that afternoon.

His stomach felt as if he'd swallowed a nest of wasps, buzzing and stinging inside him. This was probably the most important decision he'd ever made, encouraging Gramps to sell Sunshine.

It was for the best. He knew that. Gramps wasn't able to maintain it, and Sunshine deserved a better fate than falling into ruin.

He glanced at Livvy. Sunlight filtered through the leaves of the trees outside the agency, casting dappled pieces of sunlight across her dark hair.

She was so tiny.

He stopped himself. She wasn't tiny at all. She was sized just right. The top of her head came to his nose, which would put her lips—

He ended the thought before it went any further. Obviously he'd been out in the country too long, if that's where his mind was going.

She was buying Sunshine and that was it.

And, he reminded himself, once the papers were signed, it was hers. Totally hers. The only thing he and Gramps would own would be some of the glasses etched with the Sunshine name...and their memories.

He'd be off to teach, Gramps would be settled in a retire-ment home, and their lives, now intersecting with Livvy's, would head off in three different directions.

His mood began to disintegrate.

"You look sad," she said, her hand on his forearm, and her forehead wrinkled with concern. "This is rough, isn't it?"

He nodded, not trusting himself to speak for a moment. And then he gathered his emotions together and summoned a smile. "There's one sure way to chase away the blues," he said.

"Whistle?" She grinned.

"Actually I was thinking we could go fishing, but we can whistle on the way."

She looped her arm through his and the two of them began to walk to his car, trying to whistle and not laugh, and failing.

They spent the time traveling to Sunshine in the car, sharing songs they especially liked and those they absolutely hated.

"Some country," Hayden offered, "especially the old songs from the early days."

"Yes, Patsy Cline, for sure."

"A lot of classical, especially Bach."

"Bach's music is big—it takes over the room."

"Exactly! And Debussy is sweet."

"Sweet?" She tilted her head, questioning.

" 'Clair de Lune.' I have to confess though, that's the only Debussy melody I know. I took piano lessons when I was in grade school, and Miss Henrietta, my teacher, gave me 'Clair de Lune' to learn. I thought I'd never heard such a beautiful song." He smiled at the memory of sitting at the piano in his house, leaning over the keys, trying to find exactly the right phrasing for the song.

" 'Clair de Lune.' I haven't thought of that for ages! It's so pretty!"

"I played it so often that if my parents heard it on a store's audio, or on the radio, they clapped their hands over their ears. I suspect I didn't play it all that well, to be honest. I wasn't exactly a piano prodigy. I lasted through third grade, and then baseball called my name."

"I can see you playing baseball," she said. "You're a Red Sox fan, I hope."

"Sorry." He chuckled. "Around here pretty much it's the Twins all the way. Almost everybody supports the Minnesota teams, since North Dakota doesn't have major league sports. So it's the Twins for baseball, the Vikings for football, and the Wild for hockey—or the University of North Dakota in Grand Forks, of course—although hockey's so big here that local hockey is more important for most."

"I like hockey, but of course in Boston it's the Bruins that everybody roots for."

"It probably won't matter. You'll be a huge fan soon of the ObsMarWin team."

"ObsMarWin?" she asked.

"Obsidian-Martinville-Winston Consolidated School District, home of the Landers, which is short for Badlanders. It used to be the Badlanders but some kids got the bright idea to call them the Baddies, which wouldn't do at all, of course, so they became the Landers."

"The Landers. I like that!"

"They rarely get to the final rounds of any sports, but they play with all their hearts, and you've got to give them credit for that. You'll see folks around here sporting the green and gold as soon as the first puck flies."

"Green and gold being the Landers's colors, right?"

"Right. The school is here in Obsidian. It's that big prairie-style building we drove past on our way out of town. Sort of a sentinel here in the Badlands. I'll point it out on the way back."

The turn to Sunshine was still noted by a sign that had faded almost to the point of not being legible. How long had it been there? He didn't know. Since he was a boy, it had pointed the way to Sunshine. It had weathered everything from deep snows and blizzards to hot summer winds and blistering heat.

The sign, shaped like a smiling sun with once-rosy cheeks, was tilted to one side. Someone had probably taken the turn too sharply and clipped it.

He pulled over to the side of the road and tugged the sign back into place, shoring it up with one of the large stone chunks around the sign, there for that very purpose.

Livvy called through the open truck door, "That's a really cool sign. I'm surprised it's still here."

"I think Gramps just never got around to replacing it," he said as he put one foot on the running board and heaved himself onto the seat. "It's a bit out of the way for him, and I suppose other things were more important."

"I think it's charming," she said. "I meant though that I'm surprised someone hasn't taken it."

"Why would they?"

"It's old and it's retro. It would probably sell for a lot of money. Don't you ever watch those antique shows on television?"

He shook his head. "I've heard of them but never watched them. We don't have cable at Sunshine."

"Oh, they're my favorites." Her face took on a dreamy, faraway look. "Those, and the home remodeling ones, and the travel programs. One day I'm going to go to Alaska and touch a glacier with my bare hands, and then I'll go to China and see the Great Wall and try to take in how big it is, and Egypt to look at the pyramids where I'll imagine what it must have been like during the days of the pharaohs."

"You like to travel?" He put the truck into gear and edged back onto the road, now headed toward Sunshine.

"I think I would."

He shot her a startled glance. "You haven't traveled?"

"This is as exotic as it gets for me."

He hooted. "North Dakota? Exotic?"

"It is, for someone who's spent her entire life in Massachusetts."

"You never left Massachusetts? I don't believe it." He avoided a rabbit that darted in front of the truck.

"Oh, I visited other New England states, but I never got much farther west than a ways into New York. But I've always wanted to see more of the world. Have you traveled much?"

"Not a lot. Minnesota, of course. Everybody goes to the Cities at some point."

"The Cities?" she asked. "Which cities?"

"The Cities are what we call Minneapolis and St. Paul. They're the Twin Cities, you know, so most people here simply call them the Cities. It's even capitalized, so if you see a reference to 'the Cities' and the *C* is uppercased, that's what it means."

"I see," she said. "I think."

"And I have gone into Canada, but not recently. It seems like every free minute quickly becomes not-free."

He rubbed his hand over his forehead, trying to erase the frown lines that he knew had carved themselves there. The truth was that Gramps had needed him more and more, and as it became clearer that the old man was edging toward heaven, he'd in fact needed his grandfather more. Needed to be around him, needed to hear his voice, needed to see him as much as he could.

Every August, when he'd had to start spending his days inside the big tan brick building preparing for school and then teaching, he'd hated being away from Gramps. And as the year slipped onward, from summer's blazing glory to unpredictable autumn, when there might be a forty-degree variable from one day to the next, he began to dread winter's arrival.

One day last winter, driven from desperation and exhaustion, he'd sent out applications to schools along the far southeastern coast of Florida. He could see himself with Gramps on the beach, soaking up the sun and the warmth and escaping the cold and the snow and the relentless wind.

But nothing had come of it, and he'd let it slip past, and here he was, heading into another school year, and he dreaded the deep winter that was coming.

He couldn't get out to see Gramps at night then—he often had school responsibilities that kept him in Obsidian—and the weekends were iffy at best. Usually the highway to the turnoff was clear, but after that, it was anybody's guess how bad the drifting might be.

Worry about his grandfather was never far from his mind.

"You spend most of your time with him, don't you?" she asked gently, startling him as if she had been reading his thoughts. "You don't have to say it. It's clear without the words. He's why you stay here."

"No!" he objected, perhaps more strenuously than necessary, and he immediately modified the word. "Well, not entirely. My heart is in Obsidian. It's in Sunshine, and it's in Gramps."

He refused to consider the day when he would not have either of them.

Fortunately he wasn't able to continue that train of thought, for when he pulled into the yard at Sunshine, Gramps was waiting for him, a fishing pole in each hand.

"Grub!" Gramps called, as he hobbled toward the truck. "I'm ready. Even dug up a nightcrawler or two." He gestured toward a tomato soup can in the shade by the front porch.

"You got us worms?" Hayden asked, taking the poles from his grandfather. "How did you do that?"

"I took that shovel over there"—the old man gestured toward a small camp shovel with a pointed tip—"and dug."

"Well, that's the way it's usually done," Hayden said. He walked over to the can where an earthworm was making its escape out the top of it. He dropped it back into the can, where three other worms were, and returned to the truck.

"I told Livvy we'd take her fishing."

"So we shall. There's an extra pole in the blue shed, and Grub, you'd better give her one of the canvas hats so she doesn't get burned."

Within minutes, Livvy was outfitted with fishing gear and one of Gramps's old hats that was so big it insisted on sliding down over her nose.

"You can swim, right?" Hayden asked.

"Swim?" She had a look of faint panic on her face. "We're going swimming, too? I don't have a suit."

Gramps cackled. "The goal is not to go swimming."

"Not to—? Oh!" She laughed. "I can swim. I'm no Olympic gold medalist but I can get from one side of the pool to the other."

"There aren't sides to this pool. You need a life jacket," Hayden said. "They're in the boat. Let's go on down there and get things set up. I'll get the can of gasoline, and Livvy, why don't you grab that soup can? Those are the worms."

"Worms," she said faintly.

He had to smile at her reaction. "Not a worm fan, I gather. I'll put them on the hook for you."

She nodded. "I appreciate that."

Soon they were all at the boat, each one clad in a life jacket, smudged from being stored away, and thoroughly doused with bug spray. A blue and white cooler filled with root beer was tucked away next to the tackle box.

Hayden coaxed the small motor into life, and they headed out into the middle of the small lake. Sun sparkled off the water like reflected diamonds, and a light breeze ruffled the surface.

Hayden cut the motor, and the only sounds were of the river and the wind and the birds.

"Could you hand me the can of worms?" he asked, reaching for his fishing pole.

"Livvy, they're by your foot," Gramps said.

Hayden turned just in time to see the side of her pant leg catch on the can, and it fell onto its side, spilling out dirt and earthworms.

For a split second, Livvy paused, and then she leaned over and quickly scooped everything back into the can, soil and worms alike.

"I'm impressed," he said. "Some women wouldn't do that."

She shook her head vigorously. "That is so old-fashioned. Most women could pick up a worm. We might not want to, but we'll do it."

"I thought you said you wanted me to put the worm on the hook for you," he said.

"Picking up a worm is one thing. Impaling it is another." She took the rod that Gramps handed her. "That is something I can't do."

"You don't have to use a worm," he said. "You can use a lure instead."

"Worms are good," Gramps said. "Fish are smart. They know food when they see it, and they know that a plastic thing with a hook hanging out of it isn't usually something to eat."

"Now, now," Hayden chided him gently. "You're a worm guy. I'm a minnow guy. Others insist that this lure or that is the way to go."

Gramps shook his head and muttered as he reached down, picked up a worm, and threaded it onto a hook.

Hayden grinned at Livvy. "I'm guessing you'd rather have a lure dangling on the end of your hook than a worm."

"Right you are. Show me how to do this, please. Is this one going to work?" She held up a bright green lure she'd taken out of the tackle box.

"Whether or not it works is up to the fish," he said. "If it bites, it works. Doesn't bite? Doesn't work. Actually, you probably want this chartreuse one."

He leaned over her, and the faint scent of soap, clean and fresh, drifted through the sharp smell of the lake and the boat, of algae and fish and tarps.

Get a grip, he told himself. *You're in the middle of the lake with your grandfather, and this is the woman who's buying the ancestral home. And you've just had a talk about worms. Hardly the stuff of romance.*

He took her fishing rod and tied the lure onto the line. "You do it like this. See? You want it to stay on so you need to make sure it's pretty well knotted."

"Or else the fish will bite it and run away with it," she said.

"I don't think it'll run. Maybe swim."

"Okay, swim. So I tie it on. . ." She bent over the lure and examined it. "I can do that."

"Then you cast it as far as you can away from the boat, like this." He flicked the fishing rod back and forward, and the line swung out in a graceful arc. No matter how many times he did it, he loved the vision of the transparent line bowing across the water before settling under the lake.

"And then you wait." Gramps spoke from the other end of the boat.

"Hold on to your pole," Hayden added, giving her back the rod.

"Yup," Gramps added. "If it goes over, so do you. That's the rule of Sunshine. Otherwise we'd lose poles right and left. Can't afford to keep this place open if we have to buy new poles all the time. You kids, like Ellie said the other day. . ."

His voice trailed off, and Livvy shot a quick look at Hayden, her brow briefly knotted with concern before she spoke again.

"What are we going to catch here?" she asked, leaning over the edge of the boat and peering into the water.

"Crappies and sunnies, usually. Sometimes a pike wanders in."

"Crappies, by the way, are spelled with an *a* even though you'd think they should be spelled with an *o* by the way the word is pronounced. I always explain that to people who are new to fishing up here."

Gramps laughed as he moved his line back and forth in the water. "Some folks get a bit upset when they see it in print, because it sure looks like a not-nice word. But it's pronounced *croppies*."

"Why?" she asked, resuming her seat on the boat again.

"Why are the folks upset, or why is spelled that way?" Hayden asked as he watched the line play in the water.

"The spelling. I know there's a fish called carp. I thought a crappie was a misspelled carp when I saw it in a magazine on the airplane."

Hayden had to laugh. She was so genuine. A misspelled fish!

"I don't know why it's called that. Do you, Gramps?" he asked his grandfather.

The older man shook his head. "Nope. It is what it is."

The fishing lines draped into the water, the filament looking for all the world like strands of silk in the sunlight.

The three of them sat in the boat, none of them speaking. The soft sighing of the poplars along the edge of the lake and the buzz of mosquitoes were a gentle backdrop to the quiet lap of the waves against the side of the wooden boat. In the distance, a bird called to an unseen companion, and a squirrel chattered angrily in protest of the interruption.

He loved this time, drifting idly in the boat on the little lake, thinking about the Creator and wondering why He would populate such a paradise with something as nasty as mosquitoes.

He slapped one that had managed to penetrate the DEET barrier, but he wasn't fast enough. He knew that within a short time, he'd be sporting a lump.

Eventually he'd have to start the motor again if Livvy was going to catch her fish. He hadn't had the heart to tell her that a lure didn't really work unless the boat was in motion, or if she wanted to cast and recast the line. He just wasn't ready to interrupt the mood with the sound of a motor. She'd understand.

He leaned back against the torn vinyl of the seat. Many summers ago he and Gramps had taken some of the dining room chairs that Gran had determined were too shabby for the public, and they'd cut the legs off and installed them in the boat. As Gramps had said, they weren't pretty but they were comfortable, especially if they wadded up the rain tarps and used them as pillows, and rested their feet on the rubber waders.

This was a little piece of paradise, Sunshine was. He'd often thought that if anyone didn't believe in a Creator, he'd just bring them out here on a boat on a summer afternoon. Nothing could quite compare to it.

He looked over at Livvy. Gramp's old hat had slid down on one side, and she made no attempt to straighten it over her still wildly curly hair. Instead, she smiled at the sun-speckled water.

Her fingers loosened their grip on the pole, and he caught back a smile. He'd watch it to make sure it didn't slip free.

If he watched closely enough, he was sure that he could see the stresses of city life falling from her, shed into the calm of the lake and absorbed by the water.

The pole slid a bit but she tightened her hold on it. Her manicure, he noticed, was still flawless. Within a short time, he suspected that would be a thing of the past.

Was she going to be able to do it? He had absolutely no doubt in his mind that she didn't have any idea what she was tackling here, but for some odd reason he was comfortable with that.

He thought back to the moment at the café when she'd pulled the hood off and her hair was tousled. She had looked real then, he'd said—real, natural, not citified.

Last night he had prayed about selling Sunshine to her, prayed long and hard. More than anything, he needed to be sure that what was about to happen was the right thing to do. There were precious few times in life that he'd wished to have the gift of seeing the future—usually it had seemed like a dreadful burden that no one would wish for—and he still didn't, but just some way of knowing selling Sunshine to Livvy was the right thing would have been so comforting.

But there were no answers, and he had to rely upon the feeling he'd gotten, that sense of prayer offered and answered. It was enough.

Sunshine would be in Livvy's hands and, most importantly, God's hands.

He turned and motioned to Gramps to hand him a root beer. It was part of their fishing tradition, having a root beer out on the lake.

There was something about being on the lake that made his grandfather seem less confused. He occasionally got a bit befuddled, but overall, sitting in the boat was good for Gramps. His mind rarely wandered when they were out on the water. Perhaps it was the calm, repetitive slap of the waves against the boat, and the gentle rocking motion. It certainly soothed him.

Gramps opened the cooler, took out a bottle, and tossed it to him. He twisted off the cap and was about to ask Livvy if she wanted one, when a sound stopped him.

It was ever so slight.

Livvy's eyes were closed, and she was faintly snoring.

Gramps grinned and nodded. "She'll be good for Sunshine," the old man said in a low voice. "Anyone who can fall asleep with a fishing pole in her hands has the heart it'll take."

"She won't catch anything with a lure," Hayden said. "She'll have to learn all that."

His grandfather studied him, his eyes bright with insight. "I think she's already caught something, Grub."

Hayden frowned and checked her line. "Nope, nothing."

Gramps just chuckled.

Chapter 4

Livvy wiped her forehead with her arm and tried the wrench again. Tug as she might, the joint on the plumbing would not release. The basement of the house at Sunshine was cool, but she was frustrated. She'd been working on this leaking pipe for an hour with no luck.

That day of fishing seemed like three months ago rather than three weeks. So much had happened since her time with Hayden and Gramps on the lake. Now Sunshine was hers.

The men were still living there while she dog-sat Leonard. It was a nice arrangement. She was even beginning to appreciate having a dog around, although she wasn't sure that Martha Washington shared her feelings when they came to Sunshine.

Leonard would leap out of the truck and bound across the yard to the porch, his ears flopping crazily, as the resident chicken flapped back to the safety of the coop and Martha Washington stood and puffed into her formidable angry-cat shape. Leonard, having once met the wrath of the cat's claws, would temporarily abandon the overture of friendship and retire to the dirt next to the porch.

Sometimes that seemed like the best thing, soaking up the sun, and Livvy had done her share of it, but now she was determined to get busy with fixing up Sunshine.

She climbed down from the stepladder and consulted *The Complete Guide to Home Construction and Repair* once again. The photographs were clear and would have been extremely helpful if the plumbing in this house had looked anything like the plumbing in the book.

Plus the man with the wrench in the illustration, who smiled happily as the pipes cooperated and came apart with ease, had apparently never met the plumbing at this place.

"How's it going?" Hayden asked as he came down the stairs. "Gramps said there was a leak down here and you were fixing it. You sure you don't want to call in a plumber?"

She pressed her lips together to stop the retort that arose almost immediately. "I can do it."

She wasn't about to tell him that she had been stuck on "Step One: Freeing the Pipe" the entire time.

He nodded. "Do you need any help?"

"No, but thanks. I have an idea though that will revolutionize the construction industry."

"What's that?" he asked.

"Putting the pipes on the floor. Hanging them from the ceiling makes this a horrendously uncomfortable task." She glared at the offending plumbing.

"I don't know if that would actually be much help," he said, walking toward her with caution. Tools and plumbing parts were spread across the cement floor. "But it's an intriguing idea."

"I went to Cooter's this morning," she explained. "Got my own toolbox and the parts I needed."

"I see that."

"There was a leak down here so I thought I'd start with something simple and fix it."

His mouth twitched with amusement. "Something simple. That's a good idea. Are you finding plumbing to be simple?"

"How hard can it be? I mean, honestly. One pipe is connected to another pipe, which is connected to another pipe, and all I have to do is make sure that the water stays in the pipes and not on the floor, which is why I'm down here."

"That's about the best description of plumbing I've ever heard."

"Apparently though, whoever put these pipes up here stuck them together with some kind of super-powered glue." She glared at the maze of pipes overhead.

He shrugged. "Possibly."

"Anyway, I found out it was this one"—she tapped one with the wrench—"and sure enough, there was water coming from it."

She smiled at the book, which had given good advice on identifying the leak. "I turned on the water, came down here, and watched to see where it was dripping. And voilà!"

He nodded. "That's good. You remembered to turn off the water first, I hope, before trying to take the fitting off."

She resisted the urge to roll her eyes. "Of course I remembered. There's a diagram in here, on page sixty-four, of how to do that."

He nodded again, this time a bit slower. "It sure sounds like that book has it all. Do you mind if I take a look at it?"

"Go right ahead." Livvy made a face as a drop splashed on her shoulder. "Take a look at page sixty-four and tell me that's not wonderful. Meanwhile, I'll keep working on this—"

It happened all at once.

Hayden said, "Uh, Livvy," just as the coupling on the pipe gave way at last. Water poured onto the floor.

"Pail! A bucket! Get me something!" she yelled as she retrieved *The Complete Guide* from the encroaching deluge.

Hayden ducked behind the furnace and returned with a large plastic trash bin that had earlier held a collection of unused pieces of drywall, bits of wood left over from a recent window replacement, and tiles that Hayden had pulled out of the old bathroom. "Remind me to clean that up later. I had to empty it onto the floor," he said as he moved it into place. "I'll be right back."

He took the stairs two at a time as she stood, watching in dismay as the container filled with water from the pipe.

How could this have happened? She opened the book and looked again at page sixty-four. She had done everything right. She'd turned off the water to the bathroom, hadn't she?

She opened her book and again scanned the section on plumbing repairs. There was no mention of anything like this. Nothing.

Oh.

There was one tiny line, almost lost in the diagrams. *"Turn off the water to the house."*

Well, why on earth did it tell her how to disconnect the water to the bathroom if she was going to turn it off to the entire house?

She wanted to sink to the floor and cry, but all that would do would get her pants wet.

She'd taken on way more than she—and *The Complete Guide to Home Construction and Repair*—could handle. Renovating a house was way beyond her capabilities. She couldn't even manage a simple plumbing repair without bringing on a flood.

On television it was so simple. Leaky faucet? A few twists of a wrench and it was fixed. But maybe North Dakota had exotic plumbing—judging from the tangle of metal and plastic tubing in the ceiling joists, it had been put together by monkeys using leftover bits and pieces of plumbing. The whole thing should probably be taken out and redone.

But not by her.

It seemed like forever, standing in the basement and waiting for Hayden to come back. Maybe he'd left. After all, they'd signed the papers, she'd written the check, the title had cleared, and he had every right in the world to walk out of the house, get in his truck, and drive back to Obsidian, whistling the entire way. He and his grandfather were still living in the house until the housing for Gramps was set up, but there was nothing to hold them to being responsible for the antique plumbing woes that she was facing. She'd magnanimously taken that part out of the contract before signing it, telling herself that she could handle it herself.

The thought took root. Hayden was already out of the yard and headed down the county road, his grandfather beside him, and they were both delighted that he didn't have to deal with Sunshine's pipes.

Meanwhile she stood in a basement that was soon going to be filled with water unless she figured out something very quickly.

She scurried to the bottom of the stairs and called up, "Hayden? Hayden? Are you still there?" When she got no answer, she tried again, "Gramps? Gramps, did Hayden leave?"

Only silence answered.

She took a few tentative steps up. "Hayden? Gramps?" she tried again.

The house was silent. Even Leonard, who had come out from the house in Obsidian to Sunshine with her, didn't bark in response. That was not a good sign. Leonard barked at everything from a cricket to an airplane.

She bolted the rest of the way up to the main floor and quickly looked around. No one was there.

She'd have to call a plumber.

Her cell phone was in her purse, which was on the table upstairs. She bolted up the stairs and dug through her bag until she found the list she'd meticulously prepared using the phone directory that Jeannie had lent her before she left on her mission trip.

With nervous fingers, she unfolded the sheet of paper and found the listing for plumbers. She tapped the numbers onto her cell phone's keypad and heard. . .nothing. Silence.

She pulled the phone from her ear and glared at it. No wonder she couldn't get through—there weren't any bars on the display. There was no signal.

Hayden had mentioned that, and she'd forgotten it. She hadn't tried her cell phone at Sunshine before, and she put it on her list of things to get to: work out the telephone situation.

There was a telephone in the living room. She shook her head. *Way to be calm, Livvy,* she scolded herself. She'd totally spaced that out.

That telephone worked, wired nicely into the wall, and she picked up the receiver. How weird it felt to use this phone. It must be decades old. The handset was heavy and black, with a ridge along the top.

She dialed the first plumber on her list, and got a recording with the hours—they were not open on Saturdays or Sundays.

And this was a Saturday.

She tried the second number, and this time got someone. "Sunshine? You want me to come to Sunshine to turn off the water? Do you know how far I'll have to drive? Lady, that's going to cost you about $300 just to do that. You want it fixed, too? You're looking at $500, easy."

Leonard barked, a long series of happy sounds, and she sighed in relief. That meant that Hayden must not have left.

Silly her. Of course he wouldn't have gone off without telling her. She was just letting her imagination run away with her. She'd better nip that in the bud if she was going to stay out here all year round.

She realized that it had ended. The water had stopped. Hayden must have gotten the water to the house turned off. She breathed a deep sigh of relief.

She went back into the basement.

The mop was conveniently by the broken pipe. She'd been using it to swab down spiderwebs before her plumbing adventure. She shook her head as she remembered that her worst fear had been a spider dropping on her head.

It should have been water!

She ran the mop over the floor. Luckily it was concrete, so she didn't have to worry about drying out carpets or warping wooden flooring. Most of the water she chased into a drain that was near the washing machine, and within minutes she was finished in the basement.

The best place for the wet mop was in the sun, where it would dry quickly, and she hurried up the stairs, holding it at arm's length, although she realized how pointless that was. She was pretty well splattered with water from the pipe.

The barking was closer, and she heard Hayden talking to Leonard. "Settle down now. Yes, that's your ball. No, I won't throw it. Okay, I'll throw it. Now go find that dumb chicken to chase. Or Martha Washington. That worthless cat is probably asleep in the henhouse again."

She smiled to herself as she listened to him. It was like a dialogue.

"Leonard, no, I don't have time."

Bark.

"I said no. Well, just this once."

Bark bark bark bark.

There was a *thump*, which Livvy knew must be the ball hitting one of the outbuildings.

Bark bark bark.

"I have to go in and—oh, all right. But I'm serious, this is the very last time."

Bark bark.

With her elbow, she opened the screen door and propped the wet mop against the porch railing. "Hayden! Thank you so much!"

He paused, mid-throw. "Oh Livvy. I got the water turned off. I was on my way in to tell you when—" He gestured at the dog, who danced around him in gleeful anticipation.

"I understand. But what did you do that I didn't do, and would you please throw that ball before Leonard has a canine coronary?"

"What? Oh sure." He threw the ball and the dog tore off after it. "Doesn't he ever wear out?"

"Not that I've been able to tell. So how did you stop the water?"

"I used the turn-off to the house. Let me show you what I mean."

The dog followed them, yellow tennis ball still in his mouth and now covered with wet sand and dirt, as Hayden led her to the shaded side of the house.

"This," he said, pointing at a cement square set in the ground near the side of the house, "is where the main valve is. You pull on this handle, lift the cover, and there's the valve."

She shook her head. "I thought it would be inside."

"It should be, but we just never got around to it."

"Why wasn't it there in the first place? Why put it outside at all?" This made no sense to her.

"It's not uncommon out here with old houses that grew—or un-grew, if I can make up a word—without much design. There used to be a room in that spot, kind of a root cellar/pantry/storage space, all rolled into one. At least that's what Gramps said."

"Ah," she said. Now it made sense. Sort of.

"That's actually something you should take care of quickly. Gramps and I got used to knowing where this was in winter, and how to keep the pipes from freezing, but you probably don't want to get involved with it. Let's get a plumber out here and have it moved."

She laughed slightly hysterically. "Get a plumber out here. And how do I do that?" She thought of the phone call she'd made earlier, and how she'd reeled at the estimate just to come to Sunshine. Dollar signs paraded through her mind, all of them leaving her nearly depleted bank account and headed into a plumber's wallet.

"You call someone."

"I did," she said. "He said it would cost at least $500. That was just to come out and shut off the water and fix the pipe. I can't even imagine how much he'd charge to move that inside." She motioned toward the red-handled valve.

He shook his head. "You have to know who to ask. There's a fellow from church who's a plumber and he's always worked on the barter system with Gramps. He's been trying to get Gramps to take care of getting the access to the water moved into the house for a long time. I'll tell you what, let me give him a call and see what we can work out."

Her stomach sank. She'd wanted to do this herself, but she couldn't.

"What do you mean by barter?" she asked. "Oh, I know what that means, but what do I give him in exchange?"

Hayden smiled. He really did have the best smile, she thought. It quirked up on one side, and his entire face lit up. "His name is Brad Simons, and he loves fishing, but he's got two sons, and one's in a wheelchair, so he doesn't get to do it much."

"Oh, I'm sorry to hear that."

"Usually I do the plumbing—and I have to apologize for the mess that you saw down there. That was my doing, and in case you couldn't tell, I had no idea what I was up to. I would just replace stuff until whatever was leaking stopped. One time I used a whole roll of aluminum tape, which works better than duct tape, by the way, so you might notice we buy the economy pack, to hold the kitchen faucet in place until Brad could get out here."

She laughed. "So you understand my plumbing skills—or lack of them."

"I do. In the past, we've worked it out so that Brad takes care of our plumbing emergencies and we get his family out here, all of them, and put them in the boat and take them out onto the lake."

"Really?"

"Really. Of course we'd do it for nothing, but Brad's got his pride. We do the whole day up right. We have a picnic on the boat, too, and then in the evening, we have a bonfire and roast hot dogs and make s'mores. It's a nice break for them."

"Do you suppose he would do this for me, too?" She was almost afraid to hear the answer.

"Sure he would. Let me give him a call right now. Here."

The dog was waiting patiently, the ball in front of his paws. Hayden picked up the ball and handed it to Livvy. It was slimy from being carried in his mouth, and she tried to suppress the urge to shudder. This was one of the things about dogs she'd never been comfortable with—the way they slobbered all over their toys.

"Gross," she said, wiping one hand on her jeans and holding the wet tennis ball gingerly with two fingers of her other hand.

He grinned. "Keep him busy while I run inside and give Brad a call."

He vanished inside the house as Leonard stood up, wagging his tail madly, his eyes locked on the ball in Livvy's hand.

"Okay, we'll do this until he comes back, but you really should get some hobbies," she said to the dog, and she threw the ball for him.

He raced after the ball, and loped back, carrying it in his mouth and dropped it at her feet. She tossed it again, he ran after it, and brought it back to her. Automatically she repeated the scene, and as she did, in her mind she ran through what it would be like out here, without Hayden and Gramps, without Leonard.

That day in Boston when she had brazenly given her notice to Mr. Evans, the thought of being alone, responsible for a home that belonged to her, with no one around her for miles, had seemed like a dream come true.

Maybe she had taken on more than she'd bargained for, if the situation in the basement was any indication. Her beloved book, *The Complete Guide to Home Construction and Repair*, had misled her into thinking something as basic as fixing a leaky pipe would be easy.

Leonard flopped beside her, exhausted at last. His tongue hung out the side of his mouth, and he looked blissfully spent.

"What a life you have," she said to him. "As long as someone throws the ball and puts down dog chow for you, all is good. Every day is filled with nothing more important than sleeping in the sun and barking at squirrels. You don't even need to worry about your shoes or your hair or what you're going to wear."

His tail thumped and he sighed and shut his eyes.

She heard the screen door slam and turned to see Hayden coming back out. He gave her a thumbs up.

"Brad will be here in about twenty minutes. He said he could fix the pipe this afternoon, and on Tuesday he'll come out and move the shut-off valve inside. And it will only cost you an afternoon on the lake and a weenie roast, due and payable next Saturday, while he and the missus go to a wedding. I said we'd watch the boys. By the way, it's the Fourth of July, so we'll do fireworks out here, too."

"Fireworks? That's good, but it just doesn't seem quite enough," she objected, feeling relieved and at the same time vaguely guilty. "Is that a fair trade?"

"It is for Brad. He's got a lot on his plate. Speaking of plates, Gramps got some sandwiches ready for us."

They had just finished a meal of peanut butter and jelly sandwiches and root beer when a horn honked in the yard.

"Brad's here," Hayden said, draining the last of his drink.

She thought she'd never seen anyone as welcome as Brad with his plumbing tools. In his work shirt and heavy boots, he looked like an angel.

He followed her into the basement and then indicated he wanted her to stay. "Stick around," he said to Livvy. "I'll show you what you need to do."

As he fixed the pipe, he told her what he was doing every step of the way in a running commentary. "Don't blame yourself," he said as he tightened it into place. "It's just a lot easier if someone shows you how to do it. It's not brain surgery but it does have its quirks. There. See how it's done?"

She nodded, but made a mental note to proceed more carefully in the future when it came to plumbing.

"Now," he said, putting the wrench back into his toolbox, "I'll turn the water back on. Come with me, and I'll show you that, too."

Outside, he gave the red valve a twist, saying, "And the next time anyone touches this dumb thing will be the last time. You'll never have to worry about finding it out here again."

"How can I ever thank you?"

"It's all in a day's work. I'll go check on the pipe and say howdy-do to Charlie and then I'd better get back to town. See you tomorrow."

"Tomorrow? I thought you were coming on Tuesday."

"Won't you be in church? It's Sunday, you know."

"Oh. Of course."

As he went into the kitchen to visit with Gramps and Hayden, she thought about it.

Church.

She wasn't a churchgoer, not recently. How long had it been since she'd been to a service? She did some quick math and was aghast to realize it had been about ten years. Almost a decade.

It wasn't as if she didn't believe in God. Of course she did. Everyone did. How many times had she looked at a sunset, or a newborn baby, or a kitten, and acknowledged the good work of the Lord's hands?

But it was also true that the only times she prayed anymore were when she was petitioning God to let her car start or when her wallet wasn't where it should be. Certainly there was more to being a Christian than that.

She looked at the majestic panorama of the Badlands surrounding her. This had to be more than a geological accident. Someone had to have created this interplay of shape and light and color.

God? Could it be?

A hunger gnawed at her heart. She needed to know more.

The voices of the three men in the kitchen floated out to her. They all went to church. Maybe she should give it a try. What could it hurt? Nothing. And what could it help? Everything.

Her life was fine the way it was, but maybe it could be better. She'd ask Hayden about it.

Leonard, who had gotten up and come to lie across her feet, moved, nudging the ball that never left his side.

"What do you think, dog?" she asked, leaning over to let her fingers drift over his silky ears. "Dogs don't go to church."

"He would if he could," Hayden said behind her, and she jumped. "Sorry, didn't mean to startle you. Brad's leaving now, and I gather the plumbing emergency is taken care of. You up to digging through some boxes in the café? I suspect most of it can go to the dump, but let's make sure."

They headed toward the café, the dog padding behind them.

"You all go to the same church?" she asked.

"Sure do. We're all members of Trinity. My great-grandfather was one of the founders of it. Would you like to come to a service?"

"You know, I think I would."

"What church did you go to in Boston?"

Something rustled in the underbrush, and Leonard took off, barking at it.

"I didn't go to church there," she confessed. "I don't know why. Partially I was just lazy, but it's also a bit overwhelming trying to decide which one to go to."

"Obsidian doesn't offer many choices," he said. "There's Trinity. Or there's Trinity. Yup, that's it."

She laughed. "Then Trinity it is."

He tilted his head and smiled, his pale blue eyes glinting in the sun. "Would you like to go to church with us? We'd be delighted to have you there."

"I think I would," she said, and as soon as the words were out, she felt a peace. "Yes, I would."

"Great! I'll talk to Gramps. He'll think it's a wonderful idea."

"Speaking of wonderful ideas," she said as they reached the door of the café, "let's start digging."

They worked together, going through the boxes that had been stored in the dusty café. As Hayden had predicted, most of the boxes were filled with things not worth keeping. Three of the cardboard cartons contained draperies that had been the home of small creatures, probably mice. Two more boxes held tablecloths, now stained with age, and one box was filled with packets of paper napkins. These were easily set aside to be discarded.

Hayden moved another stack of cartons to the middle of the room. "We'll tackle these next week. I don't know about you, but I'm done."

"Me, too." She wanted nothing more than to clean herself up and sprawl on the couch of the little guesthouse in Obsidian and let the air-conditioning cool her off.

"If you'd like," he said to her, "I'll pick you up tomorrow for church."

"I'd like that." Just knowing that she wouldn't have to walk in alone made it easier to decide to go.

"Great. Church starts at nine thirty, so I'll see you around nine fifteen."

As she drove back to Obsidian in Gramps's SUV, which was a sight better than Trevor's truck, she looked at her surroundings, once again astonished at the panorama laid out around her. With something as spectacular as the Badlands as a backdrop to her new life, it was only fitting that she should offer praise to their Maker.

Church. She was going to church.

༄

Hayden was used to the church, but now he was seeing it as he imagined Livvy would. How different it must be from the grand cathedrals and massive churches she probably saw on every street in Boston.

Trinity was a small white-framed structure, basically unchanged in its 125 years of existence. The interior showed the importance those first church members had assigned their place of worship. A large mural of the Nativity adorned the wall behind the altar, and its hues were still as bright as they must have been when they were first painted. Stained-glass windows, handmade by an early settler to the town, shed multicolored beams on the tiny congregation.

Hayden could feel Livvy's uneasiness as they slid into the pews. He was so accustomed to coming to church every Sunday that it had never occurred to him how awkward it might be for someone not used to attending services to visit for the first time.

He smiled encouragingly and whispered, "I'm glad you're here."

"Thanks," she answered in a low voice. "I'm glad I'm here, too."

The hymns and Scripture readings were marked on the board at the front of the church, but there was also a bulletin. He noticed that she studied it closely, especially the announcements of the upcoming Men's League barbecue, and the Women's League garage sale.

He hadn't been involved much recently in the Men's League, and he reminded himself to make it to the next meeting. Maybe Gramps would like to be a part of it, especially since he would be moving into town.

The minister, Reverend Carlisle, stood in front of the congregation and motioned for them to rise for the first hymn. It was one of Hayden's favorites,

"Faith of Our Fathers."

He loved the old hymns. Singing the same melodies and the same words as his forebears had done gave him a sense of connection with the past that he treasured. He heard Gramps's wavering tenor next to him, and he put his hand on the old man's shoulder, and was rewarded with a smile.

He could sing the hymn from memory, but he held the hymnal with his free hand so that Livvy could see it, too. She followed along well, her clear soprano melding with the others in the congregation, and he could feel her relax.

At the end of the song, they sat and the minister shared the day's gospel lesson with them. It was the very beginning of Luke. "*Forasmuch as many have taken in hand to set forth in order a declaration of those things which are most surely believed among us, even as they delivered them unto us, which from the beginning were eyewitnesses, and ministers of the word; it seemed good to me also, having had perfect understanding of all things from the very first, to write unto thee in order, most excellent Theophilus, that thou mightest know the certainty of those things, wherein thou hast been instructed.*"

It was, the minister pointed out, a passage about history and faith. It was the faith of their fathers, just as the hymn had extolled, that brought them to this point of being gathered together this Sunday. Luke had his own forefathers of the church to build upon, and he had drawn upon that in his own faith journey—and what a journey it was.

Who, Reverend Carlisle asked, was Theophilus? Was he simply someone to whom Luke was writing?

The name, he explained, meant either *lover of God* or *loved by God*. Was there a difference?

The part of his name, *Theo-*, meant God. In addressing the letter to someone named Theophilus, Luke was passing his own religious heritage.

The people he was about to share with Theophilus were those who been there from the beginning, who were, as Luke said, eyewitnesses.

Reverend Carlisle leaned forward. "And dwell, if you would, for a few minutes on the last of this passage: 'That thou mightest know the certainty of those things.' Think of it. The certainty. Luke was solidly convinced of the truth of faith, and that is what we all need, knowing with certainty that God is true, that faith is true, that His love for us is true."

Hayden saw Livvy lean forward as if trying to absorb the message. Sunlight, dyed by the stained-glass windows, tinted her hair and face with blues and greens and purples.

"And when we know that this is true, that is faith. Loving God and being loved by God is an inheritance that is beyond anything we might get here on earth," the minister continued. He beamed at those gathered in front of him. "Sure beats Aunt Ethel's silverware or Uncle Ole's letter from the president, doesn't it? Not to say that those aren't important, but. . ."

He let the thought trail off as the congregation took in the meaning.

Hayden let the idea of faith and love as an inheritance settle into his mind, and through the rest of the service, he considered it. He'd always been proud of his great-grandfather for being one of the founders of Trinity, but now there was more to it. Now he was also grateful.

Too soon the congregation was standing again, and the church service was over. He turned to Livvy as the recessional began and the congregation began to chat with each other in low voices as they filed out of the small church.

"So what did you think?" he asked. He was surprised at how important her answer was to him.

"It was wonderful," she said, her face glowing. "I felt like a dry sponge in water, soaking it up."

"It was good, wasn't it?"

Gramps leaned around him and added, "I'd never thought about that part of Luke before. Grub, if you don't mind, I think I'd like to go home and study this a bit more."

Hayden looked at his grandfather in surprise. Usually they went to Clara's after church for an omelet and coffee. Gramps looked tired and drawn, as if the service had worn him out. Hayden's heart dropped. This was not good.

Livvy took the gnarled fingers of the old man in her own as they walked out of the church. "I think we all could use some time for reflection. I can walk back to my place."

Hayden wanted to object, but he could see a slight tremble in the old man's shoulders. It was a time of change, and it had clearly taken its toll on him.

"If you don't mind," he said.

"Not at all. I need to get home to make sure that Leonard hasn't gone off in search of Jeannie. After all, she's in Africa, and that's quite a walk, even for him."

He smiled despite his worry. Her words lightened his heart a bit, and he was appreciative to her for that.

"I'll see you tomorrow then."

He watched her walk away, and he turned his attention to Gramps, who nodded slowly. "She's a good one, Grub. Don't let her get away."

"She's just going to Jeannie's guesthouse, Gramps. She's not going far."

The twinkle came back to his grandfather's eyes as he said, "That's not what I mean, and you know it. She's the one for you."

"I don't—I barely know—we just met," Hayden stammered.

"Remember what Reverend Carlisle said. Certainty. It extends outside the church walls, Grub. Have a little faith. No, have a lot of faith. Have a lot of faith."

Hayden hugged the old man's shoulders lightly. "I do, Gramps. I do."

Chapter 5

Livvy walked to her little house, mulling over the worrisome tremors she'd felt in Gramps's hands. He'd looked especially frail when Hayden had picked her up, but she had chalked that up to the suit he wore. Maybe it had fit him once, when he was more muscular, but now it hung on him. Still it was sweet, she thought, the way his shirt was pressed and his tie neatly knotted. Church obviously meant a lot to him.

But when they'd left the service, his face had been pale, and his movements feeble. She had to trust Hayden's judgment. He'd take him to the small hospital if he felt Gramps's condition warranted it.

She wanted to pray for him. More than anything, she wanted him to be healthy and whole and not sick at all.

The thing was, she couldn't pray like the ministers did. She had never been able to figure out what the difference was between *thee* and *thou*. But Reverend Carlisle hadn't used those words. He had simply talked to God.

She could do that. Her attempts were halting. *Make him better, God. You know what he needs. Please get it to him. Make whatever is wrong, right.*

It wasn't pretty, it wasn't magnificent, it wasn't long. But it stated what she wanted.

Leonard barked happily when he saw her coming down the block, and she had to restrain him from knocking her over out of sheer glee when she opened the fence and came into the yard.

"I was gone an hour, you goofball," she said as she unhooked the tether from his collar so he could run freely in the yard. "A whole hour. During which you managed to knock over your water dish, spill your doggy doodles on the grass, lay across your mommy's prize rosebush, and dig a hole right next to the birdbath. You're a busy boy."

She repaired the damage as well as she could, and let him come in with her to the guesthouse. He flopped beside her as she stretched out on the futon. It wasn't that she was tired, she just needed some time to rest and reflect.

"This isn't made for both of us," she said to Leonard. "One of us is going to have to concede defeat and get up."

The dog simply sighed and settled even more deeply into the cushions.

"Well, there is something to be said for peaceful coexistence." She pushed him as far to the edge as possible, and laid on her back, staring at the ceiling fan.

She'd actually gone to church. It wasn't as if she ever had anything against going to church. It was just that her family hadn't made it a priority. They usually went when she was a child, but there wasn't much of a reason behind it. They went because they were expected to.

She rolled off the futon and retrieved her laptop. As she opened it, Leonard flung himself across the rest of the cushions. She wasn't getting back on without some pushing of doggy flesh.

Jeannie had thoughtfully continued the wireless account, and Livvy was soon able to connect with her mother.

"So," Mrs. Moore began, "how's life in North Dakota?"

Livvy laughed and told her the story of the plumbing, lightening it up so it sounded comedic—although, in retrospect, it was really kind of funny. Then she said, "Mom, guess what. I went to church today."

"Good! Did you like it?"

"I did. It made me feel peaceful, and yet there was a lot to think about, too. I'm going to go back."

"That's wonderful, honey! Did I tell you that your dad and I found a church here, too? We went initially just to see what a Swedish church service was like."

"Was it different?"

Mrs. Moore laughed. "Well, it's in Swedish. It's interesting, attending services when you aren't a native speaker. Your father and I have to listen to each single word."

"I thought you two were completely fluent."

"Not totally. We're competent but there are some gaps, especially in the Old Testament language. So we take both Bibles, Swedish and English. You don't suppose that's cheating, do you?"

Livvy chuckled. "Somehow bringing two Bibles to church couldn't be construed as cheating, I'd say."

"That's true! I hadn't thought of that. Actually," her mother said with some surprise in her voice, "I'm learning more about God by hearing the words in a language not my own. I hate to say this, since I'm a teacher, but it's amazing what you can learn if you listen to every single word."

So her parents had come back to the church. Her mother continued to talk of her social activities, and ones at the church were mixed with those from the school, or those with her friends.

Livvy thought of the Women's League garage sale she'd seen in the bulletin. Certainly in those boxes stored across the property at Sunshine were some things that she could donate—with Hayden and Gramps's permission—and that might be fun, getting involved with the women of Trinity. It would be a great way to meet people and make some friends.

After all, Sunshine was fifteen miles out of Obsidian. It wasn't like she would have a next-door neighbor to drop in and have a cup of coffee with. Even Hayden and Gramps would be gone.

Leonard sighed in his sleep, and when she ended the conversation with her mother, she returned to the futon.

She threw her arm across Leonard. He moved and pressed against her even more tightly.

There was something very calming about lying on the futon, squished between an oversized dog and the back cushions. She should get up, make some lunch, run the towels through the washing machine, and pay some bills, but all that could wait.

This was Sunday, and her soul was at rest, and soon, so was she.

❧

Hayden folded the dish towel and hung it on the rack by the sink. Lunch had been a thrown-together meal, lunch meat and cheese on bread, with pudding for desert. Afterward, Gramps had retired to his recliner, where he promptly fell asleep.

His grandfather was snoring softly and evenly, but Hayden was still concerned. Reluctant to leave Gramps alone, he tiptoed back into the living room and sat on the old green sofa. In the light that filtered through the windows, he saw how threadbare it was.

It had been there for as long as he could remember. What was the lifespan of a sofa anyway? This one had been a bed when he'd been a small boy.

It was odd, he thought, how he'd never noticed how loudly and how relentlessly the old anniversary clock on the mantel ticked. The sound seemed to fill the living room.

He wiped away a thin layer of dust on the table beside him. No matter how hard he tried, there was no way to keep the place clean, not with the wind that seemed to find every crack and gap in the house. It was amazing that the Badlands hadn't been reduced to nubs with the seemingly constant wind.

He crossed his legs and crossed his arms and uncrossed his legs and uncrossed his arms. How did people do this sitting-quietly thing? In church it was easy enough, but here, with nothing to look at but the Norman Rockwell painting by the fireplace and the little stuffed Teddy Roosevelt bear propped against the lamp on the end table, it was impossible.

He was forced to think. First about Gramps—how could he ever go on without him at his side? His grandfather had been woven into his life from his birth. For as long as he could remember, Gramps had been there for him. It had been Gramps who'd taught him about baiting a hook—that it wasn't a simple matter of sticking a worm on the barb and dropping the line into the water.

He smiled at the memory of floating on the little lake in the boat—the same boat that he and Gramps had taken Livvy out in, except it had been newer and its paint fresher. That afternoon had been filled with root beer and peanuts. Gramps insisted the turtles liked peanuts, although Hayden never saw a turtle eat a peanut. Instead, he and Gramps swigged root beer and tossed the peanuts in the air, trying to catch them in their mouths and usually failing.

Gramps had shown him the fine art of choosing a lure based upon what he wanted to catch. "Minnows, worms, or leeches for crappies, sunnies, or perch. Watch the water temperature. Warm water, you can use a lure."

He'd opened the tackle box and showed Hayden the contents. The lures were as fascinating as a treasure chest. Silvery jointed metal fish were laid neatly next to feathery hand-tied creations. Delicate flies were adjacent to brightly tasseled jigs. Lifelike frogs and ribbony strings—he had never seen anything as intriguing as this tackle box.

"This one's neat," Hayden had said, lifting up a bright orange jig, the tassels dancing in the sunlight. "I like it."

"It's pretty but it's not worth much here. You want the lure to be as close to the color of the natural bait as possible. Is there anything orange here that a fish might eat?"

Hayden recalled how sad he'd felt that the brilliant lure was basically worthless, and apparently his grandfather had noticed, because he'd squeezed the boy's shoulder and said, "You'll have a lot of shiny orange lures in your life, Grub. Just remember that a shiny orange lure may not be what you want or what you need."

It hadn't made sense then, but over the years, he'd come across many shiny orange lures, and Gramps's wisdom had come through.

He looked over at him, asleep in the chair.

Livvy wasn't a bright orange shiny lure.

His mind danced around the vision of Livvy in church, and Gramps's words came back to him. *The one.* Was Gramps right again? Was Livvy the one for him, the one with whom he could spend a lifetime?

How would he know?

He'd always heard Gramps tell how when he first met Gran, she thought he was boring and dull, definitely not a bright orange jig. If anyone had told him they'd end up married and loving each other with each breath, right up until she drew her last, he'd have said they were nuts.

But so it had happened, and a great love had been born and endured.

Was it Hayden's time for an equally great love?

He had no idea. It was too early to know any of this.

The clock ticked, and his grandfather snored, and he realized that they were creating a rhythm together. His toes tapped silently, the left foot marking time with the clock and the right foot keeping pace with Gramps.

Was it possible? Was the clock ticking louder?

He couldn't stand it. He stood and crept back into the kitchen where he opened the refrigerator and took out a bottle of root beer, wincing as it hissed when he opened it.

The *Bismarck Tribune* was on the front seat of the car. He could read that. The loose board on the kitchen floor creaked when he stepped on it, and he paused, but Gramps snored on. He went outside, catching the screen door before it could slam, and reached into the truck through the open window to retrieve the newspaper.

He repeated his silent path back to the living room, and sat down once again on the green sofa. Martha Washington, who had somehow managed to sneak inside, leaped up next to him and began to purr so loudly Hayden thought for sure that Gramps would awaken, but he slept on.

The paper had never sounded as crinkly. He spread the open paper on the coffee table and tried to turn the page, slowly, carefully, and he thought he had almost made it when his grandfather sat up and said, "Why are you being so sneaky quiet?"

"As soon as I scrape myself off the ceiling, I'll answer you. You nearly scared the wits out of me."

"Sorry," his grandfather said. "But why are you tiptoeing around like a thief?"

"I didn't want to wake you up. Gramps, are you feeling all right?"

Martha Washington sprang from the sofa to Gramps's lap, and the old man smoothed the cat's fur. "I'm fine. I was feeling a bit rocky this morning, but I think it was just because I didn't sleep that well last night."

Hayden crossed the room quickly and leaned over his grandfather, solicitously feeling his forehead for a fever. "You didn't sleep well?" he fretted. "You usually sleep like an absolute rock."

"An absolute rock, huh?" Gramps asked, his lips twitching in amusement. "Compared to a non-absolute rock? An inabsolute rock? What?"

Hayden knew the teasing was an attempt to divert him from pursuing the subject further. His grandfather did look better after his nap. He also knew better than to pursue the issue at the moment. When Gramps didn't want to talk about something, he shut down the topic.

Instead, Hayden would have to watch Gramps closely to see if he could pick up any clues about what had happened. Maybe it was nothing, but he didn't want to take the chance of dismissing something major.

He matched his grandfather's light tone. "Plymouth Rock. A moon rock. Rock of Ages. I don't know. But I should tell you I debated throwing that clock into the lake. That thing ticks so loudly it almost blew out my eardrums."

Gramps laughed. The sound was like music to Hayden's ears. It meant he was truly feeling stronger and better. "Once you're aware of it, it does seem to get extremely loud. Your grandmother put it out on the porch one time when she was trying to read. She could still hear it, so she put it out in the middle of the road by the mailbox. She said it made such a racket, she couldn't take it anymore. Lucky the thing didn't get run over."

Hayden wasn't convinced that *lucky* was the appropriate word for such an obnoxious creation, but he didn't say anything about it.

"Church was good today, wasn't it?" Gramps asked. "That Reverend Carlisle sure can dig out a deep meaning from the gospel. I dare say he's so good he could have one of those big congregations in Chicago or Minneapolis."

"We are truly blessed to have him here in Obsidian."

"Livvy seemed to enjoy the service, wouldn't you say?" Gramps looked directly at him. "She seemed to drink it up like a thirsty woman at an oasis."

Hayden folded the newspaper and leaned back. "She did. You know, Gramps, we were born into the church and we stayed. You and Gran made sure of that, and that's part of the heritage that Reverend Carlisle was talking about."

"I'm as old as Luke?" His grandfather's eyes twinkled.

"Pretty much," Hayden answered, grinning. "But I think that part of what the lesson was about is that our religious legacy goes back to the very beginning of Christianity—and before—so that even if we have a few years when we stray, we've got the path already prepared for us to step right back onto."

"That's an interesting extension of what we learned today." Gramps stroked Martha Washington's fur. "We tried to make sure you knew where the path was, Grub, so that if you did step off, you could be sure that it was there, ready and waiting for you. But we were fortunate that you stayed on it, and you've lived a life that was honorable to our Lord."

"I've tried." As Hayden said the words, he knew they were true. "I don't think that Livvy has done anything wrong, even if she hasn't been going to church."

His grandfather raised his eyebrows in question, and Hayden hastily amended his statement. "I mean that she hasn't murdered anyone, at least as near as I know."

Gramps laughed. "I think we can safely presume that she hasn't. She doesn't seem the type to be a felon. But going to church is an important part of being a Christian. And I think she realized that."

"She seemed to get a lot out of the message this morning. I'm glad she went with us."

"I suspect she needed it. We'll make sure to invite her to come with us next week, too." His grandfather studied him. "You know I'm not one to meddle in your life, Grub, but I do need to say something."

Hayden took a deep breath. Whenever Gramps started a discussion like that, the conversation was going to be intense—and honest.

"Go ahead," he said. "Meddle away."

His grandfather bent toward him, his face etched with concern. "I want to talk about Livvy."

Hayden's stomach plummeted. Did Gramps have second thoughts about turning Sunshine over to her? It was too late. The papers were signed, and she was already invested in the property, both financially and emotionally.

"What about her?" he asked cautiously.

"I may be old, but I can still see what's right in front of my face. There's something between the two of you."

Hayden rubbed his forehead. "Something between us? How can you say that? I've only known her a few weeks!"

"How long do you think it would take?" Gramps looked at him quizzically.

Hayden cleared his throat, which had inexplicably developed some kind of frog. "Well," he said at last, "a year or two."

"And when do you think it starts?"

Gramps was not going to let him off easily. Hayden parried with another question. "Do you mean when does love start?"

"Sure. When do you think people fall in love? What is the first moment? Does it hit you like a two-by-four upside the head? Or is it a gentle thing that comes over you, so slowly that you don't even know it's happening until one day you find yourself in front of a preacher saying, 'I do'?"

Gramps's tone was teasing, but underneath it was a serious note, and Hayden waited a moment before answering. "I'm not sure, Gramps. I've never been in love."

His grandfather nodded sagely. "It happens both ways. Love takes awhile to develop, and I'm not saying this is love that I see. Not yet. But given enough time, and enough care, I believe that this attraction between you two has the power to grow. Not all relationships do, but this one, I believe, does."

"Do you believe in love at first sight?" Hayden asked.

"I do, but with a rider. There is love at first sight, but love has to prove itself—no, wait. That's not right. Love never has to prove anything. Love is perfect and ideal. Let me try again. There is such a thing as an immediate attraction."

Gramps's eyes took on a faraway, dreamy look. "When I first saw Ellie I was a gas jockey in Bismarck. I was in that never-never land after school, not knowing what I wanted to do, and thinking that maybe I'd end up enlisting in the army. All my friends were doing it. And then one day, she drove into the station in a brand new 1957 Chevy. Grub, that thing was a magnificent piece of automotive history. Turquoise and white, and absolutely spotless."

Hayden settled back against the cushions of the couch. He'd heard the story before, but it was a great one.

"I looked at it, and I was going to say all the usual gas station things about the car. Ramjet fuel injection, triple turbines, V-8, rear fins, hood rockets—and then I looked at her, and all of that just flew out of my head. She may have been sitting in the most stunning car to grace America's roads, but all I could think was that she was the most beautiful woman I had ever seen and, bam, I was in love."

"So it was love at first sight."

"It was. But it wasn't the love that developed over the years. We had to learn to love each other, and, perhaps just as importantly, learn to be loved in an equal relationship. In order for a marriage to work, you need to have the same set of values. You can't be unequally partnered. If you believe in God, and

I know you do, then she has to believe in Him, too. That's vital. Without that, there really won't be love. Marriage has to have some basis or else it won't last. Grub, you know where the silver is, don't you?"

Hayden laughed. "Well that was an abrupt switch. From love to silver."

"Don't be fresh. Go get it. But first go get me a spoon from the kitchen."

From the strength of his grandfather's voice, he knew that there would be some meaning in this lesson, so he did as Gramps requested. From the kitchen he got a spoon from the drawer, and then he entered the dining area.

He crossed the room to the old Hoosier cabinet that still stood in the corner, just as it had for as long as he had been alive, and from one of the drawers, he withdrew a polished walnut box and carried it back to his grandfather.

Gramps carefully balanced it on his thin knees and opened it. He removed the cloth that covered the silverware, and took one of the spoons from its slot.

He held it up to the light. "We got this for a wedding present from your great-great-grandmother. See the glow of it? See how you can look at it and immediately know that it's good silver? Look at the patina. That satiny finish comes from years and years of use, scooping up food and who knows what else, as well as being scrubbed clean and stored away and ignored for months on end."

His grandfather tapped it against his hand. "That shine comes from years of Greenwood family dinners. And it's heavy. You can feel it in your hand when you're eating your ice cream."

He put it back into the slot in the wooden box and closed the cover reverently. He picked up the spoon from the kitchen and raised it. "Now this is the cheap stuff, the stuff we don't care if the dishwasher mangles it or if it gets left in the boat. It can easily be replaced with a quick trip into Bismarck to that big discount center."

The spoon caught the afternoon sun and sent rainbows against the wall. "Pretty, isn't it? Glittery and bright," Gramps continued, "but cheap. Even I could bend it, warp it out of shape. Scratches on the surface just make it look worse, and if its life as a spoon is too bad, we'll throw it away and get another one. And why is that?"

"Because we don't care about it, not really," Hayden answered. "It's from that set we got at ThriftyBuy for what, fourteen dollars?"

Gramps shook his head. "Sort of. Because the wedding silver is made out of quality metal and the everyday spoon is made of, well, I don't know what it's made of, but that's my point. Do you see what I'm saying? Love is like the wedding silver. The good and the bad will both add to the gleam, compared to the sharp imitation-silver spoon that can't bear any scratches. It's disposable, so we can get rid of it when we're not pleased with it."

He handed the day-to-day spoon back to Hayden. "You know, when the silverware was new, it was shiny. Not quite this wildly shiny, but shiny. I liked it shiny, but I like this subdued gloss, too. That's love. From new-spoon shiny to old-spoon gleam, it's all good."

Hayden impulsively leaned over and dropped a kiss onto the top of the old man's head. He wasn't quite ready to think of marrying Livvy, but this was excellent advice. "I'll give it some thought and a lot of prayer, Gramps, I promise. You may be right about Livvy—or you might be wrong. Either way, I need to make sure of one thing."

"What's that?" Gramps asked.

"That she's the right spoon."

Chapter 6

The Fourth of July was a jewel of a day. The faintest breeze blew away the dusty heat, until it was nearly perfect. Brad had come out with his two children, Bo and Al, and the three of them had crowded into the boat with Hayden and Gramps.

Brad's wife was, according to him, "dollying up" in preparation for a wedding in Bismarck that evening, and Brad was going to leave the boys for fireworks while he went to the wedding with his wife. He'd pick the children up around midnight.

The boys had reveled in their afternoon on the lake as "guy time." Livvy had stayed in the house, putting together the evening's weenie roast and making sure there were enough snacks to get the boys' sugar levels skyrocketing.

Al was the child in the wheelchair, and she marveled at how his brother, the wild and crazy Bo, accepted it and gave him just as much trouble as if he'd been walking.

After Brad had gone back to Obsidian to pick up his wife, the two boys tore around Sunshine, chasing the chicken and enveloping Martha Washington in sticky hugs until she finally retreated under the porch. Leonard simply ran around them all and barked happily.

Finally it was dark enough for fireworks. They could see those being shot off in Medora, the western town on the other side of the butte, but Hayden and Gramps had made sure they had enough of their own, and soon Gramps was lighting the larger fireworks.

The sky lit up as the initial volley of Roman candles exploded into a spectacular display of man-made stars.

Then it was time for the boys to have their own fireworks.

"I want one!"

"I want one, too!"

The excited shouts of Brad's children rang through the night, and Hayden laughed as their little hands greedily clutched at the box of fireworks that he held aloft.

"Remember what your mama said," he told them.

"Don't blow yourselves up!" the children chorused.

"Splendid advice, wouldn't you say?" he answered. "And that extends to parts of yourselves, too. I want to return you both to your parents intact."

"What does that mean?" Bo, the younger child, asked. "What does 'intact' mean?"

"It means with the same number of fingers and toes that you arrived with."

Livvy watched as he distributed the sparklers, spreading them out into exactly equal piles. As one child got green sparklers, so did the other boy.

The box of red sparklers was opened first.

"Light mine first, Uncle Hayden!" The younger child danced around Hayden's legs, slashing the air with the sparkler as if it were a sword.

"No, mine!" Al begged from his wheelchair. "Light mine first. Bo, you wait. You're the baby."

"You're a baby," Bo shot back.

"No, you are."

Livvy interceded. "Neither of you is a baby. You each have a sparkler, and we'll light both of them at exactly the same time."

"Thanks, Aunt Livvy!" the two boys chorused.

She grinned. Everybody was a family member to these boys. Uncle Hayden, Aunt Livvy, Gramps. It was a tremendous feeling.

Soon the children were whooping with glee and mock terror as the sparklers blazed around them. Al certainly wasn't letting being in a wheelchair slow him down. He spun in circles in his chair, waving the sparkler in great loops around him.

"I'm writing *CAT* with mine," Al said. "Aunt Livvy, did you know that we got two cats from here? I call them Tiger and Lion, but Bo calls them Kitty and Cat."

"What do your mom and dad call them?" she asked.

"Mom calls them both Hey You, and Dad calls them Bad and Worse."

Bo whirled happily beside his big brother. "Look, I'm writing my name! Watch me, Uncle Hayden, watch me!"

Hayden leaned close and whispered to her, each word tickling her ear with his closeness. "Good thing his name is Bo and not Archibald. His sparkler wouldn't last!"

She chuckled softly. Hayden was so good with the children, so patient and kind. Together they watched the boys play, enjoying the shouts of laughter and the streaks of color in the night.

Quickly the children lost interest in the sparklers and moved on to colored smoke bombs. Hayden lit them and stepped away, making sure that the boys didn't get too close to the smoking spheres, which looked fascinating but smelled horrible.

The children found them absolutely delightful.

Livvy hung back with Hayden, who began to look a bit green around the edges as the sulphurous smoke enveloped him.

"That stuff is ghastly," he said, coughing as he moved out of the colorful cloud. "I wonder why they don't scent it or something so it's not so nasty. Bo, too close, too close! Al, no, you're too close, too. It's cool to watch, but the smell—!"

"Maybe you can't have both: looking good and smelling good," she said, wrinkling her nose. The fireworks did stink.

He looked at her, his head tilted to one side. A burst of a Catherine wheel lit his face with silver and blue shots of light. "I think I can."

In the distance, the muted sounds of the pyrotechnics from Medora boomed across the night. She was grateful for the cover of darkness. It hid the flush that had washed over her cheeks.

Was he flirting with her?

The more she thought about it, the more flustered she got. She didn't trust her voice. It would probably squeak or something equally embarrassing.

Instead, she opted for shaking her head.

Her reprieve came in the form of Bo, who ran up to Hayden and tugged on his pant leg. "Uncle Hayden, Uncle Hayden, Uncle Hayden, we blew up all the smoke bombs. What else do you have? Can we blast off one of those big rocket things, please, please, please? I want to light up one of those gigantic things and watch it go zzzzzz through the air!" His pudgy little hands looped in a circle, and Hayden laughed.

"Sorry, buddy, no big rockets for you. Not even little rockets. But I have some snakes."

Bo screamed, "Snakes?" and Livvy smiled to herself. Sunset came so late in summer here, and the children were extremely overtired.

Hayden put a calming hand on Bo's small shoulders. "Not those snakes. These are black chunks that we'll light and then something really cool happens."

Livvy watched as he opened the box and placed the black piece on the concrete slab. He touched a match to what looked like a small dark piece of charcoal and stood back.

"Now watch, and remember, never touch."

The children oohed as the small black nugget began to smolder and expand into a long black curl.

"It kind of smells," the older one confided, pinching his nose shut.

"Good fireworks always smell, don't they, Uncle Hayden?" Bo asked. "Those smoke bombs were really stinkish, too."

"Yes, they do smell. But you know what smells good? S'mores!" Hayden motioned toward the bonfire. "You guys want to make s'mores?"

"Oh, I love them!" Bo shouted enthusiastically, rubbing his hands together in anticipation.

"I like the chocolate." Al wheeled over to Livvy's side and smiled at her. "Can I have double chocolate? You don't have to put the marshmallow on. Or the graham cracker."

She grinned at him. "You just want a candy bar?"

"I think so," he said, "but I'd better cook up a marshmallow just in case."

His eyelids were sagging, and she knew he'd be asleep soon. Bo's energy was getting wilder and wilder, and if her admittedly limited prior experience with children was any indicator, he'd be down for the night within half an hour or so.

The children made it through one and a half s'mores before they had to be carried into the house and put on blankets on the living room floor until their parents arrived. Gramps volunteered to stay with them, and Hayden and Livvy returned to the bonfire, which was beginning to burn low.

Still, sparks shot from the fiery logs, showering the night sky with low stars. She sat next to Hayden, cross-legged. They both smelled of summer, of bug spray, soap, and wood smoke, with a touch of marshmallow and chocolate. It was wonderful. *If Fifth Avenue in New York City could bottle it, they'd make a fortune,* she thought.

Life was good. She was in the middle of one of God's finest creations, the Badlands. A full moon glowed overhead, a shining orb more golden than a treasured coin. Only the crackle of the fire and the calls of the night birds and crickets broke the silence.

She was totally content. The hurriedness of the city—the traffic jams, the crowded sidewalks, the congested stores—seemed as far away as that moon. Nothing mattered except this fire, this moon, this man next to her.

Hayden began to sing softly, a melody that sounded vaguely familiar to her, something she'd heard many years ago. She didn't know the words but she hummed along.

As the last note faded away, she sighed. "That was beautiful."

"It's a Scandinavian hymn that every good child up here learns early on," Hayden said with a low chuckle. "Well, this child learned it. Gramps and Gran made sure of that. We closed every vesper service with it, and it just seemed right tonight to continue the tradition."

"What's the name of it?"

" 'Children of the Heavenly Father.' "

A memory slipped into place. She was sitting at her mother's dressing table, playing with an old music box that she'd used for her earrings.

It was a heavy silver rectangle, inlaid with tiny gold crosses, and it had belonged to her mother's great-aunt Rosalyn, the woman who had taken her mother under her wing when the young girl had lost both her parents in an automobile accident. Livvy had never met her, but she had heard her mother talk about the woman who had dedicated her life to raising a scared eight-year-old girl.

This was the melody that the music box had played. No wonder it sounded familiar.

"Sing it to me again," she asked.

She pulled her knees up close to her, clasping her arms around her legs, and listened as his tenor sweetened the air again with song.

"I know the melody, but I'd never heard the words," she said, and explained about the music box. "That music box has such a history. First it was Mom's great-aunt Rosalyn's repository of her numerous hairpins—my mother always said that the woman left a trail of them wherever she went—and now it holds Mom's earrings. Someday I'll use it. It's the closest thing my family has to an heirloom."

She held up her forefinger. "Wait. That's not quite true, is it? Remember the sermon Reverend Carlisle gave? About the inheritance of faith? Maybe my religious life has been spotty at best, but I'm still in line for the inheritance, too, aren't I?"

This was the ideal place for her to share her heart, between the vast dark sky arching overhead, filled with glittering showers of multicolored lights, and the night-blackened tableau shadowed in the night of the Badlands' epic majesty.

He turned to her, his face illuminated by the still-sparking fire. "You are."

"I want to be part of this." She motioned around her. "I remember when I was in youth group at church—wow, that seems like a long time ago—the leader said that God never forgets us, even if we forget Him. I—I think I have some lost years to make up, when I did forget Him. I hope He remembers me."

"He does. Trust me, He does."

Hayden began to hum "Children of the Heavenly Father" again, and she rested her chin on her knees as she listened. Could ever a night have been more perfect?

The sound of a car turning into the drive heralded the return of the boys' father. Working quickly and quietly, the children were loaded into the vehicle, never waking during the process, and Livvy walked to the truck to drive herself home.

As she pulled away from the house, Hayden waved at her, a silhouette against the last glow of the bonfire.

It had been a lovely Fourth of July. In the distance a lone firework went off, and she smiled as the sound and the light spread across the Badlands.

This was the best Independence Day she'd ever had. Ever.

⌒

"I told her that we never locked the door," Gramps said, pacing back and forth as Hayden knelt and examined the situation.

The key had snapped off and was now embedded in the lock.

"It's all right, Gramps," he said. "I'll just get a new one."

Gramps shook his head. "It's the same lock everywhere, Grub. Replace one, replace them all."

"What do you mean?" He rocked back on his heels and looked at his grandfather, who seemed oddly agitated. He spoke slowly, hoping to calm the older man down. "Each lock is different."

Gramps stopped his pacing. "Well, of course they're different. What kind of fool idea would it have been to put locks on all these doors and have the same keys for all those locks? You think I'm a bozo?"

"You're not a bozo. I'm a bozo."

His grandfather shook his head. "Bozo Senior and Bozo Junior. What I mean is that if this key breaks, that means they're all wearing out, and whether we're talking about the keys or the locks, the smartest thing would be to replace them all so this doesn't happen again. Because it will, and you know it will. That's the rule of home ownership. Remember it?"

Hayden grinned at Gramps, and together they recited it. "If it can break, it will break."

"And what's the corollary?" Gramps prompted.

"And it will break in the middle of the night on a weekend."

"That's my boy."

"You're right, Gramps, about these locks. They're all as old as the doors, which are as old as the buildings." Hayden stared at the lock with the key stuck in the hole. If he had to replace all the locks, it would mean—he did a quick mental count—seventeen of them. And assuming each one was as difficult as this one, he'd be doing this until September.

Lord, this would be a great time to dose me with patience, he thought.

The faceplate of the assembly came right off—entirely too easily, he realized, as he examined the door and found that the wood had gone bad under the metal.

The doors would need to be replaced, too.

Dollar signs danced in his head as he performed another calculation. Seventeen doors. With seventeen locks and seventeen keys.

"Gramps, you'd better get Livvy out here."

The old man scrambled off to get her from behind the house, where she was clearing a bramble-infested patch in the hope that it might be a garden area the next year.

"What's up, doc?" she asked cheerfully, pulling off her pink and yellow work gloves and wiping her hands on her jeans.

"Well, the cost of repairs, that's what's up. This door is rotten under the lock plate. See?" He showed her the damage. "I think we might end up having to replace all the doors and all the lock assemblages."

She frowned. "That's a lot."

"I'm afraid it is."

"I have my book. I think it might explain how to do it."

He shook his head. She wasn't understanding what he meant. "Livvy, I'm afraid we're going to have to buy new doors."

She crossed her arms over her chest and frowned. "Wow."

"Definitely wow. So what should we do?"

She shrugged. "There's no point in borrowing trouble. Let's take a look at the other doors. Maybe they don't all need to be replaced. And if they do, then I guess we need to go somewhere and buy a truckload of doors. And locks."

"Good idea," he agreed.

They walked around the property, checking each door, and he was relieved to discover that the cabins and outbuildings that faced east had no damage. It was only those that faced into the wind that came off the Badlands that needed help.

"That's good." She smiled happily, pulling her work gloves back on.

"Well, it's better. There are still quite a lot of them."

"Oh!" She stopped and clapped one hand, still in the silly pink and yellow flowered cotton glove, over her mouth. "I see. Well, I have the book. I can do it. How hard can it be?"

Those were, he knew from experience, famous last words. The sun was setting by the time he'd gotten back from the building supply store in Bismarck, and she'd gotten one latch replaced, and the door at least leaned against its building.

"Tomorrow is another day," she said, "and another door, and by the time I finish it'll be another year."

He laughed. It wasn't that bad. Not quite.

❧

Livvy wiped her forehead. The heat was relentless. She felt as if she were living inside an oven. The only breeze that came through was the occasional hot wind off the buttes, and it didn't improve her temperament one bit.

If this was July, she could only imagine what August would be like.

The doors were done. At least that was taken care of. Now she was doing her least favorite thing in the world: cleaning.

She made a deal with herself. If she could finish scrubbing out the cabin, she would take a break and go wading in the lake. There wasn't too much to do, just some work on the sills and prying the accumulated crud out of the corners of the mopboards.

She took a swig out of the water bottle she kept on the little table shoved up against the window. The ice in it had long since melted, and the water was very warm.

The windows were flung open, but the air inside the cabin was still and motionless. Sweat rolled down her face and dripped onto her T-shirt. She tried to think of pleasant things—mountaintops covered in snow, ice skating, making snowballs—but her mind kept reverting to the same phrase: "I'm hot."

In self-defense, she wrenched open the bottle of water and poured it over her head. For a few moments, it actually helped. She felt a smidge cooler.

She knelt and tackled a corner of the room, digging away at the stuff that had built up in there. "One day," she said through gritted teeth, "someone, probably a woman, will get smart and make a room without corners so no other human being will ever have to do this again."

"A round house isn't impossible," Hayden said from the doorway, "but it's a lot of extra work to build."

She swabbed her face with the back of her hand. "Typical man," she said. "Worrying about a few extra minutes of work."

He laughed. "We'll not fight that one out today. I thought you might be broiling in here, so I brought you this."

He held out a large plastic mug with a straw sticking out of it. "It might be a bit melted but I kept the AC on full blast on my way back from Obsidian so it would have a chance."

She took it from him and practically inhaled the contents. "Oh, this is heavenly. I haven't had a root beer float for ages."

"Yup. I got it from the drive-through on the edge of town. Take a break. You look like you could use one."

Livvy laughed. "Thanks for the compliment—not!"

"You're always beautiful," Hayden answered, and almost immediately he flushed bright red. "I mean, well, when you're clean, or not, but then, actually, um..."

He looked so miserable, stammering in the heat in front of her, that she took pity on him. "Thanks, Hayden. Beauty is as beauty does, and this is a mighty beautiful root beer float!"

Chapter 7

S hoo! Shoo! Go find a hollow tree, or wherever it is you live!" Livvy swept the chubby raccoon out of the lean-to near the house where she was stacking firewood. Indian summer was in full swing this October day. She was sweating, and having to get wildlife out of the building wasn't improving her mood one bit.

The raccoon waddled away as quickly as it could, stopping for one last snarl before vanishing into the woods, and she leaned on the woodpile, feeling for all the world like a Wild West woman.

Every day she went through cardboard boxes, plastic containers, and wooden crates. Most of it was disposed of immediately. She had learned to recognize when mice—or raccoons—had been in containers. Unfortunately they were destructive creatures, and almost everything they'd gotten into was taken to the dump.

Some of it was interesting, especially the memorabilia from Sunshine's heyday. That she put aside. Hayden and Gramps could go through it during the winter and see what they wanted to keep and which pictures they could identify. She hoped they'd let her keep some of it at Sunshine to use as a reminder of its past.

And some was sad, like Gran's clothing, which Gramps had put aside when she passed away. He'd been unable to take care of it, and unwilling to let someone else do it for him.

Now, with his permission, her clothing had gone to a charity.

There was just so much of everything.

She was trying to get each outbuilding finished before the snow came. Hayden had warned her that the first measurable snow could fall any day now, even if the days were still in the fifties and sixties, although today had climbed into the seventies. The forecast predicted a drop the next day, with the evening temperatures plummeting to the thirties, and the next week the first hard freeze was a possibility. At night, she thought she could smell snow in the distance.

Hayden and Gramps were sharing Hayden's apartment in Obsidian, and she'd moved to Sunshine with Leonard. Jeannie had decided that she wasn't coming back from Africa—her house had been sold to a young couple in town— and suddenly Livvy had become a dog owner. It was fine with her. Leonard kept her company, and she felt safer at night when the land became alive with sounds she couldn't identify.

So much had changed. She'd never been really overweight, but the labor had built up her muscles and tightened her frame. Now she could lift a box without having to empty half of it first, or call upon Hayden or whoever was handy to help her out. Her skin was tanned—naturally, without benefit of a tanning bed or a spray or a lotion.

She glanced at her arm. Not only was it tan, it was scratched from a recent run-in with the chicken that had tried to peck a bug off of Martha Washington's back. The cat had tangled with the chicken, and when she tried to separate them, they'd both clawed her.

And next to those scratches were two cuts from a run-in with a broken window, and a bruise that came about when an old radio had fallen from a high shelf and she'd foolishly tried to catch it.

She shook her head as she thought back to that morning in Boston, when a stray newspaper had changed her life. She was no longer the same person she was that day.

But the greatest changes were internal. As much as she'd always considered herself to be independent and self-sufficient, she knew now how dependent she'd been on others. If her car needed an oil change, she took it in to a mechanic.

Now she knew how to do it herself—and she did it. Plus, with her initial plumbing adventure behind her, she was able to change washers in a faucet and reseat a leaking toilet.

She began to tally what she knew now that she hadn't known before.

She could replace a light switch. Change breakers. Even bait her own hook—with a worm.

Her confidence was stronger than it had ever been before.

As much as Sunshine was responsible for this newfound strength, she knew that the majority of credit went to the peace and guidance she'd found in the church. Every week she came away from the services knowing herself better. She was truly a child of God, and just knowing that had made her feel like a new, improved Livvy.

Every evening she set aside time for her own private vespers. With her Bible at hand, she'd read and then study the passages, using the guides that Reverend Carlisle had lent her. Even though she had watched programs on the Travel Channel about Israel, it still seemed alien to her, but with this reading, she was able to get a better sense of the historical context.

What was most important though was that she was able to bridge those years, two thousand of them, and take the lessons of the past and bring them into the present day, and use them to guide her through the time yet to come.

She especially though found understanding through prayer. Talking to God helped her clarify what her life was about, and more importantly, what it could be about.

If she could only get the cloud of the future to quit hanging over her head, she'd feel much better. It still kept her up at night, tossing and turning, with sleep eluding her. She prayed and prayed her way through those wide-awake hours, asking for an answer, for a solution.

What was she going to do? That question had to be answered, and soon. She'd checked her bank balance online and was horrified to see how much it had shrunk.

She'd been hasty in packing up and moving to North Dakota. There was no doubt about that. But she could not believe it had been the wrong thing to do. Never.

Sunshine was in her soul. As the summer had moved into autumn, it had become even more enmeshed in her being.

God clearly meant for her to be there. Didn't He? If it was His intent, was He at some time going to make clear to her what she should do? Something that would be profitable?

It was too much to ask of Him. She knew that. She'd gone into this with her eyes wide open—maybe with a bit of a shadow from her fashionable sunglasses that Leonard had gnawed into a twisted, unusable piece of plastic, but open nonetheless.

She wouldn't trade back an hour of all the work she'd done for even a second of time back in her very comfortable office with the padded leather chair and the checks that made life tolerable. No, she was glad to be here, in the last shreds of warmth before winter set in.

But there was just so much to be done at Sunshine.

She'd spent so much time focusing on cleaning and repairing the buildings that she'd let her original vision for it fall aside. Now, as she was about to enter her first winter here in North Dakota, she'd have the time to work on developing it.

She had only the vaguest idea of what she wanted to do with the property. A fishing resort was the only thing she'd come up with, but that was so nebulous, it was worthless.

Initially Sunshine had appealed to her because of how different it was from the hustle of the city. Then she had met Hayden and Gramps, and the mission became different—it was no longer saving her sanity, but saving Sunshine.

And saving her soul.

Suddenly a volley of sharp barks erupted from Leonard, who, from his vantage point on the porch, had been happily watching Hayden paint the front door. The dog tore down the driveway, and continued to bark at whatever unseen menace was headed their way.

Livvy pulled off her work gloves and stepped out of the lean-to. A cloud of dust announced visitors.

It was Trevor's old truck. This was the vehicle that had brought her to Sunshine in the first place, and she started for it, a smile on her face, when the passenger side door opened, and a familiar figure stepped out.

It couldn't be. It just couldn't be.

She moved toward the truck, but Hayden was faster, reaching it before she did. Leonard growled at the stranger and protectively placed himself firmly between the man and Hayden.

"Good dog, Leonard, good dog." Hayden patted the dog's head with one hand while keeping a firm grip on his collar with the other. "Settle down now. Good dog, good dog. By the way," he said to the visitor, "I'm Hayden Greenwood."

"Pleased to meet you," the man answered, his dark eyes sweeping across the property. "I'm—"

In a split second, as she saw the familiar scan—the rapid tally, the quick appraisal of market value—a protective temper rose in her. Sunshine was hers.

She knew from working with the man that he did nothing without a firm objective in mind. What did he want from her? It couldn't be good.

Livvy stepped forward. "This is Michael Evans, my former boss."

Hayden turned to her, clearly startled by her blunt tone. "Livvy—" he began, but she waved his interruption away, and Mr. Evans laughed a bit nervously as Leonard growled again.

"Mr. Evans is here to see me, or, no, better than that, I'm wondering if he's here to see Sunshine," she said, hating that her voice was shaking. "What is it? Is there oil under the land? Gold tucked in a cave? Gemstones in the buttes?"

She tried to interject some lightness into her words, but she knew she failed. She knew him too well. He wasn't here because he was on vacation in the Badlands. Not Michael Evans. Their relationship in Boston had been very formal, very careful, very precise. Their parting hadn't been exactly cordial either.

There was some reason he was here, and it had to do with Sunshine. Or her.

He had some kind of agenda, and the most effective way to deal with it was to face it head-on, directly.

Mr. Evans looked at her, and she saw herself in his eyes. Cut-off jeans, a faded and stained T-shirt that she'd found in one of the cabins a month ago, no makeup, and hair that hadn't seen a stylist since she left Boston. To complete the package, she probably smelled like dirt and sweat and was coated in both.

"Actually," he said, his voice as smooth as Martha Washington's fur, "I'm out here because I need your signature on some papers."

"Really?" she asked, making no effort to disguise the disbelief in her voice. "And what papers would those be?"

"The Millner transfer. You didn't sign the agent's agreement."

Livvy shook her head in self-reproach. She knew exactly what he was talking about. She'd done all of the behind-the-scenes work on the account. It had been a massive amount of work because the Millners owned rental property not only in Massachusetts but also in Virginia, Florida, and Arizona. Each state's laws were a bit different, and adding to the difficulty was that the Millner family, which was spread all around the world, owned varying percentages of each property. It was the largest account she'd ever worked with. She'd left before everything was completed—the finalization had still been months away.

And yet of all the papers for her to miss, the agreement was probably the most important.

"You don't get your bonus until it's signed," Mr. Evans said, knowing, she was sure, that those very words would make her get out her pen immediately.

She'd forgotten about the bonus. It was a substantial one. With it, she'd be able to get through the winter—if nothing broke.

She took a moment and breathed a prayer: *Give me patience, strength, and understanding.*

"I apologize if I sounded rude," she said, motioning him to the door. "Come inside, and let's put ink on paper."

Gramps was at the screen door. "All that commotion woke me up from my nap," he said. His eyes were confused. "Is Ellie in the garden?"

She took his arm. "Hayden is right out here. And we have a guest, Gramps. This is Michael Evans. I worked for him in Boston. He owns one of the largest real estate management firms in the United States."

Mr. Evans reached his hand out and shook Gramps's. "Sir, it's good to meet you. This is my first time in North Dakota, and I must say it's quite a spectacular place. Sunshine has a beautiful setting."

Gramps nodded. "Sunshine is a treasure." He shook his arm free of his touch. "You can't have it."

She bit back a smile at her former boss's expression. He managed to look horrified and amused at the same time. He had clearly underestimated Gramps's mental facility, which didn't surprise her too much. He'd always sent her to negotiate with family members.

What he didn't know—had never known—was the reason she was so successful with estate work. She didn't push the family members but instead guided them to a consensus, one that they could all be happy with.

"I don't want Sunshine," Mr. Evans said in the voice he usually kept in reserve for those he considered slow.

"Then you're dumber than I thought." Gramps pulled the screen door shut and hooked the latch.

She heard Hayden gasp behind her, and in a series of great loping steps, he joined them. "Gramps, now, Mr. Evans is here to visit with Livvy. He has something she needs to sign."

The old man shook his head vigorously. "He's here to sell something. Vacuum cleaners maybe. Or toilet brushes."

A nervous giggle rose in her throat, but she choked it down. Gramps's fingers tapped nervously along the handle of the door.

"I can assure you, sir," Mr. Evans said, "that I am not here to sell anything, especially not vacuum cleaners or toilet brushes." He said the products as if the very words tasted bad.

Livvy glanced quickly at Hayden. His forehead was lined with worry. He reached toward the door but Gramps shook his head, and Hayden shoved his hands into his jeans pockets and looked upward, his face a study in frustration.

A loud rumble accompanied by blares and screeches rose behind them, and Livvy spun around to see the cause.

It was Trevor. Apparently bored by the entire scene, he'd started his car again—those were the sounds that shook the floorboards of the porch—and turned on the radio. It might have been music that he was listening to, but Livvy wouldn't stake any bets on it.

"Is that Martha Washington?" Gramps asked, and from somewhere deep inside Livvy, a bubble of laughter burst and erupted out of her. Hayden looked at her, and he joined in, too.

Mr. Evans gaped at them as if they'd both lost their minds, and as the laughter continued to pour out into the October afternoon, unchecked, she thought that perhaps he was right. She could no more stop laughing than she could sprout wings and fly around the yard.

She reached for Hayden and put her hand on his shoulder to balance herself as the laughter rolled on. It felt so good to laugh. It cleaned her. It refreshed her. And it gave her new vigor.

At last Mr. Evans coughed, a sound that shot through the growl of Trevor's truck engine and the shrill blast of guitars and drums and wailing voices from his radio, and the last vestiges of mirth died in her throat.

"Can you explain this to me?" he asked rather stiffly. "I am somewhat at a disadvantage here."

"Martha Washington is a cat," she answered, wiping her eyes from the laughing jag. "A big fat lazy cat that chases the chicken and that's about all. She purrs but not quite that loudly."

Gramps wiggled the screen door. "It's locked," he announced.

Hayden cleared his throat and approached the door. "Gramps, you locked it."

"I know."

"Now you need to unlock it."

The older man fiddled with the latch and at last it sprang free.

Hayden opened the door and motioned Livvy and Mr. Evans inside.

She took her former boss into the kitchen as Hayden led his grandfather to the couch and began to talk to him in a low voice.

Mr. Evans looked over his shoulder. "He's all right?"

Livvy nodded. "He fades in and out. Usually he's fine. He's the fellow I bought Sunshine from."

"I see."

As they neared the table, he opened the large manila folder he carried and took out the papers, looking through them, not losing a step in his stride. "I would have done this by phone, but I couldn't get through."

"No service right here. At least not for that carrier."

"And then you weren't answering your e-mail," he continued.

"No Internet out here."

Mr. Evans stopped midstep. "You're serious? No cell phone service. No e-mail. No Google."

"I'm serious. The only thing I miss is talking to my parents, since they live in Sweden, and we use the computer for that, so I go into town and use the library's connection."

He stared at her. "Amazing." He laid the papers on the scarred surface of the kitchen table and ran his hands over the faux marble top. "This would get a fairly decent price at auction, wouldn't it? Now let's see, Release, Assignment of Rights, Temporary Transfer of Title, Deed in Kind, Agent's Agreement, there we are. You have a pen? Sign by the yellow sticky note."

He seemed anxious to move the conversation on, to get out of the kitchen of this place where crazies lived, and she didn't totally blame him. She read through the document, making sure that she remembered what she had written before she signed it. It was a good agreement, fair to all those involved, but it had involved months of work, of close negotiation, of listening, listening, and more listening.

She was justifiably proud of what she'd accomplished, and she signed it with a tinge of sadness, knowing that she would probably never do this kind of work again. There weren't enough property sales or leases to make her career possible out here.

"Here you go," she said, blowing on the inked signature before handing it back to him. Mr. Evans always used a fountain pen that she knew cost several hundreds of dollars. "Signed, sort of sealed, and delivered."

"Thank you." He placed the document back in the folder and snapped the rubber band around it. "This means a lot to the agency, and, of course, to you. You deserved this bonus. I'm not one to give out compliments, you know that, but the clients have told me repeatedly how much they appreciated what you did for them. Thanks to you, the family has reunited, despite the friction of the past, and they asked me to relay their appreciation to you for your work, not just as an agent but as a human being."

She could only stare at him. This was amazing.

"Do you have a card?" he asked.

"What kind of a card?" She looked at him blankly.

"A business card," he answered, "of course."

"Business card? For what?"

"Well, for one thing, to make sure the check arrives here, unless you want it automatically deposited in the bank. Do you still have the same account?"

"I do." For once her laziness was in her favor. She'd left the account in Boston open. "Can you go ahead and deposit it for me?"

"Sure. But you should have a business card."

"Why?"

He put the packet flat onto the table. "Well, Livvy, for this." He motioned around him with a sweep of his arm. "Sunshine. You can't do this without advertising. It's the stuff of business success, after all. You'll need to start the accounts for food service, unless you want to do it all yourself, and there'll be a cleaning crew, I imagine, and a linen supply contract, just to begin."

"But for what?" She understood the words but there wasn't meaning behind them. What on earth was he talking about?

A fly roused itself on the windowsill and batted itself halfheartedly against the screen, warmed by the Indian summer afternoon. Outside the cacophony of Trevor's truck radio and engine shook the usual calm.

"For this." He leaned on the table, his black suit still spotless even after riding in the teenager's truck. She'd been in the truck just five months ago, and she doubted that he had cleaned it since. How Mr. Evans accomplished maintaining his immaculate appearance was nothing short of a miracle.

She could only shake her head.

He sat down, keeping his back stick-straight, crossed his legs, and looked her directly in the eye. "For when you reopen. You are reopening, aren't you?"

She knew Michael Evans well enough to pay attention when he was positioned like this, poised and attentive. She used to say that she could see his ears literally perk up when he sensed a business opportunity. She let him continue speaking, anxious to let him share his vision.

"This would be a splendid resort," he said.

"But it wasn't working," she objected, pretending that she hadn't been thinking of just that. The more she could learn from this man's years of cagey expertise, the better. "Plus it's not exactly Hawaii or the Riviera."

"The destination is what you create." He looked out the window, and Livvy's eyes followed his. The copper and bronze of the Badlands were framed against the bright blue of the sky. "Look at that. You name me one other place that has that. And I wager that if that teenager would turn off his truck, we'd hear only nature. Am I right?"

She nodded, beginning to feel a twinge of excitement.

"Figure out what kind of resort you'd like it to be." He stood and picked up the folder and tucked it under his arm. "I'd make it a retro theme, and market it to L.A. and New York. Big Internet splash, which is practically free. I bet that kid out there could cobble up a webpage with his eyes closed. Run off some flyers on a printer, nice full-color images with this place all spiffed up, and blast them to travel agents out there."

It sounded wonderful, and as she listened, the ideas started to take root.

"One question, Mr. Evans," she said as she walked him to the truck, nearly shouting to be heard over the music coming from Trevor's radio. "Why aren't you trying to get this from me, open it yourself, if it's such a great business proposition?"

"Me?" he asked. He opened the door of the truck and with a look of complete revulsion, flicked a bug off the seat and climbed into the cab. He placed the packet neatly centered on his knees and snapped the safety belt across his shoulders. Then he faced her squarely, and with a voice just a touch under the decibels still thundering from the radio, said, "I don't want it. But you do, and that's what counts. You have heart, Miss Moore, and that's what this is going to take. North Dakota heart."

Trevor caught her eye over Mr. Evans's shoulder and grinned, making loopy "crazy" signs and pointing at the real estate magnate.

She smiled back.

She loved this place, loved this old house, even loved this obnoxious truck and its driver and its blaring radio and amped-up engine.

North Dakota heart, indeed!

❧

The chill of autumn was definitely in the air. That Indian summer day had passed, and the temperatures had become more October-like. The leaves on the trees along the river began to dry, and when the afternoon winds picked up, they rattled together like shells, a wind chime heralding the end of summer and the time-to-come of winter.

The little apartment in Obsidian was cozy—which was a code word for *cramped*. Gramps was still with him awaiting an opening in the senior living facility, and while Hayden was grateful to have his grandfather with him, a one-bedroom apartment was just that—one bedroom. He'd given Gramps the bed, and he'd been bunking on the couch in the living room, which was about ten inches too short for any comfort.

He sat at the kitchen table, papers that needed to be graded spread out in front of him, but he wasn't seeing them. Too much was on his mind to be able to focus on the area of a trapezoid if side D was 1.3 and side B was 2.4.

Livvy had moved out to Sunshine, and they had an awkward arrangement. He'd bring Gramps out to her during the day, and he'd come back to Obsidian and teach. Then, at the end of the school day, he'd return to Sunshine, visit with Livvy and make sure everything was working well, and retrieve Gramps and the two of them would drive to Obsidian, to the tiny apartment.

He felt better knowing that Gramps was not alone during the day, but it was asking a lot of Livvy to have the older man out there all day long. And as the season progressed, he wasn't sure it would continue to work.

But it had to. There just wasn't any choice. Some things had to be the way they were, and that was simply all there was to it.

Gramps was in the living room, watching a video of an Elvis Presley movie he'd gotten at the grocery store. Why he'd chosen it from the rack of movie rentals, Hayden had no idea, but the old man had seemed delighted with the choice and was now deeply engrossed in it.

He stacked the homework into a neat pile and laid it aside. Maybe later he could get to it, but first he had to deal with what was topmost in his mind.

He picked up the envelope and removed the sheet of paper and read it once again. What should he do?

He buried his face in his hands in a futile attempt to wipe out what was in front of him. He had taken action, and now—now did he want it?

Earlier in the year, on a February day when the high was five below zero and the winds would not stop, he impetuously applied for a teaching job in Florida. He spread his fingers a tad and peeked through the opening at the correspondence in front of him. There were the letters, forming the words and sentences he had wanted to hear, and now dreaded. They had an opening and needed him to teach: Could he come for an interview?

He couldn't leave. Sunshine might be sold, but his grandfather needed him. And without a place for Gramps to live, he had to stay in Obsidian. Until a spot opened in the senior living complex, his grandfather would have to live with him.

Not that he minded. He would walk over hot coals and through burning lava for his grandfather.

Plus there was Livvy. Livvy with her cap of dark hair that curled wildly when it rained, with her eyes so deeply brown that they glowed. She needed him to help her with Sunshine. There was no way she could do it by herself, not with just that goofy book to help her. What was the name of it again? Oh yes. *The Complete Guide to Home Construction and Repair.*

He put his hands together, palm to palm. When he had been a little boy, that's what he would do when he prayed. He tried it now, asking for clarity, for comfort, for reassurance.

Usually he got a pleasant, warm feeling from his prayers, a sense that they had been heard and acknowledged, and this was no different. He came away from his brief time with the Lord refreshed and ready to face what was ahead.

Sadly, what was ahead was a stack of ungraded math worksheets.

He took a deep breath and dug in. Right now his problems were mathematical. The rest of them would have to wait.

❧

"We need a bonfire," Gramps announced one Saturday afternoon, when the three of them were at Sunshine. "One more bonfire before winter hits."

They had just finished painting the interior of one of the old cabins, and they were sitting on the porch, enjoying the notion that there was just one more cabin to refinish before they would have all been renovated. It was a pleasant feeling.

Martha Washington grunted in her sleep. She was curled on Gramps's lap in a furry ball. At the sound, one of Leonard's ears perked up, but he didn't open his eyes, apparently deeming a cat snort to be unimportant.

Livvy didn't want to move. She wanted to sit in the chair with the slatted back and absorb the last rays of the weekend sun, wrapped in the soft fleece of a blanket.

Only one cabin was left. It seemed like it had been a race against the calendar, fixing one or two cabins a week so they'd be ready for visitors in the spring. If the weather held, she could probably get the last one done in the coming week, and maybe even get the old canteen painted. She'd found another box of the old signs. They'd be perfect in there.

She shut her eyes and let her imagination roam. A clear light blue, one that matched the summer sky here in North Dakota, would be perfect for the walls. She'd leave the signs as she'd found them, a few rusted, some partially broken, others in pristine shape, and scatter them across the walls.

Café curtains would let the sun in but filter the brightness. Maybe she could find some old-fashioned chintz, with the same color of blue as the walls, and perhaps a retro theme of families enjoying themselves on the water. She'd seen something like that at one time in Boston, back in a store that specialized in old-fashioned fabric themes. They probably would send her what she needed, if she could find samples on the Internet.

The Internet. She was connected again, thanks to the wonders of technology, and life was good. A satellite dish was tastefully positioned on the far side of the house, and through some marvels she didn't understand, she had Internet, cell phone reception, and even more television channels than she could ever watch. Coverage didn't extend beyond the house, but that was all right.

Now she wouldn't have to drive into town to check her bank balances. She'd been spending her evenings investigating what kind of flowers she could plant around the house, and maybe she'd have a vegetable patch for fresh corn and tomatoes. She'd have to ask Hayden about that.

"We could," Hayden said from the porch swing next to her. "What do you say, Livvy?"

She forced her eyes open. "About what?"

"About a bonfire."

"Tonight?"

"Sure."

"Would I have to move? Or can I stay right here and you do all the work?" She closed her eyes again. There really was nothing like the late autumn sun.

Martha Washington had it right. Sleep on the porch in the afternoon. Sit back, and relax. There would be time for work—well, for her anyway. Martha's days of working were long over. She was now replaced by traps in the outbuildings, and it didn't seem to bother her at all.

"Sure. All we have to do is put more wood on the pile and put a match to it. You've got marshmallows, right?"

She nodded, not bothering to raise her eyelids. "Amazingly, I do. I was going to make cereal bars with them but that would require me to move, and that's not going to happen."

"Do you have hot dogs?"

"Nope."

"What do you think, Gramps? Should we go back into town and get some?"

The old man's chair creaked as he rocked. Apparently the motion didn't bother the cat; Livvy could hear her snoring continue uninterrupted.

"I put some pork chops in the Crock-Pot this morning," Gramps said, "so we've got them for dinner. Let's just go with the marshmallows. But you'll need to go get some more logs, Grub. Down by the river, on the north edge, I think I saw some trees that didn't make it through this last season. They'll be fine for a bonfire."

"Probably too smoky, I'd say," Hayden commented.

"Smoky is okay. We're outside. And it'll keep the bugs away."

"I'd rather use seasoned wood. There's a pile over by the orange cabin."

She could hear the teasing in his voice, and his grandfather rose to the occasion. "That's good lumber. That's not the stuff you burn. You might as well throw this chair onto the fire. Or that porch post. Maybe the kitchen table..."

Livvy let the sound of their good-natured repartee wash over her like a lullaby, a backdrop to the soft chatter of the dried leaves that still clung to the trees, and the faint splash of the river, and the distant calls of birds that still lingered before migrating south. Wrapped in a blanket in the cool evening, she was so comfortable. Who knew that this would be one of life's greatest pleasures, relaxing outside at the edge of winter? She knew she was falling asleep, but something kept nudging her arm.

"Leonard, go away," she muttered drowsily. "I don't want to throw the ball."

"You don't have to throw the ball. You just have to come in and have a pork chop." It was Hayden's voice. "Gramps got the table all set, and there's a nice salad, and he's got some goopy stuff he puts on the meat that makes it heavenly."

"What?" She sat up and rubbed her eyes, still groggy.

"I don't know exactly what it is, but it's really good. You'd better come in and try it. His pork chops are almost as good as his peanut butter and jelly sandwiches."

"Was I asleep?" she asked. "I was just listening to you and Gramps talk about the wood, and—"

"And you were gone."

She could feel the red rushing to her face. "Oh please tell me I wasn't snoring."

"Okay, you weren't snoring." He grinned.

"I was, wasn't I?"

"Maybe a little bit."

"You and Martha Washington had a regular concerto going," Gramps said from behind the screen door.

"Oh my. Oh my." She hurried to her feet. "I'm so sorry. I know I can get going sometimes, but to do it in public! I'm so embarrassed!"

Hayden smiled. "I don't know that Gramps and I really qualify as the public, but let me reassure you that it was a very ladylike little sound, just breathing with enthusiasm, actually."

"Baloney. She was sawing logs like a lumberjack," Gramps said, shaking his head. "I like that in a woman."

"You like to hear a woman snoring?" She gaped at him.

"Sure," the older man responded, holding the screen door open for her. "It shows she's no delicate hothouse flower."

"Well, I'm definitely not that," she answered, following the men into the kitchen, where the most delicious aroma in the world was wafting from. "But on the other hand, I've never been compared to a lumberjack before either."

The dinner was astonishing, and when she said as much, Gramps simply shrugged. "It's the Crock-Pot. You put a lot of interesting things in there, and the Crock-Pot takes it from there."

After they ate, the men dismissed themselves to build the bonfire. As she cleared the table and loaded the dishwasher, their voices floated through the open window over the sink.

"Big logs on the bottom now," Gramps coached, "and remember to put the twigs under the logs, that's right, but leave some sticking out so they can catch fire."

"I know, Gramps."

"I'm just reminding you, Grub. We don't want to get your lady friend out here and then have a dud of a fire."

"She's not my lady friend."

"Not yet. All you have to do though is make your move and she's yours."

"She's not mine."

The conversation had taken a fascinating turn, and Livvy put down the dish towel and eavesdropped shamelessly.

"She likes you. I can see it in the way she looks at you, and her eyes and your eyes hold, just a bit longer than most, and her face softens, and she leans toward you until you're almost touching but you're not, and—"

"Oh Gramps. You're just being silly now."

"I'm not. Your grandmother knew."

"She knew about Livvy?"

"Sure."

A sudden silence fell over the evening. Only a night bird coo-hoo'ed in the distance.

Then Hayden spoke, slowly and clearly. "Gramps, Gran is in heaven."

"I know that," the old man said. "You think I don't know that? You think I don't miss her every single waking minute? You think that sometimes it might not make me happy to think of her? And you know what? You know what? We were together for so long that I know how she thought, and what she'd say today. After you've loved someone for that long, you know. You just know."

"Gramps, I'm sorry—" Hayden began, but his grandfather interrupted him.

"You know I don't usually talk to you like this, but I know you're worried about me because I get mixed up. I do. I admit it. When you've had as many days as I've had, they sometimes run into each other and get blurry. I see blurry. I hear blurry. And I think blurry. But I do know that your grandmother isn't with me. I know that."

Something wet fell onto Livvy's hand, and she realized she was crying.

Hayden murmured something indistinct.

Gramps continued, "She did say something about Livvy. She didn't know her, of course, but she knew that Livvy was coming into your life. She told me the day she died, Grub, that there was a woman for you, someone who would love you and treasure you for all of your days, who would be there when you needed her—and when you didn't. And that she would be a child of God, just as you are. She was telling the truth. She was. That woman is Livvy."

"I know." The two words carried across the yard, through the window, and into Livvy's heart.

"And you should—Leonard, drop that stick! No, bad dog! No! Grub, do you see what that dim-witted beast is doing to our woodpile? Stop, you dumb dog!"

She grinned as the big dog crashed into the carefully piled stack of wood and kindling, digging into it with his big feet and flinging aside branch after branch.

Hayden struggled to nab Leonard, but the dog, seeing this as a grand adventure, eluded his grip, while Gramps stood on the sidelines, stamping his feet in the old patched boots and yelling at the dog.

She sniffed back the last vestiges of tears, and joined them. "Leonard baby, come to Mama," she cooed, and the dog dropped the great stick he had in his mouth and trotted over to see her.

"Leonard baby, come to Mama?" Hayden repeated. "Leonard baby, come to Mama?"

She sank to the ground and hugged the mutt. "He just wanted some attention, didn't you, sweetie?"

Out of the corner of her eye, she saw the two men exchange looks and shake their heads, and she buried her smile in the dog's fur. "All's well that ends well, right, Leonard?" she murmured in his ear. "You are a crazy creature though."

Hayden and Gramps rebuilt the stack for the bonfire as the dog, happy now, went off to the porch where he chased the chicken off the padded chair and sprawled across it himself. Martha Washington ignored the entire fracas.

Sunset came earlier than it had in the summer when the days seemed to last forever. Now they arrived quickly, and the land was covered in shadows that stretched from the buttes to the mesas to the flatlands.

Hayden lit the bonfire, and soon the entire pile of wood was ablaze. Sparks crackled upward into the darkness, and the four of them—Livvy, Hayden, Gramps, and Leonard—circled around the flames. Hayden distributed sticks and they stuck marshmallows on and let them roast until they caught fire.

"This is the best way," Livvy said, pulling her marshmallow from the fire and blowing it out. "Good and crispy and totally charred."

She waved it around until it was cool enough and gave it to Leonard, who consumed it in a single gulp, and then she roasted another one for herself.

A stray ember popped onto Leonard's paw, and he ran back to the safety of the porch. Soon Gramps yawned broadly. "This old body needs some sleep. I want to be rested for church tomorrow. Livvy, you don't mind if I bunk for a while on the couch, do you? Grub, just wake me up before you leave."

Livvy waved and watched as he headed for the house with his odd gait.

Neither she nor Hayden spoke. Only the *snap* of the logs in the fire and the sounds of the night birds disturbed the stillness. She put the bag of marshmallows aside. If she ate any more, she'd look like a marshmallow herself soon.

She didn't want to think about the conversation she had overheard between Hayden and Gramps, but it insisted, making its way into her brain.

Maybe she had misunderstood what Hayden had said. Maybe he didn't feel as strongly about her as he'd implied. After all, he hadn't even kissed her. As a matter of fact, he hadn't shown any sign that he even wanted to.

And didn't that matter?

It did to her. She hadn't let herself think about Hayden as somebody she could love, but now—now it seemed that she had skipped that part entirely and had gone straight to being in love.

The words settled into her brain.

She loved Hayden.

And now, more than anything, she wanted him to kiss her.

She looked at him. His face, lit in profile by the amber and gold flames, was that of a kind and caring man. He turned and looked at her, and they moved toward each other, knowing that they were meant to be together, meant to kiss.

So many times she'd kissed and then thought herself in love. This way though—it was perfect.

It seemed as if the world moved in slow motion, as he leaned toward her and she toward him. It was going to happen. He was going to kiss her.

Could anything be more filled with a sense of the future than the moments between the decision to kiss, and the kiss itself? The air was charged with expectation and electricity. . .and hope.

At last, when she didn't think she could bear it a second longer, their lips touched. It was a sacred time. An unspoken promise passed between them, a promise of love that had always existed, and of love that would grow to the ends of the universe. It was a promise of a commitment to a love that would hold them both to the standard of a God that loved them both, and by His love, gave them a model of how they should love each other.

"Livvy," Hayden said at last, "I love you."

"You sound surprised," she said, her voice shaking with new emotion.

In the flickering light of the bonfire, his face creased into an uneasy frown. "I shouldn't have said that."

She inhaled sharply. This was not what she wanted to hear. "Why not?"

"Well," he said, reaching up and brushing a strand of hair from her forehead, "I should have waited to say that. It was too soon. I know how it's supposed to go. We're supposed to date, and then after a couple of dates, we'd kiss, and then months later, I'd say I loved you."

"Why?" She paused for a moment. "I think your timing was perfect. Hayden, I think, I mean, I'm pretty sure, yes, I am positive that I love you, too."

He laughed. "We sound like we're first-timers at this love thing."

"Honestly, I am. I can't say that I ever was in love before this." She thought back to her prom dates, to crushes she'd had during college, and the few bad dates she'd had in Boston, mostly ill-conceived business meetings disguised as social encounters.

"Well," he said, "if we need some guides, I've got 122 high school students who are all convinced that they know what love is all about and who would be glad to advise us."

She leaned her head on his shoulder. The faint scent of shaving cream mingled with the woodsy aroma of the bonfire, and she thought she had never smelled anything quite so good.

So this was love. It was the sweetest emotion she'd ever felt.

He slid his arm around her and held her closely. He felt so sturdy, so solid, so dependable.

For the past four months, she'd relied on him for his help with renovating Sunshine, and every single day, he had been there for her, helping her with the antiquated plumbing, replacing worn window fittings, painting, cleaning, and sorting through boxes.

Not once had he complained.

He'd not only fixed up Sunshine; he helped mend her soul. He guided her back to her position as a child of God, and while she was still learning, that fact alone had brought her peace and satisfaction.

She'd changed so much since she'd come to Sunshine, and she knew even more changes were in store—wonderful changes.

Together they sat watching the flames reaching into the autumn evening. The seasons were definitely moving from autumn to winter, and from the occasional touch of cold in the evening air, she knew that winter was making its steady way toward them.

Hayden raised her chin with a single finger and kissed her again. "I think," he said, his voice husky, "that I've wanted to do that from the first time I laid eyes on you, as you drove up in Trevor's truck, the horn blaring."

She smiled at the memory. "I had my book at my side. *The Complete Guide to Home Construction and Repair*—I thought it had everything I'd ever need in it."

"Where is it, by the way?"

"It's propping up the venting from the clothes dryer, which reminds me. I've got it taped together with aluminum tape, which I think works better than duct tape, but—"

The conversation lapsed into a discussion of the merits of the two kinds of tape, but it was punctuated with a kiss, and another kiss, and another kiss, until finally the fire died down and they were forced to rake it over and splash the coals with water from the bucket that was always nearby.

He walked her to the door of Sunshine. From the porch, she could hear the sound of the late-late show. Hayden squeezed her hand. "I need to get him and take him home. He's probably asleep in front of the tube."

"I doubt it. He's fascinated by it." She peeked through the screen door, and sure enough, the old man was in his chair, with Martha Washington curled into a gigantic furry ball on his lap.

"I gather Gramps is liking the new television," Hayden said, looking over her shoulder.

"He sure is. I don't think he'd ever seen a high-definition set, and now that I've got the satellite dish, he's been glued to it pretty much nonstop when he's out here during the day. Yesterday I caught him watching an infomercial about shoe inserts. Shoe inserts!"

Hayden shook his head in mock dismay. "Well, you've seen the disreputable things he wears on his feet. Maybe shoe inserts are exactly what he needs."

"I don't know. These have magnets in them."

"Why would there be magnets in shoe inserts?" he asked.

"You've got me. I have no idea. But if you want to ask Gramps, he can tell you, right down to the cost of shipping them to North Dakota. And if you buy two pairs, you get a free eye mask that's filled with a special herbal blend guaranteed to zap headaches, neuralgia, and insomnia."

"Sounds like you paid close attention." He moved in closer to her.

"I wasn't the one who did. Ask Gramps. I heard about it all through lunch. The afternoon treat was a talk show that featured some diet guru, and Gramps quizzed me about the gluten in the pasta I used and the amount of sugar in my cereal."

"What did you tell him?" Hayden's lips were very close to hers.

"I have no idea," she answered as she bridged the last inch between them.

She slid into the warmth that was his kiss, wanting nothing to ever come between them, wanting him to hold her in his arms for the rest of their days.

All her life, she'd been waiting for him. Hayden's grandmother had been right.

"You know," Hayden said at last, when the embrace ended, "if I didn't need to breathe, I could stay here forever."

She smiled at him. He had the greatest eyes she had ever seen, the light blue of long-ago Nordic ancestors.

"No you couldn't. You need to go home," she said.

"I'll have to tear myself away." He ran his fingers down her cheek.

"You think that's going to be hard? Try getting Gramps away from his show. He's addicted to that television."

"I am not deaf!" the old man yelled from inside the house. "I have selective hearing, so I might not have heard any of those courting cooing things you said to each other, but on the other hand, maybe I did. So there, Grub."

Hayden's expression was shocked. "You did not!"

Livvy could hear the sounds of his grandfather pulling himself to his feet, apologizing to the cat as he did so— "Sorry, Martha, have to stand up"—and shuffling to the door. He grinned at the two through the screen.

"Look at you two, just as cozy as kittens on the hearth. I know what I know. I may be old but I know what's in front of my face, and I have to say that I am just tickled beyond belief."

"Gramps," Hayden said with an amused sigh, "you've got the cart way before the horse. You've taken a kiss and blown it into a marriage with two-point-five children and a white picket fence and—"

"Excuse me," Livvy interrupted before it could go any further, "did either of you happen to remember that I'm still here?"

"Oh, the kiss-ee," Gramps said.

She had to end this conversation—and quickly. "I am going to kick the both of you out of here so that you can go back to your own home, and Martha Washington and Leonard and I can get some sleep before one of us has to drive into town tomorrow morning for church. Good night."

Lightheartedly she kissed both men on the cheek, called to Leonard to come inside, and stood at the door watching the taillights of Hayden's truck as it left Sunshine.

She'd been kissed. By Hayden. And suddenly life, which had been extremely good before, took on a whole new shine of wonder.

Chapter 8

The first flakes of snow fell slowly, tiny bits of frozen sky and cloud that initially melted upon arrival, but then clung to the earth in the shadowed corners where the wind sent them. Hayden looked out the window and sighed.

"And we've got winter," Gramps said behind him.

Hayden wrapped his hands around his coffee cup, as if he could store the extra warmth for the trip out to the old resort.

He'd never been this tired in his life. Between shuttling back and forth, Obsidian to Sunshine to Obsidian to Sunshine to Obsidian, he had to fit in time to do his job in the schools and to grade assignments, talk to students, visit with parents, and serve on endless committee after endless committee.

Plus he felt that he had to constantly watch Gramps, even more so after what had happened the weekend before, when Gramps had decided to scramble some eggs, but then had gone to sleep in the chair at the kitchen table. The smoke detector had saved the apartment from a sure fire, but the alarm had nearly given Gramps a heart attack. They'd ended up in the hospital in Bismarck, with the old man hooked to monitors and machines that bleeped and blipped out endless electronic messages.

The image of Gramps in the bed, his frail and bent frame nearly lost in the white sheets and the wires clipped to his body, haunted Hayden. He'd come so close to losing him this time.

He couldn't leave him alone during the week, so the trips in the morning and the afternoon out to Sunshine had become crucial. Livvy had become a literal lifesaver. At least when Gramps was out there, he knew that his grandfather was safe.

He suspected it wasn't fair to Livvy, but she insisted she enjoyed the company, and he kept Martha Washington and Leonard occupied and out from under her feet.

Still though, still. . .

The doctor had stopped just short of an assessment of Alzheimer's. There were other possible causes of confusion, he'd told Hayden, and he'd discussed the variety of medications the old man was on. Gramps was now on a new regimen of pills and potions, and Hayden was supposed to monitor him constantly to determine if he was better—or worse—with the changed dosages.

It was too early to tell, and Hayden felt as if a heavy blanket of care was draped firmly and perpetually over his shoulders.

Even church, which had always been a source of renewal and strength for him, had become a chore. It had become one more thing in a long string of things. At night, when he finally wrapped himself in his old Cowboy Andy sleeping bag and curled up on the too-small sofa, he tried to say his prayers, but the words wouldn't sort themselves out of the swirling mass of all that he had to do.

He knew that God was aware of how much was on his plate right now, and that He saw through the garbled petitions of a tired man.

Here it was, Sunday morning, and he didn't even want to go to church. More than anything, he wanted to stay here, wrap himself in a nice warm throw, and read or watch television or sleep. He knew he'd benefit from the renewal that church gave him, but the thought of actually going through the process of getting ready for worship and then going there before he could profit from the service made him even wearier.

He had to admit it. He was exhausted.

He didn't resent any of it. Not at all. He was just tired. So tired.

Gramps's gnarled fingers touched his arm. "I know where the snowblower is," he said. "I'd better get it ready. Once the snow starts, it'll never stop."

He held back an impatient sigh. "We don't need the snowblower here. The apartment manager takes care of that. You know him. Joe, from the Cenex station? It's one of the advantages of living in the big city of Obsidian."

Gramps looked at him as if he'd begun spouting off multiplication tables in Portuguese. "Who said anything about bringing the snowblower here?" he asked. "I know Joe does all that. I'm talking about getting the one at Sunshine ready. And attaching the blade to the truck."

His grandfather had a good point. Hayden had always put off those two tasks.

The snowblower was an obstinate machine that required vast amounts of effort to get it to start—Hayden remembered with dismay how his arm would ache after he pulled the starter cord on it over and over and over, trying to get the motor to catch, and finally, when he was ready to give up, the dumb thing would finally engage.

Whether or not it would stay running until he was through snow-blowing the walkways from the house to the chicken coop and the barn was another matter entirely. It was a cantankerous and belligerent piece of work, and Hayden dreaded approaching it after every snowfall.

Putting the blade on the truck was equally painful—often literally. He'd never made it without getting several gashes on his arms and hands, and one year he'd nearly sliced off his toe. He always wore steel-toed boots after that when dealing with the blade.

It was an awkward proposition, getting the blade attached to the front of the truck, but it had to be done. Usually Gramps helped him, but would he be able to this year? He had no idea.

Hayden created a smile and pasted it on. "You're right. I don't think this snow is going to stick, but let's not take a chance."

"We'll go out after church," his grandfather said.

Church. His entire Saturday had been eaten up with a three-hour practice for the boys' basketball team at school, followed by a trip to the grocery store, running Gramps out to Sunshine to get his afternoon medication that he'd forgotten there, staying to fix a board that had come loose in the living room flooring, going back to Obsidian and fixing dinner, grading twenty-seven algebra exams and sixteen geometry worksheets, washing a load of sheets and changing the bed, and more that he'd mercifully forgotten.

Now this was Sunday, and he so desperately wanted a day of rest. Wasn't that what it was all about? A day of rest?

"You'd better start getting ready for church. All I have left is to comb my silvery locks," Gramps said, running his hand over his thinning hair.

A battle of wills began to rage inside him. His body begged for some downtime, but his soul needed some up time, an hour spent with the Lord.

God would understand. He'd—

Hayden took one look at his grandfather, who was already in his suit, his tie neatly knotted, if a bit askew, and his face shining eagerly, and he knew that the decision was made.

He'd go with the up time.

As he headed for the shower, perhaps not with the enthusiasm he usually felt on Sunday mornings, Gramps called out from the kitchen, "Hey, Grub, Livvy will be there."

Hayden stopped, midstep, and shook his head. His grandfather was never going to stop matchmaking with the two of them. And, he admitted to himself as he continued his ascent up the stairs, he wasn't sure he wanted Gramps to quit.

Children were scurrying around the front of the church, gathering the snow in their mittens and alternately eating it or dumping it on top of each other's head. Hayden grinned as he watched them. It hadn't been that long ago that he'd done those same things himself. He lingered outside, enjoying the antics of the youthful churchgoers.

Soon though, watchful parents pulled their children inside, and he followed. Gramps had already gotten himself settled with some of the other old-timers, but he stood up and hobbled over to sit with Hayden.

"You know," Hayden said to him in the moments before the service started, "you've really got to get better boots. Those things you're wearing have not only seen better days, they've seen better decades."

Gramps shook his head. "They don't make them like they used to."

Hayden started to respond but Gramps interrupted, standing up as quickly as he could and moving into the aisle. "Livvy!"

He also jumped up, banging his knee into the hymnal rack.

Livvy looked like the spirit of snow herself. Her face glowed crimson from the cold, which made her eyes sparkle with an even brighter deep brown.

"I'm freezing," she said as she slid down the pew next to Hayden, and Gramps followed her, so she had one on each side of her. "I know it's not really that cold, but the wind just cuts through me."

"It does that," Gramps said. "You're wise to wear a scarf, but you need something more substantial than that." He motioned to the airy chiffon scarf she had draped around her neck, and she laughed.

"This is just for vanity, Gramps," she said. "I have one that's out there in the entryway, keeping my coat company, that would keep out arctic breezes, let me tell you. My mom sent it from Sweden. No breeze is getting through it, trust me."

The service started, and Hayden let the words lift his cares from him.

Reverend Carlisle's theme was "Coming Home," based on, he explained, the upcoming set of holidays. As winter comes onto the starkness of the Badlands, it begins with a feast, a celebration of what has come before. The harvest, he pointed out, is the culmination of a busy season of planting, tending, and caring, before the reaping begins. The banquet is the ultimate festivity.

He leaned across the pulpit and grinned at the congregation. "Think how often we meet over food. We commemorate birthdays with a cake. Graduations, at least here in Obsidian, are marked with open houses and tray upon tray of bars and cookies and chips and dips. Weddings not only include a spectacular wedding cake, but a reception or perhaps a dinner. Even funerals end with us gathering over food."

Gramps's stomach growled, and Hayden and Livvy exchanged quick smiles.

"So we do as the song so known at Thanksgiving reminds us to do: We gather and we ask the Lord to bless us. And of course, we do this over as much food as we can possibly prepare," the minister continued. "And that leads us into what's commonly known as the holiday season, and if you look at the magazine display down at Grocery World, you'll see that probably ninety percent of the magazines offer tips on how to avoid gaining weight in this time period."

Reverend Carlisle patted his stomach. "As you can see, I am not an avid reader of these magazines."

The congregation laughed.

"Let me give you the gospel now. It's John 16:32: 'Behold, the hour cometh, yea, is now come, that ye shall be scattered, every man to his own, and shall leave me alone: and yet I am not alone, because the Father is with me.' Why, you might wonder, am I choosing this text, which talks about us being apart, not coming together? Because, my friends, it's simply this: It's easier to talk about the happy, feel-good things—what we used to call warm fuzzies back in the ancient world—but what we need to discuss is the time when those end. When we're in the January of our holiday season."

He must be more tired than he realized, Hayden thought. None of this was making sense. Why was Reverend Carlisle talking about the holidays so early, and now he was on to January?

"I want you to see this as a continuum. It's beginning now. I know that some of you are, in fact, getting ready for the winter ahead. You came in through it. Winter starts early out here; you know that. And we tear through its beginnings thinking only of celebration and gathering and togetherness. But January does come. In our lives, it'll come. The time when there aren't parties and cookies and punch. Don't think of what you've lost. Think of what you've gained in these last days of autumn, what you've stored away just as surely as the squirrel stores its acorns. These are the things you will feed on in January."

Scattered. That's what was going to happen. He had put off answering the letter from the school district in Florida, perhaps under the misguided notion that the offer would simply evaporate and he wouldn't have to deal with it, but the superintendent had called him on Friday afternoon, asking for a definitive answer.

He could go to Florida, and even take Gramps with him. Sunshine was now in fantastic shape, and Livvy could open it in the spring without his help. He could try life in the big city, and see if his career path could actually have an arc in it instead of a flat line.

He could, but he didn't want to. He knew what his answer was going to be.

He knew.

When he got home, he would write a letter to that school, turning down the job—and choosing love.

❧

The holidays sped by on winged feet. Thanksgiving gave way to Christmas, which bowed to the new year. And through it all, Livvy kept working, sending out flyers, calling travel agents, attending a travel agency gathering in Los Angeles. She'd even found a company in Valley City that would supply more orange T-shirts and blue glasses, just like the old ones.

She was determined to make this work.

And it seemed as if was going to. The phone began to ring. E-mails trickled in at first, and then increased. When she went to the mailbox, there were envelopes, some filled with requests for more information, others containing reservations and checks.

The brochure said it all:

> *Sunshine.*
> *An old-fashioned resort with old-fashioned values.*
> *We're experts at relaxation. Fish, play games, roast marshmallows,*
> *all in the safe and loving haven of North Dakota's stunning Badlands.*

No phones. No Internet. No cable.
Just land and water. . .and you.
Take it easy, here in Sunshine.
And, as we've said for generations:
At the end of the day, there's Sunshine.

But the test was going to be summertime. And when summer came, so did the guests. The cabins were full and the shouts of happy children combined with the songs at the bonfire every night, with Gramps leading the vespers. She was surprised at how quickly Sunshine's reputation grew, as a place where Christian families—or any family wanting an easy, comfortable setting—could spend a vacation.

Now it was August, and the season had been a smashing success. Livvy had had several requests to winterize the cabins so the resort could be open year-round, and she was considering it—even if her trusty *Complete Guide to Home Construction and Repair* wouldn't quite be up to the task.

Trevor had upgraded his rattletrap truck to a huge SUV and was now the official transport to the Bismarck airport—and had, indeed, managed to get a new iPod.

Her parents had come from Sweden and left with a new hobby—fishing.

Best of all, Gramps was much better. The doctor's suspicions had been right: The old man's confusion was the result of a drug interaction. Gramps was now as lively and alert as any teenager.

Life was good here in Sunshine, Livvy thought. Very good. And it was all because of what God had done. This was her inheritance—an inheritance of family and friends and love.

Hayden arrived with a delivery from Grocery World, and as they were putting it away in the kitchen, he commented on the success of Sunshine.

"I couldn't have done it without you," she said, and as she turned around, he caught her in a surprise embrace.

"Do you know what else you can't do without me?" he asked. "This."

He kissed her, squarely on the lips. "Let's put the ice cream away. I want to show you something down by the lake."

"Why? Is something wrong?" she asked, a crease of worry working its way up.

"Nothing's wrong, but it's something I think you should see."

She hurriedly put the ice cream in the freezer, and left the nonperishables on the counter.

"Come on," he said. "Come with me."

He took her by the hand and led her out of the house. Leonard followed them, his tennis ball in his mouth, and behind the dog came Martha Washington, her tail plumed as the chicken chased her, biting at her. Hayden shook his head and muttered, but he was smiling.

"What's this about?" she asked.

"Well," he said, pausing at the spot where the path opened to the lake, "I wanted a place where we might have some peace and quiet, but I didn't include the critters in the equation. And there's Gramps, out there on the dock. Well, so much for privacy. That's all right."

"What are you talking about?"

Hayden took her hands. "Livvy, I love you. I love everything about you, and I love the way I feel when I'm around you. You're the one that God has meant for me, I'm sure of that. Livvy—"

He dropped to one knee, and Leonard raced over and dropped his spit-covered tennis ball at his feet. "Not now, Leonard."

The dog nudged him, nearly knocking him over, and Livvy had to cover her mouth to keep from laughing. Hayden was so serious, but Leonard was insistent.

"Okay. Here." Hayden threw the ball and wiped his hands on his pants. "Quickly, before the beast comes back, Livvy, will you marry me?"

"I will! I will!" She knelt, too, landing squarely on the chicken, which flew upward in a great display of feathers and offended squawks, and landed on Martha Washington's back. The cat shot straight up into the air, and Leonard, seeing the great game at hand, joined in the fray.

She heard none of it. She only knew that Hayden was kissing her.

"I knew it," Gramps said from the pier, where he was fishing. "I knew it."

❧

The wedding was an autumn celebration, with Trinity decorated in the colors of the season. Bo and Al were their miniature groomsmen, and Bo flung the contents of his basket of multicolored leaves with such force that several guests were picking them out of their hair.

Gramps was there, as were her parents, and a surprise guest joined them from Boston: Mr. Evans, who gave them as a wedding present a copy of the advertisement, now framed. How he had gotten hold of it, she had no idea, but some things about love are simply magic.

Like Sunshine.